G.R. Halliday

G.R. Halliday was born in Edinburgh and grew up near Stirling in Scotland. He spent his childhood obsessing over the unexplained mysteries his father investigated, which proved excellent inspiration for *From the Shadows*. The book was shortlisted for the McIlvanney Debut Prize 2019. G.R. Halliday now lives in the rural Highlands outside of Inverness, where he is able to pursue his favourite pastimes of mountain climbing and swimming in the sea, before returning home to his band of semi-feral cats. *Under the Marsh* is his third novel.

G.R. Halliday

Under the Marsh

VINTAGE

1 3 5 7 9 10 8 6 4 2

Vintage is part of the Penguin Random House group of companies
whose addresses can be found at global.penguinrandomhouse.com

Penguin
Random House
UK

Copyright © Highland Noir Ltd 2022

G.R. Halliday has asserted his right to be identified as the author of this
Work in accordance with the Copyright, Designs and Patents Act 1988

First published by Vintage in 2022

penguin.co.uk/vintage

A CIP catalogue record for this book is available from the British Library

ISBN 9781529115468 (B format)

Typeset in 10.94/15.31pt Adobe Garamond Pro by Jouve (UK), Milton Keynes
Printed and bound in Great Britain by Clays Ltd, Elcograf S.p.A.

The authorised representative in the EEA is Penguin Random House Ireland,
Morrison Chambers, 32 Nassau Street, Dublin D02 YH68

Penguin Random House is committed to a sustainable future
for our business, our readers and our planet. This book is
made from Forest Stewardship Council® certified paper.

MIX
Paper from
responsible sources
FSC® C018179

For my mum and dad

Chapter 1

Freya Sutherland held her wristwatch up to the lamplight and checked the grey digital numbers: 00:30. It was time to go.

As if in a dream, she picked up her suitcase from where it was tucked at the side of the bed, careful not to make a noise that would wake her parents. The suitcase was heavy, but not *so* heavy for someone who was leaving their old life for ever. She looked around her bedroom – a poster of Nirvana and some drawings pinned to the wall – then reached for the note. It was hidden under her sketchbook on the dressing table. Her cat, Butter, had come into the room and was standing over the book, head tilted, staring intently at her. Almost as if he wanted to tell her something, as if he were telling her to stay. Freya stared back at him for a moment – *He probably wants food* – and rubbed the soft fur on his head one last time. Then nudged him aside, picked up the sketchbook and placed the note on her pillow for her mum to find.

Outside it was dark with no moonlight to guide her. She knew the track that ran beside the farm buildings to the road well though. Had spent hours and days, summer and winter, playing on it throughout her childhood. Splashed in puddles as a toddler, learned to ride her bike, had water fights with Dad and Jessica. She reached the end of the lane, her feet on the reassuring

1

firmness of the road, it brought another memory, the summer when it was so hot the tarmac melted. She and Jessica had run barefoot, laughing, poking twigs into the tar. They had been close as children; the year between them had mattered less. The memory drew her in and she turned back to the farmhouse. Black against the night and the dark mountains beyond. She realised then that she had never bothered to learn the names of those hills; they were always just there. The way Jessica was just there. She hadn't even mentioned her little sister's name in the note. Things had come between them, hormones maybe, certainly everything with Dad – it had become an unbridgeable gulf. She hesitated. Maybe she should run back to the house, leave a note for Jessica? It would only take a minute.

The sound of the vehicle's engine interrupted her thoughts. A moment later she could see its lights on the road, pools of yellow in the dark. She felt a pang of excitement. It was really happening, they were really doing it. She watched the vehicle draw close then pull in at the lay-by. Far enough away that there was no chance of the sounds waking her parents. Freya glanced back at her sleeping childhood home. She would send Jessica a letter the first chance she got, explain everything. Resolved, she turned and began to pull her suitcase along the road, pleased it could now trundle on its wheels.

As she approached the vehicle, she felt the first flicker of uncertainty in her stomach.

She had expected the familiar Volkswagen Golf. Instead there was a dark van, parked with its engine off. Pulled in tight beside the ancient copper beech, huge with gnarled branches – her grandad had called it *the hanging tree* when he was alive. He'd said this quiet country road used to be the main route south to Drumnadrochit. An old drove road for the Highland herders taking their cattle to market in the Lowlands. He'd said there were ghosts on the road, of thieves and killers hanged at the tree. Freya and Jessica used to hold hands and run past on winter mornings on their way to catch the school bus to Inverness.

The memory of childhood fear; the silent van under the tree. None of it was how she had imagined this moment. An expectation of excitement, laughter with her new friends as they piled into the car together. Life opening up for them all.

Freya hesitated and took a deep breath of the night air. The smell of moss from the forest, woodsmoke drifting from somewhere far away. She had an odd sense of timelessness, as if she could easily have drifted back hundreds of years into the past.

Freya felt her skin crawl, and all her instincts told her to turn round, leave her suitcase in the long grass beside the road and run back to the house. For a second, she hesitated. Then she imagined waiting for the bus to go to work at the amusement arcade on Castle Street in Inverness the next morning. Doing it every day for the next year, for the next ten years.

She stepped closer to the van, feeling the dew from the grass soaking her trainers, and tapped on the door. The metal panel was cold to the touch. There was no response at first, but she could hear a vague noise from the van's interior. A murmuring, as if someone was talking to themselves, or had a radio on at a very low volume. A hint of light from the gap at the bottom of the door.

'Hello? It's me.' Freya's voice sounded young, frightened, in her own ears. She cleared her throat as another wave of indecision rose from her stomach. Why hadn't they mentioned coming to collect her in a different vehicle? But if it wasn't her friends, then what were the chances that someone else would just show up? Of course it was them. She forced herself to bang harder on the metal. The voice inside stopped. The light went out.

Freya hesitated, unsure what to do. *Maybe they're not sure it's me? Maybe*—The door rolled open with a sound of metal on metal. It was darker inside the van. There was a reassuring smell of menthol cigarette smoke though, and without thinking Freya heaved her suitcase inside. She hesitated again, then climbed into the van. The door rolled shut behind her, the light clicked back on. As her eyes adjusted to the unfamiliar space, Freya's breath caught in her throat. The shock of adrenaline flowed through her body. She scrabbled at the door, searching for the handle. But it was already much, much too late for any of that.

Chapter 2

The serial killer had been locked up for over a decade, and mostly forgotten, on the cold morning that Detective Inspector Monica Kennedy arrived at Carselang prison. Monica closed her eyes for a moment as the heavy entrance door banged to behind her. In her experience, the sound of a prison door slamming shut seemed to be pretty much the same everywhere. *The sound's the same, but the atmosphere here's unique*, Monica thought as she opened her eyes and took in the cavernous entrance hallway. Smells seemed to ooze from the grey granite walls: fried food, bleach, sweat, the acrid stink of desperation. *Can you smell desperation?* On balance, Monica thought so – had caught its bitterness on the clothes and from the pores of enough victims and criminals in over twenty years on the force.

The prisoners in here have nothing to lose – you can never trust someone that desperate. Monica's dad had told her that once when she was a child, on one of their occasional weekend drives out to see the place. The institution had been built in 1890 to house Scotland's most dangerous offenders, and was situated in the remote Glen Wyvis, an hour's drive north-west of the city of Inverness. Her deceased father, 'Long' John Kennedy, had been a prison officer at Carselang, was proud of working there and had enjoyed showing it off to his daughter.

Monica glanced up at the sound of footsteps on the cobbled floor. An officer holding a clipboard had come out into the entrance hallway to meet her. He was dressed in dark uniform trousers and a white shirt, a heavy North Face parka pulled on over them. A concession to the chill autumn air coming down off the mountains – and something, Monica felt sure, they would never have tolerated in John Kennedy's day. The officer glanced at his clipboard, then looked her up and down with curiosity.

'You're DI Monica Kennedy?' For a second she wondered if he had worked with her dad, then took in his brown hair and realised he was probably only thirty – too young – had just been giving her the standard once-over. Monica was over six feet tall, with pale skin, dark hair and intense eyes. She rarely went unnoticed. Particularly since she had led a number of high-profile cases in the Highlands after moving back from London five years before, when her daughter Lucy was born.

Monica nodded and stepped closer. Her voice came out as a cloud of mist: 'I've got an appointment with Pauline Tosh.'

The officer looked at the clipboard again. *Surely they have a computer system now?*

'Thought your lot had given up on her. Piece of work. You're probably wasting your time; I doubt she'll see you.' The man's hair was plastered flat, his skin grey, face set tense.

'She contacted me,' Monica replied, feeling a flicker of irritation at his sceptical tone. Carselang was unique in the Scottish prison system in that it functioned essentially as two separate institutions on the same site. The west wing of the building for men, the smaller east wing for women.

'It was you who caught her, wasn't it?' The man's voice rose in the excitement of recognition. Instinctively Monica's eyes dropped

6

to his chest for his ID badge: covered by his coat. He caught the movement. 'I wasn't trying to be nosy ... My name's Tyler Mitchell.'

'It's fine.' Monica forced a smile, reminded herself that – her father aside – it wasn't anyone's idea of a good time to be working out in the middle of nowhere surrounded by Cat A offenders. It was natural the officer would want to chat to pass the day, and it paid to be on good terms with the staff when you were visiting a serial murderer in a dilapidated, underfunded prison. Tyler might be the one she would rely on to come running if things went wrong. 'I was part of the team who caught her. A while back now.'

'That's right,' Tyler said. 'I remember reading about it at the time – 2006? "The Home-Help Beast" they were calling her, wasn't it? Four they got her for. You still think she did more? That's why you're here, isn't it?'

Monica found her mind running back over the details of the case. What Tyler had said was essentially true. Four women from the Glasgow area had been murdered, their bodies found in isolated areas on the west coast of the southern Highlands. All of them strangled, dumped fully clothed. Monica had been asked to come north from London to consult. She remembered the late night, buzzed on caffeine at the old police headquarters on Pitt Street in Glasgow, when she spotted a tiny connection – all four dump sites were a few miles from caravan parks. A rainy day visiting the sites to ask about any suspicious men, staff or visitors. No result at the first two, but as Monica was about to leave the third, she impulsively asked the owner about any strange women. The man almost laughed, then shook his head and mentioned someone who brought a camper van up most weekends in the summer. Arrived late, left early. Wore work overalls even though she was on holiday. A woman called Pauline Tosh: a bit odd, but apparently harmless. She had already been interviewed as a witness. It turned out her modus operandi was to befriend isolated and vulnerable women, and eventually strangle them.

'We thought she might have killed more,' Monica replied finally. This was information that had been widely shared in the press and online; it was not exactly confidential. She left out the part about the photographs. Images they had found in Tosh's belongings – her standing alone near her camper van in remote locations in the 1990s. The suspicion was that she might have buried or otherwise disposed of more unidentified victims across the Highlands in this period. She was known to have lived in Inverness for a time.

Tyler nodded gravely. 'I read that. They could never say for sure who they were though? No real evidence.' Obviously Tyler was another aficionado of serial killers. On the rare occasions Monica went to parties or family gatherings, it was always the serial killer aspect of her work that people wanted to discuss. The modern-day monster in the fairy tale. Fascinating, darkly glamorous. But in real life, often dull and boring people. Monica wondered for a second if the young prison officer would have been as familiar with a male detective. She tried to imagine her boss, Detective Superintendent Fred Hately, or her partner, Detective Constable Connor Crawford, allowing themselves to be grilled like this. The thought must have sent a flicker of irritation across her face, because Tyler quickly added, 'Sorry, asking all those questions. I'd better take you through. Pauline can be fussy about her routine.' He turned and hit a button, spoke into an intercom. They were buzzed through the second heavy door; another officer signed Monica in then put her jacket through a scanner and handed it back to her. Tyler led her into a warren of damp corridors, low and narrow after the main entrance hall. 'Understaffed now,' he said over his shoulder as he unlocked a third heavy door, with a key this time. 'Most of it's about watching on cameras, responding if anything kicks off.'

The door clanked shut and he locked it behind them. Their footsteps echoed off the stone floor as they penetrated deeper into the prison, through two more doors and down shadowy corridors. Finally, Tyler stopped at a metal door with a peephole covered by a flap.

'There's CCTV, but if anything happens it's better if you hit the alarm button on the wall. Just in case the operator's busy with something in the west wing.' Down here the air was warm and damp, the breath of the old prison. The mountain chill a world away. 'When Pauline first came in she threw a napalm – that's what we call a mix of sugar and boiling water – she threw one in the face of another inmate. No warning. They'd been best mates up until then. Needed skin grafts, all scarred up.' Quickly he added, 'She'll be cuffed to the table of course. Best to watch her, that's all.'

Monica thanked him, though she didn't need reminding. The photos of the bodies at the dump sites were locked in her memory.

Tyler turned the key and opened the door.

Monica stepped into the small windowless room. The walls were painted an institutional green. It was lit by a single bulb in a wire cage, a CCTV camera in the corner similarly protected. In the middle of the room, sitting at the table, there was a woman. The door slammed shut behind Monica; the lock turned. Pauline Tosh raised her eyes, then she smiled.

Her hair was still thick – but mostly grey now. A narrow face with puffy cheeks. Those dark eyes, like pools of midnight water. She was dressed in blue work overalls with a DICKIES logo on the chest, the same style as the day twelve years before when Monica had knocked on the door of her house in rural Stirlingshire.

'Been a few years,' Tosh said as Monica sat down opposite.

'You look well,' Monica replied. 'I got your message.' It was Sunday; the handwritten letter had arrived at the office on Friday morning.

Dear Monica

I have discovered important information. I need to speak to you at the earliest time we can meet.

Yours Sinc.
Pauline

Stamped at the top right of the lined paper: HM PRISON CARSELANG. Tosh had never admitted to any of the crimes she had been convicted of, though the evidence was compelling: DNA in her van, victims' personal possessions in her house. This was the first time Tosh had reached out to Monica; desperate requests by the families of missing persons to share information had all been stonewalled.

'Seen your name in the paper last few years. Back in the Highlands,' Tosh said. Her accent was Lowland Scottish, a hint of Glaswegian.

'I was surprised you bothered writing to me. We get calls every other month. Professors who want to study you – you're quite unique, a female serial killer.' Monica was trying for the right blend of flattery and uninterested. The smallest hint of a smile appeared at the corner of Tosh's mouth. She folded her small, strong hands together. Monica checked that the metal cuffs were around her wrists, recalling the bruises on her victims' necks.

'They all think someone in prison's a different species. Not like me and you – we know that anyone could end up in here. Matter of luck as much as anything. I heard about what happened with your wee girl last year.' Monica felt the throb of the scar tissue on her stomach, the blend of guilt and horror – the case that had almost led to the death of her and her daughter. 'Lucy, that her name? It was in the paper.'

Hearing her daughter's name from this killer's mouth was almost too much, but with difficulty Monica maintained eye contact. 'I'm in a hurry, Pauline.' If Tosh had simply brought her here to gloat, it was going to be a short conversation. 'What did you want to tell me?' Tosh stared back at her without reply and Monica stood up, swung round to hit the buzzer beside the door.

'I've got a story for you,' Tosh said quickly.

Monica turned back to her. 'What kind of story?'

That thin smile creeping onto her face again. 'Maybe the nasty kind.'

Against her body's instincts, Monica sat back down. She tried to sound casual: 'Nasty how?'

'Well, I don't know that exactly, Monica,' Tosh said, glancing around as if someone might be eavesdropping in the small room. 'I just hear whispers through these walls, wee stories.'

'Who's been whispering?'

'Something I could show you,' Tosh said as if Monica hadn't spoken. She broke into a wider smile that revealed her small, uneven teeth. 'If you're sure you really want me to?'

Chapter 3

When she had finally passed through all those locked doors and was back in the car park in front of Carselang, Monica took a deep breath of the mountain air. Appreciating the space after staring into Tosh's eyes, feeling something like contagion from the killer.

She exhaled, and with it the thought bubbled up: *How did you do it, Dad? Work in this place every day?* Monica ran both hands through her shoulder-length hair. A disturbing case the previous spring had brought back memories of her father, forced her to reappraise her childhood. She had spent long enough mulling it over, and in the spirit of change she had recently begun looking for a relationship, tentatively signing up to an online platform after her mum had cajoled her: 'You'll never find anyone just with other police and dead bodies, Monica. Crawford says online's the way everyone does it now.'

The recollection of her partner's name brought a mix of affection and a hint of irritation. Her mum, Angela Kennedy (aged sixty-seven), and DC Connor Crawford (aged thirty-one) had struck up an unlikely friendship. Annoyingly, Angela had taken to citing his opinion on matters ranging from her favourite topics – crime fiction and police procedure – to criminal psychology. Recently there had been a diet for Albert, Monica's daughter's overweight cat. Not that it was working. She smiled as she remembered Lucy that morning, carrying the blond cat – seeming as large as her – to the bathroom scales. The grim truth that he'd actually gained weight.

Monica clicked her blue Volvo unlocked and got in, feeling some of the tension leave her body in the familiar interior. Her hand dropped to the pocket of her tweed coat, checked the plastic evidence bag was there. The thing Tosh had given her, she didn't want to think about yet. *But it'll be coming with you, no doubt about that*, her unhelpful internal voice piped up. A little piece of Pauline Tosh in your home tonight. She shook her head. Started the engine.

A mile down the road Monica spotted a familiar red Audi parked in a lay-by. It was close to Loch Wyvis, a beach, a copse of Scots pine trees. Classic Highland picnic territory. After a moment she spotted a small, thin man with red hair, then a child with blonde curls waving frantically from the shore. Her mum was sitting on the sand beside them.

She pulled over and got out. Although there was a dusting of snow on the hills, Monica could still feel the sun's warmth when it broke through the clouds.

'I was out for a drive,' Crawford said as Monica approached. 'Spotted your mum and Lucy in Tain, thought we'd drive up and meet you.'

'What were the chances of that!' Angela said. Monica had left her mum and Lucy drinking coffee and juice respectively at a cafe while she went on to meet Tosh. 'Looked up and there was Crawford!' She was delighted by the supposed coincidence, but Monica knew better. Her colleague had been there on Friday when she opened the letter and was obviously intrigued.

'What *were* the chances?' Monica glanced at Crawford, who turned guiltily away. Still, it felt surprisingly good to see him after being alone in that room with Tosh. He was dressed in dark trousers, brogues, a roll-neck sweater and an expensive-looking grey wool jacket. His red hair was combed into its regulation quiff, a smattering of stubble on his handsome face. He looked out of place – city clothes in the mountainous landscape. Monica knew Crawford had grown up on the remote west coast but had a dislike bordering on fear for the natural environment.

'Crawford's helping me build a sandcastle!' Lucy shouted from down at the edge of the water, where she was using a plastic cup to dig at the sand.

'We brought a picnic. I'll just go and get it!' Angela said, shooing away Crawford's offer of help and heading back up the slope to the Audi.

'What was the information?'

Monica checked her mum was out of earshot, then that Lucy was working on the sandcastle. 'A place for us to dig,' she whispered. 'We'll speak tomorrow.'

'Sure, tomorrow.' Surprisingly Crawford seemed placated by this. He had a tendency to go after things like a terrier when he thought information was being withheld. She guessed that even he could see a family picnic wasn't the setting to discuss a serial killer. Though her mum would have been thrilled if they had.

'I thought you said you were spending the weekend with Heather?' He had met his current girlfriend, Heather Sinclair, on a case the previous spring; they had been dating for a couple of months. Generally Monica couldn't keep up with Crawford's romantic partners, but more than a few weeks counted as serious in his world.

Crawford cleared his throat. 'I was thinking . . .' His voice died away. He sounded uncomfortable.

'Is everything OK, Crawford?' He turned to look back up the glen towards Carselang, a grey mass in the distance.

'It's just—' But before he could finish his sentence, Angela had come back down the slope carrying a tartan rug and the picnic bag.

'Who's hungry?! It's cold. This'll be the last picnic of the year probably – snow coming soon!'

Lucy shouted, Crawford glanced away, the moment passed. And much later, when she thought back on it all, Monica sometimes wondered. Would things would have turned out differently if he had tried speaking to her at a different moment? Without her mum and Lucy around? When she hadn't just come out of an interview with a serial killer? But maybe that was why he had chosen the moment. A subconscious decision that could be marked up as fate?

Chapter 4

Monica pulled the Volvo to a stop around the corner from Lucy's school, in the Crown district of Inverness. It was the morning after her visit to Carselang and she was in a hurry to get to headquarters for a meeting with Detective Superintendent Fred Hately. But when she opened the back door to help Lucy out, her daughter seemed reluctant to leave the car. Head down, hands folded around her book: an illustrated edition of *The Worst Witch*.

'Is everything OK, sweetheart?'

'I feel like I've got a sore tummy.'

Monica leaned in and shifted her daughter's curly blonde hair aside to feel her forehead. Her temperature didn't seem high and she had eaten her breakfast of Cheerios without complaint.

'When did it start feeling sore?'

'I can't remember.'

'Are you worried about something, honey?' In general, Lucy seemed to be settling in well at school, had already been invited to the birthday parties of two new friends. But when Monica thought about it, she remembered Lucy being uncharacteristically quiet when she'd collected her on Friday afternoon. They had gone food shopping at Tesco and she had barely spoken until they were back at the flat. At the time, Monica had been distracted by Tosh's letter, which had arrived that day. Monica found herself glancing at the clock on the dash: 8.55 a.m.

Monday was her mum's laundry morning; she would already be on her way to the launderette on Grant Street in Rapinch. And Monica felt that sliver of self-hatred, that she had to even consider other factors when it came to her daughter's welfare. She took in Lucy's slightly chubby face, her upturned nose with glasses balanced on it, the perfect line of her mouth, the mass of hair. Such a small creature, but already complicated.

'Would you like me to come in with you, sweetheart? To tell Miss Jennings you're feeling poorly?'

Lucy shook her head quickly. 'I think I feel better.'

'Are you sure?' Monica asked slowly, tilting her head to watch Lucy's face for any tell.

'I'm fine now.' And before Monica could dig any further, the school bell was ringing. Lucy was scrambling out of the seat, reaching for her school bag.

Half an hour later Monica was sitting with Crawford and Fred Hately. On the drive she had called Lydia, mother of Lucy's best friend Munyasa, hoping she might know if something was going on at school. There was no answer, so Monica left a voice message and tried hard to put her concern for Lucy out of her mind for now. Worrying wouldn't help.

'How did you get on with Tosh?' Hately asked, bringing her mind back to his office. Her boss was a few years older than Monica. From a Glaswegian-Italian background, neat dark hair in a side parting, wearing an expensive suit. Hately could play the game politically – a necessity if you wanted the top jobs – but generally Monica knew where she stood with him. Trusted him, up to a point. 'Waste of time?'

'Maybe, maybe not.' Monica watched the micro-expressions cross Hately's face. Getting fresh information from a serial killer had the potential to go in any direction: best outcome a cold case ticked off, closure for a missing person's family; worst outcome COPS HOAXED BY KILLER, humiliation in the media. Reopening wounds and raising false hope for families desperate to find missing loved ones. She dug in the pocket of her threadbare tweed coat and put the plastic evidence bag on the table. 'Tosh gave me this.' Inside there was a piece of paper marked with coloured pencils. 'She said it's a map.' Hately warily picked it up.

'A map to what?' Crawford chipped in for the first time.

'She told me there's something buried. Near the Caledonian Canal in Inverness.'

'The Caledonian Canal?' Hately repeated. The canal was a popular tourist spot in the city – the eastern end of a waterway that ran through the Great Glen via Loch Ness, to Fort William on the west coast. Monica looked at the map in Hately's hands. The canal was marked in blue as a straight line, the marshlands to the right of it in green. A dark rectangle and an *X* in the marsh. Tosh had pointed to it: 'Have you ever heard of the Witch's Coffin in Inverness, Monica?'

During their initial interviews in 2006, Tosh had recognised Monica's accent. It turned out she had lived in Inverness herself for a while in the 90s, and the coincidence had delighted her: 'We might have walked right past each other! What if we'd been neighbours?!'

As it happened, Monica did know the Witch's Coffin. Little more than a mile from the street she had grown up on in Rapinch. A rock shaped like a coffin. It was in a marshy pool and only became visible at low tide, covered in barnacles and black seaweed. As a child, Monica had stopped her bike many times and stared at it, transfixed.

Tosh had pointed to the map. 'Just beside the coffin.' The X was on the seaward side of the rock. 'About five feet away.'

'What's buried there?' Crawford asked.

'She claims not to know.'

'Did she draw the map?' Hately asked, running his finger over the misspelled words beside the oblong shape: WITCHS COFIN.

'She says she woke up and found it in her cell. That someone must have pushed it under the door.'

Hately sighed, rubbed his hands over his face. Like Monica, he already knew they had no choice. When a convicted serial murderer told you something was buried in the ground, you had to check it out. 'How quickly can we get this done?'

'I spoke to Clive Ridgeway this morning,' Monica said, recalling the hurried phone call with the forensic archaeologist while Lucy was eating her Cheerios. 'He says he could fit a survey in tonight if the tide times work.'

Chapter 5

Low tide was midnight, pitch-black with no moon. A dramatic time to go looking for a serial killer's treasure, Monica thought. A fog had rolled in off the Beauly Firth – the body of water separating Inverness from the Black Isle to the north – chilling its way through her coat and shirt. She felt the hairs on her arms stand up and stamped her feet to keep warm. Wondered for a moment why she hadn't thought to wear something more sensible. When Lucy went out in the cold, Monica always bundled her up in layers of jumpers and jackets. Why couldn't she treat herself with the same care?

'I heard it was an old crane base,' Crawford said from the dark beside her. They were on a narrow causeway that ran through the marshes. The path connected Ferry Point in Rapinch, close to where Monica had grown up, with Clachnaharry at the western edge of Inverness. The marshes were popular with dog walkers, birdwatchers, and – when Monica was a kid, at least – teenagers looking for somewhere to hang out, smoke, drink, do whatever teenagers did. 'The Witch's Coffin, I mean,' Crawford added. 'From when they were digging the canal. Not really a coffin.'

Beneath Monica and Crawford, Dr Clive Ridgeway and an assistant were staring at the muddy ground by the light of their head torches. Ridgeway wore shorts all winter, had once told Monica that his family took their holidays on the Western Isles to dig for Iron Age post holes. To Ridgeway, digging for secrets seemed to come almost disturbingly naturally.

Monica could just make out the shape of the Witch's Coffin in the light from their torches, darkened by strands of seaweed. Ridgeway was now fiddling with a metal detector, beginning their initial survey. After fifteen minutes of scanning he turned and slopped through the mud to the shore. He laid the metal detector on the embankment and picked up something – Monica couldn't see what – in its place. He struggled back to where his assistant was standing and started working again. After a minute he whistled, then muttered, 'Under the heath and under the trees, here lies the body of Bonnie Dundee.' Monica caught a glimpse in the torchlight, realised that he had pushed a rod into the marshy ground. He moved it side to side, pushed it in a little harder then slowly drew it out, examined its tip and sniffed at it. Finally he wrapped a piece of tape round the rod to mark the depth and slopped back towards Monica and Crawford.

'We need to dig.' He set the rod down and lit up a cigarette. 'Four and a half foot deep. I think someone's buried down there.'

Chapter 6

September 1994

On the day she'd be leaving, Freya Sutherland took care as she packed her suitcase. Crouching by the side of the bed with the case hidden as she put the clothes in. Her mum or her sister, Jessica, were liable to come bursting into her bedroom without knocking. Dad rarely came upstairs except to sleep. His accident had made climbing the steps painful; she would hear his slow progress along the farmhouse corridor in plenty of time anyway.

The accident. It felt like everything had changed since then. A dodgy tractor brake, an overloaded trailer of fence posts, a slight incline. *Just lucky it was only his legs, just lucky they heard his screams, just lucky* . . . He hobbled with a stick rather than walked now, and was often 'out working' for long hours. He would come home late smelling of stale beer and cigarette smoke, and then there was the time he hadn't come home at all. The night spent looking for him in the fields and woods around the farmhouse, her mum's phone calls to his friends, to the hospitals. Then coming downstairs in the morning to find him at the kitchen table, Mum cooking breakfast at the Aga. As if nothing had happened.

She folded the last item, a white CHOOSE LIFE T-shirt like the one George Michael had worn years before, performing 'Wake

Me Up Before You Go-Go' on *Top of the Pops*. The others had given it to her as a joke when she confessed to being in the Wham! Fan Club as a seven-year-old. She smiled at the memory; it felt good, being gently mocked like that by friends. The closeness it implied. She couldn't help but feel the familiar guilt rise in her stomach at the memory though. As if she were somehow betraying her family by being close to others. She had even hinted to them about how difficult things had been at home since her dad's accident. Afterwards that had felt like another betrayal, sharing family secrets. But was it really wrong to want to be with people who made her feel good about herself? Maybe things would feel different in Berlin?

Berlin. Despite her confused feelings, the name of the city brought a flicker of excitement. They were actually doing it, starting a new life. Maybe she could even become a different person? She closed the case and slid it back down the side of her bed. Had to stop herself from checking the money again. It was locked safely in her jewellery box, and she'd already checked it twice that morning.

Her mum shouted from downstairs. Lunchtime, but still almost twelve hours until they picked her up. Mum had made Scotch broth, served with bread at the big kitchen table. Freya forced it down despite the nerves twisting her stomach. Jessica was talking about a friend from school; her dad said something about a project he was working on, how it was unseasonably warm. It all passed in a kind of blur. The old stone walls of the farmhouse, the trees that lined the road, and the dark mountains visible through the window in the distance.

'. . . at the hanging tree?' Freya caught the end of her dad's sentence, realised that the words had been directed at her. She looked up at the expectant faces of her family. Somehow feeling like all three of them could read her mind, would ask why she'd spent the morning packing.

'What did you say?'

'Head in the clouds as usual,' her mum said, only half joking.

Jessica put on the sarky voice. 'Dad *said*, do you know who's been drinking at the hanging tree?'

'At the hanging tree?' Freya repeated, too relieved to feel irritated.

'I thought I saw someone there last night. I went for a look this morning. Someone had lit a fire, left an empty bottle,' her dad said. 'Wondered if it would have been those friends of yours?'

'What would they be doing in the woods?' Freya said, hearing her voice rise defensively.

'He's only asking, Freya,' her mum said. 'You've not exactly wanted to spend much time with us recently.'

'We're not cool enough for her any more!' her dad said. Trying for humour.

Jessica jumped on this, desperate for things to seem normal: '*You're* definitely not cool anyway, Dad!'

After lunch they went out near the back field. Her dad wanted to show them where he'd cleared away a dense clump of gorse bushes. 'Opens it up nice, doesn't it? You can see Beinn a' Bhathaich Àrd in Strathfarrar now,' he said, pointing to the newly visible mountains.

Freya had often seen this pattern since her dad's accident: excitement at some new project on the farm, a flurry of work, then an evening when he wouldn't be around for dinner, would come home late or Mum would have to go and collect him. 'Make a big difference when it's finished.'

Jessica, pleased by the return of their old dad, asked him something, and the two of them walked towards the woods.

'I bumped into Caroline Russell's mum in town the other day,' her mum said. Freya nodded but didn't reply. Caroline had been her best friend at high school, had been successful in her exams while Freya's were a disaster. Had gone to medical school in Glasgow while Freya got a dead-end job in an Inverness amusement arcade. 'Said she's doing well at uni, just starting her second year now.'

'Listen, Mum—'

'I'm just saying, Freya. Maybe you could go to college? Maybe you could resit your exams?'

Freya took in her mum's concerned frown, blue eyes, grey hair. Realised how much she'd aged since Dad's accident. 'Maybe one day you'll feel proud of me.'

Without listening to her mum's reply, she turned and started back across the field towards the house. Her dad had been right, it was unseasonably warm, and she could feel a patina of sweat on her back. She wondered for a moment what the temperatures were like in Berlin in the winter. Did it get seriously cold? She'd never thought to ask.

Freya checked the time on her watch. Almost 3 p.m. Still an age until she met them. She heard the phone ringing from the farmhouse, the sound carrying out the open front door and across the field. The ringing stopped, then almost immediately started again. Obviously someone was keen to talk. Freya hurried through the long grass, hoped it wouldn't stain the white bits on her Vans trainers. The sound ended abruptly when she was still a little way from the house. Almost as if someone had picked up the phone. Who could be in the house though? There were no unfamiliar cars outside, and any friends calling round would have seen them across the field and have surely come over.

She opened the garden gate, thought she heard a voice from the house and then a sound like the phone being returned to the cradle. She stepped inside, the house cool after the heat outside. The kitchen was still, the smell of soup drifting and the curious sense of a room recently vacated. She went to look in the hall. The phone was there, silent on its table. Why would anyone come into the house to answer the phone and then disappear? It was absurd. She dismissed the paranoid thought. Someone had called then given up, that was all. They would call back if it was important.

Chapter 7

When Monica asked how long the excavation would take, Dr Ridgeway blew cigarette smoke into the foggy night. 'Ideally we'd isolate the site and take our time, sift each layer for evidence. It's a tidal marsh though, and you know what they say about time and tide . . .'

'What should we do then?' Crawford chipped in.

'Best to move quickly,' Ridgeway replied. 'Store the excavated earth in case we need to analyse it later.'

'When can we get started?' Monica asked.

'Next low tide's about noon,' Ridgeway said, obviously relishing the task. 'We'll get it done then.'

In the end, Ridgeway's plan was almost too ambitious. By the time they'd gathered equipment and personnel they had missed the lowest point of the tide. It was an hour after when they finally began to dig. Another hour, and word had got around. From her position on the causeway, Monica could just make out a few reporters and interested members of the public watching from far back by the canal, behind the perimeter the police had set up.

'Not much of a show for them.' Crawford nodded in their general direction. The night's fog had lingered through the day, obscuring the location. Ridgeway's team had erected temporary screens around the site anyway, but in Monica's experience screens only seemed to heighten the urge to know what was hidden behind them.

'Human instinct,' she replied. 'We always need to know, to try to understand.'

Crawford thought about that for a moment. 'Not always. Some people would rather ignore it, go about their lives.'

Monica looked down at her colleague, almost a foot shorter than her. The moisture from the mist had coalesced on his red hair and eyebrows. He had brought a pristine green Patagonia jacket from his car. Not the kind of outdoorsy item he would usually be seen in; it had the look of a gift from his girlfriend, Heather. And for a moment she couldn't help wondering if Crawford was talking about the spectators or something more personal.

Further to the east, the high pillars of the Kessock Bridge spanning the Beauly Firth were just visible through the fog. Grey, ominous, and somehow a suitable backdrop for an excavation.

'We're almost there,' Ridgeway shouted. 'It's weighted with stones.'

Monica felt the tension rise as, from her vantage point on the causeway, she watched the three archaeologists around the hole. The minutes passed agonisingly as stones were photographed then handed up.

'The tide's definitely turned,' Crawford muttered, looking out at the firth. 'We started too late. It'll flood the pool.'

Monica noticed that the wind had picked up too, in from the north-west and urging the rising tide onto the marshes. As if keen to keep this treasure buried in mud and water.

Ridgeway leaned in, seemed to pull at something. Monica caught snatches of muffled conversation.

'Seems remarkably well preserved . . .'

'The face . . .'

'Refilling . . .'

'Out quickly . . .'

More torturous minutes before Ridgeway stood, up to his chest in the pit, and quietly called for a bodybag. The photographer leaned in again to take pictures, the camera's flash stifled by the thinning fog. Finally, Monica watched the utterly surreal moment as the body, shrouded in what looked like black plastic, was slowly lifted from the hole. The two assistants who had struggled through the marsh with the bodybag held it open for the corpse. As the bag was carefully zipped shut on the body, Monica caught a glimpse of the face where Ridgeway had pulled back the plastic wrapping. Long hair glued to it in strands, skin stained by the marsh mud but seemingly preserved, like a medieval relic. The wind came on stronger, whistling over the marshes. In Monica's mind, in that strange moment, it almost seemed to carry an anger. And with it the questions were already spinning. Who had they just dug from the ground? And why had Pauline Tosh so willingly guided them to this place?

Chapter 8

The chill from the marsh grave seemed to linger on Monica as she pulled up across the road from Lucy's school. The body – a woman's – had been taken to the forensics lab. Ridgeway estimated she had been buried for at least ten years. Monica had asked Crawford to begin pulling missing persons files from 2008 and earlier.

'I want to keep Pauline Tosh's name out of the press for as long as possible,' Monica had whispered to Crawford at the burial site. 'Once they connect a serial killer they'll be all over it.' Only she, Crawford and Hately were so far aware that the grave's location had come from Tosh. 'Can you ask DC Khan to draft a press release? Let her know about the Tosh connection but tell her to say we were acting on intelligence.'

DC Maria Khan was a junior detective on the team. She came from a media background and had joined the police after an unspecified disaster in her personal life. Monica trusted her, having been impressed by her ability to handle the press in previous cases.

She got out of the Volvo, crossed the road to the school. The other mums were standing in a line by the fence. Monica realised that Munyasa's mum, Lydia, still hadn't returned her call from the day before about Lucy. It wasn't at all like Lydia, who was on her phone constantly. She craned her neck to look in among the mums and the couple of dads, caught a glimpse of

Lydia in conversation. Tried to catch her eye. Instead she noticed another woman. reddish-blonde hair, standing alone beside a mud-splattered Toyota Land Cruiser, dressed in a waxed jacket. She seemed to be staring intently at Monica.

The school bell sounded. Monica turned to see the kids pouring into the playground. After a minute she spotted Lucy. She was walking alone, carrying her little rucksack over her shoulder at the back of the pack, head down. Monica felt a wave of guilt that once again a case had diverted her attention from her daughter. She crouched to take Lucy's hand and walk back to the Volvo. When she finally did glance up, the street was emptying, the woman and the Land Cruiser gone.

Monica clicked the car unlocked, opened the door and strapped Lucy into her seat. Aware of the sense of discomfort that always came on after a murder scene. As if she was tainted by the horror of what she'd seen, might somehow spread it to the people she loved. She tried to ignore the illogical notion – she hadn't been within ten feet of the body so far in this case – got in behind the wheel and started the engine. Then turned back to Lucy.

'How was your day, honey?'

'It was OK.' Lucy had picked up the illustrated *Worst Witch* book again and was staring at one of the pages. Was someone picking on her? Bullying her? Monica thought back to her own early days at school and the enterprising boys with her first nicknames: *Monumental Monica, Monica the Man*. She tilted the mirror to see Lucy's face.

'Would you like to go for food? We could go to the cinema?'

Lucy seemed to brighten at the idea. 'Can we see *Hotel Transylvania*?'

They drove to Burger King at the retail park off the Nairn

road. Monica tried very hard to pay full attention to Lucy while they ate. To stop the image of the dead woman from creeping into the restaurant with them. To stop the insistent questions about Pauline Tosh entering her head. There would be time for that later, she told herself. More than enough time to consider it all. Instead she tried broaching the subject of what was bothering Lucy again: 'You know you can tell me anything about school. It doesn't matter what it is.'

'Do you think you could cast a spell?' Lucy replied. 'I think I could.'

Lucy had a tendency to drift off into fantasy, *The Worst Witch* the latest domain for her imagination. Was it an escape from whatever was going on for her at school? Monica recalled chunks of her own childhood spent ensconced with the Famous Five or the Secret Seven. 'I don't think so, I wouldn't really know how,' Monica replied finally, resolving to try calling Lydia again later that evening.

After eating they crossed the car park to the cinema, where it turned out that *Hotel Transylvania 3: Summer Vacation* was showing. Monica even managed to keep her phone switched off throughout, avoiding the temptation to check for messages. When she finally did switch it back on a couple of hours later in the car park, there were two voicemails. One from DC Khan saying they had released a holding statement to the press. One from Miss Jennings asking if Monica could make an appointment to come to the school for a chat about Lucy.

When she had put Lucy to bed that night, Monica tried calling Lydia again. This time her friend's phone was switched off, and Monica wondered if perhaps she was having technical difficulties. If she had lost or broken her phone it would explain the lack of a response. She typed a short email: 'Hi Lydia, I'm worried about Lucy. Just wondering if you'd heard anything at school. I tried calling but couldn't get through. Thanks, Monica x'

She sent it to the email account Lydia shared with her husband and tried to stop worrying. Glanced around the living room, took in the large corner sofa, the Anglepoise lamp, the coffee table. It was moments like this that she would have appreciated having someone else around. Someone to joke with, or talk about some shared interest. In her old life in London, Monica had enjoyed going to concerts, museums, art galleries, talking about books. It all felt a world away.

You should finish filling in that online dating profile then, her inner voice piped up. How else was she ever going to meet someone? She retrieved her laptop from the bag hanging by the door, set it on the coffee table. Resolved to log on.

Instead she found herself taking an old external hard drive from the bag and plugging it in. She located the folder 'Inactive' and found the file 'Pauline Tosh'. Dragged it onto the computer desktop.

She spent the next hour re-familiarising herself with the four women known to have been killed by Tosh. Her first victim was Jean Porter, who went missing in Glasgow in 1992. Then a long gap until her final three known victims, in 2004, 2005 and 2006. To Monica this had always seemed an unfeasibly long break. In early 1993 Tosh had moved north from Glasgow to Inverness, to work as a kitchen porter in a hotel. Her exact whereabouts for the following ten years were uncertain. She was thought to have lived out of a camper van, working odd jobs for cash. Resurfacing in Stirlingshire in 2005 to care for her ageing mother and begin work as a home help.

Monica pushed the laptop shut and went to put on a record

from the collection she had inherited from her dad – *John Prine* this time. It had become a favourite. She aimed the needle for 'Angel from Montgomery', landed on 'Far from Me' instead and lay back on the couch, leaving it to play through. If the woman's body did turn out to be over ten years old, as Ridgeway had confidently asserted, then it made Tosh suspect number one, two, three, four . ... It made sense for Monica to take charge of the investigation – no one knew the details of Pauline Tosh's murders better than her.

The autopsy was scheduled for the next afternoon. Hopefully there would be some fragment of DNA that would incontrovertibly ID Tosh as the killer. Make all their lives easier. As Monica shut her eyes and began drifting off to sleep, the image resurfaced for her: the stained body being lifted from the marsh grave. In the half-dream image, the corpse's face was replaced by Pauline Tosh's. Smiling widely with her little teeth on display as she had at Carselang. Monica understood what her subconscious was hinting at. She had never seen the killer look so excited.

Chapter 9

The image of Tosh's smiling trickster face nagged at Monica through the night and into the grey autumn morning. All the way to dropping Lucy at school and driving to police headquarters in the Raigmore area of Inverness. Crawford arrived at the Major Investigation Team's office just after her, carrying takeaway coffees. Handed them out to Monica, DC Maria Khan, DC Ben Fisher.

'Nothing like coffee when you're not expecting it, is there?' Crawford said. He seemed back to his enthusiastic self. She wondered again for a moment what had been bothering him on Sunday when they'd met outside Carselang prison. Hopefully nothing important; she could do without her closest colleague hiding something from her when Lucy was acting strangely. The thought reminded her, and she made a mental note to call the school that morning and arrange the meeting with Miss Jennings. 'Colombian beans,' Crawford added. 'Meant to be a bit sweeter. What do you think?'

Monica tried the drink, which didn't taste noticeably different to any other coffee. She didn't want to dampen his enthusiasm though. 'I think it does taste a bit sweeter.'

'Did you see this?' DC Fisher piped up. He was the youngest detective on the team, dressed neatly in a suit and wearing glasses, his dark hair in a side parting. He was driven and ambitious, qualities that could be irritating but suited Monica just fine, as he was also a thorough and reliable detective, happy to shine in any kind of work assigned to him – even the detailed and boring office stuff that formed the backbone of successful investigating. During the intense case in the previous spring, Monica and Fisher had shared stories of personal troubles, but despite that moment of trust their relationship had never really progressed beyond formal.

'What is it?' She leaned in beside him, expecting to see something related to the excavated body; instead she was confronted by a picture of a burning building.

'A church near Eskadale, out west, not far from Beauly. Burned early this morning. There was a Mr Miles inside, a churchwarden. He's in intensive care.'

'Was it arson?'

'The fire inspectors are in at the moment,' Fisher replied.

'I bumped into one of the responding officers this morning,' Crawford chipped in. Her partner had a rare talent for ferreting out information, seemingly without even trying. In that regard she'd known few better in her two-decades-plus on the force. 'Jim MacLeod – know him from the gym. He said the churchwarden, Mr Miles, was talking when they carried him out.'

'What did he say?'

Crawford took a sip of his coffee, relishing the storytelling. 'Said he'd seen something. A creature, coming out the ground.'

'Out of the ground?'

'That's what he said, then he lost consciousness just afterwards.'

Probably the unfortunate Mr Miles had been experiencing some kind of delirium, Monica decided. The image was disturbing, but hopefully the churchwarden would recover quickly and the fire would turn out to be a simple accident.

*

The morgue was beneath Raigmore Hospital, just a few hundred yards from headquarters, so Monica and Crawford elected to walk. The north-westerly had persisted, banking up cloud from the Atlantic like a lid over the city. Making grey roads and buildings a notch more depressing. Not even mid-morning and already it felt like the day was mostly over. Or had never really started.

They sat waiting in the corridor outside the morgue for Dr Dolohov, the pathologist. Monica took in the chemical smell of the hospital, the flickering basement light overhead. After a moment she realised that they hadn't spoken on the walk over, that it hadn't felt awkward. The idea was strangely appealing – the comfortable closeness it implied – even if a little dangerous.

'Did you ever get in trouble at school?'

Crawford glanced up. 'My grandad was quite strict, so generally I did what I was told, or made it seem like I did.' Monica knew that her partner had been raised by his teenage single mother and devoutly Christian grandparents. 'Out of school it was different,' he added. 'Have to make your own fun as a youngster out in the sticks.' An appealing smile crossed his face at the memories, and Monica felt like she would have been happy sitting there with Crawford for the afternoon, swapping stories and never having to go through the morgue doors to the waiting body. 'Why do you ask?'

'Just Lucy. I don't know, I think she's struggling to fit in at school. I've got to go up and speak to her teacher.'

'Do you think she's being bullied?' Crawford straightened up, seemed genuinely upset at the idea.

'That's what I'm wondering. She won't open up about it.'

'Things can get out of proportion when you're a kid,' Crawford said. 'They can—'

Monica's phone began ringing. It was the school returning her call. She arranged a time with the secretary and hung up just as the door beside them was opening. Dr Dolohov stepped halfway into the corridor and beckoned them inside.

The pathologist's skin was generally pasty from a career spent underground in morgues, but on this occasion he was tanned. Greyish hair and a beard clipped short, he had a wiry physique, standing unsmiling with crows feet at the corner of his eyes and hands on his hips. The body was on the slab, covered by a sheet.

'Detective Inspector. Detective Constable.' He spoke with a distinctive half-Russian, half-southern-English accent.

'You look well.' Monica realised that her eyes had dropped to his hands; they were large, and tanned now too. More attractive than she had noticed before. She caught herself after a second and thought, *Jesus, you really need to get to work on that dating profile.* Dolohov was eccentric, at times bordering on macabre.

'Everyone says that this week. A nice thing about Scotland, they tell you when you look good; in Russia they tell you when you look bad. I've been away. Took Mother on pilgrimage to the Solovetsky Islands in the White Sea. Caught their best week of sun this year. Ate pickled fish, saw beluga whales. Mother complained. I swam in the lakes and drank vodka.'

'It suits you.' Monica realised that she liked the idea of drinking vodka and swimming in the White Sea. Feeling Crawford's amused eyes on her face and realising she was actually flirting with Dolohov, she quickly added, 'Better than being stuck down here anyway. Have you had the initial forensics through?'

Dolohov straightened up, cleared his throat. 'Oh yes! Gemma Gunn's been at it overnight. A thorough job. We take care of our victims in the Highlands!'

Gemma Gunn was the head of the Inverness Forensic Services lab. Monica knew she was thorough bordering on obsessive, had worked for the FBI before settling in the Highlands, where aside from running the lab she could indulge in her taste for mountaineering and other outdoor interests.

'Anything that stood out?' Gunn would send the report on, but Dolohov could summarise before the autopsy.

'You know that the body was remarkably well preserved by being wrapped in plastic in the marsh conditions? Gunn thinks she's been in the ground for around twenty years. Mostly based on her clothes. It'll take a few days to find out exactly when the garments were manufactured and sold.' He picked up a printed sheet. 'She was fully clothed – Levi's jeans, dark Topshop vest, two unlabelled cardigans. Nothing in her pockets, no wallet or ID. No obvious defence wounds or other signs of assault. One filling in the second upper right molar. Looks like an NHS amalgam job.'

Monica nodded at this useful information. With recent improvements in oral hygiene it wasn't unusual for younger bodies to have no dental work, making it harder to use the unique shapes of fillings as a form of ID.

'Fibres were recovered from the nasal cavity and under her fingernails. Blue, probably acrylic carpet fibres. Possibly wrapped in something pre-mortem and tried to scrape her way out.' Monica suppressed a shudder at the idea of being wrapped in a carpet, fighting for air. Not dissimilar to places she'd been in her nightmares.

Dolohov laid the printed sheet back down and turned towards the slab. Pulled on his slightly unnecessary hair covering and mask. Gestured to his assistant, who was typing something into a computer, then turned to the row of surgical implements on the metal tray beside the slab. He selected a long thin knife, removed the sheet from the body and began to cut.

Dolohov sewed the body back together as best he could. Not one of the harshest autopsies Monica had witnessed. Although the victim was young, which always made it worse, she had been in the ground a long time. Comparatively well preserved – which meant she was much more of a corpse than a skeleton – but she still didn't look fully human. If you squinted it was possible to imagine Dolohov was working on a curious anatomical model, even an ancient mummy.

The doctor removed his mask, wiped the sweat off with a towel. 'Aged about twenty, roughly five foot four, medium build, would have weighed around one hundred and thirty pounds. Death caused by asphyxiation due to manual strangulation, fractures to the cartilaginous framework of the larynx.'

'Killer used their hands?'

'Most probably. Squeezed hard enough to break the cartilage in her voice box. There's also an abrasion on her forehead, just at the hairline, that could be significant.'

Monica thought about it for a second. 'Pushed her onto the ground from behind? She hits her head?'

'It would explain the fibres in her nose and fingernails,' Crawford chipped in. He was still in the room at least, an improvement on the last autopsy they'd witnessed when he'd left halfway through. 'If she was pushed face forward she might have inhaled them, clawed at the carpet trying to turn over.'

It made sense. 'It would fit with Tosh's modus operandi,' Monica muttered. 'We'll know more when we get the carpet fibres back.' Gunn would already have sent them for analysis, and they would then be run against a vehicle database. If they matched fibres from the model of Volkswagen camper van Pauline Tosh had owned, the evidence would mount against her. Monica took a breath of the cold chemical air from the morgue, then glanced at the body, covered again with the sheet. The dental filling should make it possible to ID the victim from missing persons' reports, and if they could find a connection to Pauline Tosh then maybe the case would be tied up quickly? She could give her full attention to whatever was bothering Lucy.

Chapter 10

Up the stairs and out of the morgue, back into the same dull light as before, but Monica felt the transformation. The air was a little sharper, the day a little clearer. She'd observed the same thing previously on leaving an autopsy, concluded it was some hormonal reaction to the close proximity of death. An animal part of the brain rejoicing at escaping the monster's lair, living to fight another day. She had read a bit about it, in a book by Walter Burkert called *Creation of the Sacred*. He seemed to suggest something similar – that escaping from predators in prehistory formed the basis of our urge towards religion and sacrifice. It might explain why modern people were so intrigued by serial killers, the monsters of our times.

Crawford interrupted her thoughts: 'I always feel depressed after being in there, especially seeing someone young like that. Why the fuck do people do these senseless things?'

Obviously he didn't share her feeling of being reborn. Monica's phone vibrated in her pocket, she answered to DC Khan: 'I've just had a journalist on the phone, boss.' The detective was speaking quickly, Lowland Scottish accent coming on stronger. 'She's asking about Pauline Tosh. Thinks the body from the marsh could be one of her victims – assuming it's the body of a woman. Don't know if something's leaked to her?'

Monica swore under her breath. This would make a nice story online. Locals were probably already speculating on the Inverness

Neighbourhood Watch Facebook page – sometimes the city felt like a village. She couldn't believe any of the close team would leak it to the media. Probably Tyler Mitchell, the chatty prison guard at Carselang, or one of the other officers had put two and two together when the news of the woman's body broke. Not the most difficult deduction to make, and an easy way to gain a few extra quid.

Monica left Crawford with Khan and Fisher at headquarters, with instructions to dig into the timeline of Pauline Tosh's whereabouts in Inverness in the mid-90s and narrow down the missing persons to those filed earlier than the year 2000.

She pulled up round the corner from Lucy's school. The meeting with Miss Jennings wasn't until the following afternoon, but she had arrived a little early to try again to speak with Lydia. She walked round to the gate and the row of other mums.

'Excuse me. You're the detective Monica Kennedy, aren't you?' Monica turned towards the unexpected voice, realising it was the woman in the waxed jacket from the day before. The one who had been standing beside the Land Cruiser watching her. After the call from Khan, Monica's impulse was to assume she was a journalist. Up close she was pretty, her reddish hair tied in a ponytail, a toothy smile suggesting vulnerability – strangely it made Monica want to put her arms around her. 'You're sort of a celebrity round here,' the woman continued. 'It must be exciting . . . having a life where you do interesting things *every* day?' A question that could have been invasive, but the woman seemed naively curious, nothing like a doorstepping journalist. Aged around forty, Monica guessed. Attractive, but with a hint of sadness?

'Sorry' – Monica couldn't help returning the smile – 'what did you say your name was?'

'I'm Harriet's mum, you're Lucy's mum, aren't you. Harriet's in the year above, I think they know each other.'

After the case the year before it sometimes seemed like everyone in Inverness knew who Lucy was. Before Monica could reply, the school bell rang. She turned to see the kids pouring out. Once again Lucy traipsed out alone at the back of the pack. Head down, shoulders slumped. She seemed dejected as she came through the gate towards Monica.

'Say hi to Lucy, Harriet,' Monica heard the woman say as Lucy approached. She remembered that, before being distracted, she had been trying to speak to Lydia, and caught a glimpse of her getting into a car further down the road. She sighed and turned back. A girl with blonde hair – Harriet presumably – was standing beside her. Dutifully the girl said, 'Hi Lucy, how are you?'

Lucy was frowning but managed, 'I'm fine, thanks.'

Monica took her daughter's hand and smiled at the woman, about to leave. 'I wanted to ask you something. It's . . .' the woman blurted. 'I wanted to . . .'

Monica turned back, hearing the discomfort in the woman's voice. 'Is everything OK?'

'It's my sister.' She finally managed to get the words out. 'I think . . . Online they said a woman had been dug up . . . I think it could be her.'

Monica cleared her throat. As far as she knew, the information about how long the body had been buried for hadn't been leaked. Chances were the woman's sister had gone missing recently and she'd made a frightened assumption. 'If she's been gone for longer than twenty-four hours you should . . .' But as she spoke Monica caught that hint of sadness again, beneath the naivety. Took in the worry lines on the woman's forehead, the haunted expression. 'She's been gone longer, hasn't she?'

'Just turned twenty-four years,' the woman said. 'I'm Jessica Sutherland. My sister's Freya, Freya Sutherland. She's been missing since September 1994.'

Monica watched as the waitress brought mugs of hot chocolate to Lucy and Harriet, who were sitting together at a window seat. Smells of coffee and baking bread drifted through the boho interior of the Velocity Cafe, just along the road from the school, cosy in the autumn afternoon. The perfect quiet place to curl up in an armchair with a good book, safe from the outside world.

Instead Monica watched the tears, dammed up for over two decades, edge into Jessica Sutherland's blue eyes. Glanced down at the tumbler of water on the table in front of her, scarred white from repeated dishwasher cleaning. Wisps of steam drifted from Jessica's camomile tea, adding to the strange atmosphere. Finally Monica broke the silence: 'Can you tell me about your sister? Can you tell me about Freya?'

Jessica took a deep breath, gave a smile and said, 'Don't know what I'm making such a fuss about. There are people with no legs who get up every day and go to work.' She dabbed at the corner of her eye with a paper napkin, attempting to avoid the mascara.

'You're not making a fuss.'

'Panda eyes now . . .' She shook her head. 'Everyone was talking about there being an excavation at the marshes yesterday. I just had a strange feeling it was my sister. My husband, Barry, tried to reassure me it would be someone else. Then I read today that it was a woman . . .'

'I know this is difficult—'

'She was nineteen when she left. Dark hair, blue eyes, a bit taller than me, about five-five, average build. She went one

45

night, left a note to say she was going away with friends. We haven't seen or heard from her since.' Jessica's voice was emotionless, a contrast to her obvious upset: the missing-person recital. Monica had heard it often enough over the years from the families left behind, the lives paused at a certain moment, the details that had become marked indelibly in the mind. 'It was hard, especially for Mum and Dad. They could never really come to terms with what had happened, like we were all on hold – weeks, months, then it was years . . . It broke their hearts; they both died still wondering . . .' Monica glanced towards Lucy and Harriet sitting at the window, imagined her own daughter missing for a day, for a minute.

'It must have been terrifying.'

'Oh, I'm used to it now,' Jessica said, sounding anything but. 'At the time it was hard. We were so happy as a family, it just ruined everything.'

The timing of Freya's disappearance, her age and body size all matched what they so far knew of the victim. 'Who were the friends?' *Anyone called Pauline Tosh?* Although surely if Tosh was known to have befriended Freya Sutherland, the link would have been made back when the killer was arrested.

'She didn't say. We spoke to everyone, all her old school friends. She worked at an amusement arcade on Castle Street – Bobby's Ark? We asked there, put up posters . . . There were all these rumours, but nothing ever came to anything.'

'What were the rumours?'

Jessica dropped her eyes to the camomile tea. 'Different things, none of them exactly nice.'

Monica checked the girls weren't listening; they seemed to be watching something outside the cafe window. 'Sometimes gossip can carry a fragment of truth.'

46

'That she'd got pregnant and gone off to have someone's baby. That she was addicted to heroin in Edinburgh and working as a prostitute. That she had joined a cult.'

'And nothing ever came of any of these rumours?'

'The police weren't exactly interested.' And now for the first time Monica caught a hint of bitterness from Jessica. 'Just marked Freya down as another runaway because she left us a note. But it wasn't like her to just go; it wasn't like her at all. Someone must have got into her mind to make her leave like that. There's no way she would have just gone and left Mum and Dad to wonder where she was.'

Chapter 11

The following morning Monica drove back up Glen Wyvis and crossed the narrow bridge to Carselang prison. Close to the top of her list of places to be avoided, now here she was, back for the second time in a week. She parked the Volvo and took a breath of the mountain air, the smell of freedom drifting over the walls to mix with the fetid stink of fear and desperation. Monica couldn't help wondering if the proximity to all that wilderness was in any way comforting to the prisoners. Her father had spoken of *Carse sickness*, prisoners released after a long stretch who would lose their minds and go back to the prison. Once or twice a year they'd find an ex-inmate wandering the glen, or occasionally after a winter storm dead in the snow. For as long as Monica could remember there had been talk of decommissioning Carselang, but the idea never seemed to get off the ground and the prison remained, forgotten by most.

Monica pulled her coat a little tighter against the chill. In the distance to the south she could make out the bulk of Ben Wyvis, the huge mountain that dominated the view north from Inverness. For a moment she felt the remoteness of the place, and with it a rare sense of loneliness.

'You're a long way from home,' she muttered as she slammed the car door. In the past she had preferred to work alone when possible; today she'd actually missed Crawford's company on the drive. He was tracking down Freya Sutherland's dental records,

48

along with those of a handful of other missing persons the team had identified. In theory, ID'ing the body, finding a connection to Tosh and proving the fibres matched those from the carpet in a van owned by the killer would wrap the case up quickly.

Tyler Mitchell came bustling out of the office when he saw her. 'Read about it in the paper!' He held up a tabloid newspaper: KILLER LEADS COPS TO VICTIM'S GRAVE! Monica had read the story back in the office: 'Sources say top cop Monica Kennedy has befriended sick serial killer Pauline Tosh in a bid to locate her victims. The famous DI persuaded Tosh to give up the burial location of a so-far unidentified victim.' 'Found a body, didn't you!' His face alive with naive excitement – either he genuinely hadn't leaked to the press, or else he should be taking his acting talents to the stage of Eden Court Theatre in Inverness.

'I can't say too much about it until we can inform the family.'

'Course, yeah.' Tyler nodded gravely. 'It's the same for me – people always asking for stories about what happens up here. Have to tell them it's confidential.'

'Any idea what kind of mood Tosh is in?' Monica asked, partly seeking Tyler's opinion to keep him onside, but also because she hadn't made an appointment to see the killer. Rule of thumb: turn up unannounced when wanting to talk to a psychopath in prison. Often, agreeing to an interview then refusing to leave their cell gave them a narcissistic thrill. Better to take a chance by arriving unheralded.

'Hard to tell with her. She asked for all the papers – doesn't normally read them.'

So Tosh was excited about the coverage. This surprised Monica, as Tosh had never sought attention. No press cuttings at her home during the 2006 investigation; no communication with journalists.

Tyler led Monica through security and down the claustrophobic corridors. Then it was her turn to sit waiting in the stuffy interview room while another officer went to see if Tosh would meet her. She dug out her iPhone – the officer at security had neglected to take it – hoping for an update on the victim's ID. She quickly understood why phone security was lax: 'No Service'. She dropped it back in her pocket. Took in the lime-green paint peeling from the walls, the damp air in the windowless room. Tried to imagine spending a day, a week, in a place like this. After a half-hour wait, Monica was convinced Tosh wasn't coming. Another fifteen minutes and she began to wonder if Tyler had forgotten she was there. She was considering hitting the buzzer, when finally she heard a key turning in the door on the opposite side of the room. It clanked open and a heavyset female officer led Tosh inside, then secured the cuffs on her wrists to the table. Monica was again struck by how small but strong-looking Tosh was. Her overalls were dark green this time.

'We'll just be a half-hour or so, Moira,' Tosh said to the prison officer. 'We'll get our morning cuppa and a wee catch-up after that, will we?'

The officer nodded – 'Right enough, Pauline' – then left the room and locked the door behind her.

'Bit down being in here, Moira, so she is,' Tosh said. 'Been having a hard time at home with her eldest daughter acting up.' Her tone was that of a wise matriarch. 'They just get to that age, young women – think they know it all.'

'Are you talking about a particular woman?'

Tosh narrowed her eyes. 'We've known each other a while now, Monica. Must be what, five years?'

'Over ten years.'

'Is it really? Time goes different in here.' Tosh snapped her fingers, the cuff rattling as it came tight. 'A day lasts a month, and a year goes by like that.'

'I take it you read about the dig in the marshes, in the papers?'

'That was some bother you got yourself in, back the other year, was it not?' Tosh replied as if Monica hadn't spoken. 'You and your daughter, Lucy.'

Monica bristled internally but managed to force a smile. 'Not my finest moment.'

'You shouldn't be too hard on yourself, Monica. We can all make mistakes. A shame for your daughter right enough, thinking back to my own wee childhood.' She tilted her head slightly, staring intently. 'How bad things can make a home inside you. How they end up coming out in funny ways that you don't even understand yourself.' Tosh smiled slowly, showing her uneven teeth. 'How much can you really know about all the things in someone's mind? What a surprise my mum got with everything I used to get up to. Maybe it'll be the same with you and Lucy when she's a bit older?' Was this why Tosh had given up the location of the body? To have the opportunity to taunt the woman who had apprehended her? If so, Monica wasn't about to give her the satisfaction of showing how much the words stung.

She cleared her throat, tried to sound composed. 'I'm here in my role as a detective, Pauline. My daughter's got nothing to do with this. You know we found a woman's body buried in the marshes? I was hoping you could tell me who it is, how you met her.'

Tosh scowled then glanced away. 'Do you like reading?' Monica shook her head and stood up – clearly she was wasting her time. 'I never could read when I was wee,' Tosh continued. 'Didn't learn until I was in prison, so I did.' Monica knew for a fact this was a lie. She had seen samples of Tosh's handwriting in diaries

51

from the early 1990s, long before she was apprehended. 'Learned faster than anyone they'd seen in here, the teacher said so.'

'Take care, Pauline.' Monica hit the buzzer by the door.

'My favourite was a poem.' Tosh spoke louder and Monica turned back to see her face alive with amusement. 'A poem about the road to Mandalay. I heard it from an underworld boatman. All the way back in 1994 it would have been.'

Chapter 12

All through the drive back down Glen Wyvis and into the car park at headquarters in Inverness, Monica felt an urge to wash herself. For her this wasn't a universal response to spending time with a killer. She had met violent, even sadistic, criminals who actually conformed to the image of the charming psychopath. Much as she didn't like to admit it, Monica had even felt a ghost of a liking for some.

She swung open the door to the toilets, took in the smells of bleach and air freshener. Went to wash her face and hands in the sink, found her mind drifting to a man named Francis MacGregor. Prime example of a charming psycho – one-time leader of the Red Death, a violent biker gang, and still rumoured to head up a criminal network.

Monica and Crawford had crossed paths with him in a case the previous spring, a situation that had led to a tense stand-off and MacGregor threatening vengeance. Despite all that, and even having read about the man's violent past, Monica recalled grilling him in an interview room, running her eyes down his broad shoulders to his thick hands. Remembered feeling a flicker of animal attraction to his bright eyes, his infectious love of life.

Monica pumped the dispenser until a drizzle of soap finally emerged, scrubbed at her hands and arms, splashed water on her face. With Pauline Tosh there was no hint of attraction. Just a taint, and a bone-deep coldness. After her cryptic utterance about the poem and the boatman, Tosh had sat with a smile on her face, satisfied she had said all she needed to.

Monica straightened up. The weak electric blower seemed designed for workers who had a couple of hours to stand drying their hands. Thankfully the dryer was topped with a stack of paper towels. She grabbed a handful, dried herself off and hurried down the corridor to the office.

Crawford was sitting with DC Fisher on one side and DC Khan on the other, all three poring over something on his desk. He turned at the sound of the door opening and Monica clocked the excitement on his face immediately. 'What have you got?'

'Just Freya Sutherland's dental records . . .' Crawford was always at his most effusive when he had an audience and news to share. Apparently it was going to be a significant moment in the case, whether the records showed Freya to be their victim or not.

Monica pulled up a chair at the end of the desk beside Fisher, glanced among the paper cups of coffee, all empty, and noticed two were stained with pink lipstick. 'Khan drank yours as well. I can get you one from the pot,' Crawford said, appreciating the chance to draw out his reveal. Monica felt an unreasonable little flash of irritation towards Khan – she could have used that coffee.

Khan raised a dark eyebrow. 'Sorry, it was cold, didn't think you'd want it . . .'

'It's fine,' Monica said, feeling unbelievably petty as she glanced at the coffee pot, rejecting the tar-like liquid. 'Do the fillings match?'

Crawford cleared his throat. 'A Mr Barnes was Freya Sutherland's dentist. Still works at the Crown Dental Practice. I went over this morning. You remember at the autopsy Dolohov said our victim had one filling in the second upper right molar?' Crawford picked up a copy of an X-ray. 'This is from our victim.'

He held up a second X-ray. 'A year before Freya Sutherland disappeared Mr Barnes did her only filling. In the second upper right molar. Perfect match.'

Monica watched as he slid one X-ray sheet over the other. The white blocks of amalgam filling against the translucent jaw bones matched almost exactly. She felt a mix of emotions: grey horror at what had been done to Freya – murdered at nineteen, left in a marsh hole for a quarter-century – and a hint of satisfaction that she could at least end the uncertainty for Freya's sister. She remembered Freya's delicate hands, the nails. Could those nails really have clawed at Tosh's conscience in the darkest hours of the night, for all those summers and winters? As Monica recalled the killer's smile, she thought not.

'Tosh must really fucking like you, boss,' Crawford said, as if echoing her doubts. He was leaning back in his chair now, hands behind his head, chest pushed out so the muscles in his neck were tight. 'Why the hell did she just decide to offer us the body's location?'

Monica looked at Crawford. His white shirt had come untucked from the waist of his trousers. He seemed to have a way of looking ruffled but appealing.

'You pulled the missing person file on Freya Sutherland?'

'Got it here, ma'am,' Fisher said from beside her, pointing to a thin folder on the desk. 'Reported missing on Monday, twelfth of September 1994, last seen at her family home on the night of Saturday the tenth, wasn't there in the morning, left a note to her parents. The case went cold very quickly. Basically no credible sightings – rumours but not much else.'

Monica nodded, remembering what Jessica had said about the police treating the case as a runaway. The rumours that came to dead ends. 'Who was the investigating officer?'

'A DC Gregg.'

The name disquieted Monica. 'Duncan Gregg?'

Fisher ran his fingers over the name on the sheet. 'That's what it says.'

'Didn't realise Gregg was already on the force back then,' Crawford chipped in.

'Who is he?' Khan asked, eyes going from Monica to Crawford, catching the tension between them.

Monica cleared her throat. 'He works in traffic now; used to be a detective back when I was first on the force.' She still didn't know Khan well enough to mention the rumours about Gregg. Whispers of low-level corruption that followed him: media leaks, tip-offs to criminals. After the case the year before that had led to disaster, Monica even half suspected Gregg of passing information to a killer. 'Been a while since he worked as a detective.' She turned to Fisher. 'Anything else jump out at you?'

'Nothing obvious. As I say, it's not the most detailed. Appears that Gregg assumed Freya was safe because of the note she left.'

Monica thought back to the mid-1990s. Gregg was a few years older than her. Although he had been known to be slapdash with his detective work, he'd also had a reputation for cunning. Had closed some big cases.

'I'll try to get hold of him, see if he remembers anything that's not in the file,' Monica said, though she was sceptical. Gregg wasn't known for his generosity – unless there was something in it for him. The clock on the wall read almost 3 p.m.; she had the meeting with Miss Jennings at Lucy's school in thirty minutes. How did the hours fly by so quickly? She decided she did need that coffee after all, went to the machine and poured a mug. Treacle-dark, the splash of milk didn't touch it.

'We know Tosh moved to Inverness in 1993. She was working at the Royal Hotel as a kitchen porter, but we don't have any record of where she was living at the time.' She took a sip of the coffee, burned and bitter, and pushed the mug away. 'Can you three dig into that? Look for any crossover between Tosh and Freya.'

Monica's concern for Lucy only grew when she entered the classroom. Her mum had collected Lucy from school so she was free to attend the meeting with Miss Jennings. The teacher was dressed in a shapeless cardigan and blue wool skirt to her ankles, brown hair in a bun. Normally Monica felt warmth towards the teacher – who, unlike some memorable figures from her own school days, seemed genuinely to like children and their foibles, often greeting her pupils at the front gate in the morning with a smile. On this occasion, as she welcomed Monica and offered her a seat by the desk at the front of the class, it was her face that gave concern; set in an uncharacteristic frown.

Monica took in the little tables, the thick linoleum on the floor, the children's paintings on the walls. Funny, she could still remember the feeling of entering a similar room for the first time herself, almost forty years before. The mixture of apprehension and excitement. All the world contained in those four walls. Then the sense of disbelief as it started – the teasing and bullying about her unusual height and looks – blossoming into horror.

'I was wondering if Lucy's being bullied by some of the other children,' Monica said as she sat down. 'She's normally so outgoing, so quirky, but recently she's been subdued, not herself at all. When they were at nursery she was best friends with Munyasa; now he won't even speak to her. I've tried talking to his mum, Lydia . . .'

'It's a big change for the children,' Miss Jennings said softly. 'Starting school.'

57

'I know.' Monica glanced away to the blackboard: X IS FOR X-RAY. 'I know what it feels like, being scared to come in to school.'

Miss Jennings smiled, folded her hands in her lap. 'Lucy went through a traumatic event, a year ago?' Monica felt the words like a punch in the stomach, the second mention in the same day – the first by Pauline Tosh. Coming from the kindly Miss Jennings, it stung more.

'It's been hard for her,' Monica replied, noticing the dryness in her mouth. 'She had a thing earlier this year – she was sleepwalking, acting strangely – but she's been much better. I thought she was settling in well . . .'

'We've had a few wee incidents with Lucy,' the teacher said slowly. 'Two of the other girls got upset.'

'Wait. What?'

'She was over in the story-time corner.' Miss Jennings nodded to some beanbags and a bookshelf. 'During quiet time she told them she could make them have bad dreams if she wanted.'

Monica sighed. 'When I was at school we used to tell each other ghost stories. It's not exactly—'

'It wasn't just that, Miss Kennedy,' Miss Jennings said firmly. 'She threatened one of her classmates.'

Monica's throat went drier. 'What happened?'

'Munyasa told her he didn't want to play with her and she told him she would hurt him.'

'No, this is all wrong; they've been best friends since nursery. She loves Munyasa, they love each other . . .' Even as she was speaking Monica realised how absurd the words were. The normally communicative Lydia had failed to answer any of her messages, obviously didn't want to speak to her. This explained exactly why.

'Munyasa says he's frightened of Lucy,' Miss Jennings said quietly. 'The other children say they don't want to play with her.' Monica sat, stunned. This was so far from what she'd hoped for for Lucy. So far from being *normal*, getting on with others at school, having a lightness and ease to her life. 'She's a lovely girl,' Miss Jennings continued. 'We have such a nice time when it's just the two of us talking. What an imagination she has. I've spoken to the headmistress and the parents, and they're all understanding about everything she's been through.' Monica nodded dumbly, feeling very slightly comforted that there was no malice towards her daughter, even as she felt the dent to her own pride. 'We're all minded to try and keep Lucy in with the rest of the pupils, get this resolved in school.'

Chapter 13

Monica pulled over outside the Royal Hotel on Ness Walk, in central Inverness. The grand Victorian building was one of her favourites in the city, sitting beside the River Ness opposite the castle. On an autumn evening, when the sky was bruised purple, the view gave a sense of what Inverness would have been in its heyday – the fantasy of Sir Walter Scott's romantic Highlands brought to life. In the 1960s, a picturesque suspension bridge and historic buildings dating from the sixteenth century had been torn down. Replaced with assorted concrete structures by the Highlands and Islands Development Board. On a normal day when Monica admired what remained of the view, she reliably felt a flush of anger at this stunning lack of foresight or respect for history.

Today, as she sat waiting in the Volvo for Crawford to appear from the hotel, she felt only numb as she played Miss Jennings's words over in her head: *We're all minded to try and keep Lucy in with the rest of the pupils, get this resolved in school.* The implication being that if things didn't work out, Lucy might have to go to a different school? Be put in a separate class for those with behavioural issues? Monica realised she hadn't even asked any clarifying questions. Just sat there dumbly, trying to adjust to this new version of reality.

She spotted Crawford outside the hotel. Although it was twilight in autumn he was wearing dark glasses. Half turned away from – but talking to – a woman. Early twenties, blonde, good-looking, wearing jeans and a long black coat. Monica watched her partner's attempt at flirtation for a moment, saw the woman lift her chin and turn half away herself. It was hard to read the body language at this distance: interested or not? A beat too long and Monica began to feel like a voyeur. She glanced across the river to the castle and hit the car horn. When she looked back, the woman had gone and Crawford was jogging across the cobbled street to the car. He opened the door and got in.

'Was everything OK at the school?' Her partner smelled of the autumn cold, a hint of delicious cologne.

Monica really didn't feel ready to see his concerned face. He and Lucy adored each other. 'Can we talk about it later?'

'Course . . .' He finally took his dark glasses off and tucked them into his pocket; stretched his neck each way and pinched the bridge of his narrow nose between thumb and forefinger. She knew his body language well enough to know that he was flustered. Had the woman in the black coat rejected him, or was it something related to their case?

'Did you get anything?'

'Unfortunately the hotel's under different management now. They claimed they have no records from the nineties.'

'So they couldn't give us an address for Tosh?'

Crawford shrugged. 'I got chatting to them.' This was one of his regular preambles for having ferreted out information.

'And?'

'Turns out they've got a ton of old records stored down in the basement – didn't want to tell me about them because they're not stored properly. Worried I'd give them shit about data protection or something . . .' He shrugged again. On the bridge ahead, the traffic lights changed. Monica watched the rows of car headlamps and taillights moving against the northern gloom. 'I got the manager, good guy actually, to take me down for a quick look. Junk down there from nineteen oatcake, big picture of the Queen from the coronation, old champagne boxes from the 1800s and all sorts.' Monica nodded, 'Eventually we found a bunch of filing cabinets, inch-deep in dust.'

'You got something from them?'

'Just Pauline Tosh's address.' Crawford took out his phone and held it up. A picture of a personnel file. 'A first-floor flat on Castle Street.'

Monica recalled what Jessica had said about Freya's place of work. 'Bobby's Ark Amusement Arcade was on Castle Street.'

'That's right,' Crawford said, allowing a hint of satisfaction into his voice. 'About fifty yards from Pauline Tosh's flat.'

Monica followed the satnav's directions out of the city to the A862, west towards the mountains. Turned onto the A833 towards Drumnadrochit and Fort William, then a right turn onto a narrow country road. It was overhung by oak and beech trees, embankments on either side as if the route had been worn deep into the ground by long centuries of feet, then carts, then cars. Crawford shifted in his seat and Monica could tell the place made him uncomfortable. They went over a crossroads. A little beyond was a lay-by with the branches of a huge copper beech tree twisting above it. Further down the road, dark grey and just visible in the gloaming light, were the buildings of Fettercairn Farm.

Monica pulled into a lane beside an outbuilding, feeling the car rattle as smooth tarmac changed to rutted dirt. She parked and glanced at Crawford beside her. He raised his eyebrows but didn't need to say anything. *Brace yourself. Here we go*. Bringing the news to Jessica Sutherland: her sister had been buried in a marsh, any dreams of happy-ever-after were over.

Despite its initially gloomy appearance, up close the windows of the farmhouse were bright and welcoming. The smell of home cooking, the sound of children's voices, a muffled dog's bark drifted out as Jessica opened the door to them. A patch of comfort in the wild, until the moment Monica saw the weight of sadness on Jessica's face, who knew without needing to hear. And she thought, *Here is chaos, making a home in your little home. The crows of your worst dreams, roosting on your roof.*

Ten minutes later Monica and Crawford were seated on stools in the large kitchen. It was done in a modern farmhouse style: massive island, oak beams, Belfast sink, obligatory Aga. Like an advert in *Country Living*, a guilty pleasure of Monica's over the years when she occasionally soothed urban fatigue with fantasies of a new life in the country.

'We could come back tomorrow,' Monica said. 'When you've had a chance to process it.'

Jessica smiled sadly. 'I thought I'd be relieved . . .'

'It's a lot to take in.'

'I suppose a bigger part of me than I realised thought she'd come walking back through the door one day.'

Her husband had put their daughter, Harriet, and their two sons in the living room. He now opened the kitchen door and came back in. Monica took him in for the first time. He was attractive, tall and athletic, with dark hair. Dressed in blue jeans, a checked shirt and a green John Deere cap. He went to stand beside Jessica at the island, put an arm around her shoulders. She took his hand and squeezed it. 'I suppose that's why we ended up staying here all these years, isn't it, Bal?'

He forced a smile. 'It's not exactly a bad spot.'

Jessica gave a dry laugh. 'You're a terrible liar.' She turned back to Monica. 'Barry never wanted to be a farmer, but he agreed to take the place on when my dad died. Took my name too, if you can believe that?'

'You said it was the only way you'd agree to marry me!' Barry said, smiling shyly. And as Monica watched the exchange between Barry and Jessica, so open and natural here in front of two strangers, she had the sense of death's closeness. The way it made life precious, meaningful. Like God and heaven were just a whisper away. The feeling could be addictive.

'He must have thought I was nuts, but I had this idea that if Freya did think about coming back and heard there was a different family here, she might change her mind. Not many men would agree to that, would they?' Jessica asked, looking to Monica, who shook her head.

'I don't think so, no.'

Barry shrugged. 'I never really had a family myself growing up. Jessica's parents were more like family to me . . . I knew how important it was to Jessica, so she'd feel safe.'

Monica nodded then cleared her throat. 'I want to know about the time when Freya went missing. What was going on in her life at that point.'

'It's a long time ago,' Jessica said. Her reddish hair was tied up in a ponytail. She was wearing a cream woollen jumper; folded her arms to hug herself. 'But I still think about it every morning and every night before I go to sleep. At first I thought she'd gone with friends, because of the note . . .'

'Did Freya ever mention someone called Pauline?' Ideally Jessica would have volunteered anything related to Tosh herself, but doubtless she was aware of the recent media speculation.

64

'Or Marilyn Rosie, Barbara Dench?' Two of Tosh's known aliases.

'You're talking about the serial killer Pauline Tosh, aren't you?'

'You probably read the speculation in the press. I just want you to know that the leak to them didn't come from us; only a few detectives knew and I trust all of them. It was probably someone at the prison putting two and two together, not really thinking of the consequences.' This was important to Monica on a personal level, and surely to Jessica's faith in the investigation too. 'But they were right. Pauline Tosh volunteered the location of Freya's body to us.'

Jessica's eyes widened. 'I always hoped that if she was dead it might be an accident. Then, hearing about the dig at the marshes . . .' Her voice died away.

'Whatever happened to Freya is over now – she's at peace. We want to see justice done for her, and for your family.' The only comfort Monica could ever offer the bereaved. She glanced from Jessica to Barry, who nodded gravely.

'Did you hear any of those names?' Barry asked, looking down at Jessica and squeezing her shoulder a little tighter to comfort her, his tanned fingers accentuated by the pale cream of her jumper.

She took a deep breath. 'I don't think I remember Freya saying them; they definitely weren't names we heard at the time.'

Monica thought about it for a moment. Tosh had been highly secretive and manipulative in her relationships with her victims. It wouldn't be a surprise if the killer had forged a friendship with Freya without her family's knowledge.

Barry said, 'Your parents always thought one of Freya's friends must have known something, didn't they?'

'We spoke to everyone. Once Mum and Dad were gone, me

and Barry kept trying. We even set up a charity, Home Call, to encourage runaways to get in touch with their families.'

'I think I read something about it in the paper,' Crawford said. 'A few weeks ago?' As he spoke, Monica remembered glancing over the article in the *Highland News* while chatting to her mum. It had included a photo of Barry and Jessica.

'That's right,' Jessica said. 'A lot of young people have used the helpline. We won an award.'

'How were things between your parents and Freya?' Monica asked, out of habit as much as anything. Statistically the family were the most dangerous people in anyone's life.

'My parents?' Jessica sounded shocked. 'Everything was great—'

'They were amazing people – family was everything to them,' Barry cut in, anger edging his voice. 'They would never have hurt their daughter.'

'I'm sorry.' Monica realised her tone had been offhand. It had been a long day, and then everything with Lucy. 'I didn't mean to be intrusive.'

'It's OK, Barry.' Jessica smiled sadly up at him. More than anything she sounded tired now. 'Dad had an accident the year before, but he was much better. Then everything with Freya . . . He never fully recovered. Mum had Freya as a victim of every murderer out there, had it in her head that they would come for me next. It was hard—'

'I don't mean to be rude,' Barry interrupted again, 'but I think that's enough for now. I think we need some time with our family, to let all this sink in.'

Chapter 14

Monica could see through the hall windows that it was fully dark outside. Jessica had broken into soft heaves after Barry's interruption, the horror of the news finally overwhelming her. In the wide hallway that led to the front door, the light was switched off. Monica felt like an intruder as she listened to Jessica's muffled sobs and Barry's soothing words from the kitchen, all the while fumbling with the lock at the front door.

'I think you need to double-turn the lock,' Crawford chipped in, shining the light from his phone on the door handle.

'Can Lucy come to play?' The detectives turned together at the child's voice. The Sutherlands' daughter, Harriet, was poking her head from around a door, the light from the room casting a panel on the hall floor.

Monica crouched and whispered, 'Mummy'll be through in a minute.'

'Lucy said I could come to her house to see her cat?'

'We'll see.' Monica smiled. 'You'll have to ask your mummy first.'

'Lucy told me that she knows how to cast a spell to make an owl come to the window. Is that true?'

'She told me that too,' Crawford said. 'Still waiting for proof though.'

Monica shook her head. 'I think she was just playing,

sweetheart. You can come to visit though, if it's OK with your mummy and daddy.'

Monica dropped Crawford on Union Street in central Inverness, then drove down to her mum's house in the Marsh to collect Lucy. As they were coming back across the black bridge that led out of Rapinch, she glanced at her daughter's face in the rear-view mirror.

'Harriet was asking if she could come to play with you some time. She lives on a farm, right in the middle of the woods.'

'Harriet says she's got two cats, one's old,' Lucy replied. 'She says he's called Butter and he's older than practically anyone in Inverness.'

Through the windscreen, the lights of Rose Street car park were white against the dark sky.

'I spoke to Miss Jennings today,' Monica said, trying to keep her voice light. 'She said that she likes you a lot. She says you're a lovely girl. But she said you'd been saying things that frightened some of the other boys and girls?'

'I can't remember.'

'What about Munyasa? Did you say something to frighten him?'

'I don't think so.'

Monica sighed and glanced again in the mirror. *My parents never bothered with any of this and I turned out just fine.* Was this obsession with feelings and what children thought really necessary? How would they ever grow a skin thick enough to deal with the world? The thought was followed by memories of her own childhood, the hours and days of dreading school.

'Sweetheart, I know it's difficult, starting school. Everything's new and strange. Can you try to be nice to the other boys and girls. Try to talk to them in a nice way, like you do when you're with Gran or Crawford, or Miss Jennings?' In the rear-view mirror Lucy was lit orange from the street lights, little face screwed up in concentration.

'I think so,' she replied finally, as Monica pulled into the car park below her flat.

After putting Lucy to bed, Monica felt her stomach twist and realised she hadn't eaten all day. She opted for an indecent little treat – a cheese and tomato sandwich, dusted on both sides with cracked pepper and sea salt, shallow-fried. She ate it sitting on the sofa, watching the light of passing cars in the street outside. Her mind kept wandering back to the conversation with Miss Jennings, the strange sense of powerlessness to influence Lucy's behaviour. If her daughter decided she was going to be antisocial in the classroom, ultimately what could she really do about it? When a criminal wouldn't get in line you put them in prison. What did you do when it was your daughter misbehaving?

As an attempted diversion she picked up a novel: *The Sailor Who Fell from Grace with the Sea* by Yukio Mishima. Soon her arm was numb from propping up her head and she dropped the book, then stood up to stretch her back.

Behind the flat there was a hill covered in dense woodland. A path ran through it up towards a housing estate. As she was stretching her arms she spotted a figure under one of the street lights. It wasn't unusual to see people walking their dogs in the woods, but he seemed to be watching the block of flats, looking up towards the windows as if waiting for some kind of show. Monica had the odd impulse to lift her top up and flash her chest at him – give the creep an eyeful. Instead she waved, then reached over and pulled the blind down. 'Show's over for tonight.'

Her phone started ringing on the kitchen counter and she grabbed for it, annoyed she'd neglected turning it to silent while Lucy slept.

'You still up?' It was Crawford.

'Seems so.' As she was speaking, she watched through the living-room window as a taxi pulled into the car park and a familiar slight figure climbed out.

'Lucy's sleeping,' Monica whispered as she opened the front door to Crawford. 'We'd better keep our voices down.'

Again he brought the smell of the autumn evening and cologne, but this time alcohol was added to the mix. 'Course. How is she?'

'She's OK. I'll tell you later. Do you want a coffee?' Without waiting to hear, she started to make one. Crawford sat on the sofa, picked up *The Sailor Who Fell from Grace with the Sea*. 'Any good?'

'So far. Actually that's Heather's copy.'

'Right.' The mention of his girlfriend's name made Crawford visibly tense, and he put the book down. Monica handed him the coffee and made herself camomile tea, wondering for a moment what was going on with him and Heather.

'Had a few drinks, trying to get people talking. Trying to get hold of someone who worked at the old arcade with Freya, see if they remembered Tosh.'

'How did you get on?'

'No luck, unfortunately . . .'

'No surprise, Tosh was always—'

Crawford held up a hand to stop her. 'But . . . I thought, fuck it. Why not try Tosh's old flat.'

'They remembered her?'

'I got a lucky break – the people in the flat had never even heard of her, but the landlord still lives across the hall.'

'What did he say?'

'He's a cantankerous old bugger, in his eighties and makes out that he's deaf at first. Says he can't remember much from the 1990s. That he'll try to remember, but then asks me if I'll go down to the kebab shop on Church Street for him while he's thinking. Says he doesn't like to go out after dark these days.'

'Really?' Crawford was a good storyteller. 'Did you go?'

'Well, he seemed genuinely worried about going out. So I say, "OK, I'll go while you're thinking." He says, "Could you just nip in to the Co-op too? Pick me up milk, bread, strawberry jam?"'

Monica smiled at the image. 'It's good to help the aged. Might be us one day.'

'This is the best bit though: he says, "I've not had a chance to get to the bank yet this week; I'll sort you out later."'

'Nice work, landlord.'

'Anyway, I go and do his shopping for him. When I get back he asks me in to make cups of tea to have with our kebabs. When we finish our supper he produces this old notebook.'

'What was in it?'

'Every rent payment from his tenants across the hall for the last fifty-odd years. Cash only.' Crawford dug in his pocket for his phone, held out an image for Monica to see. It showed a school jotter with rows and columns of carefully pencilled notes. 'This' – he ran his finger down the rows – 'is April 1993. Pauline Tosh moves in.' Monica knew the date tied in with Tosh moving north after killing her first victim. 'Paid promptly every month until March 1994.'

'Wait, so she left in March 1994? That's six months before Freya disappeared.'

'The landlord said he remembered, once he'd had a chance to think it over with his kebab.'

'What happened?'

'This is where it gets weird . . . He said that she disappeared still owing her last month's rent. He went to the Royal to chase her for it, heard from someone that she'd gone off to work on a cruise ship.'

'A cruise ship?' Even as the words were coming out of her mouth Monica recalled Tosh's amused expression, her cryptic words as Monica was about to leave the interview room. Clearly the serial killer had known exactly where the investigation would lead them.

Chapter 15

She first met them after another argument with her mother. Freya Sutherland was standing under the lonely bus shelter down the road from the farm. It was July, and it was raining heavily. She watched a pothole puddle in the road, ripples spreading as raindrops hit brown water. Weird that a shitty puddle could look beautiful; sad there was no one beside her to share it with. Her mum would have sighed in exasperation if they'd been standing together and Freya had pointed it out. As she had sighed the year before when Freya floated the idea of training to be an art teacher. Her mum's response: 'Could you get anything more soul-destroying?'

Freya looked down the empty road in the direction of Drumnadrochit, wondering for a moment if she'd missed her bus. The idea brought a knot of anxiety to her stomach. She hated letting people down, even if the job at Bobby's Ark Amusement Arcade was crap. It wasn't like Bobby would sack her for being late – half the time he didn't actually open the doors until noon anyway – it was the feeling of things slipping that she didn't like. Since Dad's accident, everything had seemed out of balance. Before, he used to come to Freya's room after she'd argued with Mum. He had a way of smoothing things over, pretending to be interested in the

73

designs in her sketchbook or saying something stupid so she couldn't help laughing.

She glanced again at the empty road stretching into the mist; she probably had missed the bus. *If Bobby does sack me, Mum will be pleased at least.* Freya felt a pang of guilt at the thought. Her mum wasn't nasty like that; it was horrible to even think that way.

Impulsively Freya shrugged her backpack off and pulled her Walkman from it – she had been saving the batteries until she got on the bus – fast-forwarded to the end then turned the cassette over. 'Whole Lotta Love' by Led Zeppelin. Rain rattled the bus shelter's roof; she closed her eyes, listened to Robert Plant's voice and tried to think about sex. Something more interesting than arguing with Mum, and definitely better than sitting in a booth handing out tokens all day. Finding someone she wanted to sleep with was easier said than done though; the boys in town seemed so boring. It was probably her fault. She was too plain and boring to attract someone interesting.

After a moment Freya heard a vehicle approach then pull to a stop beside the shelter. The engine's sound wasn't deep enough for a bus though. She opened her eyes – it was a black Volkswagen Golf. She pulled her headphones off. Her reflection stared back at her from tinted glass, and she felt a pang of self-consciousness at what she was wearing: cardigan, plaid shirt, T-shirt underneath. Did it look like she was trying too hard? Totally out of place in the middle of nowhere? The window slid down and a woman looked out. She was about the same age as Freya, white-blonde hair cut short, angular features almost beautiful, almost harsh. A man leaned around her from the driver's seat to stare out at Freya. He looked tall, with dark hair that was almost shoulder-length. Freya thought she recognised them both from somewhere.

'It's Arcade Girl!' the man said, his tone between playful and mocking, and Freya remembered: they had been drinking at the bar in the arcade. He had come over to her booth and attempted to exchange a beer bottle top for one of the tokens that went into the video games. Had laughed at her when she refused. Freya looked away. Annoyed to be caught standing waiting for a bus. 'Where are you going, Arcade Girl?' His mouth was hanging open, dark stubble on his jaw.

Freya said, 'I'm going to work.' Trying hard not to let the irritated tone from her earlier conversation with her mum spill over into this interaction.

'Of course you are,' the man said. 'We'll give you a lift.'

'I'm fine.'

'I saw your drawings,' the woman said. 'In the booth. I really liked them.' She smiled and her face completely changed, assuming an appealing openness that made her almost childlike. Freya felt herself blush. 'I'm Miranda, this is Brodie, that's Joseph.' She shifted her weight so Freya could see a third person, in the back seat. A man who seemed a little younger than the others, fresh-faced and smiling shyly.

Brodie said, 'Are we going to the fucking town or not?' It was hard to tell if he was joking or angry. He reached into a handbag at Miranda's feet, produced a ten-pack of Marlboro menthols and scooped one out. Glanced around for a lighter before Joseph leaned forward from the back seat and sparked a Zippo for him.

'You'll get soaked,' Miranda said, still smiling, her accent closer to southern English than Scottish. She was wearing a floral-print summer dress and was thin – seemed almost fragile. 'Are you sure you wouldn't like to come with us?'

Chapter 16

It didn't take much longer than fifteen minutes for Monica and Crawford to track down a cruise liner from the clue Pauline Tosh had given Monica. According to Wikipedia, the *Road to Mandalay* was built by Kvaerner Masa-Yards in Helsinki, her tonnage was 71,700, and she was 'floated out' on 6 January 1990. Originally operated by Royal Caribbean International, in 1992 she was bought by P&O South Sea Cruises.

'You don't think it could be a coincidence?' Crawford asked, turning to look at Monica. They were sitting together on her sofa, the only light in the room from the laptop in front of them. On the screen there was an image of the cruise liner.

'It could be, but Tosh would love the idea of us spending time investigating her, then being able to prove she was out of the country when Freya was killed.' Monica rubbed tired eyes. It would certainly explain why Tosh had volunteered the information, why she had been so pleased with herself that morning in the prison.

Crawford stood up. 'You got anything to drink?' Without waiting for a response he walked to the kitchen, ducked down to a cupboard and found the bottle of whisky – Lagavulin – he had given her for her birthday back in June. He held it up, still unopened in the box. 'You haven't even tried it!'

'I was saving it,' Monica lied. She rarely drank alcohol and wasn't a big fan of malt whisky.

'You want a dram? You have to at least try it!' She looked up at Crawford's bright eyes and enthusiastic smile, shook her head, but found herself smiling back. 'OK, give me a small one.'

'Nice one, boss.' He opened the bottle and poured two measures. Handed one to Monica and sniffed at his own. She glanced at the clock in the kitchen: almost 11 p.m.

'What time would it be in Australia just now?'

'About eleven a.m., I think,' Crawford said. 'It's about twelve hours different.'

She put the glass on the coffee table and leaned in to the laptop, found the number for P&O South Seas Cruises on their website. Spent ten minutes on hold, then was bounced around different departments before finally being put through to a woman in HR. 'How may I help you?' She sounded like a receptionist from *Neighbours* – still Monica's mum's favourite soap.

'I'm calling from Inverness in Scotland. I'm a detective,' Monica said, turning the Scottishness in her accent up by 20 per cent. Sometimes this helped if you happened to be talking to one of the millions of descendants of Scottish emigrants. 'I'm looking for information on an old employee, Pauline Tosh. I think she worked on *Road to Mandalay* from 1993?'

'I'm afraid we only keep records of employees for the mandatory period of seven years after the end of employment.'

Monica sighed. 'Are you sure? This is an important case. Is there no chance it could have gone into storage?'

'In alignment with data protection, we dispose of all employee records after the mandatory period of seven years. Sorry I couldn't have been of more help.'

As she was about to hang up, Monica felt Crawford nudge her leg. He whispered, 'Ask about the ship's log.'

'What about the ship's log,' Monica said. 'Is it still around?'

The woman thought about it for a second. 'The ship's log is a legal document. Far as I know it has to be kept for twenty-five years.'

'Would it contain information on the crew?'

'You know, I'm not sure.'

'Could you access it for me? It's really important.'

'I believe they're registered with the national archive centre at the end of each voyage.'

Another Google search, then a call to the New South Wales office of the National Archives of Australia. Monica held the phone to her ear, anticipating more fun on hold, but unexpectedly got straight through.

'National Archives of Australia, Annie speaking, how may I assist you?'

'My name's Monica Kennedy, I'm calling from Inverness in Scotland.'

'Inverness in Scotland? Now is that near Edinburgh?'

'Sort of,' Monica lied.

'My gran was from Edinburgh.'

'Inverness is more in the Highlands,' Monica said, hoping to spark some of that diaspora romanticism.

'I'd love to visit some time. What time is it there?'

'About half eleven,' Monica said, glancing at the clock above the cooker. 'I'm really hoping you can help.'

'I hope so too,' Annie said, 'if you've stayed up all night to call me.'

'I'm trying to access the ship's log for a cruise liner, *Road to Mandalay*. I'm looking for the crew list for voyages in 1994. I'm interested in the second half of the year – September on, in particular.'

Monica braced herself for a barrage of questions about why

she needed this information, and was pleasantly surprised when Annie replied, 'Well, let me just put that request through for you.' After a minute she continued, 'They've just gone down now, so it'll be this afternoon before they go back again.'

'I'm really keen to get this tonight if possible. Is there any way you could try to push it through now? I'll show you round Inverness. My mum'll cook you haggis, all the trimmings.'

Annie laughed at that. 'Hold on, I'll try to catch the archive boys.'

'Can your mum make haggis?' Crawford sounded disturbed by the notion.

'I meant a shop-bought one . . .'

After a minute Annie came back on the line. 'OK. The boys are on it. They'll be back in an hour or so. If you give me your email I'll scan the pages and send them over. Save your phone bill.'

'I owe you one.'

'You owe me a haggis.' Annie laughed and hung up.

Monica and Crawford sat waiting on the sofa. He nudged her leg again with his elbow. 'You still haven't tried the Lagavulin.' The untouched drink was on the table beside her laptop. She picked it up – 'Cheers' – knocked it back in one and felt the heat in her throat, then her stomach.

'You're not supposed to just down it!' Crawford sounded outraged. 'You're supposed to savour it. Next you'll be adding Diet Coke to it.' He went and got the bottle from the kitchen, topped up their glasses. 'Sip it this time. *Slàinte.*' They clinked glasses. Monica rolled her eyes, then shut them as if she were a connoisseur, and took a sip. It was remarkably smooth and peaty.

'So if it wasn't Tosh, who was it?'

Monica glanced over at the closed door to Lucy's bedroom. 'We'll start with Freya's dad, work our way out from there.'

'Hately's not going to like it. Going from a straightforward addition to Tosh's kill list to a cold-case mess.'

' "Tosh's kill list"?' Monica raised her eyebrows.

Crawford glanced away, embarrassed. 'It's what some people call it online.'

'Hately'll do the right thing.'

'At first, but how long's he going to give us before it goes on the back burner, when other cases start coming in?' Crawford shifted in his seat, seeming to remember something. 'I forgot to tell you. We were talking about Mr Miles, the churchwarden at the fire?' Monica remembered Fisher showing her the images online, the odd story about a creature coming out of the ground.

'Did he die?'

'He's still in ICU, far as I know. Get this though.' Crawford turned to face her. 'I spoke to Jim MacLeod, the investigating officer, again. You'll never guess what he told me.'

Monica drank more of the whisky, feeling the alcohol warm her blood, smooth the rough edges from the day. 'What did he tell you?' She turned herself so she was facing Crawford, widening her eyes in mock intrigue.

'He said the investigators haven't been able to find any cause of fire; it's as if it just started up of its own accord. Never seen anything like it, apparently.'

It did sound intriguing. But she was long enough in the job to know how these kinds of rumours could spread between officers, then turn out to be unfounded. She would wait for the official report. 'I guess we'll find out,' she replied finally.

Crawford grunted, picked up the bottle. Monica went to

refuse but realised she was enjoying the alcohol's relaxing effects and held her glass out.

'You never told me about how things went at the school.'

'Not great. Seems like Lucy's been frightening the other kids.' She glanced over again to check her daughter's bedroom door was still closed. 'Telling them scary stories.'

'Scary stories? Like what?'

'I don't know exactly.'

'Jessica's daughter seemed to like her anyway – wanted to see her cast a spell on an owl.'

Monica laughed at that. 'She did, didn't she.' She took another sip of whisky. 'What about you – you wanted to talk about something, on Sunday at the loch after I'd been to see Tosh?'

Crawford hesitated. 'It was just . . . I don't know . . .' He ran a hand over his face. 'I wanted to ask you about something.'

'If it's about how to dump another part-time girlfriend, then I'm out.'

Crawford winced.

'Sorry, Crawford, that came across really badly. I was trying to be funny.'

'It doesn't matter, honestly.' He leaned over the end of the sofa and began flicking through her record collection.

'Are you sure? I didn't mean . . .' Monica cursed herself. Crawford rarely opened up.

'It was nothing.' He pulled one of the records out and held it up to the weak light from the laptop.

'I'm really sorry . . .' Although she was used to being tough in detective mode, Monica hated hurting the people closest to her. Through the whisky fug she realised with alarm that Crawford had drifted into this category.

'Is this any good?'

Monica sighed and leaned in beside Crawford to see the album's cover. *Sonny's Dream* by Hamish Imlach. She caught the smell of his expensive cologne, mixed with whatever detergent he used for his clothes. Felt the heat of his body through his shirt. 'I don't think I've listened to that one yet; they're mostly my dad's.'

Crawford slid the vinyl from its sleeve. 'How does it work?'

'You've never put a record on?' Monica asked, feeling unbelievably ancient.

'My grandad was fierce about his record player – never let me use it, so I just bought CDs.'

'Give it to me, child,' she said gently, taking the vinyl from his hands and putting it on the turntable. 'Just keep it low, so it doesn't wake Lucy,' she whispered.

Crawford grunted and turned the volume down. She showed him how to set the needle on the record. They both sank back onto the sofa, his hand brushing against her leg. With his other hand he reached for his glass of whisky. The music started – it was Scottish folk, not usually Monica's thing, but somehow Imlach's voice went well with the whisky. They both sank back on the sofa, Crawford shifted so he was facing her. She noticed the small bumps on his nose where it had been broken, and just how green his eyes were even in the low light from the laptop. Almost as if he were wearing contact lenses. She realised she probably hadn't looked at him this closely before. Hadn't noticed the tiny scar on his chin.

'What?'

'I don't know.' Monica glanced away. The room was shadowy, warm and contained, like it might be the only place left in the world. When she raised her eyes, Crawford was still looking at her. She watched as her fingers went to his face, traced the thin line of the scar on his jaw.

'What happened?'

'I fell off my bike when I was a kid.'

'Did it hurt?'

Crawford didn't reply, but raised his own hand to hers. He shifted closer, and so did she. Felt the heat of his mouth, the taste of beer under the whisky, rough stubble. *This is a seriously bad idea.* Even as her body wanted to sink into that rising heat. She ran a hand down his stomach, felt hard muscle, the bones of his ribs. The heat of another body. She felt Crawford's hand on her face, dropping to her hip. Monica pulled away from his mouth, glanced towards Lucy's bedroom door. It was still closed. She turned back to him. He kissed her mouth again, then her neck.

'This is stupid,' Monica whispered. 'What are we doing?'

'You know I like you,' he said.

She felt his lips on her mouth again. Took a deep breath of his cologne and ran a hand through his hair.

'Shall we go to your room?'

Yes, we definitely should. But as she pulled him closer, the memory of his face that day at the beach came back to her. Obviously he was confused about Heather – it was what he'd been trying to talk about. Somehow it had led to this.

She pulled back. 'You're still with Heather.'

Crawford paused, looking like he wanted to kiss her again. She forced some harshness into her voice. 'You don't give a shit, do you? You only think about yourself.'

Crawford sat back away from her, shaking his head. 'Fucking hell . . .' He didn't sound angry, more bemused. He straightened his shirt.

Monica realised that the top buttons of her blouse were open, and fastened them. 'I didn't mean—'

'It doesn't matter.' Crawford stood up, dusted himself down and picked up his glass. Drained what was left and poured more in.

'It's not that I didn't want to. Jesus.' Monica looked away. 'Is this just some power thing, fuck the boss?'

'No! You're intriguing, powerful . . .' Crawford was standing with his back half to her. 'I told you I liked you.'

Monica wiped a hand over her face, pulled her hair back. She was tired of sleeping alone, tired of being her own lover. All she really wanted to do was go to bed with her colleague and fuck his brains out. Why did things have to be so complicated?

'This was stupid,' Monica said. 'You should go.'

'Sure. I didn't—'

Monica's laptop pinged and she remembered why they'd been sitting in the flat drinking whisky, making terrible life choices, in the first place. She shook her head and turned to it.

'It's from my new friend in Australia,' she said, trying to force something like normality into her voice, despite the fact they'd been a few moments from being in bed together. She opened the email, scrolled through the scanned image. One of the lines was highlighted: Pauline Tosh was registered as crew on a voyage leaving Sydney on 7 September 1994, arriving in Honolulu, Hawaii, nineteen days later, on 26 September. If the information was accurate then it confirmed what Tosh had obviously known it would. There was no way the serial killer could have been involved in Freya's disappearance.

Chapter 17

Crawford had been right about Hately's response to the news that Pauline Tosh was out of the picture as Freya's killer. Monica and Crawford were in his office. When they finished filling him in, the detective superintendent stood up at his desk and swore under his breath.

'Couldn't Tosh have had an accomplice?' he asked finally. 'They took Freya, held her somewhere, then Tosh flew back at some point. Murdered her and buried her?' Hately could see the case was growing arms and legs. The media scrutiny would increase, and with it the pressure to find a culprit.

'It would really go against what we know of Tosh's MO,' Monica replied, glancing down at Crawford, who was standing beside her. He had apologised again and left shortly after the email from Australia had come through. They hadn't had a chance yet to talk about what had happened, and she could see he was wearing the same dark brown suit, the same bone-coloured shirt, as the night before. Wherever he had gone after leaving her flat, it clearly wasn't home. She felt a little knot in her stomach and turned back to Hately. 'Tosh was very solitary. Apart from anything, she was only on shore leave for a handful of days at a time in 1994 to 1995 – in Honolulu, Sydney, Singapore and Auckland.' Unable to sleep, Monica had spent a couple of hours piecing together Tosh's movements, looking for windows when she might have returned to the UK. 'It seems unlikely she could have flown back from any of those locations and committed a murder in the time available. Tosh knew we would find out she was abroad eventually. It explains why she was happy to give us the burial site; she would never have implicated herself.'

'Oh, for fuck's sake,' Hately muttered. He put his hands on his hips, shook his head as if somehow this whole mess was Monica's fault.

'We could start looking up flight records for when she was on shore leave. Just to be sure she didn't come back. But it'll take a lot of time to prove a negative.'

'How did she know about the dump site then?'

'We need to dig into that. Find out who she's shared cells with, who she writes letters to, who's visited her.' Monica had already formed one theory. 'It gets boring being locked up for decades. My dad told me that lifers would sometimes tell stories about their crimes. Use them as a kind of currency. It's possible the information came to her that way.'

'Jesus.' Hately's voice dropped in horror at the notion. But then his expression changed, his brow furrowing and some of the tension leaving his jaw.

Much later, when Monica thought back to how the case unfolded, she couldn't help but imagine that in that moment Hately had somehow caught a sense of it. Instinctively known to distance himself from the investigation. Almost mechanically, he walked round from the side of his desk, past Monica and Crawford to the door. 'Keep me posted.' He held the door open and motioned for them to leave.

Monica finished explaining about the *Road to Mandalay* and looked around the table at her team. Crawford was leaning back in his chair with his hands behind his head, outwardly relaxed but avoiding eye contact. DC Fisher was sitting attentively, hair and suit as neat as ever; he'd been nodding and making notes while she spoke. DC Khan was beside him. She was chewing gum as she listened, wearing a shapeless wool coat, scrawling a few notes in a mix of black and pink ink.

Monica cleared her throat. 'We need to keep the details of this case close, between us four.' She glanced between the three junior detectives. Despite their current uncomfortable situation she trusted Crawford with her life, and she knew Fisher's identity was bound up with being a competent detective – he would never leak information to a journalist. Khan was the uncertain quantity in the room. They had only worked together for six months and Monica still didn't feel like she knew what motived her. 'Someone leaked that we were talking to Tosh. It probably came from the Carse, but just be aware. It'll work in our favour for now if the media think the case is closed, with Tosh as the killer – buy us some time to investigate.'

They nodded in unison.

'Does anything stand out in the original investigation? Any names that ring bells? Anyone with prior convictions? Anything like that?' Monica asked hopefully. Duncan Gregg's sloppy work hadn't seemed like a major impediment when Tosh was nailed on as the killer. Now they were left trying to piece together what had really happened in a twenty-four-year-old case. Every lead gone cold a lifetime ago. Monica knew that statistically the chances of catching the killer were slim. And she was going to have to break this news to Jessica and Barry Sutherland. After decades of not knowing, when they were finally given the chance to grieve, they were instead faced with more uncertainty.

'There's really nothing that stands out, unfortunately,' Fisher said, pointing at his laptop. 'Most of the time the investigating officer didn't list full names, just "friend" or "colleague".'

Monica swore under her breath. She had hoped to avoid communicating with Duncan Gregg; now she was going to have to go to him for help.

'You want me to get hold of him?' Crawford asked, glancing at her but still avoiding eye contact.

'I'll take care of it,' Monica replied. Normally it was the kind of task her partner excelled at, but she knew enough about Gregg to suspect he would respond better to the higher-ranking officer. 'What about the note Freya left, is there a copy?'

Fisher nodded and passed her a photocopy. The note was handwritten.

Dear Mum and Dad,

I'm sorry to be leaving like this, but I felt like it would be easier this way than causing more upset and arguments. I know I disappointed you with my school results and the choices I made. I'm going with friends who care a lot about me. I can't say yet where to, but trust me when I tell you that I will be in touch soon. I've learned a lot this long summer and I'm now a different person from the one that you knew.

Love,
Your daughter
Freya xx

Monica passed the photocopy on to Khan.

'What about her dad? Could he have faked it? Or forced her to write it?' Crawford suggested. Statistically the killer was most likely to be someone close to Freya, and a male. Her dad was the obvious first suspect with Tosh out of the picture. There were problems with this theory though.

'Jessica said things were fine with the family before Freya left,' Monica said. 'Why would Freya's dad take the risk of burying her in Inverness when he lives out in the country? There would have been a million better ways of disposing of her. And how would Tosh have found out about the burial site? Freya's dad wouldn't have told her.'

Khan held up the photocopy. 'It doesn't sound like things were fine with the family. She says there were "upsets and arguments", that she'd disappointed her parents.'

Monica considered this for a moment, thought back to her own late-teenage years. The arguments, the attempts at establishing an independent life. Like Freya, she had felt that disconnect from her family, only her solution had been leaving home to join the police.

She leaned in beside Khan, catching the smells of cherry chewing gum mixed with cigarette smoke, and looked over the note again. This time she read aloud: ' "I've learned a lot this long summer and I'm now a different person from the one that you knew." ' On a second reading, the phrase sounded alarm bells.

'Sounds like something major going on for her,' Crawford offered.

'Or someone grooming her, influencing her.' Monica had heard similar things from other young people over the years.

Some who had been indoctrinated into cults, or manipulated into becoming sex workers.

Monica stood up. 'Fisher, I want you to start going through Tosh's visitors, cellmates, correspondents – anyone who could have passed her the story about where Freya was buried. I know it's tedious work, but it's important. It could be what breaks the case open.'

Fisher nodded, face set in a professional frown. She felt a pang of guilt for manipulating him so brazenly, but what she'd said was actually true.

'Anything else?' No one spoke, and Monica glanced at Crawford, who stood up.

'I was just wondering,' Khan said, 'about the location.' Monica nodded her on. 'I heard you and Crawford calling it the Witch's Coffin the other day. I was just wondering if that could have something to do with a motive?'

Chapter 18

Monica and Crawford walked down the corridor and out to the Volvo in silence. She took the driver's seat. It was another grey morning, as if ordained for an uncomfortable drive with a close colleague you had almost slept with.

'Lucy got to school OK, did she?'

Monica started the engine. 'Said she didn't want to go; I told her she had to.'

'Last night . . .'

'We'd both had a drink. It was stupid.'

'I didn't mean—'

'You didn't go home after you left?' Monica heard herself asking. Crawford cleared his throat. 'Sorry, it's none of my business.'

She pulled out of the car park and they drove in silence, west through the grimy mist. Monica had driven the road that ran alongside the Beauly Firth on hundreds of occasions. Every time it seemed different. Today the water was slack like mercury, the distant mountains of Glen Turrit, Glen Strathfarrar and Glen Affric hidden by the cloud.

'What did you think about Khan's idea?' Crawford asked finally. 'About the location of the body?'

'Most of the murders I've investigated have human emotions at the root of them,' Monica replied, pleased to be talking about something work-related. 'Hatred, anger, jealousy. Things people believe in.'

Crawford nodded. 'That's what I thought.'

There were a handful of reporters waiting at the gate outside Fettercairn Farm when Monica and Crawford pulled up. The detectives pushed past and walked down the lane to the house. Finally a stressed-looking Barry Sutherland came to the door.

'How's Jessica?' Monica asked as Barry led them into the hallway. In the daylight she could see that the walls were covered in dozens of family photos. Almost a shrine to family life – understandable when Jessica's birth family had been so horribly damaged by Freya's disappearance.

'She's shaken up. Earlier she answered the door to a man in a suit. The bastard started asking questions about Freya. Jessica assumed he was a detective from the way he was speaking . . . I wanted to go and wring his neck for him . . .'

An old trick of the at-any-costs type of journalist. 'I should have warned you both. I never thought they would find you out here.' Barry nodded, adjusted his John Deere cap, his face set in a helpless scowl. 'Is she OK?'

'She's worried in case she told him something important.'

'What did she say?' Monica asked.

'Not much, just that she knew it was Pauline Tosh. That it was a relief to finally know.'

'I know it's horrible having them out there' – Monica gestured over her shoulder in the direction of the press outside – 'but it won't last. Something else will come along and take them away.'

Jessica Sutherland was in the kitchen with the blinds drawn, and Monica couldn't help but feel a flicker of outrage that she couldn't be left alone to grieve for her sister. 'I thought I would make bread . . .'

Monica realised that she was kneading dough on the kitchen island. 'Sorry about the journalists. Whatever you said, it won't have a negative effect on the investigation.'

'Just wish they'd cared half as much when she first disappeared.'

'We've got some news about the case,' Monica said, pulling up a stool. Crawford took the one beside her. 'I'm afraid it's looking more complicated than we had initially hoped.'

The children were at school, so Jessica and Barry sat together at the kitchen island as Monica explained about the information from Australia that seemed to put Pauline Tosh out of contention as the killer.

'So now you're saying it can't have been Pauline Tosh?' Barry Sutherland sounded outraged, his anger at the journalists' intrusion now switching in the direction of the detectives. 'I thought it was all tied up; I thought we could get on with our lives now?'

'I know this must be a shock,' Monica said softly. 'I promise you, we're doing everything we can.'

'It doesn't sound like it's enough, if one minute it's Pauline Tosh, the next it's God-knows-who . . .' Barry's anger simmered.

Jessica put a hand on his arm. 'Who was it? If not Pauline Tosh?' she asked softly. 'I need to know.'

'We'll do everything we can,' Monica replied, fixing her eyes on Jessica's.

'I don't know how I can go back again to not knowing. Last night was the first time I can remember feeling any kind of peace. I need you to find the killer for me.'

'I'm going to need your help with that,' Monica said. 'I'm going to be honest with you: the initial missing-person investigation wasn't the most thorough—'

'Tell us something we don't know,' Barry cut in, his face ugly with frustration.

'You told me last night that you spoke to all of Freya's friends? That you and Barry conducted your own investigation? It'll save us time if you can share what you found out with us.'

Jessica led them up a narrow staircase to a loft office. One wall was covered by a map of Scotland, dotted with coloured pins connected by string to photos of young men and women. Another wall was covered in shelves, bowing under the weight of assorted thick files of paperwork and cardboard boxes. There was a desk with two phones on it.

'This is where we started Home Call. We've got a network of volunteers now, so we don't handle so many calls ourselves. We're still involved in the funding side though, sending applications – all that kind of thing.'

'You must have brought comfort to a lot of people,' Monica said, admiring their dedicated work.

'We just wanted something good to come out of it,' Barry said from the doorway, sounding calmer now. 'Everything that happened with Freya. A lot of young people have written to say we saved their lives.'

'That must be rewarding,' Crawford chipped in.

'Couldn't save my sister though,' Jessica said sadly. She reached for Barry's hand and shook her head. 'Anyway . . .' She crouched at the side of the shelving, opened a small cupboard door, reached in and pulled out a plastic box. 'You know I haven't looked at this for almost ten years.' The lid of the box was dusty – FREYA written on it in black marker.

'Freya mentioned friends in her letter. Do you know who they were? Can you remember their names?'

Jessica nodded. 'There were three who she seemed to be with all the time that summer – Brodie King, Miranda Salisbury and Joseph Moon.'

The first two names chimed for Monica, and for a second she wondered if she might have known them as a teenager herself. Freya Sutherland had gone to a different school to her, and by 1994 Monica was already in the police force, but they were around the same age. Inverness had been even smaller in the 90s. It was possible they had shared friends.

'Miranda Salisbury? As in the politician?' Crawford piped up, and as he said it the memory clicked. Miranda Salisbury was a rising star in the Scottish Parliament in Edinburgh.

'That's right. Brodie King became a successful chef – set up a restaurant in London. Got a few across the Highlands now too.'

'They were the same age as Freya?'

'Roughly. They weren't friends from school though; I think she met them through the amusement arcade. They were sort of arty – seemed really cool, like rock stars, when I was a teenager.'

'And you spoke to all three of them?' Monica asked.

'A few times. I always thought one of them had to know something.'

'What did they say?'

'Not much. That they had no idea where Freya had gone.'

'When did you last speak to them?'

'Years ago now,' Jessica said. 'Miranda and Brodie both left the Highlands. Joseph ended up on the streets using drugs. Last I heard he'd been admitted to Craig Dunain mental hospital.'

Monica considered the information. Four friends – two become successful, one ends up in a mental hospital, one ends up in a hole in the ground. Her detective's instinct told her there was a story here. Something had happened that summer.

'Was there anyone else living or working around here at the time?' This was Crawford. 'Lodgers? Farm labourers?'

'Nothing like that. Mum and Dad did most of the work on their own.'

Monica gestured to the plastic box Jessica had produced. 'Is there a sample of Freya's writing in there? Just to compare with the letter?'

'There should be some old school jotters, but the letter's definitely hers,' Jessica said, looking bemused by the request. 'I watched her practise her signature about a million times when we were teenagers. I'd know her writing anywhere.'

Chapter 19

Monica and Crawford stopped in the village of Beauly at Biagiotti's for takeaway coffee, then headed back east towards Inverness.

'You got plans for the weekend?' It seemed like the kind of thing to ask, to try to get things back to normal.

Crawford shrugged, sipped at his coffee. 'Not sure yet. You?'

Monica shook her head. 'I'll do something with Lucy.'

'Course. Be good for her to have a change, after everything this week.' Crawford whistled through his teeth, a nervous tic. 'Miranda Salisbury and Brodie King? Hately's going to love this – thought it was bad enough this morning without dropping an MSP into the mix. Should we try speaking to them today?'

The lights changed to red at the bridge over the River Beauly. Monica stopped the Volvo and took a mouthful of coffee. Crawford's recommendation had been spot on – it was delicious. She set the cup back in the holder. Thought about what Crawford had asked. 'It's Friday afternoon. I'll speak to Hately later.' Much as it went against Monica's instincts, she sensed it would be politically wise to run this by her boss and formally agree times to interview Miranda Salisbury and Brodie King.

'What about the other one then? Joseph Moon. Jessica said he's still up at New Craigs?'

Through the car windscreen Monica could see that the day

wasn't improving with age. More banks of cloud had drifted in over the mountains from the west and it was raining heavily by the time they arrived back in Inverness. Monica took a right turn at the lights after Clachnaharry, driving uphill on the slopes of Craig Phadrig to the Leachkin area of the city. New Craigs Psychiatric Hospital overlooked Inverness; it was an ugly, modern facility built to replace the grand, Victorian-era Craig Dunain asylum, which stood abandoned in the woods further up the hill.

The receptionist stared at Monica and Crawford's IDs for a long moment before handing them back. She seemed surprised. 'Are you sure it's Joseph Moon you're after? He's been in here since before I started – hardly left the place. His parents are virtually the only people who ever come to visit him.'

Monica told her there was no mistake; they needed to speak to him about a historical matter. The woman shook her head again, then turned to the phone, pushed a button and muttered something into the receiver.

A minute later a young man wearing chinos and a white shirt emerged, his name badge identifying him as Dr Anders Fisk. His dark hair was clipped short, his face set in a frown as he glanced from Monica to Crawford. 'Joseph's vulnerable. I don't think it will be appropriate for you to see him.'

'We really need to speak to him,' Monica replied. 'I'd rather do it here where he's comfortable, than waste all of our time dragging him down for a formal interview.'

The doctor squinted, looked over to the receptionist. 'And they say we're not living in a police state yet, eh?'

'We're investigating a very serious crime,' Monica said. Doing her best to sound apologetic.

The doctor paused at that. 'Yes. Well, we'll see what kind of mood he's in . . . He might not be capable.'

'I just want five minutes.'

Dr Fisk relented. Turning to lead them down the corridor, he spoke over his shoulder. 'Care in the Community was supposed to stop long-term institutionalisation for people like Joseph.' They passed through a set of double doors, their feet squeaking on the rubber floor. 'Doesn't always work out.'

'Hard for some people,' Crawford said. 'Making that adjustment.'

'That's right,' Fisk replied, sounding oddly relieved. He stopped outside another set of double doors with DAY ROOM printed across them. Through the wire-reinforced glass Monica could see the moving lights of a TV, and caught the sound of canned laughter. Dr Fisk waited with his hand on the glass. 'Joseph's been worse recently. He's currently on strong anti-psychotic medication. Sometimes he's too drowsy to make much sense.'

There were about a dozen people in seats spread around the day room. One woman was standing, arms spread wide in a crucifix position, staring at the wall six inches from her face. The psychiatrist ushered Monica and Crawford to the far corner, where an easy chair faced the window and the impressive view over the city below. The man sitting in the chair was bloated, his face red with patches of dry skin. What little remained of his hair was plastered to his head in greasy strips.

'Joseph, these detectives would like to speak to you.' Fisk was almost shouting. Joseph glanced up, eyes skating over the psychiatrist's face then on to Monica and Crawford. After a long moment he gave a barely perceptible nod.

'Tired today.'

Monica smiled. 'We won't keep you for long.' There was a patch of acne on Joseph's chin; white residue at the corners of his mouth. Someone started shouting out in the corridor. Fisk gave a weary shrug and turned to go. 'I'll be five minutes.'

Monica nodded, looked around for a chair and pulled two plastic ones across the floor for herself and Crawford. The heating had been turned so high, it was stifling and cast a pall over the room, increasing the sense of minds having wandered too far from home. She shrugged her coat off, folded it over a knee.

'My name's Monica, this is Crawford. We just want to ask you a few questions.'

'Someone told me you were coming,' Joseph whispered. 'Made me promise not to tell.'

'Who told you?'

'I can't say.' His voice was slow, sluggish.

'Do you remember a girl called Freya?'

'We made a big mistake.'

'What did you do?'

'You already know? Don't you?' His glazed blue eyes met Monica's.

'Did you do something to her?' Monica asked. 'Did you do something to Freya?'

Joseph Moon turned away and stared silently out at the grey day, the distant lights of the Kessock Bridge, the Black Isle beyond. After almost a full minute Monica thought he might actually have drifted off to sleep with his eyes still open. Finally he seemed to remember she was there, tilted his head a little closer and began to whisper.

Chapter 20

It was raining harder when they stepped back outside from the stifling heat of New Craigs Psychiatric Hospital. Unlike leaving the mortuary after Freya Sutherland's autopsy, this time when Monica took a breath of the cold air she experienced no feeling of rebirth.

'What do you think he meant?' Crawford asked from down beside her shoulder. 'You think they killed her?' The awkwardness from the night before was temporarily forgotten. She felt the rain pummelling her face as they hurried across the car park to the Volvo. Monica recalled the fear in Joseph Moon's voice as he had leaned close then begun to whisper: 'We made them promises.' She had noticed a line of longer hairs on his cheek, missed while shaving. 'Now we can never sleep again.'

'He's seriously unwell,' Monica said once they were safely in the car, windows misting up as they sat. She was in the passenger seat this time; Crawford could have a turn driving. 'Would you want to rely on that testimony in court? He did seem to link it to Freya though.'

After those few words Joseph had returned to staring out the window, unwilling or unable to elaborate. Crawford switched the engine on and fiddled with the fan to clear the windscreen.

'What now?'

She glanced at the time on the dash. Still only 1 p.m. Monica reached over to the back seat and opened the plastic box marked

FREYA. Opened the thick notebook on the top of the pile inside. Jessica Sutherland had mentioned a list of the names, addresses and phone numbers of Freya's friends, acquaintances and colleagues. She flicked through the well-thumbed pages of the book, wondering if somewhere it contained the piece of the puzzle that would lead them to her killer. Finally she found the relevant pages at the back. 'The receptionist said that Joseph Moon's parents still visit him.' Monica ran down the list, recorded in a mix of fading colours, her finger stopping at an address in Cromarty. 'I think we should try them.'

A picturesque coastal town on the Black Isle – actually a peninsula – across the Moray Firth to the north of Inverness, Cromarty featured narrow side streets, small fisherfolk houses and a couple of churches with old graveyards. In summer it was a favourite spot for Monica to take Lucy and her mum for picnics; today persistent rain blanketed the town.

'Feels like there should be pirates,' Crawford muttered as he followed the Google Maps directions to Duke Street.

'Let's hope not,' Monica replied as he parked outside the house.

The place was painted white, the epitome of a charming seaside home, with a display of driftwood in the tiny garden. The man who answered the door was in his seventies, had wild grey hair, and was dressed for the outdoors in blue waterproof trousers and a battered orange Gore-Tex jacket.

'Mr Moon?' There was no nameplate on the door and he didn't obviously look like Joseph. It was possible they had moved since Jessica made her notes years before.

'Who's asking?' He eyed Monica and Crawford suspiciously down a carbuncled nose.

Monica held out her ID. 'We're police. It's about Joseph.'

His expression changed from suspicion to surprised hostility. 'Twenty years too late. I should tell you to bugger off.' He had a northern English accent.

'We're investigating a murder.'

A woman's voice came from inside: 'Who is it, Brian?'

Brian Moon shook his head, frowning, but said, 'I suppose you better come in.'

Monica had to stoop her head under the low doorway into the old house. The nautical theme of the exterior was continued inside, with seascapes and prints of boats. Under different circumstances it could have been a charming holiday cottage.

'You like the sea?' Crawford asked.

'Did my time in the navy, then moved up here for it. Town named after a place from the Shipping Forecast – what could go wrong?' He gave a laugh at his weak quip. 'Don't get out much now. This is Julia.' His wife was in the adjoining kitchen, chopping vegetables into a soup pan. They went through.

'I'm sorry to land on you like this,' Monica said. Julia clanked the lid onto the pan and came to sit beside Brian at the kitchen table. Monica and Crawford introduced themselves again and sat opposite. 'Freya Sutherland, a friend of Joseph's, went missing back in 1994. She left a note, saying she was leaving with friends—'

'And now you're interested!' The years of repressed rage coming out in his voice were intimidating, despite his age. 'Twenty bloody years too late!' he repeated.

Monica had plenty of experience in facing anger, so it wasn't hard for her to keep her voice level. 'Too late for what?'

'I told your lot at the time that something happened that summer. Joseph was never the same after. He was only twenty, for God's sake. Had his whole life ahead of him . . .' Brian Moon's voice died away, anger turning to sadness.

'Who did you tell, exactly?' she asked. There was no mention of a visit to the Moons in the slim missing person file.

'The detective that came round. He was asking about the young woman, Freya,' Julia Moon said. She had grey hair cut in a bob, was wearing a white fisherman's jumper, sleeves rolled up. She squeezed Brian's arm as she spoke.

'A slimy bastard. Box-ticker. Didn't give a shit,' Brian Moon muttered, anger simmering again at the memory. His description matched some of Monica's own thoughts about Duncan Gregg.

'What did you tell him?'

Brian scowled. 'What bloody difference will it make now?'

Monica said, 'You might have heard on the news that Freya's body was discovered this week. We're trying to get answers for her family. Maybe we can get some for you too.'

Brian glanced at his wife, then back to Monica. 'Have you got children?'

'A daughter.'

He turned to Crawford. 'What about you?'

'None that I know of.' Monica glanced at her colleague in irritation, but unexpectedly Moon snorted a laugh and wiped the corner of his eye.

'They say the old ones are the best ones, eh? Reminds me of the banter we had in the service.' Moon shook his head. 'I knew from the start that Brodie King was a bad lot. Just by looking in his eyes. Something not right there. Joseph was always easily led. Meets Brodie and Miranda, thinks they're a cut above . . .'

'How did Joseph get to know them?'

'He went to art college in Inverness with Brodie, met Miranda through him. Suddenly they're spending all their time together.'

'Did Joseph ever mention leaving? Going somewhere with Brodie and the others, in the summer of 1994?'

Brian glanced at his wife, and they both shook their heads. 'We hardly saw him that summer. He was never here. If he was planning something we would have been the last to know.'

'He was living with Brodie?'

Brian replied, 'He was living somewhere. Not here though. Never thought me or his mum were worth keeping informed as to where.' He shook his head, still disturbed by the memory.

'When did Joseph's mental health begin to decline?'

Brian dropped his eyes to the table, his hands clasped together. Julia spoke, her accent English too: 'Joseph arrived back one night in October. He'd lost his keys, wallet, was rattling at the door. We hadn't seen him in months . . .'

'At first we were just pleased he was back,' Brian continued. 'He looked terrible, skinny as a whip, exhausted – stayed in his room sleeping for the first two days.'

'We hoped he'd get back to normal eventually.' Julia's grey eyes were wide at the memory. 'He wouldn't put his bedroom light off though. Ever. Hardly spoke. From October until the new year he barely left his room.'

'Did Brodie or Miranda come to visit?'

'Course they didn't,' Brian almost shouted.

Julia said, 'Eventually we sent Joseph down to stay with my brother in Bristol for a few months. He seemed better. When he came back he started taking the bus to Inverness, looking for a job.'

'What happened?'

'It was the next autumn. The tenth of September 1995,' Brian said, and Monica caught the date – the anniversary of Freya going missing. 'Phone call from the police. They'd found him wandering miles away, said he was distressed. Long and short, he gets sectioned, diagnosed with schizophrenia. Craig Dunain then and the New Craigs pretty much ever since. That's our son, that's his life.'

'I'm sorry.'

He shook his head sadly. 'Well, it sounds like Freya's family have their own version of all this. No doubt because of Brodie King and Miranda Salisbury. Heard Brodie was addicted to heroin for years after – at least he suffered too. Always boils my blood when I see Miranda on TV . . .'

'Where did the police find Joseph?' Monica asked. Hoping for an obvious link: the location of Freya's body or Fettercairn Farm.

Instead Brian said, 'Oh, it was out to the west. At Corrimony Cairn, if that means anything to you?'

'Corrimony Cairn?' The name was familiar.

'An old chambered cairn? Like at Clava?' Crawford was talking about the Clava Cairns, a Neolithic site just outside Inverness, made famous by the *Outlander* TV series.

'That's right, it's near Glen Affric.'

'Was the place significant to Joseph?'

Brian gave a bitter laugh. 'Seems to have been. Part of his delusion was that he'd made a promise to someone that he could never repay.'

'Did he say who?'

Brian Moon got slowly up from his seat and left the room. The rain drummed at the cottage's small windows. Monica caught the smell of the soup drifting from the stove.

Julia glanced down the corridor to check Brian was out of earshot, then leaned closer to Monica. 'How old's your daughter?'

'Five. Not long started school.'

'That's a nice age for them,' Julia said, smiling sadly. 'Joseph was so excited when he started school. Being an only child he was so pleased to have friends. It was like he'd do anything to fit in, to be liked.' She glanced along the corridor again. 'Brian doesn't like remembering any of that. Easier to blame Brodie King and Miranda Salisbury for everything with Joseph. Sometimes I think we must have failed him too. Something must have been missing.'

A door banged and Brian's footsteps creaked over old floorboards. When he re-entered the room he was holding something.

'A couple of years ago we finally accepted Joseph wasn't coming home and redecorated his bedroom. I found this down the side of his wardrobe.' Brian laid a photograph on the table. Monica took in the faded print. It showed three young people, standing in a triangle shape. In the distance was a large tree, and beside them what looked like a stone wall. 'That's Joseph.' The young man on the left looked absolutely nothing like the person Monica had spoken to an hour before in New Craigs. He was dressed in dark jeans and a dark shirt, strawberry-blonde hair partially shaved above the ear in a step. He was thin, pallid, but had a youthful vitality that seemed to suggest a world of possibilities. And Monica couldn't help wondering, *What happened to you, Joseph? What brought you so low?*

Brian moved his finger to the young man in the middle of the triangle, and spat, 'That's Brodie King.' He was taller than Joseph, thin like his companion but broader across the shoulders, with long dark hair. Also dressed in dark clothes, he had sunglasses pushed up on his forehead. He was frowning, intense eyes staring straight down the camera. 'The great Miranda Salisbury.' She was standing a little apart from the others. Slim, dressed in cut-off jeans and a white vest top, a purple sun hat casting her face and hair in shadow.

Monica ran her eyes over the photograph again. At first sight it felt pretentious, a group of art students posing, but something about the image carried a coldness – maybe the way the three were standing in a triangle was subtly unnerving? Or the intense and knowing look on Brodie's face. *Maybe because you know what happened to Joseph, to Freya?* Monica's internal voice chipped in.

Brian said, 'Look at Brodie's hand.'

Crawford leaned in to tilt the photograph. 'Is he pointing at something?'

Monica peered closer, wishing she'd brought her reading glasses. The thumb of Brodie King's right hand was tucked into the waistband of his jeans. Index finger extended, it looked like he was pointing at the patch of ground between the three of them.

Monica asked Brian, 'Do you have any idea where this was taken?'

'That was the only reason I kept the damn thing.' As Brian reached to pick up the print, Monica squinted at the stone wall beside the group. As the angle changed, she realised what she was really looking at. Not a wall at all, but a small standing stone.

Brian held the back of the print up for them to see. Beside the faded PRINTED BY BOOTS, handwritten in black biro was: COR-RIMONY CAIRN 1994.

Chapter 21

'You think something could be buried there?' Crawford asked when they were back out in the Volvo, his obvious horror at the idea overriding the lingering awkwardness between them – for the time being at least. Rain splashed the windscreen. The storm had picked up, and the sea was churning, an iodine stink coming in off the white water. 'Out at Corrimony Cairn?'

'I'll call Ridgeway.' Monica had spoken to the forensic archaeologist the previous day after he had completed a survey on the area around the excavation site at the Witch's Coffin, concluding there was no evidence of further burials. He had mentioned planning to take the morning ferry to visit a site on the Isle of Lewis for the weekend. 'He said he'd be back on Monday.'

Crawford nodded, wiped a hand over his face and checked the door pocket for one of his cans of Red Bull. He found one, opened it and took a sip. Offered her the can. 'There was only one,' he said apologetically.

She shook her head, started the car and checked the time. Almost 4 p.m. On Fridays Monica's mum collected Lucy from school, to take her to Lidl and the Co-op for her weekly shop. For some reason, Lucy enjoyed visiting supermarkets and helping her gran to load her small trolley.

'Must be rough for them,' Crawford said, gesturing back towards the Moons' house. 'All those years, hoping for something to change. Good folk end up in a kind of hell; bad ones live the life of Riley. Never seems fair.'

'No. It doesn't.' Monica wondered where he'd ever got the notion that life was supposed to be fair. Though one of the things she liked about Crawford was his positivity – it matched her mum's, probably why they got on so well.

'Two of them end up successful – Miranda Salisbury an MSP, Brodie King a well-known chef. Joseph ends up in a mental hospital, Freya dead. You think they killed her? Joseph's mind couldn't cope?'

'Maybe. Seems like something dramatic happened that summer,' Monica replied. 'We're going to have to find out what.'

They drove the rest of the way in silence, Crawford fiddling incessantly with his phone, the repeated buzzing sound of messages coming in. She pulled over at the bottom of Church Street in the centre of Inverness.

'You want to come for a drink?' Crawford asked as he was getting out of the car. His green eyes latched on to hers and he smiled. 'No repeat of last night, I promise.'

No, I don't want a drink, Monica thought as she stared back at him. *I want you to take me home, and I want you to fuck me.* 'I'd better go and see Lucy,' she replied.

Crawford nodded, smiled again. He seemed back to his old self, but as he went to swing the car door shut her eyes landed on the fingers of his left hand. The skin around the tips of his index and middle fingers was red-raw. She had never known her partner to chew his fingernails; now she saw they were bitten bloody.

When Monica arrived at her mum's house in Rapinch, Lucy was enthusing about a game she'd been playing at school. Monica raised questioning eyebrows in her mum's direction. Angela

Kennedy mouthed, 'Been playing with wee Harriet and her friends.' Even if the connection with the Sutherlands wasn't ideal in the midst of an investigation, it was a relief to see Lucy looking happy again. She was standing on a chair to raise her up to the level of the kitchen worktop so she could help her gran roll out the dough for Friday-night pizzas (ham and pineapple for Lucy and Angela; mushroom and olive for Monica). As Monica watched her daughter's chubby fingers press down on the rolling pin, she found herself wondering again about Crawford's hands. Why was it disturbing her that he'd taken up biting his nails? It wasn't exactly an unusual or seriously harmful habit.

'. . . said that her auntie disappeared, like a fairy? I don't think that could happen in real life?'

Monica realised that her daughter was now staring quizzically up at her. 'What was that, honey?'

Her mum cut in: 'Harriet was saying that her auntie Freya just disappeared one day, like a fairy. I was saying that can sometimes happen, like in a fairy tale.'

Monica forced a smile down at Lucy. 'No one knows exactly what happened to Freya.' Although she appreciated her mum's attempts to spare Lucy's feelings, she knew how powerful her daughter's imagination was. 'Me and Crawford are trying to find out so we can tell Harriet's mummy and her daddy.'

Chapter 22

At Carselang prison, Pauline Tosh was calling the shots. On Saturday morning Monica spent an hour sitting with Tyler, the young prison officer from her previous visits, in the cramped entrance office, waiting for the serial killer to agree to leave her cell for a meeting. The simplest way to solve Freya's murder would be to discover how Tosh knew about her body's location. Monica had to try, no matter how unlikely it was that Tosh would volunteer the information.

It turned out that Tyler had recently become a father for the first time. In between making Monica mugs of tea, he showed her a series of long videos of his son, Tyler Junior, smiling but largely inactive, on his back in a crib.

'It's a different world once you've got a kid, isn't it?' Tyler said. The electric fire was turned up high against the granite chill emanating from the thick walls. On the drive up Glen Wyvis, the mountains had been caked in autumn snow after the previous day's storm. The roof and turrets of Carselang were similarly plastered. 'Everything's more serious. If something happened to me . . .' He shook his head. 'Read about that poor woman, the one you found the other day. Her family not knowing all those years – imagined it was my child.'

Monica took a sip of tea. 'Did you sell the story to the press?'

Tyler looked like he was about to spit his own mouthful of tea over the dilapidated computer keyboard on the counter in front of him. He swallowed. 'No! Of course not! Did someone say that? I wouldn't even know how to . . .'

He sounded genuinely offended and Monica felt moved to apologise. 'The news broke when only a handful of people knew the location had come from Tosh.'

'Well, it wasn't from me.'

'But there are people up here who would leak to the press? You've heard stories?'

Tyler dropped his eyes to the countertop, shuffled a heap of visitor forms. 'I suppose you hear rumours sometimes. How you can make a few grand.'

'You know that money costs the victims' families? It's intrusive, damages their trust in the investigation.'

'I know that!' Tyler said. 'That's why I'd never do it!'

'I believe you,' Monica said, which was true. 'I need a favour though.' She dug in her pocket for one of her cards and held it out to him. 'If you hear where it came from, you see anyone able to afford a new car when they'd been moaning about having no money, or suddenly going on a fancy holiday – call me.'

The phone on the counter rang and Tyler picked it up. Listened to someone speak then hung up. 'Tosh says she's not leaving her cell today. She says you'll have to come back another time if you want to speak to her.'

This time when Monica arrived back at the cafe in Tain, her mum and Lucy were still waiting inside. *No Crawford today*, Monica thought as she pulled up outside, and she couldn't help wondering again what he'd wanted to tell her that Sunday. She sighed as she clicked the Volvo locked with the key fob. Told herself that it was probably nothing. He tended towards recurring low-level drama in his romantic attachments.

Inside the warm cafe Monica took in the cosy smell of roasted coffee mixed with baking bread. The place was off-season quiet, and she quickly spotted her mum in a corner seat, Lucy beside her, leaning over the table. The remains of an ice cream sundae beside them. Lucy looked up at the sound of Monica approaching, her face pale, one hand resting on her stomach.

'Did she eat that all herself?' Monica pointed at the dessert glass, which was almost as large as Lucy's head.

Her mum folded her arms defensively. 'She deserved a treat, been at school all week!'

'Mum, she looks ill.'

'Eyes bigger than her belly.' Angela Kennedy laughed. 'It's the only way she'll learn.'

The bored-looking Saturday waitress wandered over and Monica ordered a flat white. Sat down and felt Lucy's forehead with the back of her hand.

'I feel sick,' her daughter groaned.

Monica's mum glanced round the empty cafe, then leaned in conspiratorially. 'How did it go?' Angela Kennedy was obsessed with crime fiction, true crime, and above all her daughter's investigations. She could be dogged in her pursuit of information, often gleaning 'intel' from news sites or crime chat groups before sharing her own theories on angles Monica and Crawford should explore. The trick in dealing with her, Monica had learned, was to feed her small pieces of information that were harmless to the investigation or already in the public domain. Knowing there was always a chance that what she shared might end up on a group chat somewhere.

'Nothing. She wouldn't see me,' Monica replied quietly, looking pointedly around the cafe before adding, 'Make sure you keep that to yourself.'

'Of course, Monica, of course!' her mum said, looking round the cafe again, thrilled to have gleaned this nugget from inside the case. 'As if I wouldn't!'

Lucy soon recovered from her sundae-induced nausea, and they decided to visit nearby Dunrobin Castle. After wandering round the grounds of the magnificent house, they finally headed back south through Golspie on the A9. It was twilight when they crossed from the Black Isle over the Kessock Bridge to Inverness. It was Lucy who spotted the flames first. Angela had drifted off to sleep and Monica had her eyes on the road when the shout came from the back seat: 'Something's burning!'

Monica followed Lucy's pointed finger to the slopes of Craig Phadrig, the hill at the west of the city and site of New Craigs Psychiatric Hospital, which Monica and Crawford had visited the day before. Her first thought was that the hospital was burning – that somehow made sense, fitted with the investigation. It took a moment to realise that the fire was further to the west than New Craigs, higher up the hill. 'It's the church!' Her mum interrupted her flow of thoughts. 'It's the big one up there!'

Chapter 23

The dead-end road to the church was blocked off by the time Monica crossed the city and drove up the lower slopes of the hill. Further up she could see three fire engines surrounding the smoking building. She remembered the church was a 1970s building, mostly wood and glass. Now it was alive with black smoke and bright flames. Dry wood desperate to burn. As Monica parked at the police cordon and got out, she could see how close the church was to the dense woods that covered the hill's upper slopes. The firefighters were battling to stop the blaze from reaching the trees. Even at this distance Monica could feel the heat as the flames danced, casting curious shadows, and for a moment she couldn't help but think of satanic covens, of mischievous fairies and goblins causing chaos.

She shook her head and mouthed, 'Wait here,' through the windscreen to her mum and Lucy. Both were staring out wide-eyed, frightened by the conflagration, showing no sign of wanting to leave the safety of the vehicle. The officer at the cordon recognised Monica and didn't try to stop her, but the hot air blowing down the hill was like opening the door to a super-heated oven. She quickly understood that without the firefighters' protective equipment this was as close as she was getting.

She retreated to the cordon. 'Was there anyone inside?'

'We don't think so, ma'am,' the officer replied, shouting to be heard above the roar of the flames. 'There were no services or events planned for today.' Monica let out a sigh of relief. The thought of anyone being trapped among those flames was terrifying. 'That's the second church burned this week,' the officer added. And even as Monica felt the relief that no one was inside the building, she understood that another investigation was going to be coming the way of her team. In a strange way it even seemed inevitable.

Chapter 24

As she was crossing the car park at headquarters on Monday morning, Monica had the chance to glance at her phone for the first time since dropping Lucy at school. The slew of missed calls from Crawford was the first hint that something was wrong. She cursed herself for leaving the phone switched to silent, then hurried inside and upstairs.

Detective Superintendent Hately was already waiting for her, the door to his office open, his face closed and brow furrowed in anger. Her boss was the kind of man who had read *The 48 Laws of Power* by Robert Greene and taken notes, but like most people, under pressure he reverted to type. In his case, macho belligerence. He gestured her inside.

'Close the door,' he barked. Monica did as she was told. Stood facing him across the office, feeling her hands drop to her hips. There was an iPad lying on his desk. He pointed to it. 'What the fuck is this?'

'What?' The tablet was facing Hately, who was standing with his hands on his own hips, clearly not about to make this any easier on her. She stepped closer and turned the tablet to face her, read the headline on the tabloid news site: TORY MSP IN HIGHLAND MURDER PROBE.

'Miranda Salisbury's part of our investigation and I find out through a fucking newspaper?'

'I'm sorry,' Monica muttered, shocked herself. 'I only found out on Friday. I was going to fill you in today. Talk to you about setting up a time to interview her.' As she spoke she realised how weak her explanation sounded.

'Did you leak this?' She had worked with Hately for five years and couldn't remember seeing him this angry.

'What possible reason would I have for leaking it?'

'To put pressure on me. You were worried I wouldn't give you enough time on it, or you thought I'd hand it on to a cold-case team.'

'If you really believe I'd do that, then I don't know what I'm even doing in this office.' Despite her anger, Monica actually felt a lump forming in her throat. 'You clearly have absolutely no confidence in me.'

Hately averted his eyes. 'I didn't say that.' He ran his hands over his face, took a deep breath. 'Who then?'

Monica thought about it for a second. 'Only the team knew about this – me, Crawford, Fisher and Khan. I don't believe any of them would have reason to leak it. Jessica Sutherland told me she spoke to the press on Friday morning. She said she had only confirmed that Pauline Tosh was the suspected killer. Salisbury wouldn't have even been in her head at that point . . .' Monica's voice died away as she remembered Brian Moon.

'What is it?'

'A friend of Freya's, Joseph Moon. We spoke to his parents. His dad in particular seemed to hold a grudge against the police and against Miranda Salisbury and Brodie King.'

'You think he would have spoken to the press?'

'They said they wouldn't mention it.'

'And you just trusted them?' Hately actually sounded relieved. Better a witness leaking than a close team member.

'We can't control witnesses speaking to the press,' Monica

said. 'I'm sorry I didn't tell you on Friday. I was planning to fill you in today. I fucked up. It's not fair on Salisbury and King, but it's a high-profile case – something would have come out eventually.'

'Salisbury's solicitors are going to be all over this,' Hately said. He was staring at her again, but his tone had softened. 'You're certain the leak didn't come from us?'

Half an hour later Monica gathered her team in a meeting room. She took in the three junior detectives: Fisher with his usual neat dark hair and glasses; red-haired Crawford wearing a suit; Khan with her hair in an untidy bun, glasses, a loose white blouse.

'You've seen the story about Miranda Salisbury and Brodie King this morning.' She wasn't enjoying this any more than they were – who enjoyed having their integrity questioned? 'I'm sorry but I have to ask this. If you know how this got out, now's the time to tell me.' The three detectives glanced among themselves but none of them spoke. 'We can still fix this if it's a mistake.'

Crawford sometimes came across as a loudmouth, but he was discreet when it mattered. Fisher was a stickler for the rules; a successful police career was his main life goal. Khan? Could she have let something slip through one of her press contacts? Monica's eyes lingered on her a moment. Khan pushed the sleeves on her blouse up past her elbows, then folded her hands together and cracked her knuckles. Eyes on her hands in front of her. Monica glanced between the detectives again. No one spoke. After a minute she stood up and forced a smile. 'Let's get back to work.'

Chapter 25

The rest of the morning and early afternoon for Monica and Crawford was taken up with a long drive to Sutherland in the far north-west Highlands. Through stunning landscapes that people came from all over the world to admire. And an odd contrast for Monica: instead of contemplating the sculpted mountains and lochs, she was thinking about a hole in the ground. About Freya Sutherland, who had spent over two decades buried in it. And the person who put her there. Was it Brodie King? With Miranda Salisbury and Joseph Moon as accomplices? It would explain why Moon's mind had fractured the year after. Guilt keeping him awake? Slowly driving him mad? Whatever had happened back in 1994, King had indisputably come out of it better than Moon. Monica knew from the pictures of King's smiling blonde wife and young children on his company website that he now had a family as well as a string of restaurants. The newest was the Laxford Inn, a seafood place. Monica had spoken to a receptionist, who'd told her that King was acting head chef there, working split shifts seven days a week, and had no intention of coming to Inverness any time soon.

'You been up this way much?' Crawford asked, breaking her chain of thought. They had driven most of the way in silence, the awkwardness of the previous week seemingly destined to linger.

'Once or twice,' Monica replied. 'Enough to know this road's faster.' They'd had a minor dispute when leaving headquarters about the route to take. Crawford wanted to take the west coast Ullapool road; Monica knew from experience it was faster to take the back road off the A9 and over the mountains via Lairg.

Crawford laughed. 'Seems like you were right. Almost half-way there. How did you know?'

'I worked a case up this way. About six years ago. My dad was dying so I was back in Inverness.' As she spoke, traumatic memories of the investigation and of her dad's death threatened to surface. She clocked a subtle shift in Crawford's body language – sitting up a little more straight behind the wheel. Recognition dawning for him too.

'Shit, I remember reading about it – up at Kinlochbervie. Sounded like a bad one.'

Monica cleared her throat. 'That's right,' she replied finally. 'It was a bad one.'

Crawford glanced at her, clearly intrigued. He didn't push it though, and she was happy to let the bad memories drift away. Reminded herself: if it hadn't happened the way it did, there would be no Lucy.

Finally Crawford took the turn-off signposted for the Laxford Inn. The place was a renovated stone byre with a newly built, large glassy extension. It overlooked the Minch – the sea separating the mainland from the Western Isles. Crawford parked the Volvo between a BMW and a Ferrari and got out, flexing his back after the long drive.

Monica got out herself, feeling how her own long spine was compressed after the hours in the car. She stretched and took in the iodine smell of the sea, the comforting sound of waves breaking over sand. The glass front of the inn was actually suspended above the beach, and even though there was an autumn chill coming in off the North Atlantic, Monica could see two full tables on the balcony, drinkers wrapped in jumpers and tweeds chatting as the sun began its dip towards the western horizon. It really was a stunning view, and for a moment Monica allowed herself to imagine being the kind of person who drove the North Coast 500 in a sports car and stayed at expensive hotels. Perhaps with a rich husband.

She'd had a few serious relationships throughout her twenties and thirties. Always with men who were less dominant than an outsider might guess she would be drawn to. An artist, a historian, a psychiatric nurse. Macho uniformed characters like fellow cops or firemen had always turned her off. *Too much like Daddy*, her internal voice chipped in, and Monica didn't argue. There was no doubt she needed to be in control in her relationships. A counter to the restrictiveness she'd felt from her authoritarian father. Then the disappointment when the men she chose let her down.

She recalled a trip to Italy with the historian – his great sense of humour and the pleasure of being with someone genuinely knowledgeable about frescoes in Florence and Siena, who wanted to spend all night wandering around Rome, waiting for the sun to rise over the Colosseum. And later the same day on a quiet side street, when they'd watched a mugger knock a woman off her moped and steal her bag. Instinctively Monica had grabbed the mugger, dragged him to the ground. The woman was lying on the road beside her bike, forearm twisted at an unnatural angle from the fall.

'Help her!' Monica had shouted, only to see the historian slumped in a doorway, hand on chest, having a panic attack. Once the ambulance had taken the unfortunate woman to hospital and the Carabinieri had arrived to arrest the mugger,

Monica had spent the rest of the day reassuring him, but the uncomfortable knowledge of his vulnerability had lingered. His nervousness, amplified by the traumatic experience. His passivity during sex – the feeling that her lust could consume and destroy him if she gave it free rein. He would never be able to contain the parts of her character that were the most instinctual and feminine. She would always have to hold herself back to keep him safe.

'We going in, then?' Crawford's voice from across the roof of the car interrupted the ancient memory. Why had it surfaced today? Because the historian was absolutely nothing like Lucy's father?

'Well, I didn't come for the bloody memories,' Monica muttered, and Crawford raised his eyebrows, face alive with humour for the first time that day. He shook his head and reached into the car for his coat, checked the collar of his shirt and pulled the expensive wool garment on.

'Oh my days, abusive language to a colleague.' He shook his head in mock outrage, straightened up and locked the car. 'Bullying in the workplace . . .'

The entrance foyer was decorated with landscape photographs of the distinctive mountains and lochs of the north-west Highlands, interspersed with pictures of a man in chef's whites standing next to various famous faces. Arm around their shoulders, at least a head taller than most of them, Brodie King had the same dark hair, pale skin and dark eyes as the youth in the 1994 photograph at Corrimony Cairn. His prominent jaw, covered in dark stubble, was a little heavier, but otherwise he had changed little in twenty-four years. A marked contrast to the transformation of Joseph Moon.

The reception desk was unattended, and Monica pushed the

restaurant door open. A long bar ran down one side of the room. Mirrors and bottles behind the bar reflected the distinctive northern light. The delicious smells of garlic and mussels drifted from the kitchen. At the end of the bar, two men perched on stools looked up as Monica stepped inside. One of them was a waiter, dressed in a tweed waistcoat, white shirt and black trousers. His high-end customer service smile wavered for a split second as he took in the unusual-looking pair: the tall woman in a threadbare tweed coat; the small, preened man who appeared to have stepped out of a fashion website. Monica barely noticed though. Her eyes were on the man beside the waiter. Dressed in chef's whites with his sleeves rolled up to reveal pale forearms.

His eyes scanned her face, and unexpectedly she felt a spike in her blood. *Brodie King?* But her tongue lay still in her mouth, stilled by a feeling of raw fear she had only experienced a handful of times in life. An intuition: here was danger, a killer. Like opening a cupboard door in a dream to find a man-eating beast staring back.

'Mr King?' Crawford said from beside her a moment later.

'Who's asking?' His accent was more Lowland Scots than the softer Highland she had expected. There was a laptop open in front of him and a notepad beside it. The clock above the bar told her it was 2 p.m. The lunch service was probably just finished.

'I'm DI Kennedy, this is DC Crawford.' She crossed the room and held out her warrant card. He glanced at it, made eye contact again, and she felt that chill return, though was prepared for it this time. She stared at the end of his nose rather than into his eyes – an old trick from her first boss down in Glasgow for dealing with the psychopathic gaze. *They smell different too*, he had told her more than once when in full 'witchfinder' mode.

Different hormones released by the brain. Some women love it, get drawn to them.

King turned to the wide-eyed waiter: 'Give me two.' The waiter nodded and went to close the glass doors to the balcony. King turned to Monica. 'You never heard of the phone?' She could see he was well socialised. Operating in an environment where coldness of character would be accepted as assertiveness.

'We won't keep you long.'

'No. You won't. Saw that shite written about me this morning. Thought I might get a visit. My lawyer told me to tell you to fuck off.'

'You spoke to Miranda?'

'Don't know who you're talking about.'

'No?' Monica nodded to Crawford, who went to his coat pocket then held out a print of the photo taken at Corrimony Cairn. Miranda Salisbury, Brodie King and Joseph Moon. 'There was another young woman, a friend of yours, back in 1994. Her name was Freya Sutherland.'

Monica watched King's face closely as she spoke. His eyes were a dark grey, almost black; his face stayed completely expressionless, but his pupils widened. His hand went to the cuff of his chef's jacket and he pushed it up, revealing more of his forearm.

'She disappeared,' she continued, 'just a few months after this picture was taken. No one heard from her for over twenty years. Her body was found a week ago. You remember her now?'

'Don't remember much from back then. Had a few rough years.'

'You were addicted to heroin?'

'That's what they say.' King picked up a packet of Marlboros from the counter and put one in his mouth.

'You four were close, it sounds like. Were you and Miranda boyfriend and girlfriend?'

Brodie shrugged. 'Who knows.'

'All so close, then it all fell apart?'

'That's young people, I suppose. Passions burn out.'

'Is that what happened with you and Miranda?'

'We fucked like rabbits that summer.' He stared hard into Monica's eyes. 'Is that what you want to hear? You want details?'

'I'm more interested in how it all ended. You and Miranda become the big successes; Joseph in Craig Dunain, Freya buried.' Brodie King continued to stare at her but didn't reply. She noticed a deep white scar across the bridge of his nose, as if from a bad break. 'Did you have a car back then?' She already knew from Brian Moon that he'd driven a Volkswagen Golf. King still didn't reply. 'You ever spend time down in the Marsh? You ever hang around down in the marshes?'

'Maybe. A lot of kids did.'

'How did you meet Freya?'

'How does anyone meet?'

'She was a country girl, wasn't she? Was she naive?' Brodie didn't reply. 'Your mum had a bit of money? You've been described as entitled.'

'Poor discipline. Happens a lot with single mothers when you've got no dad.'

'Did you tell Freya you were taking her away somewhere? Did you get her to leave a note so you could kill her and no one would suspect?'

'I see the Inverness police aren't any smarter than they were twenty years ago.' Brodie laughed dismissively, but Monica could see that he had put both hands flat on the counter, as if preparing to stand up. She guessed her words had triggered a fight-or-flight response. 'Coming up here with some half-baked story.'

'Joseph Moon told us that you made a mistake. What do you think he was talking about?'

'Have you spoken to Joseph recently? Not exactly *compos mentis* from what I've heard.'

'I have,' Monica said, stepping closer. 'Your best friend. Maybe he couldn't handle what you'd done to Freya?'

For a second a flash of anger transformed his face into a fearsome mask. But before he could speak, a door at the back of the restaurant opened and the two young boys Monica had seen on Brodie's website came running in.

'Daddy!' they screamed in unison, crossing the floor towards Brodie, who got off his stool and stooped to pick them up. Following them in was the blonde-haired woman from the website, Brodie's wife, dressed in jeans and a green cardigan. Her gaze went questioningly from the detectives to her husband, obviously sensing an atmosphere.

Brodie held the two young children to his chest and met Monica's eyes. 'If I was you' – standing, he was a few inches taller than her – 'I'd think long and hard before coming all the way back up here with any more of your strange theories.'

Chapter 26

It was after 4 p.m. when they crossed the Kessock Bridge. Monica took the road west through Inverness then up onto Craig Phadrig again. Although the firefighters had succeeded in preventing the blaze from spreading to the woods behind the church, All Angels was now reduced to a charred skeleton. Foreboding under the oppressive autumn sky, Monica thought, as she passed the turn-off for the church and hit the indicator to pull into Balnafettack Terrace. When they were almost back in Inverness, a call had come in to say that house-to-house inquiries about the church-burning had turned up a young witness.

A woman in her twenties answered the door of the grey pebble-dashed house. She had straight brown hair, was neat in Lycra sportswear and ice-white trainers, and introduced herself as Sofia Dabrowski. Monica and Crawford followed her inside to a small living room. Like Sofia, the space was well put together. Brown three-piece suite, pastel-green rug matching the curtains, smelling of expensive citrus oil.

The detectives sat on the leather sofa as Sofia went to call her son down from his bedroom.

'This is Adam.' Sofia spoke with a slight Polish accent. The boy was about ten, dirty-blond hair, skinny, dressed in sportswear too – a navy-blue tracksuit and Nike Air Max trainers. He came dutifully into the room and sat down.

'You were playing in the woods on Saturday?' Monica asked, smiling. 'Did you see something?' Adam shrugged, sank a little further into the armchair, refusing eye contact.

'Just tell, Adam,' Sofia chipped in, exasperation creeping into her voice. 'He wouldn't get up for school this morning. He hasn't been right since Saturday, I didn't know why . . .'

Monica said, 'You don't have to be frightened. You're not in any trouble.'

Adam stared at the ground, skinny arms folded tight across his chest.

Crawford leaned forward, hands on his knees. 'You like Champion gear?' He gestured to Adam's chest, and Monica realised after a moment that he was referring to the logo on the boy's hoody. 'That's what all the tough guys are wearing at the gym these days.' Adam raised his eyes at that, a flicker of a smile appearing at the corner of his mouth. 'Too expensive for me though. Used to be a cheap brand back when I was a kid, you believe that?'

Sofia said, 'So expensive. Sixty-five pounds hoody, forty pounds joggers. Only thing he wants to wear though.'

'It does look good,' Crawford replied, smiling at the kid then glancing at Monica. 'You can't deny it?'

Adam was beaming now and Monica thought, *Thank you, Crawford, for male bonding rituals.* She nodded.

'Here's the thing, Adam,' Crawford said, still leaning forward, his voice more businesslike now. 'Even if you did set fire to the church, you're too young to go to prison. So you don't need to worry about—'

'I never! I wouldn't have!' Adam said, alarmed by this sudden turn. Sofia's mouth opened, but Monica cast a reassuring glance in her direction and she seemed to get the message.

'I know you wouldn't,' Crawford said. 'We just need to know exactly what you saw, so we can find out who did.'

'I saw a man,' Adam said finally, 'in the Pit.'

'Where's the Pit?' Monica asked.

Sofia answered for her son: 'It's an old quarry in the woods behind the church – the kids play there sometimes.'

Monica nodded. 'What were you doing in the woods?'

'Just making a tree swing, down the side of the Pit.'

'And you saw someone?'

'He got out a car.'

'What kind of car?'

'I think it was blue.'

'Light blue, or darker?'

Adam pointed to his dark blue hoody. 'More like this, I think.'

'Do you know what shape it was? A saloon or an estate? An SUV?'

He shook his head, looking frightened again.

'Adam's not really interested in cars,' Sofia said. Monica nodded and made a mental note to get someone to come round with a folder of car pictures. If they could narrow down the make and model it would be an important lead.

'What did the man look like?'

'He had his hood up.'

'Did he say anything to you?'

'You shouldn't speak to strange men, especially not in the woods.'

'So you stayed hidden?'

'I was in a tree, tying the rope.'

'And you were on your own?'

'Paul and Wojciech had gone home for tea, but I wanted to finish the swing.'

'What did the man do?' Monica asked.

Adam thought for a moment. 'He opened the boot and got a bag. He sort of sprinted through the woods. A bit later I was getting down from the tree to go home. He came running back to the car. Then I saw smoke from the church.'

Monica thanked Sofia and Adam, stood to leave, then turned back to Adam. 'Why were you frightened to talk to us at first? Did you think we might blame you?'

He shook his head quickly. 'It was because of what everyone said about the witch.'

'What witch?' Monica asked slowly.

'Since they found the witch's body, buried down at the canal, everyone at school says they've seen ghosts in the woods. I thought the man could have been a ghost, that he might know where I live.'

'Why did you think he was a ghost?' Crawford asked.

'I don't know. I'd never seen someone drive a car into the Pit before. It just seemed like it shouldn't have been there.'

It was twilight when they parked beside the remains of All Angels Church. Up close Monica could see wisps of smoke continuing to rise through the building's skeletal remains. Against the grey gloaming sky, the blackened wood and metal called to mind the bones of a dragon. Lucy would have loved that idea, Monica thought as she climbed out of the Volvo. She wondered for a moment how her daughter had got on at school that day and whether her friendship with Harriet Sutherland had continued to bloom.

'Stinks,' Crawford said, sniffing at the evening air. He was right: the smell of water-soaked charcoal drifted from the building. It was somehow nauseating, and Monica covered her nose and mouth with the sleeve of her coat. 'You think there's anything in what the kid said?' Crawford continued as they walked uphill together towards the nearby woods.

'About the man?' Monica was surprised her partner had to ask. Children weren't always the most reliable witnesses, but Adam Dabrowski's account had sounded reasonable.

'No, about the ghosts,' Crawford replied. Monica raised an eyebrow from behind her temporary tweed mask. He was gazing earnestly back though, and she realised he wasn't joking.

'Kids make up stories, Crawford,' Monica replied. Trying not to sound patronising as she reminded herself that he had been brought up in a family where Satan and demons were a reality. 'They like scaring themselves with ghosts and ghouls.'

Crawford cleared his throat. He stopped at a wire fence and peered into the woods beyond. 'You're probably right. Just the way he was speaking about it, after what the churchwarden said at the first fire . . .'

Monica spotted a path through the trees, so they climbed over the fence and after a minute the path opened out into a bowl-shaped quarry. 'Wouldn't take long to run to the church from here,' Crawford said. 'Fire was started at the back of the building.'

'What about the car? How did he get it in here?' They scanned the sandy floor of the quarry. It had rained heavily on Sunday and that morning, washing away any tyre marks. Monica spotted a track at the far end of the quarry – wide enough to drive a car down. They walked along it, and after five minutes it ended at a junction with a road. In the gloom, Monica could just see that the track was blocked by a metal barrier.

'That'll be why Adam was surprised to see a car in there,' Crawford said. 'The guy must have chopped the lock.'

Monica stepped closer and examined the barrier. There was still an old padlock in place and the gate was firmly closed. She dug in her pocket for a pen, used it to poke at the padlock. By the light from her phone she could see it was intact. 'Or he had a key.'

'Doesn't look like it's in regular use,' Crawford said, nodding to the overgrown track leading back to the quarry. 'There can't be many people who have access.'

Chapter 27

Lucy was still awake when Monica arrived home after dropping Crawford off. She was lying on the floor in the living room with a book open in front of her. The cat, Albert, was stretched out beside her. There was no sign of Angela, but Monica heard an unfamiliar voice speaking Gaelic in the bathroom. She felt a moment's alarm before clocking the voice's tinny quality – her mum was listening to the radio, BBC Gàidhlig.

'It's me!' Monica shouted, catching the smell of cooking. She pulled her boots off, still caked with mud from the quarry, and went to check what was on the hob. Lentil soup bubbled in a pan – one of her mum's specialities, always served with garlic croutons. Monica felt a pang of hunger and realised she hadn't eaten since breakfast.

'I was just having a quick bath while Lucy read her book,' her mum shouted through from the bathroom. 'But I left the door open so I could hear her!'

'It's fine!' The previous year Monica had firmly asked her mum to stop leaving the front door unlocked. Angela Kennedy knew it made sense but hated to be criticised. In retaliation she had launched a subtle campaign to imply Monica was a hysterical parent.

Sometimes you just have to laugh, Monica thought as she took her coat off and hung it behind the door. She made herself a mug of tea with one of the Teapigs bags she'd picked up from the health-food shop on Baron Taylor's Street, then went to sit beside her daughter in the living room. Lucy was again reading an illustrated version of *The Worst Witch* – another title in the series.

'Did you pick that from the library?' Monica asked.

'I think so,' Lucy said without looking up.

'What are the witches up to?'

'I'm just looking at the pictures.'

'Did you have a nice day at school?' Monica reached out to stroke the cat, feeling his warm fur under her fingers as he began to purr. It was nice having another creature around – the first animal companion Monica had ever lived with. Albert had come to them after a social worker colleague, Michael Bach, happened to mention one of his cats was being bullied by the others and needed a new home.

'Someone said Harriet's auntie was a witch,' Lucy replied.

'Was Harriet OK?' The rumour that had disturbed Adam Dabrowski had made it as far as Crown Primary then.

'She said she was pleased, but some of the boys were calling her Witchy.'

'Well, it's not very nice to say that.' As she was speaking Monica wondered how Jessica and Barry Sutherland were. After the news about Miranda Salisbury had leaked that morning, DC Khan had been in touch to check on them, but so far Monica hadn't heard any updates. 'Did you speak to Munyasa today?' Lydia still hadn't answered any of Monica's messages; the ghosting continued.

'We're not friends any more,' Lucy said matter-of-factly. 'We don't like each other now.'

'That's a shame.' Monica tried to keep her voice casual. This was the first time Lucy had spoken about Munyasa since their falling-out. 'What happened? You used to be best friends.' Monica thought back just a few months, to seeing them skipping out of nursery together holding hands.

'He's friends with the boys now.'

'Did you say something to him that upset him?'

'I think he just likes them more.'

Monica tried to think of the right thing to say. Whatever the hell that was. 'You know we can't always get on with everyone,' she said finally, thinking back to her own lonely schooldays. 'What's important is to be true to yourself. Then your real friends will find you.'

Lucy gazed quizzically up at her.

What exactly does any of that mean?

Chapter 28

Freya Sutherland shifted on the tartan rug, feeling the sun on her legs. Breathed in the smell of heather on the breeze, mixed with menthol cigarette smoke. She opened her eyes and sat up: blue skies over the wide Highland landscape. Brodie King was sitting at the edge of the tartan rug, staring off towards the western mountains of Glen Affric.

He had driven them to Corrimony Cairn in his Volkswagen Golf on a 'mystery trip'. Miranda and Joseph had seemed underwhelmed when they'd pulled into the car park.

'We've been here before!' Miranda had jokingly complained. 'You said it was a mystery.'

'I wanted a beach,' Joseph had chipped in. 'Girls in bikinis and donkey rides. Or my donkey getting ridden . . .'

Miranda had slapped his arm in mock disgust. 'What does that even mean?'

Impervious to their protests, Brodie strode from the car park to the cairn, laid out a tartan rug on the grass in front and unpacked a selection of sandwiches and other picnic snacks from a hamper. Unlike the others, Freya loved it. She had never been here before. The cairn had a peaceful sense of symmetry, an unbelievable ancientness. As old as the pyramids, according to Brodie.

After the picnic Miranda and Joseph drove off to find a shop in Drumnadrochit, eight miles away, complaining that Brodie had brought only one bottle of wine. It had only been a few weeks since the morning they'd stopped for her at the bus stop, but already she felt like she couldn't imagine a world without her three friends. It was like they just fitted.

'Beautiful here,' Freya said, feeling stupid when Brodie continued to stare into the distance without replying. She realised it was the first time in their weeks of friendship that they had spent more than a few minutes alone together. The thought was strange somehow: the way a group could fit together so well, but you might not really know the individuals in it. It was a bit like with her family; she and her mum always seemed more likely to argue when they were alone. She didn't want to think about any of that though, not on a day like today when summer felt timeless and pregnant with possibility.

She nudged Brodie's hip with her bare foot. 'Can I have a draw of your cigarette?'

This time he looked back over his shoulder at her. He was wearing a white T-shirt, dark glasses hiding his eyes.

'Sell you one, ten bob.'

She could never be sure when he was joking and when he was being serious. 'I just want a bit.' He took a deep drag on the cigarette then turned his wrist so the filter was facing her.

'Don't say I'm not good to you.'

She gave a sarky smile, leaned in to put her lips round the filter, laid her fingers on his hand to steady it. His skin was pleasantly dry, and she felt nerves twist in her stomach at the touch. She took a draw, exhaled and sat back on the rug. At first Freya had assumed Miranda and Brodie were a couple; they seemed so comfortable together. Miranda would frequently lay her head on his lap and they seemed to treat one another's property as if it were their own. She had never actually seen them kiss though. Over his shoulder Brodie said, 'You ever feel really guilty about something?'

'Like what?' The conversation had taken a strange turn, and again she couldn't tell if he was joking or not. 'Like something illegal?' *Shut up, Freya.*

'I don't know . . .' For once Brodie sounded reticent. 'I don't know exactly, just like something you've regretted?'

Freya thought about it for a second, recalled the time she had stolen a toy cat from the local post-office shop. Had felt waves of guilt for a week afterwards and eventually returned it. 'I felt bad when my dad was in an accident,' she said finally. 'He was trapped for an hour and we didn't know.' Freya realised she hadn't known she felt guilty about it until now.

Brodie nodded slowly, as if really taking this in and thinking about it. Finally he asked, 'Did you feel bad about it? Or was part of you pleased?'

Freya waited to see if that crooked smile would come onto his face. The part of him that liked to needle, to shock.

'I suppose—'

'Didn't even get ID'd!' Joseph's voice interrupted her. 'First time since I turned eighteen two years ago!' He was carrying a blue plastic bag in one hand, a can of Merrydown cider in the other. Beaming. Miranda was walking behind him, wearing a white dress and purple sun hat, shaking her head and smiling. They had left the car at the parking spot a hundred yards along the road. A respectable-looking family must have parked at the same time and were now just behind them, the father frowning at Joseph's shouting.

Freya glanced back at Brodie, but he was already standing up, mirroring Joseph's smile just as readily as if he'd pulled on a mask. He reached into Joseph's bag, pulled out two cans of cider and handed one down to Freya.

Chapter 29

It was another dank morning as Monica and Crawford took the A82 alongside Loch Ness from Inverness, then the A831 at Drumnadrochit towards Corrimony Cairn. Dr Clive Ridgeway had arrived back in Inverness on Monday night, the Stornaway–Ullapool ferry delayed due to a storm. He called Monica at 11.30 p.m., having just read her email about the picture of Miranda Salisbury, Brodie King and Joseph Moon at Corrimony Cairn, struggling to contain his excitement. 'We could go and look tomorrow. The site's not been properly excavated since the 1950s. At one time the locals thought it was built by fairies.'

Ridgeway's blue Volkswagen Transporter was already there when Monica pulled into the small car park. A sign indicated the cairn was a short walk further along the quiet single-track road. Low clouds blotted out the mountains that Monica knew from experience lay further to the west. Glen Affric, Glen Turrit – beautiful places, disturbing memories of police cases. *That should be your motto for the Highlands*, Monica thought drily as she watched Ridgeway getting out of his van. He waved, opened the side door and began unloading equipment. Despite the temperature on Monica's dashboard reading 5°C, the archaeologist was jacket-less, wearing just a Megadeth T-shirt, combat shorts and hiking boots.

She wound down the window, feeling the autumn chill replacing the heat from the car. 'Can we help?'

'No, it's fine.' As Ridgeway was speaking his assistant emerged and began carrying items down the tree-lined road towards the cairn. Monica wound the window back up, appreciating the warmth of the car's interior a moment longer. Remembered a summer drive for a picnic out this way with her mum, Lucy and Auntie May. Angela Kennedy had kept up a commentary, translating the Gaelic place names of Glen Urquhart: 'Rock of the Slaughterer' and 'Hill of the Unjust Killing'. Auntie May had chipped in with the story of the Hag of the Cràach, who murdered lone travellers on the moors. Monica recalled glancing in the mirror at her daughter's captivated expression, thinking, *No wonder Lucy's head's in the clouds.*

Crawford shifted on the passenger seat beside her; he had fallen asleep during the last portion of the drive. He stretched his neck until it made an uncomfortable clicking sound.

'Late night?'

He rubbed his eyes. 'You could say. Just looking into Brodie King's background.'

'Anything new?'

'Not really. A few people who knew him.' He sat forward, looking around for one of his cans of Red Bull, before giving up and taking chewing gum from his jacket pocket instead. 'Ties in with what we know already. He was addicted to heroin for a while in the nineties, went down to London to try and get clean. Few years later he's started a bunch of restaurants.'

'Where did he get the money?' Monica was no expert, but surely setting up a restaurant was expensive.

'Maybe from his mum? Dad wasn't on the scene.'

Monica thought about it for a moment. 'Did anyone know much about Miranda?'

'Nothing,' Crawford replied as Monica finally switched the

car engine off, accepting they were going to have to step out of the warmth and into the rotten weather. 'Seems like she was the politician even back then – knew how to keep her name out of things.'

'Well, she's not kept her name out of it this time,' Monica said as she fastened the buttons on her coat and climbed out of the car.

Ridgeway was crouching at the cairn's entrance tunnel, holding his hands as if framing a photo. 'Looks like they balanced the camera here,' he muttered. Monica understood he was using the small standing stone in the background of the image of King, Salisbury and Moon she had sent him, to work out roughly where Brodie had been pointing.

He nodded to his young assistant, more sensibly dressed for the weather in a Gore-Tex jacket and trousers, and directed him to the left and right until, satisfied, he held his hand up. 'Stop!' He went to stand beside his assistant and began stamping on the grass as if testing for hollowness, then made a roll-up and said, 'Here lie the bones of Elizabeth Charlotte. Born a maiden she died a harlot. She was aye a virgin at seventeen. A remarkable thing for Aberdeen.'

Monica glanced at Crawford, who raised his eyebrows. The low cloud had turned to rain, plastering his red hair to his forehead. Ridgeway walked over to a pile of equipment under a tarpaulin, reached in and pulled out a metal detector. 'Spooky place this,' he said as he fiddled with the detector's settings. 'Heard a few stories about it.'

'What like?' Crawford asked. He could never resist the opportunity to scare himself.

'A Viking prince is supposed to haunt it. He died here after a battle down the glen. One of the excavators in the 1950s dig swore he saw a shadow coming out of the ground in the middle of the cairn, said it followed him, tried to get into his body. Left the next morning and never came back, they say.' He shrugged. 'Probably just wanted to get the hell out of here.' He nodded to his assistant. 'Don't you be trying any of that.'

'Why would I ever want to leave?' the man replied from under his hood. 'Living the dream here.'

Ridgeway snorted a laugh and stood up, his soaked T-shirt now glued to his beer gut. 'It's not the Valley of the Kings, but you ever tried getting a pint of heavy in Cairo?'

Monica watched in silence as Ridgeway turned and began scanning the area he had identified, and for the first time that morning she felt genuine apprehension at what they might find buried in the ground. The ancient stillness of the place, the weight of those centuries, those thousands of years – to be the one disturbing all that felt profoundly wrong. Droplets of rain gathered and ran down her forehead to her face. She shivered and adjusted her coat; wished she'd brought the umbrella from the boot of the car, and thought about running back to get it.

Before she could make a move, she caught the shift in Ridge-way's body language. Straightening up like a fisherman feeling a bite, he narrowed his area of interest then nodded to his assistant, who moved in and sprayed an *X* on the turf. Ridgeway hurried over to his tools, returned to the *X*. Monica watched as he pushed a metal probe into the ground. Moved it back and forth like he had done at the site in the marshes. He said something to his assistant, who was now holding a small shovel. The assistant nodded and after a moment he crouched and began to dig.

Chapter 30

The cat was wrapped in plastic, inside a metal tin.

When it was alive the cat's name had been Sooky. Monica knew this because the faded pink collar around his neck had the word printed on the metal tag, along with an Inverness-area phone number. These facts weren't the most interesting things about the cat though. When forensic scientist Gemma Gunn laid the pathetic half-desiccated, half-skeletal bundle out on the table in the Inverness lab, what stood out was the piece of metal wrapped loosely round its torso.

'Looks like his neck was broken,' she said, pointing to where Monica could see that the vertebrae had been cracked. Gunn was in her late thirties but looked younger; slim with blonde hair tied back in a tight ponytail, lips painted red, fingernails blue. Indicators of her personal style, though Monica couldn't imagine the scientist dressed in anything other than the white lab coat she was wearing. 'Seeing an animal harmed always makes my blood boil – worse than humans in a way,' Gunn added matter-of-factly as she pointed at the grey metal. 'I think this is lead.'

'That's what Ridgeway thought too.' Monica remembered him digging the cat up just three hours before. His obvious disappointment at the meagre find, buried about a foot deep. Had he been hoping for something more dramatic? Another dead woman? Instead it was someone's poor little moggy. But Monica knew the psychopath's dark triad well: bed-wetting, fire-setting, animal cruelty. She was interested in anyone who killed an animal then buried it in a carefully chosen location. Particularly when one of their friends had been found murdered.

'Have you checked if the number matches the Sutherlands'?' Gunn asked, seeming to take it for granted that the detectives were incompetent.

'It's not Freya's, I checked with her sister. They've had the same number the whole time she's lived there. We tried calling it but got no answer. We're in touch with BT to get the address.'

'So you were someone else's kitty,' Gunn whispered, patting the cat's head. She shifted closer, and with her gloved hands began teasing at the piece of metal. It was wrapped like a tube around the cat's middle. 'Soft,' the scientist continued. 'Probably a roll of roofing lead . . .' She peeled the metal all the way open, slid it carefully out from under the cat and flattened it. There were still strands of ginger fur sticking to it. 'I think there's writing on the inside.'

Monica leaned in beside her. The sheet was about the size of an A4 piece of paper. Words were scratched in the soft metal, darkened by age, still partly covered by strands of cat hair. With tweezers Gunn picked away at the hairs, then she adjusted an overhead lamp so it was shining directly onto the tablet. Under the powerful light the words were now clearly readable:

BRODIE KING
MIRANDA SALISBURY
JOSEPH MOON

'As if there was any doubt,' Crawford said from across the counter. 'Nice way to treat an animal.'

Gunn was still staring down at the tablet. 'There's another line underneath. It's been scratched out though.' She pointed with the tweezers, and Monica could see where some words had been obliterated. 'The tops of some of the letters are almost visible,' she said, gesturing again. 'There's definitely an *S*.' The tweezers rattled as she laid them on the metal worktop, and she reached for the SLR camera she had used to photograph Sooky before removing him from the tin. 'An expert might still be able to figure out what was written.'

As Gemma Gunn was adjusting the camera's settings, Monica stared at the sheet of lead. It was reminding her of something or someone. After a second she realised, bizarrely, that it was her old boyfriend the historian again. Before the fateful trip to Rome, when things had seemed like they might get serious, he had taken her home from London to visit his family in the city of Bath. She remembered him proudly showing her round the beautiful architecture, and the sense of history stretching back to the ancient Romans and beyond. They'd paid a visit to the Roman baths. She recalled there had been a display of offerings to Sulis Minerva, goddess of the local hot springs: lead tablets.

'I think it could be a kind of curse tablet,' Monica said.

Crawford and Gunn both turned to look at her. 'What's a curse tablet?' She could hear the disquiet in her partner's voice.

'A way of cursing your enemies. Asking the gods to harm them in some way.' Monica thought about it for a moment, then added, 'Or asking them to help you harm someone.'

Chapter 31

'You really think they could do that to a friend?' Crawford asked as they were exiting the glass front doors of the forensics laboratory. The lab was on the University of the Highlands and Islands campus on the outskirts of Inverness, not far from the famous Culloden Moor. Like the moor, the campus was windswept, catching whatever weather came in over the mountains from the west. Normally Monica liked the location: the grand modern buildings constructed of wood and glass had a Scandinavian feel, like the university might be the hub of a future version of the Highlands. One where the ghosts of Culloden Battlefield and the dismantling of an ancient culture and society in the years after were finally atoned for.

Today the cold air somehow carried the same sense of horror apparent in Crawford's voice – that a group of young people might really curse and then murder a friend who trusted them. Monica had spent enough time as a detective to be under no illusions as to what humans were capable of, but there was still something about a calculated betrayal that felt shocking. Particularly against someone who thought they were safe with friends. Monica knew that in Dante's *Inferno* the deepest circle of hell was reserved for the Judases, the betrayers. It seemed appropriate.

'It seems possible,' she replied finally. 'Let's see where the evidence takes us.'

Her phone vibrated in her pocket. It was Hately. 'I'm just off the phone with Wednesday Donald. Can you guess who she's representing?'

Donald was an Edinburgh-based defence lawyer, feared and despised by some in Police Scotland for her belligerent courtroom tactics. Monica respected the need for a vigorous defence – apart from anything it was key to keeping police standards high – but she had witnessed Donald's aggressive cross-examination of vulnerable witnesses in rape and murder trials. In Monica's view it edged into sadism.

'What did she want?'

'She says Miranda Salisbury's in Inverness. She wants to speak to you today. They've already briefed the media.'

'We're just out of the forensic lab.' Monica guessed that Wednesday Donald wanted to rush them while also demonstrating to the media that her client had nothing to hide. 'We need time to properly prepare.'

'The meeting's in half an hour at the Mercure Hotel,' Hately replied. 'Don't be late.'

They took the A9 north towards the Kessock Bridge, then a left through the Longman Industrial Estate. It was almost lunchtime, making the traffic even worse on the always-busy roads. By the time Monica turned left at the Shore Street roundabout and headed up Academy Street, they were already cutting it fine. At the railway station, she took a right into Union Street, parking illegally in a disabled bay to the sound of honks from an irate driver. Monica waved and mouthed 'Police' as she and Crawford got out of the car and hurried down the road towards the large modern hotel at the intersection of Union and Church streets.

A man was waiting at the closed doors to the hotel's lounge

bar. Monica had to crane her neck to look up at him, he was at least six-eight, and broad as a stone column. *Bodyguard*, she thought. He glanced from Monica to Crawford – clearly a professional who had done his homework and knew who to expect, because he nodded and opened the double doors into the room for them. Followed them in then closed and locked the doors behind them. Obviously the space had been rented for the occasion.

Miranda Salisbury was sitting alone at a table by the window – thankfully no sign of Wednesday Donald QC – with a laptop and stack of papers in front of her. As Monica approached, she could see the politician was much more attractive in person than on TV. Her angular features and the white-blonde hair that had led Tory-hating internet trolls to dub her Myra, after the infamous serial killer, seemed delicate, almost beautiful. She was wearing a grey suit over a white satin blouse. Nails and make-up done, hair tidy. Salisbury looked up, gestured to the chairs opposite for the detectives to sit, then glanced at the bodyguard, who retreated to a corner of the room. Through the window Monica could see the River Ness, flowing fast and dark today. Somehow it felt appropriate.

'Sorry about my terrifying giant.' Salisbury smiled over at the bodyguard, who raised an eyebrow. 'I've had threats . . .'

Monica asked, 'What kind of threats?'

'The kind that women in politics get. From charming men who want to rape and murder me.' The afternoon light from the windows behind her cast an otherworldly glow at odds with the busy city. 'Most of them are probably confined to their bedrooms, but maybe not all.' Her accent was more English than Scottish, and she spoke in a precise way, taking care over each syllable. Together the odd light and her voice had a hypnotic quality. After the excavations at the marshes and Corrimony Cairn, the effect was almost eerie.

Monica opened her mouth to speak and realised her throat had gone dry. Crawford filled in for her. 'Any threats recently?'

'Not recently,' Salisbury said slowly. 'Unless you count journalists doorstepping me out of the blue to ask if I'd murdered an old friend as threatening?' Her tone never changed; it was cold, emotionless. 'My lawyer certainly thinks I should.'

'I'm sorry.' Monica swallowed, cleared her throat. 'You shouldn't have found out that way. The leak didn't come from us.'

'Well. It'll all come out,' Salisbury replied coldly. 'Anyway, I don't have long. You'd better ask your questions.'

Monica felt a stab of irritation at how easily the politician had outmanoeuvred them. Rules of getting someone to talk: control pace, information, location. This disaster was breaking all three, and a bunch of other ones too. She silently cursed whoever had leaked the story to the press again, but managed to keep her voice level. 'Of course. You were close to Freya Sutherland back in the summer of 1994.'

Miranda Salisbury hardly moved, but for the first time Monica caught a shift – her shoulders folding forward slightly into a defensive posture. 'It's such a long time ago, it feels like a lifetime.'

'A long time to be buried,' Monica replied. 'A long time for her family to wonder.'

'I heard that she was missing, of course. But she was . . .'

'Naive? Easily led?'

'I was going to say *artistic*,' Salisbury replied. 'I assumed that she'd left to go travelling, have an adventure. I went back to university in Edinburgh, didn't come north for years. I lost touch with everyone up here. I wondered, of course.'

'Who did you think she left with?'

Salisbury hesitated. 'I . . . never really thought about that.'

'You spent a lot of time together that summer? You, Brodie King, Joseph Moon and Freya. What did you do with all that time?'

'I can't remember much about it. I suppose we drank cider, listened to music on crappy cassette players.'

'That's funny. Brodie King said he couldn't remember either. Joseph Moon was a little more forthcoming. He said that you'd all made a terrible mistake. Any idea what he meant?' As she was speaking, Monica felt in her pocket for her phone. Still unsure whether to share the picture of the cat they'd excavated that morning.

'Joseph's been seriously unwell for a long time,' Salisbury replied. 'I'm sure you know that.'

'So you've no idea what he meant?'

'No.' Salisbury stared hard into Monica's eyes. 'I've got no idea.'

'Were you surprised when you heard Freya had been buried?'

Salisbury stood up. 'I have to go.'

Monica nodded, dropped the phone back into her coat pocket. Decided it would be better to confirm the number on the cat's collar, get the results back on the scratched-out name. Make sure to be the one in control next time they spoke.

'Just for the record, when was the last time you remember seeing Freya Sutherland?'

'You know I really can't remember.' Salisbury slid her laptop into its bag and swept up her papers.

'What about you and Brodie King? Everyone comments on how close the pair of you were. Then suddenly it's all over.'

Salisbury turned at the mention of King's name. 'We grew

apart,' she muttered finally, seeming almost to lose her composure for the first time. 'Like young people do.'

'And when did you last see him?'

The giant had crossed the room and was now smiling fixedly at Monica and Crawford, as if happy to swat them aside with one of his piledriver arms if Salisbury even hinted at the idea. The politician looked up at him, seeming to gain confidence from his proximity. When she met Monica's gaze her eyes were steely-calm again. 'You're not asking me anything new. I explained everything to a detective twenty years ago. He was wasting his time back then, same as you are now.'

Chapter 32

Back at headquarters, Monica left Crawford in the office and went to the canteen to look for PC Duncan Gregg. It was almost five o'clock and the place was busy with officers on the late, grabbing food before their shift started. Duncan Gregg had been on the force for so long that a corner booth was known as Gregg's Table. His spot to linger, gossiping with his cronies.

Three male officers were slouched around the table, dressed in regulation black Gore-Tex jackets and fleeces. No sign of Gregg though. The men were guffawing about something as she approached. The nearest clocked her, flicked his eyes at his colleagues and their laughter stopped.

'Ma'am.' The officer had grey hair and a substantial beer gut.

'I'm looking for PC Gregg?'

'He's not here, ma'am.' The officer smiled slyly at his colleagues, proud of his attempt at wit.

'Could you ask him to call me?'

'Is it about that woman they dug up? Hooker – I mean a sex worker, wasn't she? On the game and abducted.'

'Where did you hear that?' Monica asked, taking a step closer and staring down at him as she fished for his name. She made a point of remembering the uniformed officers, even the pricks. 'PC Phillips.'

His eyes widened, startled by Monica's sudden intensity. 'I – I don't know, it's just what people are saying.'

'You're right,' she said, feeling her hackles rise as she remembered Jessica and Barry Sutherland's office, the years they'd spent searching for Freya. 'You don't know what you're talking about.'

PC Phillips stared down at the table. Monica took a deep breath, realising that she was allowing her frustration at the meeting with Miranda Salisbury to spill over into this encounter. Even though Philips deserved a dressing-down, pissing off uniformed officers was best avoided where possible. She handed him a card, softened her voice: 'If you can get Gregg to call me, I'd appreciate it.'

Inverness Leisure was a large council-run sports facility at the western edge of the city. Lucy had a swimming lesson that evening, and Monica walked through to the stands by the pool where parents were watching their children. The echoey shouts and the chlorine smell took her back to the old pool on Glebe Street, now demolished, where her dad had taught her to swim. She remembered the feeling of ploughing through the water, wondering briefly when was the last time she'd been swimming. As she scanned the crowds and spotted her mum sitting in the front row, she decided it was probably on holiday on the island of Kos in Greece, before Lucy was born. Maybe she could take Lucy on holiday somewhere hot in the upcoming school break; they could go swimming together.

'Lucy's fair coming on with her swimming,' Angela Kennedy said as Monica sat down beside her. 'Turns out Harriet's in her class.'

It was the end of the lesson, when the kids got to play with balls and giant floats. Monica followed her mum's gaze. Lucy was in her orange bathing costume, goggles on and her curly mop of hair tied back in bunches, Harriet beside her. They were trying to climb onto a large float which repeatedly tipped, dumping them both back in the water.

'Stuck together like glue,' Monica replied, thinking back to her own childhood and how a bond of friendship could sometimes form so easily. The instinct to trust so much purer.

After class, Monica helped Lucy get dried and changed. The post-swimming-lesson ritual was a trip to McDonald's or Burger King. Angela Kennedy always made a point of complaining about the junk food, but Monica suspected the heavily salted French fries and break from cooking secretly appealed to her.

As they were driving out of the Inverness Leisure car park, Monica spotted Jessica Sutherland standing with Harriet by the bus stop. It was dark, had started raining again, and a strong westerly wind was driving the water almost horizontally towards them.

Monica pulled over and wound the passenger window down. 'Are you waiting for Barry to collect you?'

Jessica raised her eyes from her phone. After a moment of confusion she recognised Monica. 'Oh – no, actually we're waiting for a taxi. My car went and broke down this morning and Barry had to take the other one to Aberdeen with work.' She glanced down at her daughter beside her, lowered her voice and leaned towards the car. 'I wanted to make things as normal as possible for Harriet after everything with the press.'

'We're going to McDonald's!' Lucy shouted from the back seat. 'Can Harriet come?'

Monica smiled back at Jessica Sutherland. Despite the long day, she couldn't just leave them to take a taxi all the way out to Fettercairn on a night like this. Especially with everything that was going on. 'Are you hungry? I can give you a lift home after.'

*

After the sweet and salty goodness of a McDonald's meal, Monica dropped her mum and Lucy back at the flat then took the A862 west towards Fettercairn – it seemed like she had been on this road every day recently. They chatted about inconvenient car breakdowns, gossip from the children's school, both studiously avoiding the case while Harriet listened from the back seat.

When the conversation ran flat, Monica asked, 'What's Barry doing over in Aberdeen?'

'Oh, it's a friend's farm – he needed a hand with something. Barry never stops working. Last week, apart from everything, he was on the phone line for Home Call. Kept a girl who'd run away and was suicidal talking for over two hours until her parents could drive down and collect her in Perth.'

'Good for him.' Monica saw the white signpost for Fettercairn, hit the indicator and took the right turn towards the farm.

'He's done so much for the charity. I'm lucky. I don't know how it would have worked out if I'd ended up with someone impatient, someone who didn't understand about Freya.'

Monica pulled into the yard in front of the farmhouse. The lights were off inside and the place felt remote, surrounded by darkness.

'Would you like to come in for some tea?'

Monica really wanted to drive straight home and get ready for bed herself, but she could hear the nervousness in Jessica's voice. Her two sons had gone to a friend's in Nairn; Barry was collecting them on his way back. Leaving her and Harriet alone in the empty farmhouse felt all kinds of wrong.

'Camomile would be great.' She would keep them company until Barry and the boys were a bit closer.

Inside, Monica boiled the kettle and scouted out the kitchen for mugs and teabags while Jessica put Harriet to bed.

'Swimming seems to tire her out like nothing else,' Jessica said when she came back into the kitchen. 'She seems to really get on with Lucy. It's nice to see.'

'Lucy's been struggling a bit at school,' Monica conceded, realising it felt good to share. Better to keep a professional distance though. 'How have you been, since everything with Freya?'

Jessica tried the tea, found it too hot and went to the tap to add a splash of cold. 'It just feels surreal, so strange. One minute I feel relief to know, the next it's like this horror that it's actually real.' She shook her head sadly. 'I did what you asked me though: I was thinking about when Freya first went missing.'

'Something came back to you?'

'I thought about calling you, but it would probably be wasting your time . . .'

'Small things can be important.'

'If you're sure.' Jessica put her mug down, went back upstairs and returned a minute later holding a paper bag. 'When Freya disappeared we went through her things, hoping for a clue to where she might be.'

'Something stood out?'

'Not at the time. It was just when I heard about where her body was found . . . It made me think about this.'

Jessica handed the paper bag to Monica. She slid the object out: it was a small plastic jewellery box. She clicked it open. Inside, on a chain, was a small silver coffin.

'I'd forgotten about this – if you could see how much jewellery she had – but then hearing about where they found her, close to the Witch's Coffin. Read what's written on it.'

Monica peered closer. The coffin was about the size of a pound coin. She could see markings. After a moment she reluctantly admitted defeat and reached for her coat, feeling in the pocket for the reading glasses her optician had forced on her at the last check-up. She creased her eyes and held the thing up to the light: A WITCH'S CURSE INSIDE.

'Does this open?' Monica turned the coffin over in her hand.

'I don't know; I never thought to try.'

Monica's nail found a clasp. The little lid swung open, but the coffin was empty. 'Do you have any idea where Freya got this?'

'I just assumed that she bought it. She had a bit of a goth thing . . .'

Monica closed the locket, put the necklace back in its box. 'Do you mind if I take this?'

'No, it's fine.' Jessica turned away, then glanced around the kitchen as if remembering to look for something.

'Is everything OK?'

'It's just the cat, Bramble. With everything going on I forgot to let him in last night. He's been gone all day.' She went to the back door and shouted out into the night.

'Is it normal for him to disappear?' Monica asked, trying to sound casual even as the obvious parallel with their excavation that morning came to mind.

'He's a farm cat – he wanders a lot. I think I'm just paranoid . . .' She straightened up and wiped her eyes. 'It sounds stupid, but since Freya was found I've had this feeling like death's close by. Just little things – the car breaking down, then Bramble not coming home. If I followed my instincts I would have kept Barry and the kids at home for a month.'

As Monica was about to offer reassurance, there was the roar of a diesel engine in the yard outside, the crank of a handbrake being pulled up hard. Moments later, the front door banged open and Barry was entering the kitchen, seeming to fill the room, carrying one of his squealing sons under each arm. Jessica smiled at him, seeming to visibly relax in his presence.

'Road was quiet. We raced home, didn't we, boys! Now I was thinking I might just eat this pair for supper!' He pretended to lift one of the boys to his mouth, the kid shrieking with pleasure at his dad's impression of a fairy-tale ogre. Barry seemed to clock Monica for the first time and smiled sheepishly as he put the children down. 'Sorry . . .'

Monica returned his smile. 'It looks like fun.' But as she spoke Monica felt a flash of guilt: Lucy would never have a father who adored her the way Barry clearly did his children. She swallowed the unpleasant thought and finished her tea, suddenly feeling like her presence was an imposition. As she was pulling on her coat in the hall, she again took in the array of photographs on the walls, a shrine to a close family. The children as babies, at birthday parties, Jessica and Barry's wedding. Monica's eyes landed on an older one: Freya and Jessica together as teenagers.

Monica didn't realise Jessica had noticed until she said, 'That was my last birthday before she went.'

'Sorry, I didn't mean to pry.'

'No, it's fine.' The sisters each had an arm around the other. Monica noticed Freya was wearing a necklace in the picture. She leaned in closer, unable to see clearly in the dim light. 'Is she wearing the coffin necklace?' Having a date for when Freya owned the object could be useful. The link to her burial site in the marshes and the tablet found at Corrimony Cairn felt like more than mere coincidence to Monica.

'No, that's a different one. A fossilised shark's tooth necklace,' Jessica said. 'Practically the only piece of her jewellery I actually liked. I ended up losing it on the first day of our honeymoon in Ibiza. Barry was so sweet trying to find it for me.'

'That must have been upsetting.'

'The police were acting like, *Who's this crazy Scottish woman going mad over a crappy necklace?* She gave a weary laugh. 'Barry was out combing the beach for two days, obviously thinking, *I really have married a nutter!* It's funny though. Losing it was strangely helpful in the end. Sort of a way of saying goodbye. You know I've never told anyone that story before – always felt stupid losing it. If anyone asked, I just told them Freya must have taken it with her. She loved that necklace.'

Chapter 33

In the morning Crawford was running late, so Monica agreed to meet him at the Starbucks in the centre of Inverness. Arriving at 9.30 under slate-grey skies, there was no sign of her partner inside, so she ordered flat whites and an almond croissant for Crawford, who would presumably have missed breakfast. He came in as she was carrying the tray to a corner table. Dressed in his now-customary grey wool coat over a dark suit. He waved when he spotted her and hurried across. They hadn't spoken about *the evening* at her flat, but as the days passed the sense of awkwardness was fading. Hopefully they could get back to their normal, relaxed, if slightly antagonistic, relationship soon. As he approached she could see he was flustered – a strand of his red hair had fallen from his quiff down onto his forehead. Usually a sign that he'd had a late one.

She pushed the coffee and croissant across the table to him. 'Is everything OK?'

He sat down. 'Sorry, I slept in . . . Fucking phone alarm didn't go off.'

Monica nodded, accepting the explanation, though it seemed unlikely. Crawford was addicted to his phone. *Assume nothing, check everything* – the number-one rule for detective work – had the added benefit of making you scrutinise your colleagues' every statement, Monica thought wryly. She took a sip of coffee then filled him in on the trip to Jessica's, finally taking the box from her pocket and opening it to show him the silver necklace. Crawford took it and held the little coffin up to the daylight. ' "A witch's curse inside",' he read aloud. Then tried to open the lid as Monica had done, struggling with his bitten thumbnail.

She took it from him and clicked it open. 'Nothing in it.'

'So the curse got out already?' Crawford didn't sound entirely like he was joking. 'Do we know who gave it to her?'

'Jessica said she didn't know.'

As Monica went to put the necklace away, Crawford said, 'Maybe there's a shop label, on the box?' She put the chain and locket carefully on the table and turned the box over. The bottom was blank. 'Maybe inside, under the holder thing?'

She opened the box and pulled out the faux-velvet backing. Underneath, printed on the bottom, was CAULFEILD & SON'S ANTIQUES, ST STEPHENS BRAE, INVERNESS. Followed by an old 0463 phone number, the code before the area was changed to 01463.

'There's no antique shop on St Stephens Brae.' Monica walked up the street regularly, as it was close to Lucy's school.

'Isn't that the name of the antique shop on the Market Brae Steps?' Crawford asked. 'I bought a girlfriend a bracelet from there a few years ago. Maybe they've relocated since the necklace was bought.'

As much of central Inverness was pedestrianised, Monica and Crawford left their cars and walked through the bus station and along Academy Street to the High Street. Halfway up the Market Brae Steps that connected the city centre with the Crown district on the hill was a door marked with a small brass plate:

Monica tried the buzzer then banged on the door. Crawford checked the time on his phone. 'It's only 10.30.' They walked back down to the High Street, drank another coffee in Caffè Nero, watching through the window as a pair of young seagulls fought over a discarded sandwich. At 11.05 Monica hit the buzzer again, and this time there was a click as the door opened. At the top of some musty stairs, another door opened into a low-ceilinged room. Dark and piled high with objects: books, lampshades, boxes of coins, a row of mannequins dressed in dusty military uniforms. In her London days Monica had spent entire afternoons browsing antique shops and the stalls in Greenwich Market; this visit should have been a pleasure in the midst of a grim case, but the place had an atmosphere. Something under the tobacco and body odour, something she didn't like.

At the back of the room Monica could see a counter, a man sitting behind it.

'Mr Caulfeild?'

The man raised his head. He was heavy, wearing a black blazer, his thinning hair brushed into a side parting. 'You're after my father, I'm afraid.' He was late fifties, ruddy with bad skin.

'OK,' Monica said slowly. 'Is your father around?'

'Well, you'll have to drive down Bridge Street, about a mile towards Drumnadrochit.' Public-school accent, possibly faked. 'Take a right at the big black gates on Tomnahurich Street.'

Monica realised he was describing Tomnahurich Cemetery. 'You're saying he's dead?'

'Well, I certainly hope so.' Caulfeild was smiling, but as Monica stepped closer she could see it wasn't touching his eyes. 'Hate to think we buried him alive.'

Monica forced a weak laugh, held out her ID. 'Have you worked here long?'

Caulfeild's eyes widened and for a moment his accent slipped: 'Straight out of school.'

'So you would have been here in the mid-1990s?' He nodded slowly, clearly surprised by the question. 'By any chance do you remember a young woman called Freya Sutherland?' Monica nodded to Crawford, who held out a photo.

'The woman who was murdered?' He sounded alarmed and quickly added, 'I read about it in the *Highland News*.'

'You remember her face?'

'It's a long time ago.'

'She didn't hang around at the old shop? Maybe with a group of friends?'

Caulfeild shook his head. 'Dad would never have allowed that – more formal when he was around.'

Crawford held out the picture of Salisbury, King and Moon at Corrimony Cairn. 'You recognise any of these three?'

He shook his head again.

Monica opened the box and put the necklace on the counter. 'This was sold by you some time before September 1994.' Caulfeild reached for the necklace. For a second Monica thought she saw a light of recognition in his face. 'You remember it?'

'We sell a lot.' He picked it up with his small, soft-looking fingers, turning the coffin over in his palm. 'Maybe from the 1920s, made to look older.'

'What would this have cost in the 1990s?'

'A couple of hundred maybe? It's silver.'

Monica thought about this for a moment. For a young woman working part-time in an amusement arcade, two hundred pounds was a lot in 1994. 'Do you keep sales records?'

'Sales records?' Caulfeild sounded flustered. 'Not as detailed as when Dad was around – despite what people think, it's not a legal requirement for all antiques . . .'

'I don't care about legal requirements,' Monica said. 'I just want to know who bought it.'

'Yes, well, my father was a little more particular,' he said. 'But they were all by hand. It'll take me a while to go through them.'

Chapter 34

It had been sunny for a week on the morning Freya was walking to the bus stop. Only 10 a.m. and it was already uncomfortably hot. The wheat in the fields was ripening to a golden sea; the seed pods on the broom making popping sounds as they burst in the heat. Ordinarily she would have taken her trainers off to enjoy the heat of the tarmac under her feet, and breathed in the coconut smell of the gorse by the side of the road. This morning she barely noticed any of it. She had been up for most of the night trying to work out just what she'd done wrong.

Three days before, they'd made plans to meet after she finished work at the arcade. She'd sat waiting on the steps outside Inverness Town House for an hour before the batteries on her Walkman had begun to die, slowing PJ Harvey's voice to a treacle slur. Assuming she'd misunderstood the plan or they'd got caught up with something, she had traipsed down Church Street to the phone box. She knew both Brodie and Miranda's numbers off by heart now, tried them both twice and got no response from either of them. The phone clunked and rattled her twenty-pence coin into the tray – the unsatisfying sound of a failed call. It was so frustrating. Her friends were probably waiting for her somewhere close by, but she had no way of finding them. She dug in her bag for Joseph's number, scrawled on the back of her sketchbook. A gruff male voice, Joseph's dad presumably, came on the line.

'Is Joseph there?'

'Who's this?'

'It's his friend Freya, Freya Sutherland.'

'He's not here. Not been home since the weekend. If you see him, tell him to bloody come home. His mother's worried sick.'

Freya had rung off, promising to relay the message. What Joseph's dad had said wasn't exactly a surprise. Her friend would tell anyone who'd listen how irritating he found his father's strictness, how he couldn't wait to leave for good. She knew he often stayed with Brodie, whose mum was far more relaxed.

She'd walked back up to the arcade, Bobby's eyebrows rising in surprise when she reappeared. No sign of her friends there either. Finally she'd given up and taken the bus home to Fetter-cairn. Feeling a mix of disappointment and rejection, but expecting a message to be waiting at home – or, if not, to hear from them the next morning. There had been no call though, no message, and now three days had passed. The idea of being suddenly dumped by her new friends was almost frightening. They had made living here bearable. Road trips through the long white nights of the north Highland summer. Vodka and Coke and laughing as they ran into the sea at midnight.

The heat in the bus shelter was cloying, the air inside carrying an ammonia smell of piss. She leaned against the outside, feeling hot plastic through the cotton of her T-shirt. Looked up and down the empty country road and tried to appreciate the blue sky, the sun on the skin of her arms and legs.

Instead her mind took her back again to the last time she'd seen them – Tuesday night after work. Even as she ran over it now, everything seemed normal. Miranda, Brodie and Joseph had come into the arcade, joking about as usual. Sat at the bar drinking bottles of beer, waiting for her to finish. Freya recalled the familiar smoky interior of the arcade, the tinny recorded voices from the Japanese games, overloud and endless. Buttons being pummelled, addicts feeding stacks of pound coins to fruit machines. The atmosphere had been drilling into her head all afternoon, and at the end of her shift she'd felt half-zombie as she wandered over to them. She wondered now if she'd been offhand.

With a cringe she remembered holding out her sketchbook to show Brodie what she'd been working on in between selling tokens that afternoon: tattoo ideas. The kind of thing she knew he liked. He'd seemed interested, running his fingers over the black ink of the Celtic shapes. Had she tried too hard to impress him? Or offended Miranda by too obviously seeking his approval? Once again Freya tried to recall Miranda's expression. She'd been sitting on a bar stool – loose jeans, linen dress and sandals. At least one silver ring on each of her fingers. As usual managing to look supremely cool, even in the arcade's dingy bar. She had glanced over as Brodie flicked through the sketchbook, given a quick smile then continued to chat to Joseph beside her. Freya remembered Miranda was wearing a chain with a locket. Her hand had gone to it, begun to rub it between thumb and forefinger. Was it a nervous gesture? A sign that she was pissed off with Freya?

The distant sound of the bus approaching carried across the fields.

At 3 p.m. Freya finished her shift, and called home from the office to check if anyone had been in touch. Jessica clearly took delight in telling her, 'No, no one's called for you, Freya. I've been at home all day.'

Freya remembered then that Brodie had mentioned working on a painting at college. The next bus back to Fettercairn Farm wasn't until after 5 p.m. The idea of being desperate – hunting down people who wanted nothing to do with her – was hideous, but a small part of her felt angry at how they were treating her. She at least wanted to ask why they'd dropped her without explanation. She headed down the High Street, cut through the railway station then along the dual carriageway to the ugly concrete college buildings. It was still hot, and by the time she pushed through the double doors into the cool interior, sweat had pooled in the small of her back.

The art department had paintings on the walls. An old THATCHER'S POLL TAX protest flyer printed in black and white was still visible on the pinboard, partly covered by newer Greenpeace and Rape Crisis flyers. Classical music was drifting from an open door at the end of the corridor. She started towards it but stopped, suddenly overcome with self-consciousness.

'Oh, you gave me a fright!' She turned and saw Miss Rossetti, one of the art lecturers who she had met on a previous visit with the others, stepping out of the small kitchen. Freya hadn't noticed her when she passed.

'I'm sorry . . .' With horror, Freya realised that she was about to start crying.

'What's the matter?' Miss Rossetti stepped closer. 'Come in and have a cup of tea, love. Your friends were here earlier, but they've gone now.' She hustled Freya into a studio, sat her down and pushed the mug of tea she had been making into her hands. Freya could see the large canvas Brodie had been working on over the summer – purple shapes against a dark landscape. They'd been here but not bothered to tell her. 'What happened?'

'It's nothing.' She could feel the hot tears on her cheeks, no doubt making her mascara run. *How pathetic.* She recalled her attempt at a cool persona when they first met, telling the lecturer she had enjoyed *The Outsider* by Camus, was reading Foucault. Now she was blubbering like a schoolgirl over friends dropping her. 'I think I've ruined everything with Miranda and the others. I just want to know what I've done.'

Miss Rossetti smiled and nodded, sympathetic but detached. As if Freya was just being childish. Freya felt even more stupid as she wiped the tears from her eyes. She put the tea down, stood up and walked out of the room.

In the months after, and for the remaining years of her life, Miss Rossetti would occasionally wonder. On a hot day when she was drinking tea alone, when her mind wandered back to the brief interaction. If she'd asked the right question, adopted the right tone, would Freya have had a different life?

Chapter 35

Monica was pleased to take in the fresh maritime air when they exited the stuffy interior of Caulfeild & Son's Antiques and walked back down onto the High Street. Two things she liked about Inverness: the air always seemed to carry a feel of the nearby sea, and the mountains were often visible from the city centre. Until she'd moved back after years in London, Monica hadn't even realised she'd missed those hints of close-by wildness.

Beside her, Crawford was talking on the phone to DC Fisher. Their colleague was still working through the prison records to narrow down a list of Pauline Tosh's contacts. Hopefully this would help them deduce how she might have come to know the location of Freya's body.

Crawford covered the mouthpiece and turned to look up at her. 'Says there's mountains of them. It's taking ages, was in until two a.m. last night.'

'Tell him "well done",' Monica replied. 'He's doing a great job.' She took a deep breath, enjoying the feel of the air in her lungs, wondering about what she'd picked up on in the antique shop that had disquieted her.

'The boss says well done, you're doing a great job,' Crawford repeated into the mouthpiece. He said something else Monica didn't catch, then turned to her again. 'Fisher says an address has just come in for the cat's collar.' First thing that morning in the office, she had asked DC Khan to chase BT on the number.

'Anything interesting?'

Crawford said, 'Number 2 Macleod Cottages, out near Muir of Ord, not all that far from Dingwall.' Monica watched as he nodded and sucked air through his teeth. 'Really? Are you sure?'

'What is it?'

Crawford mouthed 'Two seconds' to Monica, bent back to the phone. 'No, yeah, definitely. Seems to make sense.' Monica felt a childish impulse to grab the iPhone from her partner and get Fisher to tell her immediately what he'd discovered. Still, at least Crawford and Fisher seemed to be getting on better; sometimes they were barely on speaking terms. 'Still no answer? OK, I'll check with the boss. Thanks.' Crawford hung up, turned to Monica. 'Right, get this. Fisher did a Google Maps search. Macleod Cottages are part of a farming estate. Right across the field from them, not even five hundred yards away, there's a place called Carnoch House.'

Monica squeezed her brain, wondering if the place should mean something to her. 'Give me a clue.'

'Carnoch House is a big detached Victorian villa, sold a couple of years ago, so Fisher was able to find the particulars online.' Crawford could never resist elaborating, to draw out the tension of a reveal. 'Offers over a million, not sure what it went for in the end.' He then spotted a man he knew smoking a cigarette outside Poundland, waved and shouted something. The man started laughing. Monica knew her partner well enough to know that showing frustration would only encourage him. She wondered for a second, though, if he would be so cheeky with a male boss; if their getting too close might be affecting her work in other ways. Finally he turned back to her and said, 'Carnoch House was owned by the same family from 1950 up until it was sold in 2016. Childhood home of one Miranda Salisbury.'

Macleod Cottages were two adjoining semi-detached homes. Harled and painted white, surrounded by fields. In the distance to the west, shrouded by clouds, was the mountain of Sgùrr Mòr, part of the Fannich range. The area felt similar to Fettercairn Farm, but was ten miles further north, near the village of Muir of Ord. Number 2 was marked by a tarnished brass numeral on the gate. Beside a wooden fence sagging under a weight of honeysuckle, Monica parked the Volvo.

'Looks like it might be abandoned,' Crawford said. The garden seemed like it hadn't been attended to in months. A sharp contrast to the neighbouring house's neat lawn. Monica walked down the path to the door and knocked, but there was no answer. Through the window she could see sun-faded pink curtains, a thin layer of dust gathered in their folds. After a few minutes she gave up and scribbled a note on one of her cards, then pushed it through the letter box.

They had more luck next door. In fact, its inhabitant had obviously spotted them passing his window and was already opening the door to them: in his seventies, tired-looking but keen to talk. He introduced himself as Mr MacAdam, invited them in. The house had an air of sadness, and Monica wondered if Mr MacAdam's wife or partner might have died in the past few years.

She asked, 'Have you lived here long?'

'Bought the place in 1981,' Mr MacAdam replied. 'Always wanted to live in the countryside.'

'It's a beautiful spot,' Monica said. 'You must get to know the neighbours well?'

'I saw you going down Mrs Dunsmore's path next door. You'll not get her for a while. She's on holiday in Spain. Takes long trips to visit her grandchildren, leaves her garden to go wild through the summer.'

'Do you have a contact number for Mrs Dunsmore?' Monica asked hopefully.

'Oh no, nothing like that.'

'Do you know how long she's lived here?'

'Since before me. She still rents from the estate, mind you.'

Monica nodded – that would explain why the landline hadn't been registered in her name. But if she had lived here since before MacAdam arrived in 1981, it meant the cat out at Corrimony Cairn would have been hers.

'Means she doesn't care if *her* garden's a mess. Doesn't think of the plants blocking *my* view.'

'You're allowed to cut them, if they're overhanging your garden,' Crawford said helpfully.

'Well, I don't see why I should have to,' MacAdam replied.

'Fair point,' Crawford said.

'You've heard of Miranda Salisbury?' Monica cut in. 'The MSP? She lived in Carnoch House as a child.'

'Oh yes, I know her, of course.' He pointed through the window, across a field to a copse of trees. Beyond them Monica could just make out the roof and chimney pots of a house. 'That's Carnoch through there. Big place. Sold for a million, they say.'

Monica asked, 'Do you remember Miranda as a teenager?'

MacAdam nodded. 'We'd pass her on the road sometimes; she'd be out walking or in a car.'

'Was there anything about her that stood out?' Monica asked, and Mr MacAdam sucked his lips in, his face tense as if facing a tough question on one of the afternoon quiz shows which the fifty-inch TV on the wall suggested he might well structure his days around. Monica gave herself a black mark for stereotyping the older man and tried to help him out. 'Anything at all?'

'Well, I remember she dressed in loose clothes, sort of like one of those hippies. Not professional-looking like she is now.'

'Do you remember her friends? A young man, tall and thin, about the same age, who came round sometimes?'

'There were more kids around here then,' MacAdam replied defensively. 'My daughters were already grown up and left home, you see, so I never paid as much attention.'

'So there was nothing else? Nothing that sticks in your mind?'

MacAdam sucked his lips in again and Monica started to stand up. 'Thanks for your—'

'I'm not one for gossip,' MacAdam cut in. 'I used to work as an engineer, you see. Over at McDermott's, and there were some there – terrible gossips.'

Monica sat back down. 'We're not looking for gossip.' Her eyes landed on the mantelpiece and the framed photograph of a younger Mr MacAdam. He was standing beside someone who Monica assumed was his wife, and two young women – presumably his daughters – one of them dressed in a black graduation gown. 'You might have read about it in the paper. We're investigating a young woman's murder. She was a friend of Miranda Salisbury's. She disappeared in 1994.'

'A murder?' MacAdam sounded surprised. 'I don't read the paper much now.'

'What came to mind for you? About Miranda?'

'My wife never liked her. Didn't trust her. Once when she was just a girl, about ten, we found her in our kitchen. We always used to leave the door unlocked – had our own girls and their friends coming in and out from the garden all the time so we never bothered. When they left for uni we just carried on. Then Susie, my wife, she started to notice little things going missing.'

'What kind of things?'

'Silly things. Once an old SodaStream bottle went from the fridge. I used to leave change from my pockets in an ashtray on the windowsill, then there would be less than I'd left. I never really noticed, it was only afterwards. One evening, Susie went through and found Miranda standing in the kitchen with her hand in the money.'

'What did your wife do?'

'She was shocked. They both looked at each other for a second, then Miranda just smiled at her, turned and walked out like that, with a handful of coins.'

'Did you call the police?'

'Oh, nothing like that, we didn't want to make a fuss.'

'You didn't speak to her parents?'

'Susie called and tried speaking to her mother – Anna was her name – but that was no good. Didn't want to hear it. Told Susie to mind her own business, that she knew best how to raise her own child. Spoiled she was, entitled. We just kept the back door locked after that.'

'What about her dad?'

'He was never around. Supposed to have a girlfriend down in London he mostly lived with, worked in banking or something with money.'

'Anything else that stands out?'

MacAdam hesitated and then said, 'I was surprised when Miranda got into politics. Didn't believe it was the same girl when I first heard her name. Like I said, Susie caught her stealing that time, and the impression I had was she was out of control. I'd be driving home late from work, see her going out. Spoiled, allowed too much freedom. My girls were always home by eight, and I always knew where they were.' He added proudly: 'Eldest a schoolteacher, youngest an accountant.'

Monica smiled, and part of her liked his old-fashioned pride in his daughters' achievements, even as she disliked the simplicity of his thinking. She sensed there was something else though, something about Miranda that he wasn't telling. The clue was how emotional he sounded about her.

'Did something else happen? When Miranda was a teenager?'

MacAdam dropped his eyes to the carpet then looked up at Monica again. He seemed embarrassed. 'Well . . . once, I wasn't looking or anything . . . I'd been out walking the dog – there's a path that goes close to Carnoch House. It was getting dark and I just happened to glance up. Miranda was standing at the window. She was . . . well, she wasn't wearing anything. I looked away and then looked back up, and she was just standing there like that, not trying to cover herself up or anything. Staring down at me until I walked away.'

'Was there—'

MacAdam kept talking though. 'A few weeks after we were on the same walk – I had my wife with me, didn't like to do it on my own after that. This time we heard voices from the garden. Someone swearing: F-ing and C-ing.'

'Did you hear anything else?'

'It was a girl's voice – Miranda, I'm sure. She was saying, "I just want her to die. I want that F-ing C dead and in the ground."'

'When was that?'

'It was harvest time, August or September. I remember because it was close to my wife's birthday. The time of year you first feel the winter creeping in. My youngest had just started her first big job in Edinburgh after her training; we'd been helping her move in. That would have made it 1994.'

Chapter 36

August 1994

On the bus home to Fettercairn after her humiliating visit to the college, Freya's upset turned to simmering rage. As she stared out the window at the flat calm waters of the Beauly Firth and the blue skies, she fantasised about writing poisonous letters to them all, wishing there was some way to let everyone know just how horrible they were.

But by the time she'd walked back from the crossroads to the farm, through the dusty afternoon heat, the energy of her outrage had faded. Mum and Dad were out, probably working in the fields somewhere. Jessica was at a friend's for dinner, although tonight Freya would have appreciated the chance to argue with her sister and let off steam. No note again on the pad by the phone. Of course there wasn't. Her 'friends' had dropped her, that was clear now. She stood for a moment in the hallway. In the shafts of sunlight from the windows, dust was drifting. Why did watching those particles hanging there feel so melancholy? Maybe because they seemed so delicate? So fragile? The way that a human was fragile. Hanging around waiting for a phone to ring. Was there anything more pathetic?

Freya shook her head and went upstairs to lie on her bed. She took in the room: her jewellery box, the lava lamp; Brodie's sketch he had given her – a fairy-tale woman standing in front of

Corrimony Cairn. She'd pinned it to the wall, thinking it represented their friendship. Impulsively she scrunched it up, opened the window and put a lighter to it. She held it between thumb and forefinger until it was almost gone, then let the last scrap float off into the gloaming.

Her eyes caught a hint of movement in the distance. Down the road she walked every day to the bus, close to the hanging tree. She strained her eyes, half hoping to see a familiar Volkswagen Golf in the lay-by. For a moment she actually thought there was a shape, a figure standing by the tree, staring up at her window. She blinked and the shape was gone, lost in the evening haze. After the heat of the day, the night was edged with chill. Freya shivered, left the window open but crawled under the covers on her bed. She closed her eyes and listened to the sounds of the birds in the woods, the occasional car passing the crossroads. Despite her upset she drifted off to sleep.

The sun was shining on a quiet place in the mountains. Beside a loch with old schoolmates she'd never met. In the shallows of the loch there was an ancient suit of armour, partially rusted but shiny silver in places. As she stepped into the water for a closer look there was movement beside her. A stranger, leaning in over her shoulder.

Freya sat up in bed, blinking herself awake. A noise rattled through the house – knocking at the front door. She felt sick after waking abruptly from the deep sleep, and lay back down and pulled the covers up against the cold. It was dark now, and the strangeness from her dream lingered with the shadows. Her arm was numb from where she'd been sleeping on it. Staying safe under her blankets felt right, but then the knocking came again. Loud and insistent.

What stranger could be knocking at my door? The words drifted into her mind – maybe she was still dreaming? After another moment she understood that no one had gone to answer the door; her parents must still be working. She crawled out of bed, still in her shorts and T-shirt from earlier, and went downstairs. Floorboards creaking through the unlit house.

When she opened the front door, Brodie King was outside. He was wearing a black leather jacket and staring down at her. His familiar expression, somewhere between amused and angry.

'Have you got time to talk?'

Chapter 37

As they were arriving back in Inverness, Monica's phone buzzed in her coat pocket. She went to dig it out and realised the tweed was worn through, her phone poking halfway out of the hole.

'You'll lose that eventually,' Crawford said, glancing over at her. 'Time for a new coat.'

'It's fine,' Monica replied. Though in fact the coat was over twenty-five years old.

She looked at the phone, a text message from an unfamiliar number: 'Meet me at Cafe Grill in one hour.'

She dropped Crawford back at headquarters, asked him to help Fisher with the work on Pauline Tosh's contacts and drove to Cafe Grill, a truckers' stop on the Longman Industrial Estate, the grim stretch of warehouses that met visitors from north, east or south arriving in Inverness. Two HGV lorries were parked outside, beside them a marked police car.

Inside the cafe it was weekday-afternoon quiet, a few tables occupied by men reading newspapers. Country music drifted from the kitchen. PC Duncan Gregg was sitting at a corner table at the back, in uniform. He'd been a detective in the 1990s and early 2000s but was working traffic these days. Fiddling with his phone, he lifted his head at the sound of the door. Face set in a tight frown, corners of his mouth turned down, forehead creased suspiciously.

'The great Monica Kennedy,' he said, attempting bonhomie as

she sat down opposite. 'Best detective in the north. To what do I owe the honour?' Up close his skin was grey, a yellow tinge to his eyes. He looked ill.

She smiled. 'Why do you think?'

A nervous waitress appeared. Monica ordered a black coffee. Gregg furrowed his brow harder, staring at the cup in front of him.

'The girl in the paper?' he said finally. 'That's what everyone's been talking about. Saying she was one of Tosh's?'

'Her name was Freya Sutherland,' Monica said. 'You investigated her disappearance back in 1994.'

'Did I?' Gregg dropped his eyes to the table. 'Hard to remember, such a long time ago.' But Monica had caught the shift in his body language. She took the picture of Freya Sutherland from her inside pocket and put it on the table in front of him. 'She went missing from out at Fettercairn Farm, not far from Beauly.' Gregg didn't have a reputation for being helpful, unless there was something in it for him.

He picked up the photo, held it at arm's length. 'Pretty. It was a big place, wasn't it? Big farm. Be worth a lot now, with the way house prices have gone in the Highlands.'

'That's right.' Monica was pleased that Gregg was at least talking.

'Dad was disabled, crushed by a tractor. Remember him telling me about it.' The waitress brought Monica's coffee over, and another pot of tea for Gregg. 'Aye,' he said slowly, putting the photo back down on the table. 'It was a funny one that, right enough. Freya Sutherland. Left a note, didn't she?' He splashed tea into his cup, added milk and sugar.

'I just wanted your take on it.'

Gregg rubbed a hand over his chin. 'Aye,' he repeated,

obviously considering how much to share. 'There was something about that. Something not right.'

'In what way?'

'It was one of those. Nothing obvious, seemed a straightforward runaway, left a note.' He sipped at his tea. Despite how ill Gregg appeared, Monica could tell his mind was sharp. 'Thing was, it was out the blue. Freya had never done anything like that before. Her parents were beside themselves. Not much I could do really. She was over eighteen, entitled to go where she wanted. But it got under my skin, so I did a bit of digging.'

'Who did you speak to?'

'Same as you, probably,' Gregg said with an unappealing smile. 'Miranda Salisbury, Brodie King. Both done well for themselves. Doesn't surprise me exactly; they were a crafty pair even then.'

'Why do you say that?'

'The mum and dad were convinced they were involved somehow. Freya hadn't even met them at the start of the summer, then they're spending all their time together. Next thing she's gone and they're still around, claiming they know nothing.'

'There was no one else she was close to?'

'Not from what they said. Salisbury, King, the other boy – waste of space, Boon?'

'Joseph Moon,' Monica corrected him.

'Right, thick as thieves all summer. When I track them down they're all playing dumb. Say they'd talked about going somewhere together, but it had never come to anything. Thing is, Miranda Salisbury's mum, she alibied the three of them for the night Freya left. Said they were all out at her house.'

'Carnoch House?' Monica offered.

'Yeah, big pile, out near the Muir.' Gregg sipped at his tea again. Monica was surprised by how forthcoming he was being. Surprised too that it sounded like he'd made a genuine attempt to find out what had happened to Freya, even if this wasn't reflected in the notes he'd left in the file. 'I just had a feeling about it all. Brodie King especially. The boy had a coldness to him, you know?'

Monica nodded. She did know.

'I spotted him walking down in the Marsh one time, took him for a drive out to Abriachan, put the guilt trip on him about Freya's family. He was still adamant he'd got no idea. I . . . I was younger myself then.' Gregg's hand went to his forehead. 'You know what it was like back then. Got a bit out of hand, ended up giving him a few slaps. Dumped him out there to walk home.' Monica didn't reply. Applying pressure had been standard Scottish police approach in 1994: obtain confession, then worry about evidence afterwards. 'Anyway, I thought, *I'll burst the weakest one, Joseph Moon.* Got him on his own too, quizzed him hard, still nothing. I took it more personal back then. Had the bit between my teeth for a while. Determined to find out what was going on.'

'Did you get anything solid?'

'Brodie King and Joseph Moon were both doing art at the college. I went asking around, just fishing for something. Spoke to a few of the lecturers. One tells me a story.' Here Gregg stopped and looked around the cafe. Content that the two truckers were safely absorbed in their newspapers and the waitress was in the kitchen, he continued: 'Said she'd seen three friends of Freya's – King, Moon and Salisbury – getting dropped off outside the college by someone driving a black Rolls-Royce. Thought Freya might have known the driver too.'

'Could it have been Miranda's mum or dad?'

'I checked. They owned a few different motors, but no Rolls.'

'Can you remember the lecturer's name?'

He thought about it a moment. 'Not coming back to me. She'd be dead now; on her last legs back then.'

'Did you get an ID on the vehicle?' Monica tried to sound casual – she realised now that finding the owner might be key. But if PC Gregg wanted to trade on his piece of information, this would be the time for him to clam up and start asking for what he wanted in return. Unexpectedly though, he kept talking.

'Well, I'd been on the case a while, working it in the background. Feeling like I'm making a breakthrough with this piece of intel. Thinking it shouldn't be hard to track a Rolls-Royce down. Start digging into it.' He met Monica's eyes. 'Can you guess what happens?'

'Someone shut it down?'

'Bill Quest calls me in.' Monica remembered Bill Quest, an old-fashioned detective superintendent who had retired a couple of years after Monica joined. Dropped dead of a heart attack a few years later.

'What did he say?'

'He warned me off. "What the fuck are you doing on a wild goose chase?! Proper work to do!" Some other case he wanted me on.'

'You think he was protecting someone?'

'Maybe. I don't know. Could be he was genuinely pissed off. Was different back then: they'd scream in your face if they were having a bad day. You must remember though, you're old-school?'

Monica nodded, intrigued that she felt a flush of pride at being recognised in this little way. 'But it niggled at you?'

'You know what it's like, those questions that won't go away. Six months later, I was working another case, coincidentally I'm looking for a black car. Took the chance to scoop in the owners of black Rolls-Royces in the Highlands.'

'What did you get?' Unconsciously Monica lowered her voice and leaned closer. She had picked up on the uncertainty in Gregg's tone. It actually sounded close to fear.

'There were a handful, but one that definitely stood out.'

'Who?'

'William "Buggsy" MacIvor.'

'MacIvor?' The name was vaguely familiar to Monica, but it took a moment to bring it to the surface. 'As in the actor?'

'Calls himself a comedian now,' Gregg replied, picking up his phone to check the time. 'Never found him funny myself.'

'What was he doing picking up a group of students?' As she was asking the question, Monica's mind ran back over what she knew of the man. In the 1980s and 90s he had been well known across the UK, appearing in a long-running sitcom in full Highland dress with his own camp catchphrase: 'Oohh it's a long way to Inverness!'

Gregg replied, 'Who the hell knows. He was a big thing up here back then. Lot of charity work, chieftain of a few different Highland games. Knew the higher-ups on the force, had them round to his house for dinner, parties.'

'Didn't he own a place to the south of Loch Ness? Balnakine House?' Even as Monica felt a wave of surprise at the direction the investigation had taken, something else fluttered into her conscious mind. 'Something happened out there, didn't it? In the 2000s?' At the time Monica had been in London, trying hard to forget about her home town: *Oohh it's a long way to Inverness!*

'That's right, it was a haunt of the rich and famous in the nineties. Always rumours about the place – drugs and whatnot – but like I say, MacIvor was connected, and he's not doing any harm so they don't bother him. Then, Hogmanay 2003, we get a callout. A young woman's gone missing from a party at the house, found floating face down in Loch Ness.'

'Jesus.' Monica remembered it now.

'Buggsy ended up successfully suing a bunch of papers over it. The woman's death was officially declared misadventure.'

'How old was she?'

'Her name was Sally MacFarlane. Early twenties. Addict, prostitute, booze and coke in her system, no family that were bothered about her. That was in MacIvor's favour at least. Still, he was *persona non grata* after that. No more appearing on *TFI Friday* or in your sitcom when you're linked with something like that.'

'Another young woman,' Monica said, 'Freya's age.'

'It did cross my mind at the time,' Gregg said, finishing the last of his tea and slowly standing to go. 'But it was all in the past by then – what difference would it make?'

Chapter 38

When she arrived at her mum's house to collect Lucy, Monica was surprised to see Auntie May sitting at the kitchen table as her mum applied the finishing touches to a pie she was about to put in the oven.

'Bumped into May and I invited her down for supper,' Angela Kennedy said by way of explanation. Monica could tell from her mum's tone that the pushy and hypercritical May had more likely invited herself.

'Still working every hour God sends, are you?' her aunt snipped. May was in her mid-seventies, grey hair, and sharp as a knife. She was Monica's dad's sister. They had looked alike and were similarly forceful.

Monica joked, 'Someone has to keep the streets safe.'

'Well, it sounds like you need to be telling Lucy off a bit more! Else people'll need the streets kept safe from her!'

Monica raised her eyebrows at her mum, who avoided her gaze. 'I was just saying to May – what a fuss people make about things!'

'Oh?' Monica could feel her hackles rising. The last thing she wanted to hear about in front of May was more of Lucy's misdeeds.

'Some of them just looking for things to be annoyed about,' her mum continued.

'What exactly are you talking about?'

'Well . . .' The part of her mum that loved gossip was rising to the surface. 'I was at the school to pick her up earlier, and one of the mums was complaining about Lucy and Harriet.'

'What happened?'

'She said they'd frightened her son, told him they'd put a spell on him so he'd wake up in the middle of the night and his dead granny would be there under his bed pulling his feet.'

'For God's sake.'

'They're all so sensitive these days, can't take a bit of fun. We used to say there was trolls under the bridge and run home rare excited!'

'Running riot, so she is,' May chipped in. 'It's all that curly hair – God alone knows where that all came from.'

Monica jerked round to glower at May, who shrank back. Then she turned to her mum. 'We've been over all this before, about what's in Lucy's head and what's real.' She was referring to a troubling period the previous spring when Lucy had claimed to be communicating with Monica's dead father. 'It's not healthy. Focusing on all this, believing in magic. It's not good for her.' She turned back to May. 'And don't you dare ever talk about Lucy like that again.' May smirked and crossed her arms defiantly. Monica felt her simmering disquiet from the conversation with PC Gregg turn to fresh anger. 'You might want to think about why my mum's the only person in the family willing to talk to you. And God knows why she gives you the time of day!'

Without waiting for a reply, Monica pulled her coat back on, then marched upstairs to the spare bedroom. She picked Lucy up and carried her out to the car.

*

Back in the car park of her own building, as Monica was opening the child-locked back door of the Volvo, Lucy shouted, 'Look, Albert's watching us!'

She turned and followed her daughter's pointing finger to the second-floor window. She must have forgotten to switch the living-room light off that morning, because the room was lit up bright against the night sky. The cat sitting on the windowsill inside was looking piously down at them, like a fat little god.

'He'll be hungry,' Monica said. 'He's not keen on the dried food.' As she was speaking Monica wondered about Jessica's cat, Bramble. Whether he had come home yet. She helped Lucy out of the car and reached across for the bags of groceries from the Marks & Spencer section of the garage shop down on the Longman estate. As she straightened and turned back towards the block of flats, her eye was drawn to something in the woods behind. A man was standing beside one of the lamp posts that lined the path through them. Monica watched for a moment, expecting him to turn and shout for a dog or start walking. He didn't move though, and seemed to be staring back, his face shadowed from the orange light above.

'What is it, Mummy?'

Monica glanced down at Lucy and impulsively picked her up in her free arm, noting almost subliminally how heavy she was getting. By the time Monica turned back to the woods, the man had disappeared into the shadows and the rain.

'I like food from the microwave better than normal food,' Lucy said as she poked a fork into the carton of Marks & Spencer cauliflower cheese. Monica had begun spooning the food onto a plate, but Lucy had insisted on eating from the container.

Well, that's good, Monica thought, *because Mummy's a terrible parent who never cooks for you.* 'Gran makes a big effort to give you nice food. She puts a lot of care into it.'

Lucy considered this for a moment. 'I just like it better when you buy it.'

'Well, don't tell Gran that.' Monica felt an indecent little spark of satisfaction at beating her mum in her daughter's eyes, and tried to cover it up: 'Her home cooking's much better for you.' Lucy furrowed her brow, thinking this over as she chewed. Monica had microwaved a vegetable curry for herself, but now felt sick after having not eaten all day and pushed it aside. 'Gran told me that you and Harriet have been saying things to one of the boys in school? Upsetting him.'

'Freddy kept saying that Harriet's auntie Freya was a zombie. He said he'd seen her in a cupboard in the boys' changing room at Inverness Leisure.'

'So you told him his granny was under his bed?'

'We said we'd made a spell, so she would come tonight.'

'And did you do a spell?' Monica couldn't quite believe what she was asking.

'We took some of his pencil sharpenings, and mixed them with dust and worms.'

'OK,' Monica said slowly, unsure what to make of this. 'It might seem like fun, but playing with magic can upset people. Will you do me a favour and just try to stay away from Freddy?'

When Lucy was in bed, Monica opened her laptop and began reading the old news reports of what had happened to Sally MacFarlane out at Buggsy MacIvor's house. After the meeting with Duncan Gregg, Monica had called Crawford, keen to get him on the case. He hadn't answered his phone, and when she tried the office he had left early for the day. Instead she'd spoken with DC Maria Khan. As she scrolled through the reports now, Monica recalled hesitating before sharing the information about the Rolls-Royce and MacIvor's possible involvement. Wondering again if Khan could be the leak to the press. Finally Monica had decided she couldn't operate while doubting her closest colleagues – she'd been there before in the Met, and it was no way to work. She had asked Khan to look into the unnamed art lecturer, and find out if there was any chance she was still alive and could ID the driver of the Rolls.

She looked back at the laptop. MACIVOR: DEAD HOOKER ON DRUGS was one headline.

The stories seemed to tie in with what PC Gregg had told her. Sally MacFarlane had gone to a Hogmanay party out at MacIvor's house in 2003, drowned in Loch Ness, had alcohol and cocaine in her system. Details of what exactly had happened at the party were vague. After an hour Monica closed the laptop; she would have to pull the police files and autopsy report in the morning to find out more. She picked up her phone, realising Crawford still hadn't returned her call from earlier. That wasn't like her partner at all. She went to dial his number; it would be good to talk over everything Gregg had told her. She hesitated then dropped the phone back on the table. Crawford coming round late the other night hadn't ended well. They would be able to talk first thing the next morning.

Chapter 39

After dropping Lucy at school, Monica drove to headquarters. In the Major Incident Room, DC Maria Khan and DC Ben Fisher were both already at their desks. No sign of Crawford yet. *Running late two days in a row?*

Monica sat down alongside the junior detectives; she hadn't had a chance to properly catch up with them since the previous morning. 'Where are we up to?'

DC Ben Fisher had been speaking on the phone when she entered the office. He hung up and sat back in his chair, making a point of taking his glasses off and wiping tired eyes. No doubt this was partly for her benefit, to show how hard he'd been working. 'That was someone calling me back about the Pit.'

'The Pit?'

'You remember, up on Craig Phadrig?' It took Monica a moment to bring the church-burning case to mind – the disused quarry in the woods that the fire-setter had accessed. She had been so focused on the revelations of Buggsy MacIvor's possible involvement in Freya Sutherland's murder that she'd almost forgotten they were also investigating this.

'What did they say?'

'The quarry is owned by a construction firm who used it when they were building the estates. That was the secretary on the phone. They don't have a list, but she thinks there shouldn't be more than a dozen people who have keys. She's going to get the names over to me.'

'Good work.' If they could clear up the fire-setting case quickly it would at least keep Detective Superintendent Hately off her back. The addition of infamous celebrity Buggsy MacIvor to the Freya Sutherland investigation was sure to add to the media storm. Something her boss was going to love. 'Have you made any progress on Pauline Tosh's contacts?'

'There's a lot to get through,' Fisher replied defensively. 'She's had more than you'd expect.'

'That's fine, Fisher. I know it's a lot to get through.' Sometimes her younger colleague's perfectionism and need to see her as an authoritarian boss could be tiresome. 'Just keep working on it. I expected it to take a while.'

'I was in until late last night. DC Crawford was helping me in the afternoon, but then had to leave early.' This was a not-so-subtle dig at her partner, Monica realised.

'Did he say where he was going?' The wall clock told her it was 9.30 a.m. It really wasn't like Crawford to be so late two days in a row.

'I assumed he was chasing a lead.'

'Chasing pussy more likely,' Khan chipped in.

Although she was clearly joking, Monica felt protective. 'I'm sure he'll be in soon. He can fill us in,' she snapped back. 'Was there anything else?'

'Actually, I received an email from forensics in Dundee just before you arrived,' Fisher said. 'About the carpet fibres recovered from Freya's body.' As well as Gemma Gunn's local forensics lab, the team made use of Police Scotland's central lab located further south in Dundee. 'We were testing for a possible match with a Volkswagen Golf, which Brodie King was known to own at the time,' Fisher said as if Monica might have forgotten this.

'And?' This could be an important piece in building a circumstantial case.

'No match with the Golf,' Fisher said.

Monica swore. 'Could they have come from a Rolls-Royce?'

'They ran the fibre and dye types against their vehicle database. It didn't come back with anything. It looks like they didn't come from a vehicle.'

'Was there anything useful?' In such a long-dormant case with little in the way of witness testimony, building compelling forensic evidence was going to be crucial.

'Possibly. The fibres are from an industrial-style carpet. It was only sold in Scotland by a handful of wholesalers for about a year in 1987–88, before being discontinued. I'm working on the list of stockists.'

'Good work,' Monica said. 'I'll get Crawford to help you with that when he gets in.' Hately had already refused her request for extra bodies, claiming they were needed on other investigations. Though Monica suspected that at least part of her boss's motivation was to slow their investigation after the recent heat from Miranda Salisbury's lawyer. 'Anything else?'

Khan cleared her throat. 'I think I got the name of the lecturer, the one from Brodie King and Joseph Moon's college? A Miss Rossetti.'

Monica remembered what PC Gregg had said about the lecturer being elderly back in 1994. 'I assume she's passed away?'

'No,' Khan said, sounding surprised as she pushed her dark hair behind her ears. 'She's alive, in a nursing home.'

*

Monica turned into the car park of the Culloden Nursing Home and spotted Khan's black Honda Civic. The younger detective had had another appointment so had come in her own car. As Monica pulled up, she saw the Honda's door was scuffed with white paint, the window was down and Khan was smoking a cigarette. She was wearing a black baseball cap and, despite the grey autumn day, dark glasses. Monica got out and walked over. Inside she could see Khan's passenger seat was covered in a heap of CDs, fast-food wrappers and empty Coke bottles. In among them lay what appeared to be a small baseball bat. Khan got out. She was dressed in dark jeans and a fake fur coat. *One thing's for certain*, Monica thought, trying hard not to stare into the car. *Next time you need someone undercover, Khan's unique style means no one will ever guess she's a cop.*

The Culloden was a grim bungalow clad in grey pebbledash. Inside it was more welcoming: high ceilings, white walls, a smell of baking bread and the pleasant sound of Radio 4. Nursing-home hot of course, prompting Monica and Khan to both immediately shrug off their coats as an assistant led them through to a day room. Contrary to PC Duncan Gregg's confident assertion that the lecturer would be dead by now, the aged Miss Rossetti was very much alive. Sitting at an easel by a window, working on a watercolour of a turquoise mermaid. The old woman turned when the assistant said her name. She was stick thin, but her white hair was thick, her skin a healthy olive. Her eyes were bright as they ran over Monica, then down to Khan, where they lingered. 'I love your coat.' She put her paintbrush carefully into a jar then reached out a wrinkled hand to feel the fake fur Khan was holding.

'I'm sorry this is out of the blue,' Monica said, sitting down on the chair the assistant offered. 'But did you lecture at Inverness College?'

'That's right,' Miss Rossetti said brightly. 'Art, art history, art theory, everything art.' She laughed. 'Ever since I was a little girl.'

'I was wondering about some students of yours from back in 1994?'

'This is about Freya, isn't it?' Her accent still carried a hint of Italian. 'Freya Sutherland.'

'You met her?'

'Oh yes. They were a little group – they came to the studios during the summer when the college was closed, so I got to know them a little. Freya and Miranda Salisbury, and two of my students, Brodie King and Joseph Moon.'

'We're investigating Freya's murder,' Monica said quietly. 'Her body was discovered recently.'

'Yes.' Miss Rossetti's lips went thin. 'I saw it on the news. It's so horrible.'

'What was your impression of the group?'

'At the time they just seemed like normal young people,' the lecturer said. 'Trying to find their way, I suppose.'

Monica nodded. She had heard the neighbours and colleagues of more than one serial killer describe how 'ordinary' or 'normal' they were, so Miss Rossetti's assessment didn't surprise her. Most folks found it hard to accept that people they knew and liked might be linked to murder.

'It seems that the other three were already friends when Freya joined the group?'

'Yes, I didn't meet her until later. The others seemed quite tight; I got the impression that she was maybe a little on the outside.'

'Anything that stands out?'

'Actually, yes. I've thought about it over the years, whenever there was something in the press from Freya's family, looking for her. It's probably unrelated, but . . .'

Monica asked, 'What happened?'

'Freya came to the studios one day in the summer.'

'Can you remember when?'

'August, not long before classes were due to begin again. It was the start of my last year before retirement so I remember it well.'

'What did Freya want?'

'She was looking for the others. She was upset, thought they were ignoring her. I'm afraid I was a bit casual. I wasn't expecting it and didn't really take her seriously.'

'Had they done something to her?' Monica remembered what Mr MacAdam had said the previous day – hearing Miranda Salisbury shout about wanting a woman dead. The timings would match.

'No, it was nothing extreme. They had stopped returning her calls, missed meetings with her, I think. I'd seen the same kind of upset a million times with students over the years.'

'So you never found out what they'd fallen out about?'

'The next week they were all back together, friends again. Next thing I hear is that Freya's missing, then Brodie King and Joseph Moon just stopped coming to college. I did wonder what had happened.'

'I believe one of my colleagues contacted you?'

'No.' Miss Rossetti's face changed. 'That's not what happened.'

'Oh?'

'I called the police, then it was weeks before they bothered to come down and speak to me. The detective was very off-hand.' This contradicted Gregg's version, in which he had skilfully hunted the lecturer down. Probably it also explained why he had been so insistent that the lecturer would be dead by now.

'What did you want to tell the police?' Monica asked.

'That I'd seen Freya's friends getting out of a car, a black Rolls-Royce! I thought it might help them trace where she'd gone.'

'When was this?'

'About a week before she disappeared.'

'I know it's a long time ago, Miss Rossetti,' Monica said, 'but do you remember any of the number plate?'

'I never noticed that,' she replied slowly. 'But I can tell you exactly who was driving. The same thing I told that detective back then. I'd seen his face on TV a thousand times. It was that comedian Buggsy MacIvor.'

Chapter 40

When Monica and Khan arrived at Caulfeild & Son's Antiques halfway up the Market Brae Steps, Caulfeild Junior was sitting behind the counter, hands folded on his stomach.

'No luck so far, I'm afraid.' His face broke into a schoolboy grin. 'Records are a nightmare; Senior's revenge on Junior from beyond the grave. If you try back at the end of next week I might have something.'

Monica again took in the untidy piles of objects, the oppressive smell of the place, and unexpectedly felt a flash of anger at his blatant stalling. 'You recognised that locket, didn't you?' She watched as Caulfeild's expression shifted from self-satisfaction to alarm.

'I'm sorry. What?' He tried to stand, but his knees were trapped under the counter and he fell back in his chair. Monica stooped to lean over the top so her face was inches from his. She could see the flour on his lip from his breakfast roll, smell the sweat from his stained shirt.

'The locket. You recognised it. I think you know who bought it. You thought you could spin us along, invent some bullshit story about missing records. Am I wrong?'

Caulfeild stared up, transfixed by her fury.

Monica took a breath, suddenly aware Khan was watching, wide-eyed behind her dark glasses. It had been a while since Monica had allowed herself to get this agitated at work. Not good. With an effort she calmed herself. 'Listen. This isn't going away. The girl who owned that locket was found in a hole in the ground. It was sold in this shop. I've got an office geek who will dig through every file associated with your business, every tax return.'

'I told you, the records are a mess. I just haven't had a chance. I'll need a few days—'

'You know who bought that thing; you don't need to look up any records to tell me.'

'It . . . It's not someone . . .' As he was speaking Monica realised that in her anger she had missed the subtle cues: a bead of sweat had rolled down the side of his face; his hands were shaking slightly. Caulfeild was obviously terrified.

'You're frightened of the person who bought that locket, aren't you?'

Caulfeild nodded almost imperceptibly.

Monica softened her tone. 'This can stay between us. We already have a name; I just need you to confirm it.' He wiped the sweat from his forehead and muttered something. Monica leaned in closer. 'You need to speak up.'

He narrowed his eyes at DC Khan, then looked back at Monica, whispered the name again: 'Buggsy MacIvor. It was him who bought it.'

'Are you sure?'

'He used to come in here to talk to my dad – he was interested in antiques.'

'What kind of antiques?'

'Nasty ones.'

'In what way?'

'Ones that were made with nasty intent. Ask any antique dealer and they'll tell. You've eaten in a bad restaurant, practically tasted the contempt with which the food was made?' Monica thought about it for a second, then nodded slowly. 'Objects carry something of how they were made too. You tune in to it when you're around them all the time.'

'You think the coffin locket was one of them?'

'Well, you touched it. What did you think?' Monica's rational impulse was to dismiss the idea, but then she remembered that she had locked the necklace in the glovebox of the Volvo over-night rather than bring it into her flat. She nodded again. 'Some people are more attuned to objects that come from the darker side of a creator's imagination. Some people like them. Buggsy MacIvor's one of those people.'

Chapter 41

'Sorry about that, I shouldn't have lost my cool,' Monica said as they left the shop and started down the High Street. She realised now that her rage was fuelled by PC Duncan Gregg: he had blatantly lied about Buggsy MacIvor. Miss Rossetti had told Gregg back in 1994 that she had seen Freya's friends with the comedian, and Gregg hadn't done anything about it.

'It was amazing,' Khan replied, apparently without irony. 'Especially the bit about an "office geek".' Monica looked down and for the first time saw genuine admiration in her colleague's eyes.

It had started raining again, but Monica had left her umbrella in the back of the Volvo at Rose Street car park. It felt like that kind of day.

'Not really,' Monica said. She realised now that Auntie May's niggling, Lucy's difficulties at school and the complications with Crawford had all fuelled her anger. 'You let your frustrations influence your work, you miss things. It can be dangerous. Believe me, I know.'

'Of course,' Khan replied. 'That makes a lot of sense.' But worryingly the little smile at the corner of her mouth persisted. It suggested an attraction to mischief. And as Monica wondered just how deep that impulse ran, she paradoxically felt herself drawn to Khan. Funny – one day working in the field, you learned more about a colleague than six months in the office.

On the way to the antiques shop Monica had messaged Fisher and Crawford to meet them at MacGregor's Bar at the bottom of Church Street. Fisher was waiting, laptop open at a quiet corner table, but no sign of Crawford. Monica looked at her phone; her partner still hadn't responded to any of her messages. 'Have you spoken to Crawford?'

'He called just as I was leaving the office,' Fisher said, looking up from his laptop. 'Said he's caught up with something.'

' "Caught up"?'

'That's what he said. I just assumed it was part of the investigation.'

'Well, I'm sure he'll fill us in.' As she was speaking Monica realised that she was now covering for her partner. What was going on with him?

She sat and looked around. Only one other table was taken, in the opposite corner of the bright room. MacGregor's Bar was one of her favourite places in Inverness. Named after the owner, a traditional musician, and unconnected with notorious local-criminal-turned-businessman Francis MacGregor. She let Khan fill Fisher in on what Miss Rossetti and Caulfeild had told them about MacIvor's involvement. The comedian had apparently given Freya a necklace. A young woman of a similar age to Freya had been found dead in Loch Ness near his home years later.

Finally Khan turned to Monica. 'So Miranda Salisbury and Brodie King presumably knew Freya had spent time with Buggsy MacIvor, but never mentioned it during the investigation in 1994.'

'Does this suggest a conspiracy?' Fisher offered.

In Monica's view it did. Especially combined with the other evidence: the curse tablet at Corrimony, Mr MacAdam's report of Miranda Salisbury's threats. Something had happened that summer – something that led to the death of Freya and radically changed the trajectory of Joseph Moon's life. Was that thing Buggsy MacIvor?

'What do we actually know about MacIvor?' Monica asked, glancing over to check that the occupants of the other table weren't listening. Fiddle music was drifting through from the back room and the couple appeared deep in conversation over their beers. Satisfied they wouldn't be able to hear, she continued, 'Beyond his public persona?'

'Not a great deal,' Fisher replied. 'Just what's online. He was famously convicted of the armed robbery of his local post office, back in 1979 when he was a teenager – no one was hurt, used a plastic gun. No offences since then. Before the woman in the loch in 2003, his reputation was spotless up here.' Fisher passed his phone to Monica. It showed an image from a newspaper. Buggsy MacIvor, a wide – almost cartoonish – smile on his face, was a head taller than the others in the picture, with a thick ginger beard and wearing a Bonnie Prince Charlie outfit. It was captioned 'Local hero returns as games chieftain' and the accompanying article was headlined NOT SUCH A LONG WAY TO INVERNESS!

'This is from 1993,' Fisher said. 'MacIvor would have been thirty-five at the time.'

'So nothing else?'

'Not so far,' Fisher said.

Monica thought about it for a moment. Ideally she would bring MacIvor in for questioning and search his house for any links to Freya. It was unlikely that forensic evidence would survive from 1994, but if what Caulfeild had said about his interest in unpleasant objects was true, MacIvor might be the type of killer to take trophies. Monica had a hunch that finding something belonging to Freya at MacIvor's house would be their best chance of connecting him to her murder. But getting a search warrant without a compelling link wasn't going to be easy. Hately was already looking to slow the investigation; he wasn't going to sanction a search of MacIvor's house without a compelling reason.

Out of the window it was a grey day, and it felt strange having the meeting without Crawford. In a weird way he was the glue that held the team together. And of all the cops she had worked with, he was one of the best at ferreting out information. If anyone could dig up something useful on MacIvor, it would be him.

Time for a white lie. She stood up. 'I have to get my daughter.' In fact her mum had sent a brief message minutes earlier to say she had collected Lucy. 'I'll be in touch this evening.'

Monica pulled the Volvo to a stop in Huntly Street on the western bank of the River Ness in the city centre, opposite Crawford's place. She scanned the street for his red Audi; could see no sign of it. The curtains were open in his second-floor flat, but there was no sign of movement within. Monica sat watching as a group of Japanese tourists crossed the nearby wobbly bridge, jumping on the famous tourist attraction to make it bounce then shouting in excitement. *At least someone is enjoying Inverness in the rain*, she thought as she got out of her car, remembering the umbrella this time. She crossed the street and hit the buzzer on Crawford's door. It occurred to her that she'd never actually been inside his flat, just picked him up on the street. As she waited, Monica wondered for a moment what the interior might be like. She recalled him mentioning an expensive espresso machine, and a games console he'd bought when recuperating from a gunshot wound the previous year. The flat would certainly be neat: she imagined a Japanese interior, with tatami mats and minimal prints. Wondered if the idea had been planted in her psyche by the tourists she'd just seen, or if Crawford had mentioned Japanese decor in connection with his enthusiasm for martial arts?

Well, I'm not going to find out today, Monica conceded with a mix of hurt and anger. Whatever was going on with Crawford, he clearly didn't want to speak to her about it. She hit the buzzer a final time and waited a further five minutes, rain pattering off her umbrella, then headed back to the car.

Monica drove the short distance down Greig Street, then along Telford Road into the unfashionable part of Inverness where her mum lived. She pulled into the driveway of her mum's council-built house. Feeling like a schoolgirl as she pondered what kind of reception she might expect. Other than her mum's brief text message they'd had no communication since Monica had stormed out of the house the night before. Fortunately Angela Kennedy wasn't a woman who bore a grudge. She did like to have her say though, Monica knew.

'You can't just be saying whatever comes into your head with an elderly person, Monica.' Her mum was working at puff pastry with a rolling pin when Monica stepped into the kitchen. Sleeves up and handsome face down, avoiding eye contact.

Monica craned her neck to see if Lucy was listening from the living room. She seemed to be absorbed in a book. Monica leaned in close to her mum. 'May's a fucking bitch. She's always been a bitch.'

Angela tutted, furiously shaking her head.

'I've put up with her sniping about Lucy for years.'

'It's your dad's sister you're talking about, Monica. He'd be turning in his grave.'

'Well, she was happy enough moaning about him when he was alive.'

'It's not the point. She was in pieces at his funeral, and let me tell you, she was black affronted yesterday after what you said to her. "Never been so offended," she said. Miracle she didn't take one of her turns and end up in Raigmore again!'

'No doubt.' Monica put the kettle on and sat at the kitchen table. May had a long history of 'taking turns' at convenient moments.

'I'm just saying, Monica, sometimes family's all you have.'

'Well, I'm finished with her.'

'You can't just always be cutting off from people, Monica.' Her mum paused. This was the part where she probably wanted to say, *That's why you've not got a man.* Instead she said, 'You never let people be human. It's always sugar or shite with you!'

'Sugar or shite? Charming.' She couldn't remember the last time she'd heard her mum swear.

'Well it's true. Only, the truth hurts, Monica. You've always been like that!' Angela snipped. 'Expecting too much of people then using it as an excuse to cut them off before they get too close.'

'Thanks for that.' Monica wasn't in the mood for cod psycho-analysis. She tilted her head to look at what her mum was preparing. 'What kind of pie is it?'

Angela Kennedy sighed, still shaking her head, but Monica

knew she could never resist talking about cooking. 'It's beef bourguignon with puff-pastry tops, only made with something called seitan from the health-food shop so we can all eat it. Crawford told me about it – says you can't taste the difference from meat.'

'Have you heard from him at all?'

'Crawford? Not in a few days, why? Did he want to come for supper?'

Chapter 42

August 1994

Freya stared up at Brodie. Finally he repeated, 'Have you got time to talk? It won't take long.' In her half-awake state Freya felt strangely disappointed by his appearance. As if, deep down, part of her enjoyed drifting alone, like those specks of dust in the sunlight. 'Actually I don't. I was sleeping.'

She didn't close the door of the farmhouse though, and found herself wondering how she looked to him. Cute? Rolled out of bed with her hair tousled up, wearing shorts and a T-shirt. *I burned your drawing.*

'I'll give you a free cigarette.' A mocking half-smile.

'Fuck off.'

'I know you like free stuff.'

'No, I don't. Where have you been?'

'How much money do you have saved?'

'How much money? Why?' She wrapped her arms around herself against the evening chill. 'Why didn't you call me back?'

'Come to the car with me. I just want to talk.'

'I'm not wearing any shoes.' She pointed to her bare feet. Brodie turned and crouched, motioned for her to get on his back.

'You're not carrying me.'

213

'I've got free sweets in the car too.' She slapped him on the shoulder, but found herself climbing onto his back. He grabbed her legs, pretended to stagger under her weight, then straightened up and carried her easily across the yard. She leaned her head into the back of his neck, felt the cold leather and breathed in the smells of smoke, deodorant. The Golf was parked just down the lane, engine still running. She had expected to find Miranda and Joseph inside, but it was empty. Freya climbed off Brodie's back into the passenger seat, grateful that he had left the heating on high. He got in the other side behind the wheel, lit two Marlboro menthols and handed one to her.

'Do you want to stay here for ever?'

'You said you were going to tell me why you didn't call.' But as she was speaking, Freya realised that she wasn't even angry with him now. Somehow it felt good just being in his company.

'I'll explain. I promise. But I need to know if you want to come.'

'Come where?' The way he was talking felt like she really was still in that dream.

'Somewhere hot. A different country.'

'What's happened? Did I do something to offend you all? It was like you just disappeared.'

'I told you, we'll explain everything later.' Brodie was staring straight ahead through the windscreen. He sounded angry now. 'I just need to know if you're interested.'

'Where would we go?'

'We'd just drive. Just take the ferry to Europe.'

'You told me last week that you didn't have any money,' Freya said, recalling the conversation when she'd lent him money for petrol. 'I've got about fifty quid saved.'

'What if we did have money? Would you think about it then?'

'I don't know.' As she was saying it, Freya imagined another year of living at home, another ten years. 'Probably.'

For the first time that evening Brodie's face softened into a smile. 'There's someone I want you to meet. A friend of ours.'

Chapter 43

As usual with Angela Kennedy's cooking, the fake-beef bour-guignon, served with peas smothered in butter and crunchy potatoes straight from the roasting pan, was delicious. After they'd eaten, Monica did the dishes, watching through the window as the street lights on the road outside turned from pink to orange in the evening gloom. The silhouettes of the chimney pots against the bruised sky familiar from childhood. Monica wondered just how many times she had stood in this same spot as a teenager, pondering all the ways her life would be better once she'd got the hell out of Inverness. Had Freya Sutherland been thinking something similar on the night she walked away from Fettercairn Farm?

Monica was about to tell Lucy to get her shoes on for the drive home when her phone started ringing from her coat pocket. She answered.

'This is PC Kai Smith. We've got a note to contact you for any calls coming in about prowlers in the Inverness area?'

Monica remembered asking Crawford to get in touch with the call-handling team about the church-burnings case. 'What have you got?'

'Out near Connachton. We've got officers responding now.'

'Remind me where Connachton is?' There were so many places with similar-sounding names across the Highlands, it was easy to confuse them. Although she appreciated the call, the chance of a prowler being linked to their fire-setting case was slim.

But PC Kai Smith said, 'Just outside Inverness, south of the loch,' and Monica realised this was the same vicinity as Buggsy MacIvor's place, Balnakine House. She felt those rare fingers of intuition.

'Can you message me the address?'

Connachton was a hamlet set among vast plantation forests. The roads were quiet and Monica drove fast – made it in just over fifteen minutes. She identified the building before she even reached the hamlet, because it was already burning. Sending a glow up into the evening sky. She turned a corner and saw a low stone construction, set back from the single-track road. A marked police car was at the end of a driveway, blocking the road, lights flashing. Monica pulled up alongside the two uniformed officers standing by the car. She recognised PC Phillips, from the canteen, and beside him PC Duncan Gregg. Gregg did a double take when he saw her getting out of the Volvo.

He was speaking into his radio: 'Yes. Immediate assistance from the fire service.'

Monica shouted, 'Is anyone inside?'

Gregg finished on the radio. 'We just got here. Saw the place on fire.'

Monica pushed the gate open and ran up the driveway towards the building. As she approached she could see it wasn't a church this time, but a barn conversion. Flames were twisting out of a broken window at the far end of the house. Casting eerie shadows in the forest. She tried the front door. Locked. Clocked the sign by the door: COTTON LODGE BARN. She rammed at the door with her shoulder; it didn't budge.

'Let me try.' Gregg had followed her up the path. He kicked the door twice, his considerable weight behind the blows. On the third impact it swung open. Hellish smoke and glowing red, the crack and whisper of dry wood aflame.

'There's no car parked outside!' Phillips was shouting to be heard over the fire's roar. 'It could be empty!'

Monica yelled into the house, thinking, *God, I hope so.* The noise of the flames made it impossible to hear any returning cry. She could just make out shapes in the room – a bookcase, framed paintings on the wall. She stepped over the threshold, but the heat and smoke forced her out. She fell back, gasping for air, and ran to the far end of the house. She grabbed a large stone and lobbed it at the window. It bounced ineffectively off the double glazing. Gregg appeared a moment later and had more success with his baton on the glass, which cracked and then broke. He cleared the remaining glass from the window frame then shone his torch inside. There was no smoke at this end of the house yet, and Monica could see a double bed – empty, not even made up.

She shouted, 'Try the other window, just to be sure,' and Gregg moved further along and smashed the glass out. A room with bunk beds. Thankfully empty again.

'Holiday home?'

It appeared to be. *Thank God no one was here*, Monica thought. The fire was taking over. Moving with frightening power down the building.

'Service are on their way,' PC Phillips shouted. Barely a minute had passed since Monica had arrived at the scene, but already the blaze was noticeably more intense. She felt the growing heat, and turned away to shield her skin.

It was then that she spotted the shape in the trees. A figure among the shifting shadows. She blinked, expecting the shape to dissolve into the darkness. Instead it became clearer. A person with a hood obscuring their face.

'This'll need to get put out!' Gregg was mouthing off beside her to Phillips. 'Tell them if they're not here soon the whole fucking forest could be up!' She reached for his shoulder, nodded towards the person in the trees.

Monica could see now that the figure was crouched, staring at the flames. A moment later the person – a man; Monica was sure from the body shape – must have felt their eyes on him because he seemed to shift, glance up. Monica took a step towards him. He stood, staring back a moment, face still hidden.

She stepped forward and shouted, 'Stop! Don't move!' Sometimes this actually worked. Not tonight though. A beat and he was gone.

Monica stared after him for a second then gave chase. The ground was sloping, rough underfoot. Thirty seconds into the dense forest and the darkness was disorientating, thick all around despite the light from the fire. She sensed movement, turned as the blow landed, glancing off her shoulder onto the back of her head.

Next she knew she was lying among pine needles, staring up. A torch clicked on, its beam in her face. Dazzled, Monica could just make out someone standing over her. Watching her face.

'Brodie?' Her voice sounded heavy. 'Brodie King? Is that you?' Under the stink of the smoke she could smell pine sap, moss. She wondered dimly why she'd said Brodie's name – and if it was him, why the hell he was randomly setting fire to buildings. What was the connection to Freya's murder? The man seemed to hesitate. Her mind told her to kick out, to fight, but the light was strangely hypnotic.

Another moment and she heard shouts through the woods. 'Kennedy?! Is that you, ma'am?' The light shining in her face clicked off. The man stared down at her in the darkness for a moment longer, then he was gone.

Chapter 44

It was 11 p.m. before Monica made it back to her flat. Lucy had gone to bed at her gran's, who had volunteered to drop her at school in the morning. She felt the back of her head again. It throbbed, but there had been no blood. It seemed that she had turned at just the right moment, making it a glancing blow, thankfully only knocking her off balance and momentarily stunning her. Though if the fire-setter had wanted to do more harm, he'd had ample opportunity as she lay at his mercy on the forest floor. Perhaps Gregg's approach had put him off?

In the woods, Monica had got gingerly to her feet, dusted herself down. For some reason as Gregg approached she hadn't even told him what had happened. Just said, 'I lost him. Can we get a patrol to visit the lay-bys on the A9?' Her thoughts were still murky, but her voice sounded clear. She knew that the forest backed onto the busy A9, which joined the Highlands with central Scotland. The road was their best bet. 'Get the details for any vehicles parked up.'

'Will do, ma'am.' Gregg was breathing heavily. In the distance she could hear the reassuring wail of approaching fire engines.

As the fire service tackled the blaze, the neighbour who had called the police emerged from a nearby house. Monica went over to the edge of the police cordon to talk to her. The woman, Mrs Jane Roberts, was in her fifties, wearing an orange waterproof and with a small busy spaniel on a lead.

'What did you see?'

'I was out walking the dog, and he was in a funny mood, just seemed agitated. We were coming round the corner' – she gestured further down the road – 'and I spotted someone trying the door of Cotton Lodge.'

'Have you seen the person before?' Monica asked. The fire behind her cast an orange glow on Jane Roberts's face. With her recent blow to the head this gave the questioning a dreamlike quality, and she wondered again why her half-conscious mind had jumped on the idea that the fire-setter was Brodie King. Simply because he had a similar build and she had been thinking about him all day? There was certainly no logical reason to believe it was him, or that the fires were connected to Freya's murder. Monica blinked, realising she had missed the woman's reply. 'What was that, sorry?'

'I said I've never seen him before. His face was covered anyway, with a hood.'

'Why were you suspicious of him?'

'I know the owners of the house – they live in Birmingham and only let it out to friends and family. Sometimes people come out here from Inverness, looking for unoccupied places to do over.'

Monica thanked her and said that someone would be in touch the following day to take a proper statement. She watched for another half an hour as the firefighters got the blaze under control. As she was walking back to the Volvo she felt PC Gregg's presence alongside her.

'Funny you turning up out here, after seeing you yesterday. What are the chances?'

Monica forced a smile. 'Yeah, unlikely.'

'The patrols on the A9 haven't spotted anything so far. Still a few places to check.'

Monica nodded, feeling the throb at the back of her head. 'Well, keep me posted.' She turned to go, intent on making it home for a hot shower and a rest, but Gregg stepped closer and grabbed her arm.

'Not got your partner with you tonight?' he asked, frowning. 'Crawford, isn't it?'

Monica looked down at his hand on her arm. 'Not tonight,' she said slowly. 'I was home when I got the call.'

'Right enough.' Gregg nodded, checked PC Phillips was safely in the marked car out of earshot, then leaned closer. 'A tip. Just watch that one – Crawford. Just watch him.'

Gregg gave a wink, turned and was already in the patrol car alongside Phillips before Monica could muster a reply.

Monica took in her empty flat, and for about the fiftieth time replayed the moment. What had Gregg been getting at? Simply trying to niggle her, or was there genuinely something he knew about her partner? She trusted Crawford implicitly, but why had he disappeared? Why wasn't he returning her calls? For the first time, she allowed the obvious suspicion to touch her conscious mind. The case had been dogged by media leaks. Crawford didn't know about the MacIvor connection, and so far this part of the story – the juiciest part – had stayed out of the press.

'For fuck's sake,' Monica muttered. She went to the freezer for a bag of peas, held them to the back of her head and ducked to the cupboard for the whisky they'd been drinking the other night. She poured two fingers into a glass.

It made absolutely no sense. Crawford liked nice clothes, having a nice car, but he wasn't motivated by money or status. He 100 per cent wanted to do a good job in the police, she had no doubt about that. What, then? She downed the whisky in one, closing her eyes against the burn.

As she did, Monica remembered the time they'd drunk it together. She realised Crawford had been trying to tell her something. She had turned it into a joke, and then he'd fallen back on his favourite defence mechanism: replacing emotional intimacy with physical. He had immediately attempted to seduce her. Monica felt a strange new wave of embarrassed horror at the memory. As if she had been somehow abusive to her colleague by letting it happen.

She refilled the glass and took another long pull.

Chapter 45

Monica woke, still on the couch, feeling the first waves of nausea. Dimly she recalled having messaged someone on Plenty of Fish, offering sex. She stretched her right arm out and felt around: the leather of the sofa, the familiar fabric of the cushions, but mercifully no sleeping body. Finally satisfied that she was alone, she opened her eyes. Her laptop was still open on the coffee table, the empty bottle of whisky beside it. *Jesus, you really are becoming a caricature of a detective.*

As she stood under the shower, turned down as cold as it would go, Monica tried to remember the last time she'd had a hangover. Not since before Lucy was born. Last time she'd had to work with a hangover? A long time . . . She forced down a mug of instant coffee, then immediately went to the toilet to throw it back up. She thought about calling in sick, but remembered the fire-setter, Freya, Buggsy MacIvor . . . The team was already under-strength. Finally she dragged on a pair of dark trousers, a white T-shirt and a grey cashmere jumper, needing the comfort of the soft wool on a day like today.

The cool air outside was revivifying, but when she got into the Volvo the steering wheel seem to shift in her hands. She went to start the engine, then recalled the horror car crashes she'd attended during her stint working traffic the winter before. One young man pleading, 'I just had a couple of pints, thought I'd be fine. They're going to be OK though, aren't they?' He'd just blown hot on the breathalyser at the scene of a crash on the A9 which led to the death of two elderly tourists. Monica got out of her car and went to sit on the wall by the road until the taxi arrived.

Khan was already in the office, but still no sign of Crawford. Or, for that matter, DC Ben Fisher.

'Crawford left a message,' Khan said as Monica sat down beside her, doing her best to seem fully sober. One good thing about having a consumptive's complexion: no one noticed if you were dying of a hangover.

'What did he say?' Monica asked, feeling too ill in that moment to actually care or even think about what Gregg had insinuated the night before.

'He's unwell, not going to be in today.'

'Unwell?'

'That's what he said.'

'How did he sound?'

'I don't know, he called it in to the desk sergeant. I could ask him?'

Monica shook her head and dug out her own phone. Still nothing from Crawford. *What the hell is going on?* 'Sorry I wasn't in touch last night,' she said finally. 'I got a call-out – there was another fire.'

Khan nodded. 'I heard about it. You saw the fire-setter?'

Obviously PC Gregg had filled the whole station in on the excitement. Monica put a hand to the lump on the back of her head, pleased that he didn't know that part of the story. Though as she remembered the chase, it occurred to her to wonder why the fire-setter had sat watching them. Wouldn't he have known they would spot him eventually? Was that part of the thrill? Or did part of him want them to see him, to catch him? Occasionally this really was the case with criminals.

Finally Monica replied, 'He moved fast through the woods, seemed to know the area.'

'I wonder why he targeted that house?' Khan asked.

Monica pondered the question herself. The first two fires had been churches – this one a holiday home. 'Maybe because he knew it was empty,' she replied, surprising herself with the idea. 'He wanted to watch it burn without anyone bothering him.'

'Or he didn't want to hurt anyone?' Khan suggested.

Monica thought about that for a second. The throbbing pain at the back of her head suggested otherwise, though she had been at his mercy and he hadn't hit her again. 'Where's Fisher?'

'He was in here until three a.m. working on the Tosh stuff. Left a note to say he'd be in late because he's chasing a lead.'

'Did you get anywhere with intelligence on Buggsy MacIvor?'

'Nothing too useful,' Khan conceded sadly. 'Not been on film or TV since the early 2000s. He still lives out at Balnakine House but doesn't do much locally now. Keeps himself to himself.'

If she hadn't been so hungover Monica would have been angry with Crawford. This was definitely a case for him to be digging into. She realised then just how much she'd come to rely on him.

'So we don't have anyone who knew him back in 1994? Anyone who could link him more firmly with Freya?'

'No one so far.'

'Do we know what he does with his time now?'

'He still does stand-up and he's on Twitter.'

'Dead woman in the loch outside his house not enough to put people off?'

'He's incorporated it into his act.' Khan turned her laptop and opened a YouTube video titled 'Fucked Up Non-PC Comedy'. It had 150,000 views. She hit Play. A dimly lit club, mid-act.

'When I was on TV I used to say it was a long way to Inverness. You heard me say that, huv ye aye? Oohh it's a long way to Inverness! Aye, well no, now it's no – fuckin' stuck in Inverness permanently now. Want to know why? I'll tell ye. Any other part of the country you wake up with a dead hooker floating out your back garden they'll tell ye te fuck off.' MacIvor was a large man, still with a red beard, and wearing a kilt. 'Up in the Highlands they don't give a fuck up there. "Aye, oh well, a hooker dead is it, aye – oh it'll be Nessy that got her, good for tourism so it'll be." Ah'll tell ye, up there they don't give a fuck.' He was walking back and forth across the stage like an agitated child as he spat angrily into the microphone, kilt flying up around his legs. 'Dead girl in Loch Ness and that's me, *persona non grata* down in London now. Oohh it's a long way to Inverness! Someone should have said that to her before she tried swimming home from my house, I might still have a job then, fuck's sake—' The video ended.

'What a charmer,' Monica said, remembering the photos of Sally MacFarlane's body floating face down in the dark waters. MacIvor's act was clearly narcissistic, though she had to concede he still had a dark charisma, a stage presence. She leaned over and ran the short video back to the start, played it again without the sound this time and watched his eyes. There was a coldness there; he seemed almost to be revelling in what he was describing. A monster hiding in plain sight? Getting a thrill out of openly talking about a woman he'd murdered?

'I take it we haven't been able to track down any of Sally Mac-Farlane's family or friends?'

'No, she was an only child. Dad not on the scene, mum died

228

when she was two. Grew up in foster care. Homeless, in and out of hostels, struggles with addiction.'

'Poor woman.' With the weight of her hangover Monica felt the sadness of Sally MacFarlane's short life more poignantly. Trying to find comfort in this cold world and instead being met with exploitation, with murder?

'I checked Sally MacFarlane's autopsy,' Khan said. 'She was twice the old drink-drive limit; diazepam in her system as well as the cocaine.'

'Any signs of violence?'

'She had bruises on her arms and legs. No obvious defence wounds flagged. Sounds like she was out of it from the drugs and booze.'

'Any witnesses?'

'No one who spoke to the police. There were a lot of guests, some of them rich and famous. No one saw her going into the water, no one remembered seeing her in the house. She normally worked the streets down at the Longman – it was never explained how she ended up out at Buggsy MacIvor's house.'

Monica said, 'Being close to two young women who died in tragic circumstances is a lot for one lifetime.'

'What next? We go and question MacIvor? Get a search warrant?'

Monica thought about it for a moment. 'All we actually have connecting MacIvor to Freya Sutherland is a locket that he might have given her, and someone who saw Freya's friends with him. After everything with Miranda Salisbury's lawyer, it's going to be difficult to get a warrant without something clearly linking MacIvor to Freya. Particularly since he successfully sued newspapers over the allegations about Sally MacFarlane.'

'So what do we do?'

Monica cleared her throat, wished her brain wasn't so whisky-fogged. What was she thinking, getting drunk in the middle of a serious investigation?

The door of the office banged open and DC Ben Fisher bustled in. He held up a Costa Coffee cup carrier. 'I thought since DC Crawford wasn't in, I would do the honours.'

As she took in her geeky young colleague, Monica felt something akin to love through her hangover. How bizarrely exciting the promise of a coffee in a fancy paper cup could seem on an otherwise grey day.

Fisher extricated the cups from the holder and handed one to Monica, another to Khan. 'It's with hazelnut syrup,' he said nervously. 'I asked for it in mine but they put it in all three by mistake.'

Monica took a sip, the sickly sweet caffeinated drink perfect hangover fodder. 'Delicious.'

Fisher nodded and adjusted his glasses, clearly delighted. 'Khan said you were chasing a lead?'

Generally fieldwork wasn't Fisher's strong point, but with Crawford out of the picture and the investigation seeming at a dead end, she was willing to listen to anything.

Fisher adjusted his glasses again, cleared his throat. Obviously excited by whatever he'd discovered. 'You remember we spoke about cultivating contacts?'

Monica nodded, dimly remembering a conversation with Fisher a few months before – after he'd been down to London for a course on intelligence-gathering. For some detectives like Crawford, getting people to talk came naturally. For others it was harder. Fisher definitely fell into the latter category.

'Well, I asked DC Crawford for help . . . We started exercising together, going to a gym. After everything in the spring, you remember?' He dropped his eyes and Monica nodded again. How could she forget the infamous case that had brought memories from her own childhood so strongly to the surface? At the time it had felt like she and Fisher would become closer after sharing details about their personal lives. In the end it seemed he couldn't handle that kind of intimacy at work, and had since drawn back into himself and his high-achiever persona. 'I thought the gym would be a good environment to practise building a contact network.'

Monica nodded. 'Good habit to get into.'

'Yes, well, I remembered talking to the manager of the Royal Hotel. DC Crawford and me met him once at the gym.'

Monica nodded again, intrigued now – the hotel was the one where Pauline Tosh had worked as a kitchen porter.

'It occurred to me that in the nineties it would have been one of the more prestigious places to be seen in Inverness. Before the city embraced mass tourism I believe there were only a handful of equivalent bars and restaurants?'

'That's right,' Monica said, wishing the long-winded Fisher would get to the point.

'I thought if Buggsy MacIvor were in the vicinity of Inverness at the time, there was a chance—'

'He might have met Pauline Tosh there?'

Fisher was struggling to keep the smile off his face. Proof that MacIvor and Tosh had known each other would open up the possibility that this was how Tosh had known the location of Freya Sutherland's body.

'And?'

'I spoke to the manager. He said they used to have pictures of the staff with any celebrities that came in, but they took them all down ten years ago because the new owners thought it was tacky.'

'But you found something anyway?' There was no way Fisher would be looking so pleased with himself if not.

'One of the old chefs. Worked at the hotel for twenty years – Peter William. Retired when the new management came in. I got his contact details.' Fisher had puffed his chest out, and weirdly his tone was very similar to Crawford's as he told the story. 'Tracked him down. Lives up near Dingwall now. He took all the old prints when they were going to chuck them.'

'What did you get?'

Fisher laid his briefcase on the desk and clicked it open. Inside was a picture, still in its frame. It showed a youthful Buggsy MacIvor, behind a bar as if serving. He was wearing a red and orange Hawaiian shirt and a Glengarry hat. On one side of him there was a blonde barmaid smiling brightly; on the other, wearing an awkward half-smile, was a familiar face. Dark eyes staring into the camera.

Khan whistled. 'Ben Fisher nailing it!'

Fisher flushed, and tried to cover up his pleasure by clearing his throat and deepening his voice. 'Does this give us what we need? For a warrant?'

Monica thought about it for a second. The photo clearly put MacIvor and Tosh together. 'MacIvor probably had his photo taken with a thousand people in Inverness in the nineties,' she said, imagining out loud what Hately would say if she walked into his office with the picture.

'What, then?' Khan asked. 'Just rock up to Carselang prison and ask Pauline Tosh to tell us all about Buggsy MacIvor?'

Chapter 46

When Monica walked into the interview room in the Carse, Pauline Tosh was already sitting at the table, hands folded in front of her. Instinctively Monica's eyes went to Tosh's wrists, to check she was secured. When she glimpsed the reassuring metal handcuffs Monica allowed her eyes to go up to the killer's face. Her dark hair looked freshly washed, and was brushed into a centre parting. She was wearing her dark blue overalls, a smile playing around her mouth. During the drive to the prison – Khan behind the wheel – and right up until she was in the room with Tosh, Monica had thought the trip would most likely be a waste of time. The chances were it still would be, but at least Tosh had agreed to see her.

Monica smiled, nodded at the two white takeaway coffee cups she was holding. 'Do you mind if I sit down, Pauline?'

Tosh's eyes went to the cups, transfixed. 'One of them for me, is it? The wee guard told me you'd brought me one.' Tosh had been imprisoned for over a decade; Monica had thought a take-away coffee might intrigue her.

'I brought them from Inverness, a place just off the High Street.'

'On the High Street, is it? Right enough. Wait until the girls hear about this.'

'It was cold by the time I got here, but the screw heated them in the microwave for us.'

Monica sat and slid one of the cups across the table, cardboard scraping wood. Tosh regarded it suspiciously. 'You push the plastic bit on the lid down, and then you can drink it through the hole.' Monica demonstrated with her own cup. Awkwardly, with hands cuffed to the table, Tosh did the same. 'Careful, it might be hot.'

In truth, Tyler Mitchell had been conservative when heating the coffee, mindful Tosh had previously scarred an inmate for life in an attack with boiling water mixed with sugar. Tosh took a cautious sip and tilted the cup to look at it, the chain on her wrist pulling tight.

'Got the name of the place on it and everything, so it does. That's what they do now, is it? Used to be that polystyrene cups you'd get your coffee in. Not nice like this though.' Tosh slurped at the drink, blew her cheeks out. 'Getting treated today, so I am.'

Monica felt the folded-up piece of paper in her pocket: the printed picture of Tosh with Buggsy MacIvor. 'That was a rare trick you played on us, Pauline,' Monica said, feigning nonchalance. 'Had us running round thinking you'd murdered that woman in 1994. Turns out you were on the other side of the world.' She watched Tosh stiffen. 'Lucky for me you gave me that clue. Sailing the seven seas on the *Road to Mandalay*. Never would have thought to check on the boats if you hadn't said that.' Monica forced a laugh, and Tosh gave an odd half-smile. Then sucked at the cup, dark eyes fixed on Monica's face.

'I wasn't sure if you'd get it. That's why I said about a sailor teaching me. Like a clue.'

'It took me a while, but I worked it out in the end.'

'I like the puzzles – crosswords in the paper.'

'I'll bring you a book of them next time I'm in.'

Tosh said, 'Aye, right enough,' her face screwing up. Monica realised she had said the wrong thing: assumed there would be a next time. She quickly changed tack. 'What do you think of the coffee?'

Tosh tilted her head to look at the cup again. 'Must cost a bomb this, does it, Monica? Special cup and everything.'

'Well, you've found me out,' Monica replied. 'Truth is I wanted to get on your good side.'

'Is that right, is it?'

'I need a favour, Pauline,' Monica said, looking directly into the killer's eyes for the first time. They were cold and dark like a midnight grave. 'Could you tell me who murdered that Freya Sutherland?'

Tosh stared back and for a second Monica thought she might actually give her a name. Instead she puffed out her cheeks. 'I'd never know about all that. Me stuck in here.'

Monica took the printed image of Tosh and MacIvor from her pocket, put it down on the table. 'You remember him – Buggsy MacIvor? He knew you back when you worked at the Royal?'

Without looking at the print Tosh said, 'Did he, aye?'

'Was it him who told you where the woman was buried?'

Tosh's eyes roamed over the peeling green walls, then she whispered, 'I heard stories about that Buggsy MacIvor.'

'What kind of stories?'

'That he liked his wee games.'

Monica felt a cold chill run up her spine. 'What kind of games?'

'I wouldn't know about anything like that,' Tosh said, face screwed up in disgust. 'Turns my stomach.'

'Who told you?'

Tosh said, 'I'm not one for gossip, all the details. I just hear whispers . . .'

'Give me something.'

'I hear other whispers.' A malignant smile crept to the corner of her mouth. 'These walls keep secrets.'

'What secrets?'

'About you. About your girl.' Monica felt the blood drain from her face, her eyes lose focus. 'Stories about who her daddy is. Stories that you tried to get rid of her back a couple years ago because of it. That true, is it?'

Rage turned Monica's blood hot. She wanted to take Tosh's head in both her hands and ram it onto the table. She blinked. Tosh was staring at her, genuinely curious. Jessica Sutherland's distraught face came into her mind; those decades of not knowing. That was why Monica was here, after all. She sensed what Tosh wanted with her question: to indulge the fantasy that the two of them were similar.

Finally Monica whispered, 'You never know, Pauline. Who's to say what the monsters inside us really want?'

'Just like two peas in a pod, us pair.' Tosh smiled widely, showing her small yellow teeth, and for an instant Monica was staring at a demon. 'Down by Loch Ness, so I heard. A big old house, so I heard. Liked to record it all, loft all set up for his games.'

Chapter 47

Monica hurried down the corridors and through the locked doors. Out into the yard. She wanted to put as much distance between herself and Tosh as possible.

'Mrs Kennedy! Erm, officer!'

While she'd been inside it had started snowing – winter coming early in the mountains. Flakes caught in the wind blew in tight swirls, landing as specks of white on the cobbles before melting to black.

'I mean, ma'am!' She turned at the voice, and saw Tyler Mitchell jogging after her across the courtyard.

Monica patted herself down, assuming she'd forgotten something in her rush to sign herself out. The young prison officer didn't appear to be holding anything though.

When he drew near he said, 'I did what you asked,' his breath coming out in clouds. He was wearing his North Face parka, hood up against the snow. Monica hunched her shoulders and turned her own collar up, but the wind cut through the threadbare material. After all these years it might really be time for a change of coat.

It took her a moment to recall that she'd asked Tyler to investigate the source of the leak to the press. At the time she had assumed he would forget the request as soon as she was gone.

'What did you hear?' Monica felt a knot in her stomach. If Tyler had identified the source of the leak in the prison, it would put Crawford in the clear.

He glanced around at the walls and windows overlooking the courtyard, as if the prison itself was listening. 'Strange here,' he said, 'the way gossip spreads. I never used to listen to it. Kept myself to myself and did my work, wasn't interested in it all.'

'But you've been listening now?'

'Doesn't feel good, hearing all these things.' Tyler sounded genuinely upset.

'What like?'

'One of the boys who retired a few years ago, he'd sometimes pay the female inmates to sleep with him. It's not right. They say that they used to make the inmates fight each other, sort of as a punishment.'

Monica swallowed the unwelcome associations with her father's time working at the prison. The case that had led to their estrangement. *Jesus, this is turning out to be a shit day.* She felt the wind blasting icy shards of snow at her face. And with it, guilt that she had caused the naive Tyler to be exposed to the darker aspects of human behaviour. Finally she replied, 'People are complicated, Tyler. It doesn't mean they're all bad.'

'You get criminals, and I understand that they're the bad guys – they need locking away – but some of the things . . . It's not right.'

'What are you talking about, exactly?'

'One of the other officers was talking about how he'd won thousands in a game of cards last Christmas. The guy he won it from was addicted to gambling. Had to sell his car to pay what he owed. He seemed pleased about it. Another one said he'd fed his alcoholic neighbour a trifle with sherry in it, got him drinking again. Thought it was funny.'

'We all have a shadow side. We're all capable of doing unpleasant things.' He nodded, but his wide eyes told Monica he hadn't taken any of what she'd said on board. 'Did you find anything out about the leak to the press?'

Tyler shook his head quickly. 'Nothing. None of them seem to trust the press.' Monica's heart sank. 'They said there had been stories published about the Carse in the past, blaming the staff for its problems. I don't think any of them would have leaked to the press.'

Outside, DC Khan was leaning against the Honda in the lee of the wind. Smoking a cigarette with her black baseball cap pulled down low and her fur coat wrapped tight. Strands of black hair flicking out around her face.

'Tosh wouldn't see you?' Khan asked as Monica arrived at the car, peering at her downcast expression.

'She saw me,' Monica replied, feeling close to zero excitement after Tyler's depressing news. 'We'll get our warrant for MacIvor's place. Now let's get the hell out of here.'

Chapter 48

Freya stepped out from the gloomy arcade into the evening sun-light. Heat was rising off the tarmac, the sky a perfect azure. She knew she should have been elated to be spending another even-ing with her friends, but somehow things didn't feel right. She stared back down Castle Street towards the centre of Inverness. No sign of the black Rolls-Royce yet. As she adjusted the strap of her shoulder bag where it was digging into her neck, Freya couldn't help thinking of a fairy tale Mum used to read to her and Jessica, 'Hansel and Gretel' – the house in the forest made out of gingerbread, and the old woman who lived there. Somehow it felt like that with Buggsy MacIvor. Why was he so generous towards them? Inviting them out to his huge house, giving them gifts, free food, free drink? It didn't seem to bother any of the others, who seemed content to accept it as natural generosity from a friend.

Freya sighed and lit one of her Gauloises Blondes. The smoke was ghostly blue in the summer light, as if an apparition might take shape from it. She remembered how strange it had felt at his huge old house on the banks of Loch Ness. Like you should be paying an entrance fee to visit. Seeing Buggsy for the first time, there on the wide stone porch, he'd been much bigger and broader than she'd expected. With shoulders like a bull. He was dressed in Levi's jeans, a blue Teddy Smith sweatshirt and tan

Timberland boots. More like someone who would hang around at Bobby's Ark feeding pound coins into a fruit machine than the man she'd watched for years on TV. She remembered his way of talking: never quite looking you in the eyes, always at an angle. He hadn't exactly been funny either – had seemed more agitated than anything. Moving continually around the huge living room, and when he did speak he was abrupt: 'Another fucking drink then.' Or, 'You want to smoke, get your arse outside, Brodie.'

Freya had assumed Buggsy didn't like her, but the following day Brodie, Miranda and Joseph had picked her up from the farm. They'd driven into Inverness and sat on the Ness Islands – a scenic group of isles in the River Ness – eating ice creams and sharing a bottle of Mad Dog 20/20 kiwi flavour.

'You've got a fan anyway,' Miranda said, laughing. She was wearing dark glasses under her sun hat, making it difficult for Freya to read her expression.

Freya glanced at Brodie. Since the night the week before when he'd come to speak to her outside the farm, they hadn't been alone together. She still didn't exactly know what the others had been doing during the days they'd disappeared. Brodie had mentioned that Miranda was upset in some way, but never expanded on it. And Freya didn't want to pry. Miranda was always kind and charming to her, but she sensed part of her was off-limits. Freya knew that feeling – knew she wouldn't want anyone asking her about the difficulties with her mum, or how things had been with her dad since his accident.

Brodie was wearing dark glasses too, his long legs stretched out in front of him in dark jeans. 'Yip.' He took a mouthful of the Mad Dog. 'You definitely turned Buggsy's head. Said he liked your style.'

Freya dropped her eyes to the grass they were sitting on. Bizarrely pleased at the affirmation, even though she hadn't felt drawn to the comedian. 'I didn't think he liked me; he hardly looked at me.'

'That's just Buggsy's way,' Miranda said. 'Took him months to speak to me.' Unexpectedly she reached into her shoulder bag and picked something out. 'He wanted you to have this – was too nervous to give it to you in person. He's kind of a shy boy. A big teddy bear underneath it all.'

Miranda handed a small box to Freya and she opened it. Inside there was a coffin-shaped locket. She held it up uncertainly, and Brodie began to laugh. 'Classic Buggsy. Nothing signifies friendship like a coffin.'

Freya felt herself blushing; thankfully Joseph then laid an open magazine on the grass between them. They all turned to look at it and she slipped the box into her pocket.

Joseph said, 'Berlin's the city to go to.'

'Why Berlin?' Miranda asked, smiling indulgently at Joseph. And suddenly they were talking about what Brodie had asked her. About leaving Inverness and going to live somewhere else together.

'It says here it's at the forefront of house music, art. They've got this thing called the Love Parade, a free party right in the middle of the city. It's supposed to be cheap to live there too. There are loads of squats, and even if you rent a flat properly it's really cheap.'

'We still need money though,' Miranda said. 'To get there and everything.'

'Buggsy will give it to us,' Brodie replied.

'Why would he just give us money?' Freya had asked.

*

Outside the arcade, Freya became aware a car was pulling to a stop beside her. The almost-ghostly black Rolls-Royce. She hesitated for a moment. The memory of Hansel and Gretel and the gingerbread house; the lesson of things coming too easily. It occurred to her that she hadn't mentioned anything about Buggsy MacIvor to her parents, even though they were huge fans. They would have been beyond excited to hear about him. Why hadn't she told them? Because they would be worried? Because they wouldn't approve?

The window slid down. Brodie was staring out at her, a sardonic expression on his face. He smiled and she got into the car.

Chapter 49

It was 6 p.m. by the time Khan dropped Monica home after their trip to the Carse. Lucy was at her mum's house, so Monica put in a call to headquarters, spun a quick story and got the address she needed. The house was a detached new-build in the Tornagrain area, to the east of Inverness. Two cars outside most of the houses, neat lawns. A new suburban zone that felt close to the fantasy of middle America.

It was twilight when she pulled up outside 15 Firthview Street. The lights were on inside and she could see a family through the kitchen window. An attractive woman with long brown hair stirring a pot; a kid with its back to Monica at the kitchen table. She fished out her phone, found PC Duncan Gregg's number and dialled. The first time it rang out, so she dialled it straight back. Finally a flustered-sounding Gregg came on the line. 'What you calling me for? I thought I told you only to text.'

'Because I need to speak to you,' Monica replied, not about to argue that he hadn't.

'It's not a good time. I'm with my family, we're just about to eat.'

'I know, I'm watching you.'

Gregg swore under his breath and hung up. Through the window Monica watched as he appeared in the kitchen from the back of the house and peered out at the Volvo. He said something to his wife, who put her hands on her hips and tilted

244

her head. Body language that said, *What, really?* She shook her head in irritation, and Gregg came bustling out the side door of the house wearing blue Crocs, jeans and a white polo shirt. He came down the driveway and got into the passenger side of the car, bringing a strong floral smell of fabric conditioner in with him.

'What you doing, turning up here?'

'Same thing you did to me the other night – dropping a bunch of shit on your head.'

'Wait – what?'

'What you said about Crawford. Dropping that on me and then taking off without explanation.'

Gregg sighed, hung his head. 'Wife doesn't like me having a phone. Forgot to switch it off.'

'Why doesn't she want you to have a phone?' An alarm bell went off in Monica's head. Denying a partner a phone was often an indicator of coercive control. Though, given what she knew of Duncan Gregg, the idea seemed absurd.

He shook his head sadly. 'I've had a few problems with gambling. Got into debt. Wife's old man had to dig us out or we were losing the house – never lets me forget it. Thinks I'll be on the phone to the bookies, back gambling . . .'

'I won't keep you long,' Monica said. 'I just need you to tell me what you heard about Crawford.'

Gregg shifted uncomfortably in his seat, looked out into the wing mirror. 'This just between us?'

'I'll keep you out of it.'

'Thought I was doing you a favour telling you.'

'You might be able to work with people you don't trust. I can't.'

'I heard rumours about your boy.'

245

'What kind of rumours?'

'That debt I owed?' Gregg said. 'It was to Francis MacGregor.' It was Monica's turn to shake her head. MacGregor was rumoured to have ties to the underworld across Scotland. Gregg continued: 'I've got a friend close to MacGregor, keeps me posted on what he's up to. Said he saw your boy meeting with him.'

'Crawford was meeting with MacGregor?' It made absolutely no sense. Crawford hated MacGregor, had pointed a shotgun at him. And did this meeting with MacGregor relate to the case leaking to the press? What was Monica missing? 'When was this?'

'A few days ago.'

'You're sure it was him?'

'My contact's got no reason to lie. Said they were talking for an hour. MacGregor was putting a proposal to him, my contact said.'

'Who's your contact? I need to speak to them.'

'I shouldn't even be telling you this much.' Duncan Gregg actually sounded frightened. 'MacGregor finds out someone close to him's passing on information, they're dead.'

Monica thought about how oddly Crawford had been acting recently. The fact he'd tried to speak to her that night at the flat. She really had let her personal feelings mess up her work. If she'd been more disciplined, maybe she could have stopped this from happening. 'What did you hear?'

Gregg glanced at the mirror again, then reached for the handle to go. Monica snaked an arm out to grab the door handle herself, trapping him. 'Fuck's sake!'

'Why were they meeting?'

'I don't know. Business, they said.'

None of it made sense: why Crawford would meet with

MacGregor without telling her; why Gregg would volunteer the information to her, at risk to himself. Monica leaned forward to get a proper look at his face. She stared into his eyes, hoping to see some spite or trickery that would indicate he was lying. If anything, there was sadness in them.

'Hurts when it's someone close to you, eh? Aye, it's a cold harbour, this kind of work – cold comfort at the end of the day, not being able to trust your colleagues. Been there myself.'

Monica looked away through the windscreen to the pools of yellow from the street lamp on the cul-de-sac's dark tarmac. For a horrible second she thought she was going to tear up. She turned away, towards Gregg's house. His wife was now looking out through the kitchen window at them.

'I'd better go.' Monica realised that she was still gripping the door handle, her arm over Gregg's stomach to box him in. She caught the smell of his bad breath mixed with deodorant. Lynx Africa, favoured by an old boyfriend of hers.

'Why did you tell me?'

Gregg sighed, looking past Monica towards his wife. 'I heard about all that last year – what happened with your daughter. Didn't like the thought of anything happening to you. Not after everything she's been through.'

These days Monica was usually able to compartmentalise the stress of work. But the anticipation of an early start for the raid on Buggsy MacIvor's house the following morning, mixed with everything about Crawford, meant she barely slept that night. When she did drift off, images from the case flitted between dream and consciousness. Ancient coffins and dead cats merged with versions of her teenage self. She and Crawford were the same age, travelling through a grey land to start university somewhere. The dream had a sexual undertone, as if they were inevitably going to sleep together at some point, and she woke in a state of agitated arousal. It was a long time since she'd felt so confused, a long time since the boundary between her work and personal life had felt so weak.

Chapter 50

The first big storm of the autumn arrived the next morning. As dawn broke, thick banks of sleet were railing off the North Atlantic onto the west coast of the Highlands, and driving northeast up the Great Glen. Turning Loch Ness into a mess of whitecaps.

The fleet of marked police vehicles headed along the B852 on the southern side of Loch Ness, towards Balnakine House. It had been built by an aristocratic playboy in the 1920s. A fire that led to his death gutted the place in the 1950s, leaving it derelict until it was renovated twenty years later. It had been bought by Buggsy MacIvor in the early 1990s.

'No Crawford again?' This time there was a hint of concern in DC Khan's voice.

Monica was pleased to be steering the Volvo, eyes fixed firmly on the road as the windscreen wipers battled to keep pace with the driving rain. They both knew Crawford would never have missed the excitement of a raid like this unless something was seriously wrong.

Monica shook her head. 'Must still be sick.' She hadn't yet decided what to do with Duncan Gregg's unwelcome revelation. The by-the-book side of her wanted to go straight to Detective Superintendent Hately and get Professional Standards involved; have Crawford summoned for a formal interview. That had been her intention when she'd walked into headquarters early that morning. For some reason she'd hesitated. Could she really shrug off the ties to her closest colleague so easily?

'Maybe I'll try calling him later?' Khan offered finally, when she realised Monica wasn't about to add anything.

Up ahead, the B852 turned away inland to the left. The lead cars in the column slowed for a right-hand turn into a driveway guarded by high wrought-iron gates. Monica watched through the rain as an officer got out of a car, the wind catching the vehicle's door, then ran over and hit the buzzer of an intercom. After almost five minutes of waiting, during which a queue of cars had built up on the road behind the Volvo at the back of the convoy, the gates finally swung inward.

Built to resemble a traditional Highland castle, Balnakine House was a large structure at the end of a tree-lined driveway, almost overhanging the loch on one side. As Monica got out of her car, water whipped up into foam by the storm was being blown onto the steps at the front of the house. The officers at the head of the convoy had already served the warrant and were making their way up the steps and inside.

A man was standing at the top of the sandstone steps. Partially sheltered from the storm by the stone porch. Monica climbed towards him. He was a big man, taller than her, with shoulders like a bull and thick forearms to match. Buggsy MacIvor still had a thick ginger beard, and a large gut. Monica found herself hesitating as she approached him. She realised she would have liked Crawford there beside her – had come to rely on him as a presence she could trust. Great joke. Still, at least she had Khan with her.

'Mr MacIvor?' He turned at the sound of her voice. He was wearing Adidas tracksuit bottoms and a white vest with a grubby purple dressing gown pulled on over it. Monica realised that she had subconsciously expected him to be in his usual kilt, black jacket and red tartan sash, as she'd so often seen him dressed on TV. His face was puffy red, but there was a sharpness in his eyes. Behind him, sitting close to the wall, back from the rain, were a man and a woman on a bench. Watching the action as the police officers entered the house, with expressions somewhere between excitement and concern.

MacIvor turned away, speaking to Monica almost from over his shoulder. 'Buggsy's not in the mood for talking. The fuck is this?'

He had a kind of animal quality, Monica thought as she reached the top of the steps. A feral hunted look – more dangerous because of it.

'Why do you think we're here?'

Buggsy MacIvor grunted and walked away, shaking his head. Monica had seen the same little-boy-lost body language in numerous violent men over the years: the two-hundred-pound man who had just beaten his wife bloody, wandering around like a frightened two-year-old.

'Buggsy's not in the mood to speak,' the woman piped up from the bench. 'You won't get anything out of him now. Better to leave him alone or he'll kick off.'

MacIvor had walked to the far end of the porch and was now staring into the distance. His purple dressing gown flapped behind his bulk in the breeze. It was a strangely disturbing image.

Monica turned to the woman. 'I'm sorry, what's your name?'

'We're the caretakers,' the man said, cutting in. 'I'm Mike Brundell; this is my girlfriend, Mairi Ross. We look after the place for him. So he doesn't have to think about it.' Monica took the couple in. Both appeared to be in their forties; both wearing green raincoats, shirts and baggy blue jeans. Monica got an impression of them having washed up at the house dressed in Britpop's finest fashion in the 1990s, and never changing their style or leaving since.

'How long have you worked for Mr MacIvor?'

Mairi glanced at Mike, who looked to check that Buggsy was out of earshot before answering. 'Since 2003. We've been friends with Buggsy for years. A lot turned their backs on him after all the lies—'

Mairi couldn't contain herself. 'We saved his life,' she said proudly. 'That's what he always says. If it wasn't for us he'd be dead now.'

Monica was unmoved by Mairi's story of redemption as she found her eyes drawn again to Buggsy's wide back. The rain was blowing directly over him, soaking his dressing gown dark. 'Were you ever here in the mid-1990s?'

'Maybe. I can't hardly remember the nineties now . . .' Mairi emitted a strange little chuckle that turned into a defensive laugh.

'I first met Bugs in '99,' Mike said. 'Introduced Mairi to him a year later. I was having a rough time myself and he took me in. Youse are wasting your time in here, by the way.' His voice was rising and his face went tight. 'Whatever you've heard about him isn't true. We've only been with him every day for the last ten years! We'd know!'

Monica looked down at Mike. Wondered for a moment about the need some people had to be a sidekick, to be a prop to a larger personality, then turned and nodded to the two uniformed officers who had come up the steps behind her to make sure MacIvor didn't go anywhere.

Monica paused at the front door. Music was pumping through

the house. It took her a moment to recognise the singer as Hamish Imlach. She had one of his records in her dad's old collection; Crawford had put it on when he had come round *that* night. He was singing 'The Reprobate's Lament'. Strangely creepy comedic lyrics about an overweight and heavy-drinking man. Monica felt eyes on her, turned and realised Buggsy MacIvor was watching her from the end of the porch. He was moving his hips and thick body in a snake-like dance, eyes fixed on her face. He ran a hand down his chest, pausing for a moment at his nipples, then over his stomach to the waistband of his tracksuit bottoms, pushing his hand down the front as if to fondle himself. Staring hard at Monica all the while, he licked his lips and blew her a kiss, then produced a phone from his pants. He jabbed at it, and the music coming from the house switched to 'Celebration' by Kool & the Gang. MacIvor did a spin so he was facing away, then dropped the dressing gown off his shoulders in a parody of a provocative gesture, looking back with mock-sultry eyes at Monica.

She stared at him then stepped into the house. One of the officers must have found the power for the stereo because after a moment the music cut out. Replaced by the howling wind from outside and voices as the officers began the slow job of searching the house. Back at headquarters Monica had briefed the team on what to look out for. Any objects that might have belonged to a young woman in 1994 – but especially Freya's sketchbook, which Jessica was certain had been with her when she left her home for the last time. It was the type of keepsake a misogynistic killer would find difficult to dispose of, carrying so much of a victim's character and identity in it. Though items belonging to Freya wouldn't be enough on their own and could be explained away by any competent defence lawyer, so Monica was even more interested in solid evidence that put Freya in the house.

She raised her voice. 'Remember, any scrap of industrial carpet that could possibly match the fibres we recovered from Freya's body. We want photographs and samples. Any old VHS tapes, any cassettes, we're examining them.' Unnecessary prompting, as she had already emphasised their importance in her briefing, but it wouldn't hurt to remind the officers, who paused for a moment to listen before continuing the search.

Monica walked around the ground floor of the house. It was a mess. Judging by the assorted empty beer and spirit bottles, caretakers Mike Brundell and Mairi Ross spent more time drinking with Buggsy MacIvor than keeping on top of the cleaning. The main lounge was decorated with pictures from MacIvor's illustrious early career. On stage as an *enfant terrible* in full Bonnie Prince Charlie outfit, winning the Perrier Comedy Award at the Edinburgh Festival Fringe in the early 1980s; then a little older, in *Better In Than Out*, the sitcom role that had made him famous. A clutch of awards from his heyday, dusty now in a cabinet. Slowly Monica's eyes adjusted to the poor light. She realised that there were virtually no antiques. Surprising, given that Caulfeild had emphasised what an enthusiastic collector MacIvor was.

'Boss.' Monica turned at the sound of DC Khan's lowered voice. She had come down from directing the search of the upper floors. Today the younger detective was wearing a suit with a battered orange and red Marmot jacket over it. Droplets of rain still sat in her dark hair; some of them coalesced into a larger drop and ran down her forehead towards her ear. She didn't seem to feel it – evidently she was agitated about something. 'There's something you should see, upstairs.'

Chapter 51

Monica followed DC Khan up the wide stairs, rain drumming on the glass skylight above the stairwell. The sound of rain was something Monica normally loved – but not today, as she contemplated what might have happened to Freya Sutherland in this house. Lured here by friends? Dazzled by the glamour of celebrity? Had things got out of hand? Or had killing Freya been the point all along?

There was a pool of water on the first-floor landing; evidently the skylight was leaking. Perhaps it helped to account for the smell that Monica was now aware of, drifting through the upper floors of the house. Mildew, rot, corruption; pungent but subtle. They carried on upstairs.

Khan led Monica into a room lit by wall-mounted electric lights, with narrow windows facing north out over Loch Ness. There was no one in the room, which was taken up by a billiard table. 'Over there.'

Monica's eyes followed Khan's outstretched hand. On the opposite wall was a large painting, reaching almost to the floor, of a crouched Minotaur. Monica walked over. She had been obsessed with the Greek myths when she was at school and should have found the painting enthralling, but as she approached, her body experienced a visceral reaction. Her shoulders tensed and her stomach tightened. Almost like a predator were present there in the room with her. Monica could now see that there was something unpleasant about the way the monster was observed. As if the painter had purposely made the creature's limbs subtly unbalanced and lacking in grace. When Monica peered closer, she saw with horror that the paint had been mixed with what looked like strands of human hair, and in places fingernail clippings. For a moment she wondered if the picture had something directly to do with the murder of Freya Sutherland, but the frame was aged, the paint faded. Monica leaned in and saw a date of 1879 on the frame.

'The painting's on a hinge,' Khan said from beside Monica. 'It's not exactly hidden – there's a handle.' With a gloved hand, Khan reached out to a small metal handle fixed to the frame. The painting swung away from the wall to reveal a door made from plain plywood. It was closed by two padlocks.

'Tosh was telling the truth,' Monica whispered. 'Can you get someone in here now to open this up?'

As Monica was waiting she took a longer look around the room. There were various things mounted on the walls. Small oil paintings, often with a mythological theme, but other things too. Using her phone torch, Monica began to inspect them. There was a horrible bronze sculpture by one window – a stork with an arrow through its chest. Beside it, a roughly carved wooden mask, old and sticky with dust, the dark eyeholes covered in wire. Then a small glass case. Monica peered in; behind the glass there were two dried-out objects. A strip of paper lay beside them with words printed in faded letters: FINGER & JAWBONE OF BILLY JAMES, MURDEROUS HIGHWAYMAN.

Involuntarily Monica stepped back from the case. The smell of corruption that drifted throughout the mansion seemed strongest in here. Almost as if she was now standing close to the core of the house's unpleasantness. She remembered what the antique dealer had said about the dark character of some objects. In that moment she understood and suddenly really didn't want to be in that room alone. Monica took a deep breath of the fetid air and tried hard to suppress the illogical feeling. She forced herself to have another look around. The floor was varnished wood, no chance of a link to the carpet fibres recovered from Freya's body. Whatever had happened to Freya, their best bet seemed to be to follow Pauline Tosh's advice up into the attic.

'They're just coming with the tools.' Monica jumped at the sound of DC Khan's voice from the open door. 'Sorry I took so long. DC Fisher got me on the phone. You know what he's like.'

Monica nodded, then started over to where DC Khan was standing. Pleased to have an excuse to head towards the door.

'What did Fisher have to say?' He had remained at headquarters to continue with the ample office-based work the two cases of Freya Sutherland and the fire-setter had generated.

'He's finally got that list through. The people who had a key for the quarry, close to the church that was burned?'

It seemed like an age since Monica and Crawford had spoken to young Adam Dabrowski and his mum Sofia. In reality it had only been a week. 'Anything that stands out?'

'Not straight away, but he spoke to the owners of the house that was burned, Cotton Lodge Barn. They've had a lot of work done on the place in the past few years; he's getting a list of the contractors to see if there's any crossover.' Khan then dropped her eyes to her feet – she was wearing heavy black military-style boots. 'He also said that DC Crawford called in, left another message. Says he's still sick.'

What was Crawford playing at? Monica opened her mouth to say something, but two officers came bustling up the stairs, one carrying a crowbar, the other bolt cutters. She insisted that all four of them pause to don Tyvek suits before entering this inner sanctum. If there was any chance of recovering forensic evidence to prove what had happened to Freya, Monica was convinced it would be in here.

Monica led them back across the billiard room. Pulled the painting of the Minotaur to the side and motioned for the officer with the bolt cutters to open the door.

Chapter 52

It took just moments for the officer to cut through the steel of the padlocks. Then he drew back the bolts and pulled the door open. On the inside it was padded with some sort of vinyl material, possibly soundproofing. The smell hit Monica, and she had to put a hand to her mouth to stop herself from gagging. Damp, mildew – the atmosphere of the house distilled further. The door opened on to a narrow staircase, padded with foam on both sides.

Monica took the torch offered by the second officer and started up the unlit stairs. At the top was another door, of old unpainted pine. It had no lock or keyhole, just a round handle. Monica took a breath, wondering for a moment what horrors she might find behind it, then pushed it open. There were no windows or skylights. Monica swung the torchlight around in the gloom. Low on one side, where the slope of the roof met the floor, the space ran the entire length of the house and appeared completely empty. She shone the beam on the floor: plywood sheets. No sign of any industrial carpet. Monica swore under her breath, stepped further into the loft. The source of the stink became apparent when she saw the patch of damp on the stone wall to her right. What appeared to be orange fungus was growing from it. She leaned closer and poked the wall, which was so damp that her finger actually went into the stone – more like wet sand now.

'What the hell's that?!' DC Khan had ventured further down the long narrow attic. She had stopped and was staring at something. Monica followed the light of her torch. There was an object in the corner, at the end of the space. It seemed to be hanging from the rafters.

The officer who had chopped the bolts was standing beside Khan. He muttered, 'Previous owner killed himself, didn't he? Went bankrupt and hanged himself.'

Monica hadn't heard this story until now. She walked past her colleagues towards the thing. A black shape in the light from her torch. The shape of a body, she realised, suspended from a rope.

'Is that a person?' Khan's alarmed voice sounded hollow in the enclosed space.

Monica forced herself to continue over the creaking floor. Finally she reached a hand out to the hanging object. It felt soft to the touch. She stepped up close.

The thing was three-quarters life-sized. Noose around its neck, hanging from the rafters. Coated in a thick layer of dust as if it hadn't been moved in years. A grotesque doll dressed in a Bonnie Prince Charlie outfit, with a ginger wig and a beard painted onto its white china skin. An effigy of Buggsy MacIvor left hanging in his own emptied den.

The search of Balnakine House didn't conclude until almost 9 p.m., but after she had seen the doll hanging there in the otherwise empty attic, Monica knew they weren't going to find anything linked to Freya in the house. If what Tosh had said about the attic once being used for MacIvor's 'games' was true, it had obviously been thoroughly cleared out years before.

The search returned nothing but a handful of bank statements and receipts from the mid-1990s. Monica ordered them checked for a potential confirmation of the purchase of the necklace given to Freya. If their flimsy case ever did make it to court, such details might be important. But there had been no VHS tapes, no cassettes, not even a single computer in the house.

When Monica followed the last of the officers back outside, it had finally stopped raining. The moon had risen and its reflection was floating in the water of Loch Ness. On any normal day she would have loved the opportunity to stand on the porch, taking in the iconic view. The ruins of Urquhart Castle were just visible in the moonlight on the loch's northern shore. Tonight the panorama was tinged with horror as she contemplated the memory of the doll hanging in the attic, and wondered what might have been done in there. Buggsy MacIvor seemed to fit as Freya's killer – probably Sally MacFarlane's too. And it looked like he was going to get away with it.

'Come on, boys and girls, you know you want to! It's on your uncle Buggsy!'

Monica turned at the comedian's voice. He was still wearing his tracksuit bottoms and purple dressing gown, but had apparently undergone a character transformation. Judging by the pile of boxes on the porch he had ordered in a mountain of takeaway, and he was attempting to hand slices of pizza and bottles of Heineken to the departing police officers. Monica walked over. He held out a bottle of beer to her.

'Not tonight, Buggsy, I'm working.' She watched his face, illuminated by the overhead light. Despite his hearty voice he seemed furtive now, avoiding eye contact. Monica caught a smell off him too, as if his clothes had taken on the sourness of the house.

'Right enough,' he grunted. 'Just doing your job, I suppose. Nothing personal.'

Monica said, 'I saw your doll, up in the roof. Did you leave part of yourself up there?'

This time Buggsy MacIvor met Monica's eye, and stared at her for a second. She sensed he actually might want to tell her something.

'Come on, Bugs.' Mike Brundell nudged at his elbow. 'Let's get inside. Getting cold out here.'

The interruption seemed to snap Buggsy MacIvor out of whatever thought he had gone into, because his expression shifted to a scowl. He glared hard at Monica for a second, then shouted, 'Help yourself to pizza and beer, then fuck off out of my house! Tell those paparazzi bastards they can fuck off too!'

As Monica and Khan drove out of the gates, the press were camped out on either side. Monica ignored them, hit the indicator and turned left back towards Inverness. Not even ready to think about what kind of reaction all of the media attention was going to generate. DC Khan had done a good job handling the press queries during the day, but famous comedian Buggsy MacIvor and a murdered young woman was a huge story. Add serial killer Pauline Tosh and politician Miranda Salisbury, and it became the kind of frenzy that no one could control.

Chapter 53

By the time she'd dropped Khan back by her Honda Civic at headquarters, it was well past Lucy's bedtime. Monica decided there was no point in rushing round to her mum's to try to see her. Instead she found herself back on Huntly Street beside the River Ness. The street was quiet, the stone pavement still dark from all the rain, and it carried something of the emptiness of that space high in Balnakine House. If Freya had been killed up there it was long hidden, long forgotten. Any proof was going to be hard-won. If MacIvor had kept video evidence of the murder, then where was it? His only property was Balnakine House and it had been thoroughly searched, along with its outbuildings. Could an accomplice have stored evidence for him? Or could it be hidden in a deposit box somewhere? If the evidence hadn't been destroyed, the chances of finding it now were minimal. MacIvor had cleared out the loft space long ago; had he left that part of his life behind him?

Monica pulled into a loading bay. The lights were off in Crawford's flat. She wished he was sitting there beside her and they were discussing the case. As she stared up at the darkened windows, she felt a hollowness in her stomach.

'Crawford, you fucking prick.' There was a sadness to her voice, and it took Monica only a moment to realise that under her anger she was desperately worried. Fuck the work side of things; the truth was she'd come to have intense feelings for her partner. An inappropriate mix of fantasy lust and genuine care. She cursed herself again for letting things develop the way they had that night at her flat. She should have followed her mum's advice sooner and hooked up with someone via the internet if she'd wanted a romantic partner.

She got out of the Volvo, crossed the street, and pushed the Service button until finally someone responded and the front door clicked open. Upstairs, she rattled the door to Crawford's flat. Unsurprisingly there was no reply, just the sound of the wind, faint through the thick sandstone walls of the building. She ducked to peer through the letter box, but the interior was too dark.

'Can I help you?'

Monica turned at the voice from behind her, and the woman on the opposite side of the landing shrank back, a look of alarm on her face. Monica couldn't help but imagine seeing herself from the woman's perspective: the ghoul who glowers through your letter box. Pure urban myth. The woman said, 'The police . . .' Seemed to check herself and said, 'You're Monica, aren't you?'

'Did Connor mention me?' Monica took the woman in – brunette, about thirty.

'I don't . . . I don't know . . .' Her alarmed expression suggested she was regretting opening her door in the first place.

'I really need to know where he is.'

The woman nodded slowly, eyes going to the darkened stairs. Monica realised that she seemed genuinely frightened. When she spoke it was a whisper: 'Is this about the debt collectors?'

'What debt collectors?'

'They were here a few days ago, looking for Connor. He usually pops in every couple of weeks for a cup of tea, but I hadn't seen him for a while. I heard something in the corridor, thought it was him, so I came out to say hi.'

'But it was someone else?'

'There were two men.'

'What did they look like?'

'One of them was big, dressed in a long black jacket. The other was older, long greyish hair and a beard. It was strange though – he seemed young. I don't know if that makes sense?'

The description fitted Francis MacGregor. Monica recalled her own encounters with him. He certainly did have an unsettling quality of agelessness. 'What did he say?'

'It was weird . . . He stared at me and for some reason I just stood there. I don't know . . . I wanted to close the door but I couldn't. He walked right up to me.'

'What did he say?'

'He said, "Tell your neighbour it's time to pay the piper." '

And as the woman was speaking it triggered a memory for Monica. The previous spring, when she and her partner had first crossed paths with Francis MacGregor, his last words to Crawford were: *I'll see you again. I'll see you again.*

'When was this?'

'A few nights ago.'

'And you haven't seen Connor since then?'

'No. I texted him to tell him, and he messaged back to say not to worry. But I haven't seen him since.'

Chapter 54

Back at her flat Monica sat drinking camomile tea, staring blankly at the open laptop in front of her. She was aware she should try to do something useful on the Freya Sutherland case, but her mind kept circling back to Crawford. Could he really owe money to Francis MacGregor? It didn't fit with what she knew of her partner. Money had never seemed like a big motivator for him; if it was, why was he in the police? Besides, he was dating one of the wealthiest women in the north of Scotland. Couldn't he have borrowed money from her if he was desperate? Unless the debt wasn't financial? Monica had a number for Francis MacGregor, the one they had used to track him six months before. MacGregor was famously difficult to pin down, and unsurprisingly when she dialled the number it had been cut off. She tried Heather Sinclair's number next – straight to voicemail.

Albert slouched over from the radiator, and spread himself on the sofa like spilled clotted cream. He exposed his belly and Monica ran her fingers through his fur. 'Your diet isn't working, by the way.' The cat purred, paddling his feet in mid-air. It was a moment of simple domestic comfort, and Monica wondered what it meant that she was experiencing it alone instead of with Lucy, her mum, a friend or a lover. Maybe she was the kind of person who would always be alone, in their own world?

It had felt different with Crawford. Like the two parts of her life could finally meet. A stupid fantasy, a mistake – letting him get close. If any other colleague had been missing she would have felt desperate concern, but it would have fitted firmly into the work category; she would have gone straight to Hately. With Crawford it felt more complicated.

She sighed and went to put a record on, her finger landing on an album: *Return of the Wayfaring Stranger* by Burl Ives. She set it spinning on the record player and lowered the needle randomly. Appropriately, Burl was singing a sad farewell to his 'honey'. 'For fuck's sake.' After thirty seconds Monica lifted the needle and sat in silence instead.

What exactly was Crawford running from? Monica knew enough of Francis MacGregor's background to know he was capable of doing serious harm to anyone. He had sworn revenge when Crawford pointed that gun at him. Perhaps he'd waited until now, at the height of a high-profile case, to exact retribution? Forced Crawford to leak stories to the press? But it made no sense. And as she turned to look at the moon out of the window, Monica felt a sickening indecision. What if MacGregor already had Crawford? All of her partner's recent communications had been via phone or text. All relatively impersonal. Out beyond the confines of the city, in those wide moorlands and deep lochs, the possibilities for disposing of a body were limitless. The idea sat like a weight in her stomach. If she called Hately and they instigated a search, would MacGregor kill her partner? If they found Crawford's body they might be able to prove MacGregor was responsible, but it would be cold, cold comfort. Or was her imagination running away with her?

As she turned the situation over in her mind, trying to tease out the best course of action, Monica realised that what PC

Duncan Gregg had told her had turned out to be true. He had been the one to alert her to the connection between Crawford and MacGregor. Suddenly it seemed obvious. She needed to know who had given him the information. She needed to know who had seen Crawford.

Chapter 55

PC Duncan Gregg's phone was switched off when she called him. She sent a text message, telling him that she needed to see him asap. Then she lay on the couch with the phone in her hand, drifting in a half-sleep. In the morning she tried him again. His mobile was still switched off; evidently he was now adhering more closely to Mrs Gregg's wishes. On any other day she would have driven straight to his house first thing, but she was aware the Freya Sutherland case was hanging by a thread. Despite her concern for her colleague, she couldn't let Jessica Sutherland down. No doubt the added drama of Buggsy MacIvor's involvement would be increasing the stress on her and her family. Monica knew that DC Khan had been in touch with them yesterday, but made a mental note to also call them herself.

When she reached the office Fisher was at his desk, hair scuffed up, shirt loose at the collar and sleeves rolled up. Three empty cups arranged neatly by his keyboard. Someone who had been in the office all night and perhaps wanted everyone to know it. Given her own sleepless night of paralysed inaction, she felt genuine gratitude towards her diligent young colleague. For the entire case he had been grinding away at detailed, unglamorous work without complaint.

She sat down beside him. 'What have you got, Fisher?'

'Well, first the bad news.'

Monica nodded. A sinking feeling – another dropper on top of the seemingly endless stream that came with this case.

'The carpet samples we recovered from Freya's body? It turns out the carpet was more widely sold than it had initially seemed.'

Monica swore under her breath. She had been hoping only a handful of people in the Highlands had bought it.

'It turns out they sold it off cheap to lots of small businesses. I'll keep digging, but it's starting to look less useful.'

Fisher didn't seem too downcast though. 'You got some good news?' Monica asked.

'You know I was working on Pauline Tosh's contacts?'

'Of course.' In truth she had almost forgotten this in all the drama of the case. Asking him to go through the hundreds of cellmates, visitors and correspondents Tosh had had contact with over the years was the epitome of needle-in-a-haystack police work. Only, Fisher was almost beaming now, suggesting he'd found the needle. 'What did you get?'

'It's taken a lot of work, digging into employment records and finding addresses, dates. Frankly I thought I would never get there.' Despite all her worries, Monica couldn't help feeling genuine admiration for Fisher's commitment and attention to detail.

'I owe you one, Fisher.'

Her young colleague could barely contain his smile. 'I've managed to narrow it down significantly.'

'Remind me of the criteria you were using?'

'I focused on anyone who lived in or close to Inverness in 1994 at the time of Freya's disappearance who then had contact with Tosh within the last three years. I know it's not exhaustive, but I thought it probable she had been in relatively recent contact with whoever told her about Freya's location.'

Monica nodded again, though she wasn't as confident as

Fisher about this point. The serial killers she had known or studied seemed to enjoy reflecting on seemingly minor details of their crimes for years. But still, Monica reminded herself, something must have drawn Tosh to get in touch at this particular point. So Fisher's reasoning seemed as good as any. 'How many did you get?'

'Seven people,' Fisher said proudly, handing her a printed sheet. Monica's eyes ran down the list. No Buggsy MacIvor, Miranda Salisbury or Brodie King, obviously. But could one of the names on the sheet be the key to unlocking the case?

'I take it none of them had links to any of our suspects?' Although Monica was sure Fisher would have highlighted this, it paid to never assume.

'Nothing obvious,' Fisher replied. 'I've not really had the chance to investigate them properly.' She caught the undertone: *Give me a chance, I've only been working all night.*

Monica ran down the list again, hoping inspiration would hit and a name jump off the page.

The door to the office opened and DC Khan stepped in, wearing her fake-fur coat and baseball cap – quirkily glamorous, but Monica could see she was tired. Knew she had driven out again to Fettercairn Farm to talk to Jessica and Barry Sutherland late the previous night.

'How were they?'

'Crying. Upset.' Khan shrugged. 'Press on to them non-stop, asking about MacIvor, calling up their charity line and asking about Freya.' She rubbed her eyes and yawned.

'I'll visit them later,' Monica said, feeling a pang of guilt that she'd left Khan to go alone. Wished she could explain to her about Crawford, but didn't want to go there yet. Not until she'd spoken to PC Duncan Gregg.

Fisher cleared his throat, filled Khan in on the carpet samples, then the list he'd compiled.

'What, then?' Khan said when he'd finished. 'We start digging into these names? Look for someone with a crossover to MacIvor or the others?'

Monica thought about it for a second. In the midst of all the worry about Crawford and the confusion of the case, it suddenly seemed so obvious. 'I'm bored of all this.' She stood up and picked up her coat. 'I'm going to get Tosh to tell me who gave her the location.'

Chapter 56

Monica set the paper coffee cups on the graffiti-covered table, feeling a sense of the absurd as she put the box of six assorted doughnuts down beside them. Bought from Perk on Church Street in Inverness, Monica had reasoned that the coffees might not be enough on their own this time. Though God knew what tribute might be required to get Pauline Tosh to see her if Monica needed to visit Carselang again. She looked at the empty seat opposite, the lime-green walls, felt the damp on her skin as the distant sound of a door slamming shut echoed in the room. The prison was one of the last places Monica wanted to have anything to do with, yet here she was again. Almost as if she was drawn here subconsciously.

She checked the time on her phone: after noon. PC Duncan Gregg hadn't replied to her messages, and by the time she'd left the office Crawford still hadn't been in touch. Monica had already decided that, if she hadn't resolved the situation by the end of the day, she was going to Hately. There was no other choice.

The key turned in the lock of the opposite door. After a moment it clanked open and Tosh was there in her green Dickies overalls. The guard ushered her into the room, cuffed her to the table and then left, locking the door behind him. When he'd gone, Tosh finally made eye contact with Monica.

'Box of doughnuts?' Her eyes wide in childish delight. 'Six of them for me?'

'Don't eat them all at once.'

'Oh, I couldn't eat all of them,' Tosh replied gravely. 'Appetite like a sparrow so I have. I'll share them out with the other girls, that's what I'll do.' With difficulty, cuffs drawing tight, she opened the lid. Her hands were now obscured from Monica's view.

'Do you want one, Monica?' Tosh asked, moving her head from side to side in a curious gesture.

'I'm fine, thanks, I'll just have a coffee.'

'Cannae beat a wee coffee when it's cold outside. That's what I always said.' But she made no movement towards the cup. Monica didn't notice this little detail, still distracted by everything with Crawford as she stared down at the table. Eyes running over the words scratched into the surface: FUCK PIGS, ALBA GU BRATH. She felt in her pocket for the list Fisher had collated. If Tosh confirmed the source of Freya's burial site was one of those names, it would open the case right up.

'Last time I was here, you were a big help.'

'Have I got something on my nose?' Tosh twisted her face up, as if trying to amuse a child. From any other person it would have been comical.

'I don't think so,' Monica replied.

'Must have gone,' Tosh said, wriggling her shoulders as if shivering. 'Felt like someone walked on my grave. Sorry, Monica, what were you saying?'

'I need your help again, Pauline. I've got a list of names – friends of yours. I need to know who told you where Freya was buried.'

'Wouldn't that be breaking confidence?' Tosh was now sitting very still.

'I really need to know.'

'I told you, I just hear whispers.'

Monica took the printed sheet from her coat pocket. She began to read the names. 'Josephine Bryan, Cameron Jackson, Rolf Stilger—' She caught the almost-imperceptible shift in Tosh's expression at the mention of the name. 'Rolf Stilger? Was it—'

'What's that!' Tosh shouted.

Monica glanced away for just a second before her subconscious registered the movement. As she turned back, the impact came hard on the side of her face. Monica landed on the stone floor, understood a moment later that Tosh was loose from her handcuffs – had launched herself across the table. Time seemed to slow. She pictured all those doors. All those narrow corridors. A beat and she felt Tosh's surprising weight land on her chest. Knocking the breath from her lungs. The killer's small strong hands found their way to Monica's throat, thumbs searching for her windpipe. The smell of Crabtree & Evelyn hand lotion, the same kind Auntie May used. The smell of garlic breath, damp on her face. Her eyes met Tosh's – cold and demonic.

The world throbbed. She knew it took mere moments to render someone unconscious through strangulation. The edges of her vision blackened as she struggled to shift Tosh's weight. She tried to say, 'Please, my daughter,' but the words sounded garbled, almost comic.

'Shhhh . . .' Tosh whispered. 'Shhhh . . .'

Monica realised that this was how it must have been for all of Tosh's victims. A false sense of safety. Then the ambush. Tosh hadn't even had to try hard, she thought sadly, as she pedalled her legs, trying desperately to get them underneath her. She gasped, tried to scream. Stared into Tosh's dark eyes. The blackness was coming on quickly, fading in from all around. Monica felt the strength ebbing from her body.

Chapter 57

In desperation, Monica twisted her head hard to the left. This weakened Tosh's grip for a moment, allowing a fraction more oxygen to reach her brain. Enough to buy her seconds. She gasped for air, grabbed at Tosh's fingers, dragged them down towards her chest – the way her dad had taught her to escape from attempted strangulation years before. This shifted Tosh's weight forward slightly. Enough for Monica to free her leg. She bucked her hips, rolled hard towards the wall. Somehow it worked, and Tosh ended up underneath her.

Monica grabbed for her throat with both hands. Tosh's neck was thick and strong, but Monica's thumbs fitted snugly around her windpipe. She squeezed as hard as she could. Feeling the strange intimacy, the warmth of this other human being, so close. Monica felt heat move down her forehead – only knew it was blood when she saw Tosh's face splattered with red. She straightened her arms and pushed down with all her weight. Tosh went purple, desperately pulling at Monica's hands. Kicked her short legs, jerking frantically to relieve the pressure.

Monica never wanted to stop. Wanted to feel the last moment of life leaving the killer's body. *And then you'll never know*, the voice in the back of her head piped up. *Neither will Jessica Sutherland.*

'It was Rolf Stilger, wasn't it?' Monica said, loosening her grip slightly. Tosh made a frantic attempt at a nod. Eyes wide in her purple face. Monica let go. Sank down on the floor beside her. The killer seemed barely conscious, ran a hand up to her neck – the bruises were already coming up and both her eyes were bloodshot. She was making a soft moaning sound. Monica felt the blood on her forehead and dug in her pocket for a napkin to stem the flow. She guessed that Tosh had hit her with an elbow that had split the skin.

'What did Rolf Stilger tell you?' Monica said, staring hard at Tosh, but there was no need now for intimidation. The killer inside Pauline Tosh respected the law of the jungle. Monica had proved stronger, and now she would submit.

'Rolf was a fan,' Tosh said, her voice coming out as a croak after the pressure on her windpipe. 'Used to write me stories – "nasty wee stories", he called them.'

'A fan?' Monica heard the rasp in her own voice, though as yet there was no pain through the adrenaline. She heard the distant sound of a door buzzing open at the end of the corridor. Presumably someone had noticed what was happening on a monitor. Not that they would have been in time had Tosh kept the upper hand.

'Interested in serial murderers, he said. Read every book about them. Wanted to meet one, and I was closest to Inverness – and Scottish like him.'

'What did he tell you about Freya?'

'Nothing. Just told me a story about how he'd been working on the railway in the marshes back in September 1994. He was the night watch, said he saw someone getting buried.'

'He saw the body being buried?'

'It's what he said.'

'Did he kill Freya?'

'Always said he didn't have the temperament for killing.' Tosh rubbed at her throat. 'Practically killed me, Monica. Aching.'

Monica ignored her. 'Where does he live now?'

'Said he was going to finish telling me the story next time I saw him. Seemed pleased about it. I told him I wasn't interested in his filth. He said, "Just you wait. You'll want to hear this." Next I heard he was dead in a house fire. That's why I contacted you – wondered if he really had seen someone being buried.'

'He never gave you a name?'

Tosh shook her head. Still cowed, but already regaining some of her composure as the oxygen returned to her body. Monica stood up, wanting to put distance between them.

'He told you about Buggsy MacIvor's attic?'

'That was all rumours I'd heard at the Royal. Bit of mischief on my part,' Tosh croaked out with a cold smile.

Monica heard the sound of running footsteps in the corridor outside, then the key turning in the lock. She took a deep breath. As the adrenaline ebbed, she felt the pain throb in her throat for the first time. The box of doughnuts was still on the table. Bizarrely, she thought about taking them to eat in the car. Decided to leave them for the guards. She took a step back as the door swung open and two officers came in. 'You keep an eye on your wee daughter,' Tosh said, getting slowly to her own feet. 'Being around the likes of you or me, who knows how she could end up turning out.'

Chapter 58

It was snowing heavily when Monica finished recording a statement about what had happened with Tosh and was finally able to leave the Carse. On the road, visibility was reduced to fifty yards , the moor coated white, the loch a black streak. She drove with the windows down, relishing the cold air and the feeling of being alive after coming so close to death. Being on that knife edge was strangely addictive. She realised after the Volvo went into a skid on a sharp corner that she was driving far too fast for the treacherous conditions, though her body barely responded as she straightened the car. Evidently her adrenaline stores had been well and truly used up for the day. She pulled over into a passing place. Even the throbbing pain in her throat felt strangely satisfying.

She dialled the office, got Fisher. 'We heard what happened. Are you all right?!'

Monica reassured him that she had never been better. That she just wished she'd brought the doughnuts with her as she was starving after all the excitement.

'OK,' Fisher said slowly. 'I've been doing some more work on the individuals who contacted Tosh. This is really weird—'

'One of them died in a house fire,' Monica said.

'Yeah, how did you know?' He sounded deflated.

'Rolf Stilger. It was him who told Tosh about the location of the body.'

'Was he the killer? Or an accomplice to MacIvor and the others?'

'Tosh didn't think he was involved. Apparently he was working as a nightwatchman for the railway, and just *happened* to see someone burying Freya.'

'Why the fuck didn't he tell someone?!' DC Khan's outraged voice came over on loudspeaker.

'He sounds like a ghoul,' Monica replied. Watched the chunks of snow splatter the windscreen. 'Obsessed with serial killers – that's why he contacted Tosh. But it sounds like he was on to something. He told Tosh that the next time he saw her he was going to tell her who had buried the body.'

'Then he died in a fire?' Khan asked.

'That's right. That's why she wrote to me.'

'Why didn't she just tell us?'

'She's a serial killer,' Monica said.

'So the fire-setter could be connected to Freya's murder?' Fisher chipped in.

'It seems possible.' Monica remembered the sense of familiarity on the night out at Cotton Lodge Barn; the notion that she had met her assailant before. That it was Brodie King. 'Let's find out all we can about Rolf Stilger – if he left any information with friends or family before he died.'

Monica hung up. The time on the dash said it was already 4 p.m. The hours had passed like minutes within the prison walls. Far down the glen, dim street lights glowed through the snowstorm. A vehicle was driving towards her, a yellow snowplough, keeping the road to the Carse open for the moment. She looked at her phone. Now she had reception Monica saw that she had a series of missed calls and messages. Nothing from Crawford, but Duncan Gregg had agreed to meet her. Worryingly there were also four missed calls from her mum.

'Is everything OK?'

'Why didn't you answer your phone, Monica?!'

'I had to go up to the Carse. What's the matter? Is Lucy OK?'

'She's fine. It's Albert. He got out when I came by at lunchtime and he's not come back in. We've been looking for him everywhere.'

Monica was relieved that Lucy was OK. But then she remembered Jessica's cat Bramble had also gone missing. Had he ever come back? Not to mention the poor cat buried out at Corrimony Cairn. It was certainly out of character for Albert, especially on a miserable day like today. When they let him out he usually spent five minutes sniffing uncertainly at the trees before miaowing to be let back inside.

The cafe was already closed when Monica pulled into the car park. The temperature was well above freezing in Inverness, the snow from the mountains falling as heavy rain. An unmarked BMW was waiting, engine running. Monica pulled up alongside. After a moment Duncan Gregg got out, glancing around suspiciously before climbing into the Volvo beside her.

'There'll be accidents tonight, I'll tell you that for nothing. Boy racers getting scraped off the roads left, right and centre. Don't know how to drive in the wet.'

Monica stared at her hands on the steering wheel. They looked strange in the dim light, as if they belonged to someone else. If she concentrated on them she could feel the stiffness in her thumbs, from where they had dug into Tosh's throat.

'What happened with Crawford?'

'Nice to see you too,' Gregg huffed, shaking his head. 'Should never have mentioned it to you – thought I was doing you a favour. This instead . . .'

Monica sighed. 'It's been a rough day.' She tilted her head and pushed her hair back so Gregg could see the cut on her forehead. He whistled through his teeth, and Monica caught a hint of his bad breath.

'That's the side of the job they don't tell you about in those adverts. Getting used as a punchbag by Tom, Dick and Harry and their mates.'

'I think Crawford's in danger,' Monica said.

'No shit, Sherlock,' Gregg replied. 'Anyone within five miles of Francis MacGregor is in danger. Never mind getting tied up in something with him.'

'Crawford's a cop though.'

'Cops have accidents, just like everyone else. Sometimes they even disappear, don't they?'

'Who told you about him? I need to know.'

Gregg shook his head. 'Fucking hell. It was a girl, all right?'

'What kind of girl?'

'A dancer I suppose you'd call her. You know Fingertips?' Fingertips was a grimy strip bar above a nightclub on the High Street. Monica nodded. 'It's supposed to be owned by Francis MacGregor through one of his contacts.'

'She told you Crawford had met MacGregor?'

'That's what she said.'

'Why did she tell you?'

Gregg took a packet of Polo mints from his pocket, thumbed one out and put it in his mouth,

'I've kept an eye on her for a while,' he said finally. Monica wasn't sure if she wanted to know exactly what this arrangement involved. 'Made sure she's safe.' He shrugged. 'Sounded like she had a thing for your man. Maybe she was worried, seeing him get close to Francis MacGregor like that.'

Chapter 59

In the woods behind Monica's building it was cold and dark. She had stopped in at the flat, hoping to find that Albert was back inside with her mum and Lucy. But her mum's concerned face had told her he wasn't before she even spoke. 'I shouldn't have let him out!'

'It's not your fault, Mum,' Monica had replied, mustering up the energy to go and look for Albert in the dank woods. On a day when a serial killer had come close to taking your life, everything else had a way of feeling insignificant. Before she went up to the flat, she had found a beanie in the car, pulled it on to cover the cut on her forehead. Fastened her shirt collar to hide the bruises on her neck. She would explain what had happened to her mother at some point. Just not tonight.

Why did everything happen at the same time? The old rule her granny used to live by: *Things come in threes, never forget that.* How many 'things' did she have on her plate? More than three, she decided as she swapped her tweed coat for a Gore-Tex jacket. Stalled investigation, Tosh's attack, Crawford's involvement with MacGregor, Lucy's troubles at school, and now Albert going missing to top it off.

'Should we come and help?' Angela Kennedy had asked as she handed Monica the torch from under the sink and a packet of Albert's beloved Dreamies.

'Just stay here,' Monica replied, glancing over to where her daughter was looking out of the living-room window, hoping to see Albert appear from the woods. 'Last thing I want is Lucy seeing him dead on the road.' Her mum's eyes opened wide with horror, and Monica reminded herself, *Not everyone's on first-name terms with death today*, so she added quickly: 'I'm sure he's fine. Just in case.'

Outside she clicked the torch on and shone it around. The storm had picked up, rain spiralling among the dancing shadows. Any other day it would have felt intimidating out here; today she felt invulnerable, and she wondered if it was some ancient hormonal reward system. A feeling of triumph at having bested a predator. *Well, it won't be much of a triumph if you find out tomorrow that Crawford's been kidnapped, or he turns up dead.* PC Gregg had given her a first name for the dancer who had told him about Crawford – Emily – but claimed not to have a phone number or address. Monica was going to have to track her down through Fingertips; she just hadn't worked out how yet.

She shook the bag of Dreamies, shouting Albert's name into the wind, which carried her voice off through the trees. She had already checked the surrounding roads and thankfully found no sign of him. Perhaps the cat had been frightened by the storm and was hiding somewhere? Surely no one would have hurt him?

The rain was running off her jacket and soaking the legs of her trousers; she could feel icy damp on her thighs. The smell of decomposition rose from the ground as her steps disturbed rotting leaves. The woodland was really just a narrow strip separating the blocks of flats from a housing estate at the top of the hill, but at that moment it seemed strangely remote. A slice of urban wilderness, a borderland. At the idea, Monica felt her body tense. The hair on the back of her neck stood up. Residual tension from the afternoon? Body still primed for action? But there was an unmistakable feeling of being watched. Looking back towards the flats, her mum and Lucy were clearly visible at the kitchen window, peering out into the storm. It reminded her of the man she thought she'd seen on the pathway through the woods a few days before. Watching the flat. Obviously he could easily have seen inside from his vantage point higher up the hill. Or seen Albert looking out of the window for that matter. Had he lured him into the woods?

Surely not. What would be the point? *Well, what was the point of burying a dead cat out at Corrimony Cairn?* her internal voice fired back. Monica shouted for Albert again. And again the wind carried her voice away. It muffled other noises too, the sound of twigs snapping underfoot, of leaves shifting.

Monica sensed something. But she didn't hear the man approaching. When she finally registered his presence he was close enough to touch her. Monica turned towards him, flinched and dropped the torch, its beam jabbing into the trees. She felt the hand on her arm and instinctively let fly with her right knee. It connected hard. The man gasped and fell forward, arms around her waist.

'Wait! Monica! Fuck's sake!'

Pushing him away and turning to run, she recognised the voice. Caught the faint smell of aftershave.

'Crawford?' She bent to pick up the torch, shone it into his face. He blinked, still clutching his stomach.

'Fucking hell, you winded me.'

Monica felt an overwhelming sense of relief that he was alive and seemed to be OK. She grabbed him and squeezed him hard, feeling his skinny but muscled body through the leather jacket he was wearing. Then pushed him away and shouted, 'What the fuck have you got yourself into, Crawford? Why the hell didn't you call me?'

'I'm sorry. Things got out of hand.'

Her mix of emotions bubbled over – overwhelming relief, affection, frustration, disappointment. She remembered the days of worry, of covering for him, and chose anger: 'You'd better start talking fast, or you can explain all this formally to me and Hately tomorrow.'

Crawford nodded quickly, still holding his stomach. 'Is there somewhere we can go to talk? I think I've got evidence. I think I can prove who killed Freya.'

'Why the fuck didn't you phone, Crawford? Where the hell have you been?' But Monica's anger was already dissipating, inevitably changing to curiosity. And Crawford knew her well enough to know that she would listen to him.

'I'll explain everything, I promise.' He looked warily around among the trees. 'But can we just not do this here?'

Chapter 60

Monica stared at Crawford for a moment, her soaked trousers icy against her legs. The search for Albert was clearly not going to yield results tonight. She prayed he was hiding in someone's shed or outbuilding – had been locked in. She would print some flyers asking people to check, and hand them out the next day.

'I've just been out looking for Albert,' she said finally. 'He escaped.' Before Crawford could reply she pushed the keys for the Volvo into his hands. 'Just give me five minutes.' She hurried back inside to change into dry clothes, reassure Lucy that they would find Albert in the morning and explain to her mum that she had to pop back into the office for an hour.

Crawford had already started the engine and turned the heating up high by the time Monica got into the car. She appreciated the warmth, and with the jeans and old high-necked fisherman-style jumper she had pulled on in the flat, it actually felt cosy in the car. As Crawford pulled out onto the road she took in his profile. His beanie was soaked, hair poking out from under it. With his high cheekbones and haunted expression, he made Monica think of Al Pacino's character in the movie *Serpico*.

She said, 'I could have brought you a jumper.'

Crawford grunted a response, clearly edgy as he glanced into the wing mirrors. The street was dark and empty behind the car.

'No one's following us.' Monica had to stop herself from reaching out a hand to touch her partner's neck. She took a deep breath and turned deliberately to look out of the window, still getting over the fight at the prison. *What a strange day.* She twisted her neck and felt the throb where Tosh's fingers had bruised the skin, then straightened up and tried to inject some authority into her voice: 'Where are we going?'

At the Shore Street roundabout, Crawford hit the indicator to turn right. 'We're going to the Marsh.' He stared straight ahead as he spoke, taking the exit onto the metal bridge that led across the river to Rapinch. And Monica felt the distant cousin of alarm. Why was he taking her down there? Had she been desperately naive just getting in the car with him? Her judgement impaired by the clash with Tosh? She reminded herself that he was mixed up with Francis MacGregor.

'Crawford, are you planning on harming me?'

For the first time since she'd got in the car he turned to face her. He looked shocked. 'What are you talking about? Course not. You're the one that kneed me in the stomach, remember?'

And you're the one that sold information to the press, aren't you? The one who owes a debt to Francis MacGregor? Monica didn't verbalise the thought though. She wanted to savour this moment of strange closeness – maybe the last one, because once she asked the question nothing would ever be the same between them.

They drove down Grant Street, where punters huddled, smoking outside the rough bars. Before the turn for her mum's house Crawford went left, then left again into the Maze, a labyrinth of narrow streets, small terraced houses and larger blocks of flats from the 1970s. Pebbledashed in greying white. More than one marked police car had been burned out in here, drivers disorientated and finally boxed in by local youths – then forced to flee on foot, sometimes under a hail of rocks and bottles. Monica had grown up a few streets away, knew the area as well as anyone; a reassuring thought. Even if she knew there were plenty of people from round here who'd be glad to never see her again. Mercifully the storm was raging, keeping anyone who might recognise her inside.

After another five minutes, glancing continually into the mirrors as he navigated the narrow roads, Crawford pulled into a car park beneath a block of flats. Got out and led Monica through another maze of alleyways to a different block, then up a dingy stairwell, their footsteps echoing off concrete, wind funnelling rain in through a broken window. On the fifth floor Crawford paused, held a finger to his lips and listened. After a moment he seemed satisfied and hurried down a corridor to a door.

'It's not much, but it's home,' he said, smiling at Monica as he unlocked the door. Inside the place stank of stale smoke, ammonia and deep-fried food. The carpet was sticky underfoot; woodchip wallpaper had peeled off in some places and was graffitied in others. The light of a television was flashing at the end of the hallway from what was presumably the living room, along with the sound of someone blasting their opponent in a video game.

'Who is it?!' A male voice carried over the din.

'It's just me.'

'Who's me?'

'It's Crawford.' The reply was met with more electronic blasting. He shrugged, turned to Monica. 'Archie from outside Poundland? You remember?' She recalled Crawford talking to a man begging on the High Street. He led her into the small kitchen, no more salubrious than the rest of the flat. 'I'd offer you a coffee . . .' The sink was full of dirty dishes, with more stacked along the worktop.

Monica watched Crawford's face. Part of her still didn't want to ask the questions – strange when she wanted to know so badly. Her partner showed no signs of beginning the conversation though, so finally she said, 'What happened?'

'You're not going to believe it . . .' Crawford took out a cigarette, leaned to light it on the gas stove. She couldn't recall seeing him smoke before. 'Fucking crazy. I can't really—'

Monica cut in, 'I know those stories in the press came from you. Don't fucking bullshit me.'

When Crawford looked up his face was pale. 'I've seriously fucked up.'

Strangely, after her desire in the car she now felt repelled by him. 'Keep talking.'

Crawford sat down, wiped his hand over his face. 'So fucking stupid. Everything with Heather was getting on top of me, like it was too serious. I ended up at a bar.'

'Which bar?'

'A strip bar, it's called Fingertips, on the High Street.'

Monica looked away. Through the window the lights of the city spread out below, ending abruptly at the dark waters of the firth nearby. Somewhere to the west were Fettercain Farm and the mountains of Glen Turrit, Glen Affric, Glen Cannich and Glen Mullardoch. An urban outpost surrounded by so much wilderness.

'I got talking to one of the girls. She liked going to the gym. One thing led to another . . .'

'Who was the girl?'

'Emilija.'

'So, what? You were sleeping with her?'

'Yeah. I don't know. I really liked her, like she had a good sense of humour. She was fun, took her for a drive to see the mountains – she said she liked them.'

'While Heather thinks you're moving in together?'

'I fucked up. It didn't feel right. I tried to talk to you about it, that night at your flat.'

Monica recalled the conversation. She had sensed at the time that her partner was trying to open up. Instead they had almost ended up sleeping together. *Jesus, it would be funny if it wasn't so tragic.*

'What happened?'

'She asked me to meet her, at Fingertips. When I get there, it's closed up so I buzz to get in. Who do you think's sitting inside?'

'You tell me, Crawford.'

He wiped a hand across his face again, lit another cigarette from the gas then reached into his jacket pocket for a flat bottle of Co-op vodka. Took a pull on it and creased his face up.

'Francis MacGregor,' he said finally. 'Smiling himself silly. A couple of monsters with him. He says, "Do you remember you pointed a gun at me? Well, I've been pointing something at you." Sits me down and shows me a video. Me and Emily in bed. I was talking to her. Telling her about the investigation.'

'For Christ's sake, Crawford, how could you be so stupid? A stripper just decides she's desperate for you?'

'The weird thing was, it was like I knew? Once they started showing me the video? You ever feel like that? Like you know you're going to fuck things up but you do it anyway?'

'What does MacGregor want?'

'Revenge for pointing the gun at him. To ruin my life then get me to work for him.'

'What did you say?'

'What do you think? I told him thanks but no thanks. He just thought it was funny – told me I could get kicked off the force, or I could get paid cash to help him out from time to time. Could work for both of us, he said.'

Monica knew all about these types of arrangements. During her time at the Met, infiltration by drug dealers had become endemic.

'Why didn't you come to me?'

'My head was spinning.'

'You were thinking about his offer?'

'I couldn't imagine not being a detective.'

'What did you decide?'

'Come on, Monica. I'm here speaking to you, amn't I?' He sighed and took another mouthful of the vodka. 'I get a message, anonymous number. I'm guessing it's from Francis MacGregor.' He went to the pocket of his leather jacket for his phone, held it up for her to see the text: 'Check out Buggsy's boat.' 'I had absolutely no idea what it was about, then I hear about the raid on Buggsy MacIvor's place yesterday morning.'

'Francis MacGregor gave you information about Buggsy MacIvor?' Monica recalled that Crawford had told her he had information on the case.

'I couldn't find any boat registered in MacIvor's name, so I went down to the Muirtown Basin.' He was referring to the docks at the end of the Caledonian Canal, close to where Freya's body had been recovered. 'Started asking around. Harbour master didn't know, but he told me about a boy – Alan's his name. Lives with his mum at the metal bridge, the one that opens?'

Monica nodded. She had occasionally been forced to wait for the metal bridge that crossed the Caledonian Canal to swing back into place after letting boats through. There were rows of council-built houses overlooking the picturesque canal locks.

'Turns out he's sort of the boat equivalent of a trainspotter.

Knows all about the different boats and the names of the sailors; keeps a record of them all in his "Captain's Log", he calls it.'

'You got MacIvor's boat?'

'Registered under a company, but Alan tries to speak to the captains when he can, get a bit of the history of the boats. Spoke to MacIvor a few times. Boat's called *The City of Inverness*.' Crawford opened a picture on his phone of a large white motor cruiser. 'I think the name's supposed to be funny?'

Monica nodded. In 2000 the town of Inverness had been made a city. At the time it was something of a local joke.

'You found it?'

'There was no sign of it in Inverness, and Alan said he hadn't seen it in five years. Hasn't missed a bridge opening in all that time.'

'So?'

'Well, Alan said some of them just stick to the Caledonian Canal and the lochs in the Great Glen if they're not experienced sailors. I tried the different docks, tracked it down over in Fort William. Drove there last night.' He tilted his head to listen for a second; then, reassured by more blasting sounds, went to the cupboard under the sink. He reached around inside to the pipes at the back, and finally he pulled out a plastic bag closed up with masking tape. From the sleeve of his jacket he produced a hunting knife and sliced through the tape, peeled the bag open. Then laid an envelope and a plastic audio cassette on the table.

'What's in there?'

'I haven't listened to the tape yet, but judging by the pictures in that envelope I think it's a recording of Freya's murder.'

Chapter 61

It was after 11 p.m. when they arrived at headquarters. Tonight there was no sign of DC Ben Fisher, who must have been taking a well-earned rest after his series of late finishes. Monica was pleased not to have to explain about Crawford yet. She hadn't had a chance to think through the implications of his story, in particular whether it meant his career as a detective was effectively over. They could deal with all that after.

She clicked the lights on, took in the office. The smells of copier ink, coffee burned into the walls and ceiling; the background hum of computers, noticeable in the quiet. In the corner of the room were a couple of rarely used sofas – supposedly for informal meetings but in practice for exhausted detectives to crash out on for a couple of hours when they were too busy or tired to drive home.

She put the bag down on the coffee table between them while Crawford went to put some coffee on. It was a strange feeling – Monica in her jumper and jeans, Crawford wearing a leather jacket and hoody – like being at school after hours. She found a pair of forensic gloves and opened the envelope. Inside there was a silk purse. Monica held it up to the light. It was black, decorated with Japanese-style erotic images. It fitted with the other things they had seen out at Balnakine House. As Crawford crossed the room carrying mugs of coffee, Monica asked, 'Were there computers? Laptops or anything on the boat?'

'There was an old computer. I didn't want to risk carrying it across the yard – thought these would be enough on their own.'

'First thing'll be to get a warrant and seize that.' As Monica was speaking, she wondered for the first time how Francis MacGregor had known they were investigating the comedian. Gregg was the most obvious source, she decided. He'd known about Buggsy MacIvor's involvement since 1994. Anyway, it was a question for another day. This was about nailing MacIvor; they could pick up the pieces after.

As she opened the purse, Monica caught a faint hint of perfume. Realised after a second it was Charlie Red, a cheap and cheerful product that had been popular with young women in the mid-1990s. It seemed relatively fresh though. Monica knew that smell was one of the most reliable triggers for memory. The idea of MacIvor driving to Fort William to sit on his boat and reimagine Freya Sutherland's murder was horrifying. Likely he had cleared the attic out after Freya, and the boat had become his new den. It explained why they'd found nothing in the house.

Monica went to slide the photographs out, then caught Crawford's eye. 'How bad are these?'

'Not the worst.' He slid the quarter-bottle of vodka from his pocket, splashed some into his coffee. 'But bad enough.'

The first of the photos showed Freya Sutherland fully clothed, sitting on a sofa with Brodie King on one side, Miranda Salisbury on the other. Then one of a large man, topless, hairy stomach and chest visible from waist to neck. The next showed his face. Or what was visible of his face. It was hidden by the mask of a bull, reddish like Highland cattle. It might have been comic, if not for the eyes of the person who was wearing it. Staring out with a mad intensity. The next was a blurred image of

Freya Sutherland, still fully clothed but with a man's thick hands around her neck. What appeared to be shock on her face.

'Jesus Christ,' Monica whispered. Ten similar pictures. Finally, another series of blurred images, this time of Freya with her hands tied. Monica studied the background to see if there was anything that might definitively ID the location as MacIvor's house. Though both Miranda Salisbury and Brodie King were clearly pictured, none of the photographs actually showed MacIvor's face, and frustratingly the background was always blurred.

'Do you think we could enhance them?' Crawford asked.

Monica wasn't hopeful. The images were low-resolution and poorly lit. 'Maybe we won't have to.' She stood up and went over to the walk-in cupboard in the corner of the room. Spent five minutes fishing through boxes until she recovered an aged cassette player. Tried to remember the last time she'd used one during an interview. The machine brought back ancient memories. The hundreds of interviews she had conducted down in London. Before that, listening to music with friends on the Ness Islands in the summer – INXS or Guns N' Roses – imagining some better future.

Better than this? Monica thought wryly as she looked over to where Crawford was flicking through the photos again, the vodka on the table in front of him.

She plugged the cassette player into the power, slid the tape in and hit Play. For long minutes there were only indistinct sounds of music, fragments of voices.

'That'll be shining bright!' Buggsy MacIvor's distinctive voice came bursting onto the audio, mid-conversation. 'Know what your type are like . . . Fu-ckin' helllll!'

'What do you mean?' A girl's voice, soft Highland accent. The voices were hard to make out, barely audible through the crackling. It suggested to Monica that the cassette had been played frequently over the years.

'You know what I mean. Girls like you, my mother warned me what you were like.'

'I don't know what you mean . . .'

'Fuckin' right you do!'

'Why would you say that?'

'You're a whore, aren't you? A fuckin' slut?' Monica glanced at Crawford, whose face was set hard. 'You think I'm fuckin' joking? Think I'm a fuckin' clown?'

A pause.

'No, I don't think that.'

'Think I'm some fuckin' joke. Someone you can walk all over?'

'I don't think that, Buggsy.'

'You want me to fuckin' choke you unconscious? Want me to do that to you?'

'No.' The girl sounded terrified. 'No, I don't.'

'You think I should choke Freya over here?'

Another girl's voice came on the tape: 'I don't know, Buggsy. She might enjoy it. Maybe that's what she wants.'

'Do you hear that? Miranda says I shouldn't choke you because you might just enjoy it. Is that what you're like? Is it?'

There was a long pause with just the sounds of breathing and sobbing before the tape mercifully clicked to a stop.

Chapter 62

William 'Buggsy' MacIvor wasn't going to come quietly. The morning after listening to the audio recording, Monica and Crawford stood watching as uniformed officers marched up the steps of Balnakine House. The comedian was waiting for them, dressed again in his purple dressing gown. Scowling down at Monica from under his scraggly ginger hair.

As the arresting officer began to speak, Buggsy dropped his head and threw a wild haymaker. It landed behind the officer's ear and she fell sideways, landing hard on the steps.

'Fuckin' bastards!' He swung at the second officer, who ducked the punch and caught him around the waist. Somehow the comedian ended up on top though. Screamed and bit the officer's face then stood up, a smear of blood around his mouth. 'You can all get to fuck! You can all get to fuck!'

His eyes landed on Monica. 'Fuckin' whore!' He started down the steps towards her. Eyes burning.

Monica had no doubt that, if he could, he would kill her there and then on the steps of his house. She tensed as the adrenaline flooded her system, ready to meet him. He never made it close. The first officer, still prone on the steps, kicked out and caught MacIvor's leg, knocking him off balance. He landed in a heap of purple and ginger, and more officers piled on. Monica watched as it took two officers to drag each of his thick arms behind his back and cuff them. MacIvor continued screaming, attempting to bite, like a giant two-year-old. Finally the officers half dragged, half carried him to the back of the waiting van.

'What's happened?! You can't do this!' The caretakers, Mairi Ross and Mike Brundell, had been watching from the front door. They came down the steps, eyes wide. Mairi shouted, 'Bugs hasn't done anything! Where are you taking him?!'

Mike stopped at the bottom step as the van door slammed shut on MacIvor. He turned to Monica. 'What's happening? What'll happen to us?'

Monica told him that she didn't know, then felt her phone vibrate in her coat pocket and turned away to answer. It was Fisher. 'We've got Salisbury. She was at home, came easily.' Monica hung up and dialled DC Maria Khan's number. The young detective had driven to the far north-west to oversee the arrest of Brodie King.

'King's not here. His wife won't even speak to us, but the staff at the restaurant say he's not been there for the last two days. It's like he knew we were coming for him.'

Monica swore under her breath. Wondered whether Brodie King had just got spooked and taken off after they'd visited him. Or if he'd known they were getting close and would eventually find something solid.

'I've started looking into his friends and colleagues, anywhere he could be holed up,' Khan added.

Monica thanked her and hung up. The caretakers had trudged back up the steps by the time she turned to Crawford. 'King's taken off.'

'There goes our clean sweep,' he replied, rubbing tired eyes. He looked exhausted, his normally handsome face haunted. She wondered how long it had been since he'd been able to sleep properly.

'Brodie King spent years down in London; he might have property or connections there.'

As she was speaking Monica wondered again about the fire-setter. Could the death of Pauline Tosh's contact Rolf Stilger in a fire have been a coincidence? And if not, why now? She hadn't had the chance to properly consider the horrifying implications of Stilger's claim to have witnessed Freya's burial. Her first task was to examine the report on his fiery death – had he been killed by Brodie, MacIvor or Salisbury? The photographs and audio recordings were strong evidence – albeit they would have to side-step the issue of how they were obtained – but they weren't a smoking gun. Proving one or more of the three had killed Stilger to keep him quiet would solidify the case, not to mention bringing justice for him.

Monica turned to look at the loch, and thought: *If it hadn't been for Stilger then Freya's body would never have been discovered. Even a ghoul deserves justice.*

Chapter 63

Monica sat down opposite Miranda Salisbury and her infamous lawyer, Wednesday Donald. Just the three of them in the cramped, shabby room, which was painted lime green with industrial carpet on the floor. Monica had chosen the room herself. Miranda Salisbury came from money, was a Conservative MSP, was used to being treated with deference – to her face at least. As Monica made the introductions for the recording, she observed Salisbury. She already seemed diminished compared to their previous meeting in the hotel: her face drawn, washed out against her white-blonde hair. She was wearing jeans and a sweatshirt, no belt, no laces in her trainers.

Monica opened with, 'We know most of what happened now, Miranda.'

'My client is being victimised again here!' Wednesday Donald cut in. It was only 11 a.m. The lawyer must have jumped in her car and headed north from Edinburgh the moment she heard her star client had been arrested. 'We've already filed a complaint with Professional Standards at Police Scotland about the blatantly political leaking of information to the press.'

Monica stared back at her, thinking, *One thing my fuck-up partner is not is political.*

'This feels like another attempt to intimidate my client. If you've got any evidence then lay it on the table.'

Monica cleared her throat. Even though it felt like she had the upper hand at this point, with the audio evidence and the photographs, she knew that Wednesday Donald would be all over any screw-up in their procedures. One of several reasons that DC Connor Crawford was now on his way north to assist DC Khan with the search for Brodie King. Even though Monica would have appreciated having him by her side for this interview, she wanted him as far away from the formal side of the investigation as possible.

'You know as well as I do, Ms Donald, that we're under no obligation to reveal any evidence to you at this stage. If we press charges and this case ends up in court then you'll have plenty of time to prepare your client's defence. At the moment I just want to ask your client a few questions about her friend Freya Sutherland, and also about her relationship with one William "Buggsy" MacIvor.'

Monica watched Miranda Salisbury's face – there was a flicker at the corner of one eye – while Donald's brows furrowed for a moment. Clearly this connection was news to the lawyer.

'I'm particularly interested in any audio recordings that your client might have participated in.' The colour drained from Miranda Salisbury's face. Her lips pressed tight together. Wednesday Donald clearly had to stop herself from turning to look at her client. Instead she scribbled something in a notebook, then looked up at Monica as if everything the detective had said was exactly as she had expected.

'Well, it'll be hard for my client to provide anything useful without understanding the context.'

Monica replied, 'Your client knows her rights.' Then she tilted her head to look at Miranda Salisbury. 'It was a strange summer for you, wasn't it – 1994?'

Salisbury turned to look at Wednesday Donald, who nodded. Salisbury's voice was barely a whisper. 'No comment.'

'You and Brodie King come out of it with some money. He starts a restaurant; you're at university, then into politics. Never look back. Wasn't like that for Freya Sutherland or Joseph Moon, was it? One ends up dead, the other in permanent psychiatric care.'

'No comment.'

'Was that just down to luck? Talent? It seems odd to me, given that you'd all been so close. Then it's like you never wanted to see each other again.'

'No comment.'

'Can I give you a theory?' Monica let the words hang for a moment. 'You and Brodie got to know Buggsy MacIvor, maybe you ended up at his house for a party and stayed in touch? I think you needed money. I know your family were wealthy, but I don't think they looked after you very well. I think you and Brodie started doing things for Buggsy MacIvor, to make money. Sex work maybe. Maybe just posing for pictures.' Salisbury's hands were shaking, and Monica knew at least some of her words were hitting the mark. 'Does that sound right to you?'

'No comment.'

'I think things got more intense. I think you had a problem with Freya Sutherland. Maybe you didn't like her, or maybe you just told yourself that you didn't because you knew what you were going to do to her?'

'No comment.'

'MacIvor wanted to take things up a notch. Act out his fantasy of killing a young woman? He offered to pay you to bring him someone. That's why you befriended Freya Sutherland. She was vulnerable at the time, not exactly sure of her—'

'That's not what happened,' Miranda Salisbury said, her voice a whisper.

Before Monica had the chance to reply, Wednesday Donald cut in: 'I'd like time alone with my client. She's clearly in no fit state to be questioned, after the stress she's been subjected to in the last week by the persistently heavy-handed approach of the police. We would have arranged a time to come in for questioning. The circus this morning was entirely inappropriate. I'm concerned for the well-being of my client and would like her to be examined by a medical professional for signs of trauma before we continue.'

Monica tried not to let the frustration she was feeling at the lawyer's blatant stalling show on her face. With a different lawyer present, Salisbury would have been talking by now. Probably why Wednesday Donald earned the big bucks. These were the moments that a case could turn on. 'We'll arrange for a doctor.' She said finally as she stood up, 'But these questions aren't going away.'

Chapter 64

Monica stopped at the office to take a breather after the frustration of the interview with Miranda Salisbury. Obviously a confession from the MSP would have made things feel much more certain, but she didn't have time to dwell on it. Next up was Buggsy MacIvor. Ideally she would have had one of the junior detectives conduct the interview while she watched on. But the already stretched team was under extra pressure with the search for Brodie King under way.

Apart from DC Ben Fisher, the office was empty. She made herself a coffee and went to sit beside him.

'Khan's just been in touch,' he said. 'They've found Brodie King's BMW abandoned by the pier in Lochinver.'

'Suicide?' As she said it, Monica recalled Brodie's face as his kids and wife had come into the restaurant. Clearly his family adored him; just for that reason, she hoped he hadn't killed himself.

'Khan doesn't think so. A barmaid says she remembers seeing him get into another car with someone. A couple of nights ago.'

'Did she notice the registration? Anything about the car?'

'Unfortunately not.'

'Do they have any leads, any idea where Brodie King might be?'

'DC Crawford says he knows some people over on the west coast. He's "digging into it".' Fisher used the words like they were foreign, and Monica had to stifle a laugh. It was good to have Crawford back on the team, even if his future was uncertain. First priority was to conclude this case; everything with Crawford could be dealt with later.

There was a knock at the door, and a uniformed officer stuck his head into the room. 'Buggsy – sorry, I mean William – MacIvor's waiting in the interview room, ma'am.'

When Monica entered the room, MacIvor's demeanour couldn't have been more different from the spitting, raging man-child they had arrested that morning. He had tipped back his chair to balance it on two legs and was tilting it back and forth. Wearing jeans and a sweatshirt, hands folded over his ample stomach, his wide face set in an impudent smile, he resembled a naughty schoolboy who had spent the morning outside the headmaster's office and was now going to spin a yarn and be home in time for dinner.

Not likely, I'm afraid, Monica thought as she sat down opposite MacIvor and his solicitor.

'Do you mind if I call you William, or would you prefer Buggsy?'

'Only if I can call you Taggart? That sound fair?' He nudged his solicitor with a thick arm. 'She look like a Taggart to you?' He adopted a thick Glaswegian drawl: '*There's been another murder!* Scared the shit out of me, that programme did. Fuckin' dead bodies clogging up the Clyde practically. Miserable bastard detectives.'

Monica forced a smile. 'You don't like women much, do you, Buggsy?'

He nudged his solicitor again, stage-whispering, 'She's met my mother, hasn't she? Fuckin' hell, eh!' He craned his neck, pretending to look around in fright, now in full comedic persona. 'She better not be out there now. Chuck me in jail for life – just don't let her in here, for fuck's sake!'

'I want to ask you about a young woman. One you spent time with back in 1994.'

'I spent time with a *lot* of women,' MacIvor replied, licking his lips lewdly. 'An *awful lot*. Had money back then, you see. Funny thing about women – when you're rich and famous they say it's not about the money, they just love the taste of your knob. Try getting a blow job when you're down and out though. Fuckin' hell, must be something about having all that money in your wallet – just happens to make your dick taste a lot better! Am I wrong?' He nudged the solicitor beside him again, a buttoned-up man with neat dark hair and glasses who was now blushing red. 'He knows – fuckin' solicitor, hourly rate – he knows what it takes to keep a woman happy. Eh?'

As Monica listened to MacIvor, her mind wandered back to the recording. The mix of MacIvor's comedy persona and the much darker motivations beneath. Proximity to him made her skin crawl. 'I want to know about a woman called Freya Sutherland. Was she ever at your house?'

'Who knows,' MacIvor replied, his voice still casual. But he had stopped tipping the chair, was now leaning forward. 'All sorts came to my place back then.'

'You ever do anything to her? You ever touch her?' Now MacIvor was looking hard at Monica but he didn't reply. 'You ever hurt her?' She leaned across the table so her face was close to his. Still he didn't reply. 'You enjoy hurting women, don't you?'

'I'd like to hurt you.' And for a second MacIvor's eyes were set cold before he started guffawing, then turned to his solicitor and slapped his thigh. 'Told you this bitch thought she was Taggart. You've searched my house, and you got fuck all.'

'You ever make any recordings of Freya?'

'What are you talking about?'

Monica took her phone from her pocket, opened the voice memo function and pressed Play.

He listened to the first few moments of the recording before standing. 'Fuckin' turn that off. Where the fuck did you get that? That is fuckin' private!' His solicitor reached for his arm to calm him. MacIvor threw him hard against the wall then turned to Monica, small eyes flaming in his red face. 'Fuckin' bitch!'

Monica stood, facing him across the table. 'You're going to have to come up with something better to explain this.'

'I'll fuckin' explain it.' He made to throw the table aside, realised it was bolted to the floor and instead lunged over it for her. At the same moment the door burst open. The four uniformed officers she'd asked to wait outside hustled in and dragged him to the floor. Not exactly displeased at the opportunity to manhandle the comedian back to his cell after he had left their colleague with a broken shoulder during his arrest that morning.

Chapter 65

Hately was waiting for Monica back in the Incident Room. For the first time in the course of this case, something approaching satisfaction was written on his face. Obviously he had been watching as she played the recording to Buggsy MacIvor. Against the odds it now seemed like they had a high chance of at least seeing MacIvor, Salisbury and King in court for Freya's murder. Any cold-case conviction was a major win.

'Good work, DI Kennedy, this is looking like a big result,' he said. Following it up with another cliché: 'Shows no one's above the law.' He hesitated, obviously considering how much he wanted to know before curiosity won out. 'The tape and the pictures? You said they were handed in?'

Monica cleared her throat, looked away. 'A contact of Crawford's – kid from the Maze, down in the Marsh – thought he'd bought some fetish kink. Got freaked out when he recognised Freya from the pictures in the press.'

Hately nodded slowly at this, looking around the room. 'Where is Crawford, anyway?' When the case had seemed like a disaster zone, the detective superintendent had kept a distance. Perhaps he really hadn't noticed Crawford's absence, and there was a chance he would never find out about her partner's entanglement with the press and Francis MacGregor. 'He's with DC Khan, tracking down Brodie King.' Hately nodded again, and Monica glanced away before adding, 'We've had some intel.

Buggsy MacIvor owns a boat, down in Fort William. There could be evidence on it.'

Hately frowned, forehead creased, and looked at Monica for a moment before saying, 'Course, I'm on it. I'll organise press for later.' Then he turned and jogged out of the room towards his own office. Happy to be front and centre in the investigation now it looked like they were on to a winner. Well, that was fine by Monica, it had been a long time since she'd sought the limelight.

DC Fisher was still hard at work on his laptop. 'How you getting on?' The clock on the wall told Monica it was after 2 p.m. already. She would soon have to collect Lucy. It occurred to her that she still hadn't made up the flyers for Albert. She hoped he was OK.

'I've been examining the files on Rolf Stilger – his death.'

'Did he have a record?'

'Benefit fraud, a few vehicle offences. Nothing serious or violent.'

As she was listening, Monica opened up her own laptop, transferred a recent photo of Albert the cat from her phone to it and quickly set about making up a flyer. She fiddled with the word-processing program, which seemed designed to make this kind of task as frustrating as humanly possible. *Or maybe you should have watched the tutorial first*, her internal voice piped up.

'Can you help me with this, Fisher?'

He looked over, surprised. 'Erm, I think so.' He turned the laptop to face him. 'Hmm . . . Pages. I'm more familiar with Word . . .'

'What about the house fire that Rolf Stilger died in? Anything suspicious?'

Fisher screwed up his face behind his glasses, dragging the

picture of Albert around the page. 'Nothing in the report. Stilger had been drinking, fell asleep with a fire still burning without a guard. A log fell out and ignited a heap of newspapers. Died of smoke inhalation.'

Monica thought about it for a moment, watching as DC Fisher resized the text on the screen.

'How's that?' The flyer read: CAT MISSING – ANSWERS TO ALBERT. Monica's address, phone number and email beneath.

'That's great, thanks.' She clicked Print, fifty copies, reasoning that she worked so much unpaid overtime the force could pick up the tab for the flyers. 'Did you get the list of contractors who had worked on Cotton Lodge Barn?'

'It came through this morning from the owners. They've had a lot of work done over the years, so there were quite a few. I've not had a chance to compare them with the companies who had access to the Pit.'

Monica nodded. Could it really all be a coincidence? She certainly wanted to know more. As she walked over to the printer and picked out the pile of warm flyers, something occurred to her. She put the heap of paper into an empty box and turned back to Fisher. 'Pauline Tosh said that Rolf Stilger was a night-watchman out at the marshes while work was being done on the railway. She said that was how he knew a body was buried there. Could you find out the names of any contractors working on the railway at that time?' It was a long shot, but it felt like there was the ghost of a pattern between the three incidents. Building contractors working nearby or having previously had access. 'Check for any connections with the contractors who had access to the Pit behind the church, or who worked on Cotton Lodge Barn.'

'Of course. Oh, I almost forgot – Mr Miles, the survivor of the first church fire out at Eskadale? One of the nurses called to say we should be able to speak to him in the next day or so. He's out of the ICU.'

As she was leaving headquarters, Monica's phone buzzed: a message from her mum saying that she was on her way to collect Lucy, and they would walk to the flat. Monica realised she'd forgotten they'd agreed this via text the night before. Her brain had almost ground to a halt.

At least it's stopped raining, Monica thought as she parked back at the flat and started her search of the nearby roads. The drains were full of yellowed leaves – some mulched to brown after the recent storm – but mercifully no sign of Albert. The air smelled of far-off coal smoke, drifting in the autumn afternoon. She felt a welcome chill on her face after the long night and day spent mostly in the stuffy office. After checking the roads, she wandered into the strip of woodland again, the new layer of yellowed leaves satisfyingly crunchy underfoot. She shouted for Albert for ten minutes. A friendly woman walking her Border terrier stopped to ask if Monica had lost a dog. She explained about Albert and the woman took her number, said she'd keep an eye open for him. When there was still no sign of the cat, Monica went back to the Volvo for the flyers and spent the next hour delivering them to nearby flats and houses. A couple of people came to their doors. They were sorry to hear about Albert but hadn't seen him. They would certainly be in touch if they did though. One of them was an administrator for a local Facebook group and promised to post about him.

Back at the flat, Monica's mum turned at the sound of the door. Judging by the excitement on her face, she had heard the news about the arrests of MacIvor and Salisbury, which had spread like wildfire around Inverness.

'Must have been a busy day for you.' Despite Angela's obsession with all things crime, these days she knew better than to start firing off detailed questions. Instead she generally satisfied her need to feel that she was part of the investigation by keeping Monica well fed and dropping not-so-subtle hints to the other members of her crime fiction book group that she was privy to top-secret inside information. She had started work on dinner, while Monica could see Lucy was in the living room, running around with a painted stick, pointing it at things as if casting spells. Outwardly she seemed quite unconcerned about Albert. Monica watched her jumping around, wondering if this was normal for a five-year-old. Could it indicate a lack of empathy? Maybe she just didn't want to think about Albert not being around.

'You could say that,' Monica replied finally when she realised her mum was awaiting a response. She sat at the kitchen table, feeling an ache in her long legs, and realised her shoulders were tight too. It really had been a long day. She was getting too old for this. When she was thirty, the thrill of the chase could keep her up without sleeping or eating for days on end. Not any more.

Her mum glanced over to Lucy, then put a lid on a pot, leaned in close to Monica and whispered, 'I was speaking to Lydia outside the school,' referring to Munyasa's – Lucy's ex-best-friend – mum.

'Really? What did she say?' Since the kids had stopped playing together, Lydia had ignored all Monica's attempts at communication.

'She just asked how Lucy was. I felt like telling her to mind her own business!'

'But you didn't?'

Angela harrumphed. 'Well, no. I didn't think it was fair on Lucy, in case her and wee Munyasa ended up as friends again.'

'What did Lydia say?'

But before her mum could respond, Monica heard her phone ringing from her coat on the rack. She sighed and hauled herself to her feet. She had asked Crawford and Khan to keep her updated on the search for Brodie King – maybe there was news? But when she pulled the phone out it was a local number, one she didn't recognise.

'Hello, am I speaking to Detective Inspector Monica Kennedy?' The speaker was female, and sounded elderly.

'You are,' Monica said. 'How can I help?'

'I've been away, you see. I was over visiting my son and his family, then he brought me back yesterday. I saw your card had been put through my door but I didn't think anything of it, but then I spoke to my daughter-in-law. She said that if you'd put your card through my door there would be good reason and that I should call you back.'

'Sorry, what did you say your name was, ma'am?'

The woman spoke very slowly, as if to an idiot: 'My name is Mrs Robin Dunsmore, and I live at 2 MacLeod Cottages.'

Monica racked her brain then remembered: Mrs Dunsmore, the cottages across the field from Miranda Salisbury's childhood home. The woman whose cat had been killed by Miranda, Brodie King and Joseph Moon, then buried out at Corrimony Cairn.

Chapter 66

Monica stifled a yawn as she parked outside MacLeod Cottages. Wondered for a moment how long she had been going without sleep or food. It had to be at least a couple of days now. When Mrs Dunsmore had called an hour before, Monica had been tempted to brush her off, to tell her it wasn't important or that the case had been resolved. But partly because of her own missing cat, and partly because Mrs Dunsmore lived alone and sounded vulnerable, Monica knew she had to drive out and explain in person what had happened to her cat. Besides, the photograph at Corrimony Cairn could turn out to be important in proving a motive for the murder of Freya Sutherland. In painting a convincing picture of who Miranda Salisbury and Brodie King were in 1994.

She killed the engine and finished off the can of sugar-free Red Bull she'd picked up at the garage on her way out of Inverness. The caffeinated drink didn't seem to be achieving much, other than giving her nausea. Darkness was gathering now, woodsmoke from the cottage settling in the still air. In the distance through the trees she could just make out the chimney pots of Carnoch House. Monica slammed the Volvo's door and looked around at the dark fields, the copse of trees. In the half-light they seemed ominous, and Monica couldn't help thinking that she would hate the thought of her own mother living alone out here.

Mrs Dunsmore must have heard the car pull up outside, because she was waiting at her front door when Monica pushed the gate open. She was in her seventies, with white hair and tanned skin, and seemingly unperturbed by Monica's looming presence at the end of her garden path.

'I recognised your name from the paper!' Mrs Dunsmore said with a laugh, once Monica had followed her inside to a living room cluttered with ornaments and framed paintings. 'All that happened last year. It must have been terrible for you and your daughter!'

'It's hard, but I try not to think about it too much,' Monica replied, caught off guard. She had expected to find a vulnerable old woman; instead Mrs Dunsmore seemed a bundle of energy, hurrying through to the kitchen for a tray of tea and biscuits after sitting Monica down in a chair by the fire.

'Yes, well, sometimes that's for the best.' She poured tea for them both then sat down in another armchair. 'But you never know when the past'll come rearing back around for you.'

'I guess that's me today, turning up on your doorstep,' Monica replied, surprising herself by taking one of the thick chocolate biscuits from the tray. And as she did, she couldn't help wondering if Pauline Tosh had been allowed to keep any of the doughnuts. Probably not – she would likely be in solitary confinement. Involuntarily Monica's hand went to her forehead to check her hair covered the cut.

'Well, every stranger is a possible friend, that's what my mother used to say,' Mrs Dunsmore replied. She leaned down to pick up a log from the basket and threw it onto the fire. 'Just back from visiting my son in Spain. Feeling the cold.' She laughed.

'I hope my card didn't startle you,' Monica said. 'This might sound a bit strange, but I wanted to ask you about a cat of yours.'

'A cat?' Mrs Dunsmore was clearly puzzled.

'One from a long time ago. He would have gone missing back in 1994?'

Slowly Mrs Dunsmore shook her head. 'I never had a cat. My eldest was allergic to fur so we never could have pets in the house once he came along.'

Monica felt just as puzzled herself. 'You never had a small, ginger cat?'

'A small, ginger cat?' Mrs Dunsmore hesitated for a second, then said, 'You're not talking about Sooky, are you?'

'That's right!' Monica had forgotten the cat's name was written on the ID tag.

'Sooky wasn't ours; he belonged to one of our neighbours.'

'Which neighbour?' There weren't many nearby houses, and the cat had had Mrs Dunsmore's phone number on his tag.

'It was Miranda's, Miranda Salisbury's. She used to live across the way. She's a politician now, quite famous.'

'Sooky belonged to Miranda Salisbury? Are you sure? The cat I'm thinking of had your phone number on its collar.'

'That's right!' Mrs Dunsmore sounded excited by the memory. 'Miranda loved wee Sooky. She'd bring him up to the window and wave his paw at me.'

Monica nodded dumbly. 'Why did it have your number on its collar?'

'Well' – Mrs Dunsmore's lips narrowed – 'I shouldn't gossip really . . .'

'Have you been keeping up with the news recently?'

She shook her head slowly. 'No, I don't read the papers any more, why?'

'I'm investigating an extremely serious case. Miranda Salisbury has been implicated in a murder.'

'A murder? Miranda would never have hurt anyone.'

'Why was your number on the cat's collar?'

'Miranda was worried about it going missing. Worried about something happening to it.'

Monica considered this for a moment. So Miranda Salisbury and Brodie King had killed her own cat. A creature she apparently loved. 'Why was she worried about it?'

Mrs Dunsmore sighed. 'Miranda was an unusual girl.'

'In what way exactly?' Monica remembered what Mr Mac-Adam, Mrs Dunsmore's neighbour, had previously told her: about Miranda stealing from his kitchen, and standing naked at her window and staring at him.

'Well, her family were sort of upper class, but didn't always seem to take good care of her. She was sort of allowed to run wild?' Monica nodded. 'I had my own kids, who were a bit younger, but I sort of worried about her. Seeing her wandering in the woods, just a wee thing. Sometimes when she was young she'd come and stand by the garden and I'd give her something to eat. I think her parents forgot to feed her sometimes. Sort of left her to fend for herself.'

'How old was she at this point?'

'Oh, this was when she was young, about ten. I didn't see her as much once she was at the school. I think she boarded some of the time. But that last summer – I think she'd come back home from university? I found her in the woods, she was crying.'

'Did you speak to her?'

'Yes, I brought her back here. She had the cat with her. She said she was worried about it. I don't think things were great at home for her then. She asked me if she could put my number on the cat's collar. I said of course. She seemed happier after that.' Mrs Dunsmore gave a half-laugh. 'You know, I suppose that was the last time I saw the cat, or Miranda for that matter. Not until years later when she was on TV as a politician.'

Chapter 67

When she was back outside MacLeod Cottages, Monica felt renewed confusion. Exhaustion, the complex investigation, Crawford and now this. Another unexpected angle to the case. As she climbed back into the Volvo she wondered if it made a difference. Miranda had killed her own cat for some reason. Did it matter? Was it relevant? Monica knew from bitter experience that an investigation had the potential to become dangerous at a moment like this. When the stakes were high for those involved and there were elements to the case that you didn't understand.

Monica started the engine and squeezed her tired brain. She recalled the lead plate around Sooky's body – the curse tablet. It had had some writing scratched out on it – they'd thought most likely Freya Sutherland's name – with the *S* at the start of a word clearly visible. Last time Monica had checked with Gemma Gunn at the forensics lab there had still been no confirmation from the handwriting expert. She dialled the lab and left a message chasing it up, although Monica was sure Gunn would get in touch immediately when she had anything to share. Her impulse was to drive to headquarters and ask to speak to Miranda Salisbury, but there was no hurry. They had already been granted an extra twenty-four hours to question her and Buggsy MacIvor before having to press charges or release them.

Instead she decided to call Fisher for an update. He seemed to appreciate it when she acknowledged his work by keeping in touch. When he answered there was classical music playing in the background. After a moment Monica recognised it as a section of Wagner's *Tristan and Isolde*. 'Oh, sorry, just let me turn that down,' Fisher said, and as with so much about her younger colleague, Monica couldn't help but wonder if he had planned the music for effect. The heroic lone detective working late into the night listening to Wagner.

'You like Wagner?'

'Of course!' For once Fisher sounded genuinely enthusiastic. 'I went on a school exchange to Bayreuth – they have a Wagner festival. Fell in love with him. Wakes me up when I'm tired.' The music stopped, and Monica wondered if she was projecting her own pretentiousness onto Fisher. She recalled wandering around central London late at night, listening to classical music on her headphones when seeking some insight into a difficult case – had she been playing a role back then? 'Actually I was going to call you.'

'What have you got?'

'I found a link – a contractor called Hume and Sons, who had access to the Pit, the quarry on Craig Phadrig. They also did the driveway at Cotton Lodge Barn. Their office is closed, but I've sent a request for a list of employees. I've not been able to get hold of anyone who can help me with the work done on the railway line at the time of Freya's disappearance. I'll get on to it tomorrow.'

Monica thanked Fisher, rang off and made a third call. To Crawford this time. He answered after a couple of rings. Again there was background noise – what sounded like the chatter of a busy bar. 'Where are you up to?'

'We're in Ullapool, been doorstepping some of Brodie King's acquaintances. Emphasising how serious it all is, so hopefully someone'll get frightened and tell us something. There's always someone who knows something in a town this size.' Monica heard a voice, then laughter in the background. 'Khan says hello. We've just stopped for food.'

'Say hi back,' Monica said, feeling weirdly irritated that the two younger detectives seemed to be having fun in a bar while she was alone in the wilds of rural Inverness-shire. *See how much fun you have if Francis MacGregor releases that recording to the press, Crawford,* Monica thought. Officially, Khan was heading up the search for Brodie King with Crawford there to advise. Monica needed all hands on deck at the moment, but this way his presence wouldn't compromise the investigation if and when the story broke. 'Have you got lists of King's employees? Friends in Ullapool and the surroundings?'

'Sorry, boss, the reception's not great.'

Monica repeated herself.

This time Crawford replied, 'Affirmative. We're all over it.'

'Just . . . just be careful,' Monica said. 'Brodie King's desperate. He must know by now that we've arrested MacIvor and Salisbury. He could be dangerous.' But before she finished speaking, the phone beeped three times in her ear and cut out.

Chapter 68

The following morning Detective Superintendent Hately was waiting for Monica in the corridor outside her office. Hands on hips, well-cut suit, hair neat. He looked like a senior detective in control of his investigation, happy and well rested, which Monica certainly wasn't. Her anxiety and the uncertainty around the case had followed her into her dreams: a night of grey and brown palaces underground, endless doors and tunnels.

Hately said, 'I'm in favour of moving to charge Salisbury and MacIvor with Freya Sutherland's abduction and murder. I've spoken informally with the Crown. I think we should finish collating the evidence this morning then move ahead. If we find something more solid on MacIvor's boat, then great. But the audio and the pictures seem like enough to me, combined with the other circumstantial evidence.'

Perhaps unkindly, Monica thought she could practically see her boss's ego inflating. Well, it wasn't every day you came close to clearing a case from over two decades before and which happened to involve a famous politician and a notorious comedian.

Monica said, 'I want to speak to Miranda Salisbury again first.'

Hately cleared his throat, the tic at the corner of his eye going off. 'Why exactly? I just told you that you've nailed it. We're looking to press charges.'

'Call it intuition.'

Hately's brow furrowed. 'We don't have time for that. You've done a great job, now let's get to work on collating the evidence to make sure this goes smoothly.' He turned and marched down the corridor towards his own office. Monica felt the frustration rise; the feeling of not being seen or listened to took her right back to being a child. Dad laying down the law, no matter how random or illogical.

Impulsively she ran after Hately and grabbed the handle of his office door so he couldn't open it. 'It'll be five minutes. Either she'll talk to me and I'll get a confession, or she won't.'

Hately looked down at her hand, seeming to weigh up his response.

She spoke quickly: 'Look, Brodie King doesn't appear on the audio recording. He could claim not to have been there. If I can get Miranda Salisbury to talk, we can get it all wrapped up today.'

Hately stared hard at her, but she already knew that the prospect of solid evidence against Brodie King as well would be too much for her boss to refuse. If you want someone to agree to something, appeal to their self-interest. Finally he barked, 'You've got half an hour,' before brushing past her into his office.

Miranda Salisbury had been in custody for almost twenty-four hours now. Enough time to really feel the beginnings of her new reality. Her old life was over – what politician could survive being arrested on suspicion of murder? Let alone the eventual release of the audio recording to the public. Although Monica hadn't played it to her, Salisbury had to know at least some of what was on it, even if MacIvor had recorded it without her knowledge.

Monica sat down. Opposite her, Salisbury looked like she was in shock. Her eyes were bloodshot, her body language hunted: shoulders hunched, arms folded.

'Do you have nightmares, Miranda?'

Salisbury seemed surprised by the question, and made eye contact with Monica.

Wednesday Donald said, 'My client has nothing to say at this point.'

Monica ignored her. 'We've got a compelling case against you. My boss doesn't even want me in here talking to you; he wants to send our evidence—'

The solicitor cut in: 'Well, why *are* you in here then?' Obviously hoping that Monica was bluffing.

Not this time, Monica thought. For once she had the upper hand: the case against Salisbury was solid. 'Because there are details I want to understand. I think there could be more to this case. I don't understand why you killed your cat. I spoke to an old neighbour of yours, who told me you loved Sooky.'

Salisbury looked up again, startled perhaps by hearing the name of her long-dead pet, and began to say something. Wednesday Donald interrupted: 'I've explained my client has nothing to say.'

'What happened that summer? Why did you kill Freya?'

Softly, Miranda said, 'We didn't.'

'Who did then?'

'I prayed. For a long time I prayed to God.' Donald tried to interrupt again, but this time Salisbury snapped, 'I'm talking,' and suddenly Monica was back in the room with the powerful politician she had often seen on TV. Wednesday Donald QC slumped back in her chair and began scribbling furiously in her notebook.

Monica asked, 'Why did you pray?'

'To get him to stop it.'

'Buggsy MacIvor?'

Salisbury didn't seem to hear. 'Then one night I cut myself and I prayed to the devil instead. And the next day he sent Brodie to me. He was standing in the garden, all dressed in black. At first I thought he *was* the devil. I was ready to give myself to him.' Monica watched Miranda Salisbury closely; it seemed she was almost in a trance state. 'He told me we were brother and sister. He knew what had happened to me because my dad had hurt him, done things to him too.'

'Brodie's dad was your father?'

'That's right. My father had at least two families. Mine and Brodie's. Brodie found out where he lived and watched the house. Saw me.'

'What did he do to you?' That horrible collection of words. 'Your dad?'

'I suppose he hurt me,' Miranda said, and when her eyes met Monica's there was a kind of glazed incomprehension. 'He used to hit me and had strange rules. I wasn't allowed to close the bathroom door, I wasn't allowed a door on my bedroom, I wasn't supposed to eat except when he said. Sometimes we'd go out for the day together, just me and him. I had to pretend to be his girlfriend – hold his hand in shops and cafes.'

'What happened with Freya?'

'I started spending time with Brodie and Joseph. Brodie liked Freya, and we ended up becoming friends. It felt like they were the first friends I'd really ever had.'

'And then you betrayed Freya?'

'No! We never hurt her. I swear to God.' Her hand had gone to an ugly prison-style heart tattoo on her wrist, previously hidden by her sweatshirt sleeve. She was rubbing it with her index finger. 'We had planned to leave – me, Brodie, Joseph and Freya. We were going to drive down to London, the ferry, then get the train to Berlin. Lose ourselves there, start a new life. We'd planned it all.'

'This all sounds great,' Monica said slowly, 'but I've heard the tape. I know what you and Buggsy MacIvor did to Freya.'

'We needed money. MacIvor was a pig, he was horrible, but he didn't hurt Freya, at least not when we made that tape. We went to his attic, and he took pictures of us. We told ourselves it was a bit of fun. Like being in a play at art school. We were desperate. Everyone assumes I grew up rich, but my dad never gave me money. We made those horrible recordings because we wanted to leave. Nothing actually happened that night. Buggsy was impotent, voyeuristic; he talked a good game about how many women he'd slept with, but he just wanted to see us with our clothes off. It was like it made him angry that he couldn't get it up. Like he enjoyed being humiliated, saying those horrible things but not doing anything.'

'Why didn't you go then?' Monica said softly. 'If you didn't hurt Freya, and you were planning on leaving together, then what stopped you from going?'

For a long time Salisbury stared at the table. Finally she whispered something that Monica didn't quite catch. She leaned in closer. 'What did you say?'

Her solicitor tried again to interrupt, but Miranda shook her head. More loudly this time, she said, 'Because of our father. He tried to stop us. That's why we weren't there to leave with Freya.'

'What happened?'

Miranda Salisbury's index finger went to the tattoo again. Monica could see her hands were shaking. 'Brodie and Joseph came to get me the afternoon before we were leaving. Dad was supposed to be away with work, but he must have found out somehow because he was there waiting. He had a shotgun. He hit Brodie with it, broke his nose, started beating him up, like he was going to kill him. I just wanted to stop him. I hit him with something over the head. I don't remember what happened next, but Brodie must have had a knife because it was in Dad's neck and then there was so much blood. I couldn't believe it.'

'You killed your father?' Monica asked softly.

'Afterwards we tried to clean up, buried him in our garden.'

'Where?'

Salisbury looked as if she didn't quite understand the question for a moment, then said, 'Near the back wall, between the two big beech trees.'

'Why didn't you go off to Berlin?'

'My mum was there. She saw what happened, helped us bury him. I think she hated him, was even pleased he was dead. She said she'd call the police if we ever saw each other again. She hated Brodie of course, because he reminded her that her husband had a secret second family.'

Monica thought about all this for a second. 'So why did you kill your cat? Because you were leaving? Some kind of sacrifice?'

'We didn't. I came home and Sooky was dead. Dad was there, but he said he didn't know what had happened. I could see in my mum's eyes that she knew he'd done it, she denied it though. In a way that hurt more, seeing her lie. I was so angry – told Brodie that I hoped she would die . . .'

Monica recalled what Mr MacAdam had said, about Miranda wishing a woman was dead and in the ground. He must have overheard this outburst. 'There was a tablet,' Monica said, 'around the cat's middle.'

'It was a curse tablet,' Miranda replied. 'Brodie and I were both drawn to those ideas – the occult, magic – even before we knew each other.' She shook her head. 'I suppose we both felt powerless. It was a way of having some control. We cursed our father. We both wanted him to die, I never thought it would actually happen.'

'His name was on the tablet?' Monica remembered the *S*. They had assumed it began the name Sutherland; actually it was Salisbury.

'My dad, Patrick Salisbury,' Miranda said.

This all sounded plausible, if extraordinary. There was a big part that didn't make sense though. 'Why didn't you tell Freya what had happened? She left her house late that night to meet you. You said it was the afternoon that you killed your father, right? So why didn't you tell her?'

'We did! It was madness at first, clearing everything up and hiding the body.' A faraway look came into Salisbury's eyes as she replayed the memories. 'You can't believe it's actually happening. But after a while it was like waking up. Brodie phoned Freya. I watched him.'

'He definitely called Freya?'

'I'm sure of it; he wouldn't have just left her.'

Monica thought about it again. 'Did Buggsy MacIvor know that you were leaving?'

Salisbury shook her head. 'No. It was just between the four of us – me, Brodie, Joseph and Freya.'

'And you weren't surprised when Freya just disappeared?'

'She had our money. Two thousand. It was a lot back then. We thought Freya had taken it and just gone on her own.'

Chapter 69

Monica's head was reeling as she left the interview room. Salisbury's story was so odd that it sounded true; besides, it could easily be verified. Clive Ridgeway would be more than happy to dig for Patrick Salisbury's body, and there was the evidence from the curse tablet when the handwriting expert finally came back. She wished she could feel a sliver of professional satisfaction that her instinct that Brodie King had killed seemed correct.

'What the fuck was that?' Hately was standing in the corridor. Hands on his hips again but looking seriously deflated this time. His recently solved cold case opened right up in front of him again.

Monica rubbed both hands over her face. *What a mess.* 'It would have come out eventually. Better now than our case falling apart in court.'

This was undeniably true and Hately sighed. 'What now, then?'

Monica thought about it for a second, trying to make sense of the crazy situation. 'According to Miranda Salisbury, Brodie King spoke to Freya on the day they were supposed to be leaving. What if Freya mentioned to Brodie who she was with that day?'

Hately asked, 'Brodie might think he knows who killed her?'

'It seems possible.'

'Well, why the hell didn't he say something at the time, when Duncan Gregg was questioning him?'

Monica replied, 'They thought Freya had taken the money and gone to Berlin. Miranda says they genuinely had no reason to believe Freya was dead. Maybe he's only realised now, wants to get to the person? Force them to talk?'

'Who then? Buggsy MacIvor?' Hately said.

'But he has to know Buggsy MacIvor's in custody. It's all over the press.'

'So someone else then? Someone we're missing?'

Monica squeezed her brain, needing some fresh insight, because if Brodie King made it to the person before them, they could be looking at another murder. She wondered again about the fire-setter, the possible connection to the death of Rolf Stilger – who had passed information to Pauline Tosh. Monica had wondered if Brodie King could be responsible, but if not him then who?

Monica's phone vibrated in her pocket. She swore, but pulled it out anyway. It was Crawford.

'This'd better be good.'

'Nice to speak to you too.' The signal was patchy; it sounded like he was driving. 'We didn't get anything from the house-to-house inquiries, but this morning I got chatting to someone down the docks. Gave me the name of one of Brodie's seafood suppliers, got a boat down at Loch Side – that's the opposite bank of Loch Broom from Ullapool?'

'OK, so?'

'Told me Brodie King's friendly with him. We took a drive round. Long way and the road's—'

'Crawford, can you get to the point.'

'Brodie was staying there,' he said huffily, irritated he wasn't able to elaborate on his story.

'Have you got him?'

'No. He left early this morning. Stole a weapon, a shotgun.'

'Did the guy say where he was going?'

'He doesn't know. Just said that Brodie seemed angry. Irrational even.'

Monica hung up and turned back to Hately. He was going to love what she told him next. 'You know the fire-setting case?'

'The church burnings?' She didn't bother to correct him that the third property was a barn conversion.

'I've been working on a theory that they're connected to Freya's murder.'

'What?'

'They started just after we discovered her body.'

'So?'

'Rolf Stilger, who first told Pauline Tosh where Freya was buried – so started the whole case . . . he died in a house fire. I wonder if he knew who the killer was? Knew who buried Freya's body? He told Pauline Tosh he was going to find out and tell her. Then he died.'

Hately barked, 'Why haven't you focused on this link already?'

Monica stared back at him. She felt like really letting him have it then. Pointing out that he had been absent for most of the case. Had been frightened of creating a big story in the press and had held back resources when she could have used them to investigate this more thoroughly days ago. She took a deep breath – there was no sense in point-scoring now. 'DC Fisher's on it,' she replied curtly, before turning to walk back to the Incident Room. He could follow if he wanted, or he could piss off; she would solve the case with or without his support.

Fisher looked up from where he was sitting in front of his laptop, a startled expression on his face as his boss, then *her* boss, came bursting into the room. A vision from the career-orientated officer's nightmares.

His hand went instinctively to his glasses. 'Is everything O K?'

Monica quickly brought him up to speed with what Salisbury had revealed. He seemed to relax on realising that he wasn't in trouble.

'I'm waiting on the list of names from the contractors who worked at both the Pit and Cotton Lodge Barn – Hume and Sons,' Fisher said. 'They were making a thing about data protection, but finally said they'd give me them if I sent a formal request via email.'

'Tell them we need it now. Brodie King might be on his way there already.'

'Course, ma'am.' Fisher picked up the phone.

Monica ran back over the case, trying to force her brain back from Miranda Salisbury's story and 1994 into the present. There had to be something, some clue they were missing. Her mind landed on the first of the fires, the one out at Eskadale. She remembered that Fisher had told her the churchwarden had recovered somewhat. Was out of intensive care. She waited impatiently while Fisher spoke on the phone to a secretary at the contractors. When he hung up she asked, 'Has anyone been over to speak to Mr Miles, the churchwarden at the first fire?'

Chapter 70

Rather than drive the short distance across to Raigmore Hospital, Monica went on foot. The huge hospital served most of the Highlands and Western Isles, and its car park tended to be full during the day anyway. It was mid-afternoon by now. Grey with thick cloud capping the city like a lid. The kind of autumn day where the sun never really seems to rise. After a frustrating few minutes of confusion at the reception desk, Monica discovered that Mr Miles was now located on the third floor of the sprawling building.

A nurse led Monica into the small ward. She felt the eyes of six patients land on her, the familiar sense of being a walking curiosity: *Is this the grim reaper, here among us?*

The churchwarden was propped up in bed. He was younger than Monica had anticipated, only in his fifties. His face was grey and drawn, but he seemed alert as Monica tried for a reassuring smile.

'This is a detective, DI Monica Kennedy, Mr Miles,' the nurse said. 'Here to ask about your accident if you're able to talk.'

He furrowed his brow, actually looking angry. 'I've told you, it was no accident.' The nurse nodded and smiled as if her patient was delusional, offered Monica a seat, then hurried out of the ward. 'I've been saying for three days that it wasn't an accident. No one seems to give a shit.'

'I know it wasn't an accident,' Monica replied. 'There's been a lot going on, and we're understaffed.' Never a nice thing to have to tell the victim of a crime, but there was no point in lying. 'I'm here now. Can you tell me what happened?'

Mr Miles shifted in his bed, brow still furrowed, but Monica could sense he was pleased to be finally taken seriously.

'I was at the church late. Beautiful old building. I'd been tidying up, and sometimes I'll just sit there and let it get dark. Fall asleep even. It's peaceful. You ever just sit in a church?'

'I used to, sometimes,' she said, taken aback by the direct question. She remembered times in Glasgow when she would sit thinking in the crypt of the cathedral. The idea of falling asleep down there was frightening though. 'Not for a long time.'

'No, well, I don't suppose many do now.'

'What happened?' Monica knew that a near-death experience could lead anyone to re-evaluate their lives, ask the big questions. Right now she needed to guide Mr Miles towards the smaller ones.

'I was sitting there, and I heard a vehicle pull up outside.'

'Did you see what kind of vehicle?' Monica asked hopefully.

'No. There are no windows on that side. It was unusual because the church is so remote – hardly anyone comes. I got up after a few minutes because I could hear the engine still running, and went to have a look.'

'Who did you see?'

'At first I thought it was an animal, then I realised it was a man. I saw him through the window. He was standing at the old oak tree.'

'What did he look like?'

'It was almost dark so I couldn't really see him, but he had a hood up. He seemed to be fiddling with something on the tree. It was very strange. I thought maybe he was trying to take a cutting or something . . . But then I smelled the smoke. I ran through to the church hall and saw there was a fire. I went for the fire extinguisher, tried to put it out. I must have passed out from the fumes. Next thing I remember is being carried outside by the fire brigade.'

Monica pulled up outside the charred remains of the church hall, twenty miles to the west of Inverness; the church adjacent to it was virtually intact. The fire brigade must have arrived in time to save it. It was almost dark, even though it was only mid-afternoon. The grey stone of the church matched the slate skies and the mist. The oak tree was easy to spot at the back of the graveyard, ancient and gnarled, with branches hanging low. Monica walked over to it. She ran her eyes over the branches, mostly bare of leaves after the recent storms. There was nothing obvious, no mark cut into the bark. Probably she was wasting her time, allowing Mr Miles's memory to give her hope that the fire-setter had left some clue. But then she remembered the way he had sat watching from the edge of the forest as Cotton Lodge Barn burned. The suspicion she'd had that part of him wanted to be caught. At the time she'd intuited it was Brodie King – if not him, then who? She walked back up the slope then worked her way down, looking carefully at each of the oak's branches in turn, wishing she had brought the powerful torch from the car. She was just about to walk back to get it, when her eyes landed on the thing. Hanging from one of the lowest branches, delicate and hard to see in the low light. She reached for it, felt cold metal, saw it was a necklace. A black shark's tooth, hanging from a silver chain. She stared at it in disbelief for a moment as the pieces slotted together in her mind. Then, moving quickly, she grabbed her phone from her pocket, found the contact and dialled.

Chapter 71

Brodie King pulled the Golf to a stop at the little lay-by close to the hanging tree. Further from the house than he normally dropped Freya off. Generally he seemed to like pulling into the farmyard; last time he had got out and she'd shown him the chickens in the barn, introduced him to Butter the cat, who he seemed to like.

'Why are you stopping here?'

'I just wanted to talk to you.'

It was hot, like an Indian summer, though Freya had never really understood what the term meant. Both the car windows were wound down. He killed the engine and lit a menthol cigarette, then offered it to her. She was far enough from the house that no one would see. Freya took it, but held it down by her knee. Her parents would worry if they saw her smoking. Though probably they'd be out in the fields anyway, Dad working on clearing the gorse. In not much more than twenty-four hours, they would be leaving for Berlin. It was still hard to imagine it was actually happening.

'What did you want to say?'

'Things have been hard for Miranda recently. It'll be easier, once we've gone.'

'Like in what way?' For some reason Brodie's words felt like a final welcoming in. As if there was some subtle shift between them, a new openness. 'Is she OK?'

'She will be. I'll explain it all later, when we're in Berlin.'

'We're actually going to do it.'

He reached across her to the glovebox, opened it and pulled out a padded envelope, handed it to her.

'The money from Buggsy?' she said.

'Two grand. He'll transfer more to us. He's rich and generous.'

Freya nodded. Everything with the comedian had been weird, creepy, but she'd never actually felt threatened. Maybe because Brodie was watching, like he wanted to make sure she was all right. It had felt more like they were actors in a particularly odd play.

'My mum has a habit of going through my things when I'm not around. Can you keep it until tomorrow? Don't be stealing it.'

Freya made a face. 'You won't see me for dust.' She put the money into her bag. It didn't feel like there was anything else to say, so she got out of the car. Leaned back in through the open window. 'Tomorrow night then. One in the morning.'

Brodie said, 'I've put a spell on you. To keep you safe.'

She smiled at him.

He gave her that crooked smile back and for a second she thought he was going to kiss her. Instead he said, 'Don't go running off with that money now. I know you like free things.'

'If I don't turn up, then you'll know I've gone to Ibiza instead. Prefer the heat.' And before Brodie could reply she leaned across the passenger seat, put a hand on his jaw and kissed him quickly on the cheek. She turned and walked from under the shadow of the hanging tree down the ancient road to Fettercairn Farm. Without once looking back.

*

Brodie King watched her. He liked the way she moved, and actually opened his door and got out of the car so he could see her take the last steps before she turned into the farm. Partly he hoped she would turn back, see that he was watching. Partly he hoped she wouldn't, that she would pretend not to care. Back and forth like a dance, the way everything was a dance. He lit another cigarette as Freya stepped out of view.

There was still a lot to do before they left. He turned to get back into the Golf but heard something: a rustle, the sound of a foot on dry leaves, just off the road. Brodie hesitated a moment, then took a step closer, curious. He blinked as his eyes adjusted to the dim light. There was a man sitting at the foot of a tree, looking straight at him. For a moment Brodie actually thought it was some kind of creature raised from the underworld by his amateurish attempts at spells and curses – but, looking closer, he could see it was a young man, maybe still a teenager, dressed in blue jeans and a faded old Timberland sweatshirt. He had an odd expression on his face: smiling, but under that he seemed frightened. Brodie felt sorry for him. He walked over.

'Want a cigarette?' He held out the packet as the younger man looked up at him with wide eyes. Brodie saw that despite his subdued body language the man was large, strong across the shoulders. For some reason this made Brodie doubly sad for him. He must have had a shit life to be so cowed, and Brodie knew what that felt like. He smiled again. 'Here you go, buddy.' Before turning back to the car he handed him a second menthol cigarette. 'You keep that one for later, pal.'

Chapter 72

Monica was already back in the Volvo and starting the engine when Jessica Sutherland answered after the third ring.

'Do you remember we spoke about a photo, at your house?' Monica said, trying to keep her voice level. 'In your hallway. I think you said it was of your last birthday before Freya went missing?'

'Yes, that's right, why?' Jessica sounded utterly bemused by the question.

'Freya was wearing a necklace? A shark's tooth?'

'That's right, one of the only things she had that I actually liked. I think it was a fossil.'

'You told me you lost it? On your honeymoon?'

'Why are you asking me this?' Jessica said slowly, as Monica navigated the tight turns in the road with one hand on the steering wheel while holding the phone to her ear.

'I'll explain, I promise.'

'Yes, I lost it.'

'Where's Barry?'

'Barry? He just got home, he's through with the kids, why?'

'Listen, Jessica. I need you to leave the house.'

'Leave the house? What the hell are you talking about?!'

'I'll explain, I promise. Just keep talking and go outside.' She had reached a particularly winding section of the road, so Monica dropped both hands onto the wheel, slowed to a crawl. Lifted the phone back to her ear once she was through. 'Jessica? Are you there?' There was no response, the line was dead. She slowed, connected the phone to the car's Bluetooth function, then called again. It rang for a long time. Finally someone answered, but there was only silence at the end of the line.

'Jessica? Are you there?'

'I'm here.' It was a man's voice.

'Barry, where's Jessica? Where are the children?'

'They're going.'

'What are you talking about? Put Jessica on the line.'

'It's too late for that. It's much too late for all that.'

Chapter 73

Monica dialled Fisher. 'I've just had Crawford on, ma'am. He's been trying to get through to you. They've apprehended Brodie King on his way to Inverness. He's got a story—'

'About Barry Sutherland being the one who killed Freya. I know. I need fire, ambulance and armed backup to the Sutherlands' place at Fettercairn Farm, right now. Barry Sutherland's going to burn the place down, and probably kill his family if he hasn't already done it.'

Monica hung up then dialled Crawford. 'I've been trying to get hold of you. A couple of traffic cops spotted Brodie King, and we managed to apprehend him. He had a crazy story—'

'I know, his story's true.'

'What?'

'Barry Sutherland's the one who's been burning the buildings. He killed Freya. He's going to kill his family rather than let them know what he did. Where are you?'

'I'm still with Khan – just outside Beauly.' He was closer to the farm than Monica, who had a few more miles to drive.

It was dark by the time Monica took the turn-off past the hanging tree. The glow was visible through the trees.

'No, no, no.' Monica gazed in horror at the outline of Fettercairn Farm, now ablaze. 'No, no, no.' She was too late; they were all dead. After a moment she realised that she had taken her foot off the accelerator. The car had slowed to a crawl. She had failed. But then she remembered Crawford and Khan, and she could see Crawford's red Audi pulled in off the road. She parked behind it and ran towards the house. Khan was standing outside, phone pressed to her ear, shouting to make herself heard over the growing roar of the fire.

'. . . need them here now!' She looked up as Monica approached. 'Crawford's gone inside!'

Monica ran to the front door. Smoke was pouring from the first-floor windows, but wasn't yet as thick downstairs. She could see movement. After a second she realised it was figures, wrestling on the floor.

Monica ducked inside. The heat was stifling, the air like fire in her lungs. She crouched. Blinked and realised the figures were Crawford and Barry Sutherland. Sutherland was on top; he seemed to be getting the upper hand. Without thinking, she grabbed the farmer and hauled him off. Crawford struggled to his knees, punched Sutherland in the face, hit him again and again until he stopped moving.

'Where are the kids?' Monica shouted.

Crawford spun round wild-eyed, as if he didn't recognise her, blood running down his face. 'I think they're upstairs!'

The heat was unbearable, smoke thick as night. Monica took a step towards the stairs. Saw black for a second, felt the heat in her lungs. Took another step, because she had to save those children. Her hand found the banister. She took a scorching breath. Dragged her foot forward again.

The floor seemed to slide away into dark infinity.

Chapter 74

It seemed like years later when Monica felt something. Strong arms around her waist. Someone was dragging her somewhere she didn't want to go. She opened her eyes and saw the flames. After a second she remembered: the necklace, Barry Sutherland, the fire, the children. Dimly she understood that she'd passed out. She took a breath, felt the cooler air and realised she was back outside. There were firefighters wrestling with a hose.

She stood up, legs shaking. Sutherland was beside her; she stooped and grabbed him by the collar. 'What did you do to them?' she screamed. Thinking of Harriet and her brothers. In that house. Dead.

Sutherland stared up at her, not even trying to resist her grip. His face was a mess and there was blood all over him. She looked down and saw that he'd tried to cut his wrists. She felt heat in her hand again and understood that she was injured too.

'You killed them!'

'I couldn't do it,' Sutherland shouted. 'I tried. I really tried.'

'Where's Jessica? Where are the children?'

'In the barn,' Sutherland said. 'I didn't want them to see me.'

Monica looked around. The barn was connected to the end of the farmhouse. The fire was being blown in that direction, and it was probably already filling with smoke. She ran towards it, still feeling the ground tilt underfoot. The heavy barn doors were chained closed. Over the roaring of the fire Monica was sure she could hear voices inside. She pulled ineffectively at the doors. A moment later Crawford was there beside her, blood still leaking down his face as together they tried to wrench the doors open.

Monica realised it was useless and ran back towards the fire engine. The firefighters were fully engaged with their hoses and didn't seem to hear her shouts. She saw an axe attached to the engine, pulled it off and ran back to the door. She swung it at the chain, missed and swung it again. This time it connected and sparked, but the chain didn't break.

'Hit the handle!' Crawford shouted. Monica swung the axe again. The metal handle snapped back. Crawford dragged the chain away and pulled the door open. Inside, the smoke was gathering, funnelled through from the burning house. Monica shouted, looked around. The space was lit by electric lights high in the rafters.

The family was huddled together in the far corner of the barn. *Dead, of course they are.* But then Monica saw them moving. She ran over and her eyes met Jessica's, her panic and incomprehension boring into Monica's soul. The questions there: *Why? What? Who?* Nothing Monica could answer, and surely Jessica Sutherland would go on asking them for the rest of her life.

Chapter 75

Much later that night, Monica and Crawford were sitting in Raigmore Hospital casualty waiting room. She could see the pair of them reflected in the window they were facing. Both stained grey by the smoke. The knife wounds on Crawford's arm and neck were thankfully not deep, but they needed cleaning and stitching, as did the cut on Monica's hand.

After the drama they finally had a chance to reflect. Crawford spoke first: 'When I ran inside, Barry Sutherland was just sitting there. It was weird.' His voice was matter-of-fact, but his green eyes were alive at the memory. 'The house was burning, and I just wanted to find out where Jessica and the kids were. Then I saw the blood. He'd cut his wrists. It was like he was just waiting there to die. It looked . . .' Crawford lowered his voice. 'For a moment I thought we were actually in hell. Does that sound far-fetched?'

Despite her best efforts, Monica couldn't stop a chuckle from leaving her lips as she took in Crawford's wide eyes in his grey face.

'I'm glad you think it's funny,' he said, turning away.

'I'm sorry, Crawford. I know it's not funny.' Again Monica couldn't stop herself laughing though. She bit her tongue hard, knowing her behaviour was totally inappropriate. Her partner was genuinely superstitious, had been raised on fire-and-brimstone religion, and here she was laughing openly at his fears. 'Sorry, it's been a long week.'

Crawford harrumphed but turned back to face her. One good thing about her partner: he never stayed annoyed for long. 'I was on my own; Khan was on the phone for backup. One minute I was asking him where the kids were, next thing I know he's on top of me. Farmer. Strong as a bull. Thought I was dead for sure until you showed up.'

Monica didn't reply, just closed her eyes for a moment. Sank down into the uncomfortable seat, feeling the deep tiredness in her bones. Her old tweed coat stank of smoke, was singed black in places. She conceded that this time it really was killed in action. First order of business when she had a free day would be a trip out to Campbell's of Beauly to get fitted for a new one before winter. She wondered what tweed she would choose from the gorgeous selection on offer. Allowed her mind to wander into fantasy: a trip with her mum, Lucy and Crawford to Campbell's, then Cafe Biagiotti across the street for their amazing Tuscan bean soup, then cake and coffee. She was sure Crawford would love seeing all the tweeds. *That's if he's even still on the force*, her internal voice piped up. *If he's not been kicked off for gross misconduct.* And Monica realised that she had been blanking out everything about Crawford's fuck-up. One thing she'd always been good at: cutting herself off from the things she didn't want to think about.

Crawford must have been thinking along similar lines because he said, 'When should I tell Hately? Or will you tell him?'

Monica looked around the waiting room, mostly empty now. Just the sleeping drunk with a bandaged head who had come in thirty minutes before, offering everyone chips from a styrofoam tray; and a boy with his mum, dressed in pirate pyjamas, arm wrapped in a sling, still nibbling at a chocolate bar Crawford had got him from the vending machine. Her partner had screwed up, no doubt about it. But did he deserve to be kicked out? Maybe. Probably, because once you started making exceptions, once you started bending the rules, where did things end up? But by the same standards, she should have been sacked years ago herself.

Finally she replied, 'Let's just get this case wrapped up first. We can worry about that later.'

Crawford nodded, stretched his thin legs out in front of him. He was still wearing the old leather jacket and black jeans that made up his undercover disguise. He'd lost his hat somewhere in the drama, and his hair was plastered onto his forehead, stained grey from the fire.

'How did you know Barry Sutherland killed Freya?' Crawford asked, obviously as keen as Monica to forget about the guillotine hanging over his head. 'When Brodie King told us, we thought he was insane. I didn't even think Barry Sutherland knew Freya's family until after she'd gone missing.'

'He didn't meet Jessica until later. I've still got no idea how he ended up killing Freya,' Monica said. 'I found an old necklace of Freya's outside the church at Eskadale. Jessica thought she'd lost it on her honeymoon.'

'Why would he leave it there for someone to find? Why did he set the fires in the first place? None of it makes any sense.'

'Hopefully we'll find out tomorrow. Maybe he thought we would get to him eventually,' Monica said. 'Burn those remote buildings, then burn his own house if he had to. Kill himself and take his family with him. Try to make it look like someone else was responsible?' As she was speaking, Monica realised that she hadn't consciously considered this possibility until now. Although, it seemed to fit a pattern she had sometimes seen: insecure men who got all of their validation from their family, who would rather destroy that family than risk losing it. She recalled an old case down near London – a successful businessman who shot his wife, two daughters, horses, dogs, then himself, rather than admit the truth that he was facing bankruptcy and a fraud investigation. Mercifully, in the Sutherlands' case everyone had survived.

Crawford nodded. 'Feel like burning my own house down with me in it at the moment, rather than face what's coming my way. I can tell you.'

Monica looked down at him and couldn't help laughing again. 'Well, you're still alive for now, Crawford.'

'One thing I don't—' The door to the interior of the casualty ward opened. The triage nurse stuck her head out and called the little boy and his mum through. Monica sighed, supposed it was procedure to treat the young first, even though they had been waiting longer. Crawford continued: 'I don't understand how Brodie King knew it was Barry Sutherland. That part makes absolutely no sense to me. If he had nothing to hide himself and knew Sutherland was guilty, then why didn't he come forward years ago?'

Monica stared into their dark reflections in the window. The large grey woman, the small grey man. The lights of the car park outside and the sleeping drunk with the tray of cold chips balanced on his chest. She realised that she hadn't had a chance to fill Crawford in on what Miranda Salisbury had told them that afternoon.

'You want to hear a weird story?'

Chapter 76

The next morning, when Monica entered the interview room, Barry Sutherland was sitting alone at the table. He wanted to talk and had waived his right to legal representation. Monica put a mug of coffee down in front of him – milk, no sugar. She had barely slept after getting home late from the hospital and showering, her lungs still tight after the fire, her mind buzzing from the hectic day.

'It's strange,' he said after Monica had made the introductions for the recording. 'I slept better last night than I can remember.' His face was red, his chin covered with three days of stubble. Without his regulation John Deere baseball cap he was mostly bald. He looked younger, uncertain like a little boy. His arms were bandaged; the self-inflicted cuts to his wrists had been relatively minor, not even requiring stitches. Clearly there was a large part of Barry Sutherland that desperately wanted to live. Monica looked at the padding on her own left hand: two stitches. Crawford had ended up with six between his two wounds on neck and arm.

'Why was that?'

'I guess it was a weight off, at the end of the day.'

'You mean about Freya?'

'That's right. Not having to pretend any more.'

'Can you tell me what happened?'

'It was an accident. I never meant to hurt her.'

'And so you buried her?'

'I was trying to stop her.'

'Stop her from doing what?'

'From leaving her family. She didn't know how lucky she was, having all that.'

'How did you know Freya's family?' Jessica was adamant she hadn't met Barry until after Freya went missing.

'I worked with my uncle for a few days. Repairing the track outside their farm. None of them noticed me, but I saw them, how they all got on. The way they would sit and eat lunch and dinner together. I'd never really had any of that. I kept going back once we'd finished there. Just to watch, see how a normal family lived. There's an old tree near the farmhouse, the hanging tree – it's easy to climb. From up there I could watch them. Mrs Sutherland would bake, Mr Sutherland would come home from the fields. It felt nice, just seeing all that. What would it be like to be a part of it all? It was all so perfect.'

Monica recalled her first meeting with Barry, the emphasis he had placed on being part of the Sutherland family, what he'd said about his own, which suggested a broken home. The fact he had changed his name to Sutherland. She hadn't thought to ask his birth surname when they first met – at the time it had seemed certain Pauline Tosh was the killer – but now she knew it was Hume. He still sometimes worked for his uncle's business, Hume and Sons. Had worked at Cotton Lodge Barn, at the church at Eskadale, had access to the Pit.

Monica asked, 'You knew Freya was planning to leave?'

'It started going wrong when she met that group of *friends*.' He practically spat the word. 'Miranda Salisbury, Brodie King – the other one, Joseph Moon. Mr and Mrs Sutherland didn't approve of them. Up until then everything was great. Freya changed though. Started coming home late, drinking, smoking.'

'How did you know she was leaving?'

'I overheard. I was in the woods when a car pulled up beside me. The windows were down. I wasn't eavesdropping, but I couldn't help it.'

'What were they talking about?'

'Brodie King said he would pick her up the next night at one. He got out of the car and saw me, gave me a cigarette, acted like we were friends. But I knew he was trying to break the family up. I knew it would break Mr and Mrs Sutherland's hearts. The next day I waited until the Sutherlands were all out in the fields and crept into the farmhouse. I was going to leave an anonymous note, telling them that Freya was planning to leave. Then the phone started ringing.'

'You answered it?'

He nodded.

'Who was it?'

'He said it was Brodie, asked to speak to Freya. I told him I was Mr Sutherland. Told him Freya wasn't there. He asked me to give her a message – the plans for this evening were off. He would be in touch again tomorrow.'

Monica nodded slowly. 'You didn't give her the message.'

'I . . . I heard them coming back. I heard their voices and I wanted to tell them. Just stand there and tell them who I was. But I was in their house. They'd think I was a burglar or I was mad. That I'd just made it up. I didn't want to get Freya in trouble either. I mean, I thought it would be better if I could talk to her, explain how upset everyone was going to be. So I got out by the back door.'

'So you came back. That night?'

'I had the keys for my uncle's van, so I took it and waited under the hanging tree. I wasn't sure if she would come, but then

I heard her tapping at the door. I realised I'd made a mistake and should go, but I couldn't just leave her there, so I let her in. She was surprised at first, started asking, "Where is everyone? Where's Brodie?" I told her I was a friend of her parents. That what she was doing would break their hearts. Her face was all screwed up, all ugly, like she couldn't understand any of it. Then she said, "I know you. You're that boy, the one who was doing the track. You don't know my parents." She tried to leave, and I grabbed her arm to stop her. I just wanted to explain. I knew that if she told them what had happened, then I would never be part of the family.'

'And so you strangled her?'

'I just held her on the floor. When I let go she wasn't moving. She'd gone so pale. I drove her to the hospital, but when I got there she still wasn't moving.' He looked up at Monica then, his face drained of colour as he relived the memory. 'Jessica won't come in to see me, will she?'

'No' – Monica shook her head slowly – 'not if you don't want her to.'

'I always thought how different it would have been. If I hadn't gone there that night. I never did have any luck. That was the thing. My brothers all had it so easy.'

'What did you do,' Monica asked, 'when you saw she wasn't moving at the hospital?'

'I closed the van door back up and drove to the Muirtown Basin. I was working there with my uncle at the time. I wrapped Freya in plastic and put her in a rubble sack, then carried her down over my shoulder. She weighed nothing.'

'Did you see anyone there?' Monica asked, remembering Pauline Tosh's story about Rolf Stilger.

'There was the nightwatchman. He shone a light at me, must have recognised me because he just asked, "What you got there?"

I said the first thing I thought of, that I was burying some old junk from the van. He didn't seem to care, went back to his cabin. I took Freya out of the sack. There was already a hole, so I just put her in and shovelled rocks and mud over her. I stayed in bed all the next two days. I was sure the police would be at my door in no time. I got up on the third day and decided I couldn't bear it any more – I was going to hand myself in to the police – so I walked up to the station and I sat outside for the whole day. Waiting for someone to come and ask me what I was doing there. But no one ever came. So I thought I should go and check on the Sutherlands. I thought they would be worried by now so I would tell them what had happened. But when I went to get the van, my uncle was there and really angry, wondering where I'd been. There was work needed doing, did I think he was a fucking joke?'

'And so you never told anyone?'

'It didn't seem right. After all that.'

'What did you do next?' Monica asked, feeling deep numbness at Sutherland's matter-of-fact account.

'I just worked. Did what I was supposed to do. It's all a man can do, after all.'

'But you didn't want to make amends? Didn't want to let her family know what had happened to Freya?'

'Telling someone the truth isn't always fair on them,' Sutherland said. 'Just because you want a clear conscience doesn't mean they need to hear it.'

'You befriended the family?'

'There was a thing in the newspaper. About how they were raising awareness of Freya's disappearance. I volunteered to distribute flyers and ended up getting paired with Jessica. We walked round Inverness together. I had this strange feeling that

Freya might be waiting at one of the doors or watching us from a window. Even though I knew there was no chance. That she was buried at the other end of the city.'

'And you started going out with Jessica?'

'It was like we had a connection. Somehow we both knew that Freya was a long way away. Like Jessica sensed it from me. I had seen her wearing an Oasis T-shirt – the band, I mean. I got one too and told her that I'd bought their album *Definitely Maybe*. She said she liked the song 'Live Forever'. That it was her favourite. I said it was my favourite too even though I wasn't sure. I'd liked things like Nirvana and Pearl Jam more up until then. That was what Freya listened to. I ended up liking Oasis though, and Blur too – like the way you didn't have to think about anything when you listened to them? You know?' Monica didn't think she did know, but she nodded anyway. 'I guess we sort of bonded, like we both knew life would never be the same again with Freya missing.'

'Did you say any of this to Jessica at the time?' Monica asked. It hadn't occurred to her until now that there was a chance he had actually confessed to Jessica. But *stranger things have happened*, as Monica's mum was fond of saying.

'No!' For the first time, Barry Sutherland sounded shocked. 'She never knew anything about what happened. She could never know.'

'So you decided to kill her and your children instead?'

'I couldn't do it in the end. I'd been planning it since you found Freya – how to make it look like someone else killed me, Jessica and the kids. I don't understand exactly, but it was like some part of me thought if I left the piece of jewellery on the tree and burned the churches and the empty houses, everyone would just think the murderer had come back and killed us all. They say psychopaths like to start fires, don't they?'

He looked up at Monica, and after a moment she realised it was a genuine question. Nodded. She remembered her intuition that at least part of the fire-setter wanted to be caught.

Barry continued, 'If I'm honest I wasn't thinking clearly. But I thought it would seem like someone else killed us, like a pattern of fires with us dying at the end. At least that way people would feel sorry for us, remember us as a good family. No one would ever know about my accident with Freya.'

'Why did you take the shark necklace? Jessica said she'd lost it on your honeymoon.'

'I couldn't stand to see her wearing it, knowing it was Freya's. It reminded me of everything. So I hid it in the lining of my suitcase. I never touched it again until I heard about you digging up Freya. It was in there every holiday we went on, every time we went on a trip. It was like part of me wanted Jessica to find it, to somehow see the part of me that stole it, the part of me that did that thing to Freya, and then I wouldn't have to lie. I followed you home too, stood in the trees behind your house. I was going to confess if you spoke to me, and then that time at Cotton Lodge Barn I could have really hurt you if I'd wanted. I think part of me wanted you to see it was me – that's why I waited. Maybe that's part of the reason I started the fires? Left the necklace in that tree that reminded me of the hanging tree – so someone would catch me, stop me. It's like there are two sides of me. One wants to be a good family man, forget the past. Then the side that wanted to admit what I'd done. It became such a weight. Knowing that you'd come for me eventually. I think I just wanted it all to be over.'

'How did you know we'd come for you in the end? You'd got away with it for over two decades.'

Barry Sutherland looked surprised at the question. 'Because of the nightwatchman, Rolf Stilger. He was the only one who knew where Freya was. So when I heard the news that she'd been found, I knew he must have told someone and it would come back to me eventually. But at first I hoped Brodie would end up getting the blame.' He put his face in his big hands. 'That was wrong – he's got a family too – but I was frightened.'

'You killed Stilger?'

Sutherland looked up. 'I had to. It was a couple of months ago. We'd won an award for our charity, Home Call. The *Highland News* ran a good-news piece about how Jessica and I had met, how it was nice that something good had come of Freya's disappearance, how we both still hoped she would come back. I'd always been careful about being photographed. I'd forgotten though; it all seemed so long ago.'

'He saw the picture of you?'

Sutherland nodded, his eyes wide with horror at the memory. 'The next week he was waiting for me. Under the hanging tree, all hunched up in the rain like a little imp from one of the fairy tales we read the kids.'

'What did he say?'

'He was just standing there, smiling at me. I thought he might need help, so I pulled over. I always try to help, never pass someone who's in trouble. I didn't recognise him and I asked if he was OK. He just kept smiling, like we shared a joke, then he said, "You don't remember me, Barry, do you?"'

Monica recalled the story Pauline Tosh had told her at the Carse, about Rolf Stilger knowing who had buried the body in the Marsh. About coming back with more information. He must have approached Barry Sutherland around that time.

'He asked if you'd killed Freya?'

'Not exactly, just hinted at it, like it was a big joke. "Funny, your sister-in-law going missing, you burying something in the marshes round the same time." I couldn't believe what I was hearing. I'd sort of stopped even thinking of what happened, like it was from someone else's life. He said he wasn't interested in money, just wanted to hear the full story and write it down. He wouldn't tell anyone, he said.'

'Did you agree to meet him?' Monica knew that Stilger had lived further south, in Argyle, hence why the team hadn't initially connected his death with the other fires.

'I just told him he was mad and drove away. When I got home I was sick in the kitchen, stayed in bed for two days. In the end I found out where he lived, went to explain.'

'And ended up killing him?'

'The front door was unlocked. He was passed out, drunk. The place was like a hovel. I just rolled a log out of the fire onto the floor, added some paper until it got going. It seemed like the best thing for it. Then, seeing the flames from outside, it was beautiful, like my problem was being burned away.'

'But he'd already told someone.'

'He must have – I didn't know who though. I thought if I burned the churches and left the piece of jewellery then at least no one would ever know it was me. All our friends knew I hadn't met Jessica or her family until after Freya was missing.'

Monica stared across the table at Sutherland. If it hadn't been for his cack-handed attempts to cover his tracks with the fires then they might never have caught him. Monica sensed that part of him really had wanted some kind of absolution. Even as it battled with the side that wanted to end all of his problems with the simplicity of fire and death. As she watched him, Monica tried to muster up outrage at what he'd done to Freya – all the years of hurt he'd caused her family. How would Jessica and the children ever come to terms with these terrible truths? She couldn't imagine how Jessica would feel about having married her sister's murderer. But instead she couldn't help feeling sorry for Barry Sutherland – seeing what an incomplete person he was. How everyday human feelings of shame and inadequacy had coalesced for him. If he hadn't made the mistake of meeting Freya that night . . . if he hadn't been in the farmhouse when Brodie called . . . But, on the other hand, his pathetic tale was rather convenient. And she wondered how many other *mishaps* had befallen him.

'How many other people have you killed, Barry?'

He looked shocked, ran a hand over his bald head. 'None, no one. I'm not a murderer. It wasn't my fault. I never meant for any of it to happen. You believe that, don't you?'

Monica gazed at him, trying to read those eyes. Ultimately he looked like an ordinary man, someone you would pass on the street, someone you'd glance over at once in a petrol station while you filled your car and never think of him again. Finally she said, 'You'd know better than me, Barry. The things you did are on your conscience.'

'Do you think any of the charity work and the helping people – do you think that would make up for what happened with Freya?'

'No,' Monica replied. 'I don't think you can ever make up for taking a life. It sounds like you've tried in some ways. Maybe that counts for something. But I'm no judge.'

Chapter 77

Hately was standing at the open door to his office. His expression was not what you'd expect of a detective superintendent who had just cleared up a complex cold case. Monica understood why a moment later, when she saw Crawford sitting inside.

'You knew about this little love affair with one of Francis MacGregor's dancers?' Hately said as Monica stepped into the office.

Before Monica could speak, Crawford said, 'She didn't know anything. I called in sick, kept it all from her. It'll all be logged on the system. It's all on me.'

Hately raised his eyebrows, looked from Crawford up to Monica: *You think I'm fucking stupid?*

'I take it you've seen this?' He held up a copy of a tabloid newspaper for Monica to see. She took in the front cover: a bloodied Crawford with the burning farmhouse behind him. Presumably taken by some enterprising local, with the headline: HERO COP SAVES MURDER FAMILY. The first paragraph contained a vaguely accurate story of Crawford fighting with Sutherland and saving Jessica and the children. There was mercifully no mention of Monica's part in the drama; she could live without more attention. Obviously her partner had decided there wouldn't be a better opportunity to throw himself on Hately's mercy than on the back of this acclaim. 'You're suspended, Crawford. This is going to Professional Standards. You'd better pray nothing else comes out. If you're seriously lucky, you might make it through this shitshow still as a detective – one with a terrible record and a reputation for being a fuck-up.' He shook his head.

Crawford said, 'Thank you, sir.'

'Get the fuck out of my office.'

'Of course, sir.'

Monica followed Crawford down the corridor to the empty Incident Room. He pulled his grey wool jacket on, wincing as the collar brushed his stitches. 'Well, that went better than I thought.'

Monica managed to smile. 'I'll do what I can – tell him the truth.'

'Don't. If we're both involved it'll look like a conspiracy. At least if it's just me they can put it down to shit judgement.'

Monica nodded. It didn't sit well with her not to step up for her partner, but what he was saying made sense. He looked around the office as if for Fisher and Khan, probably because he wanted to say goodbye, but they were both out.

'I'll speak to them later,' he said, grey circles under his eyes from the long night.

She felt as tired herself, had only managed an hour's sleep, infested with dreams of fire and shallow graves.

He looked around again as if taking in the office for the last time, then put his hands on his hips, spread his coat out wide and said, 'Are you hungry? I haven't eaten yet today.'

Her mum was delighted to see Crawford when they arrived back at Monica's flat. She was in the midst of preparing a shepherd's pie (made with Quorn mince for Monica's benefit).

Lucy was in the living room, reading one of her books. 'I

spoke to her about wee Harriet,' Angela Kennedy said conspiratorially. Delighted to be part of the team. 'I did what you said and didn't go into the details, just said her daddy was a bad man. Had tried to hurt them all, but Crawford had saved them.' She smiled at Crawford. 'She was back playing with Munyasa today, since Harriet wasn't around,' Angela announced proudly. 'Weren't you, Lucy?'

Absorbed in her book, Lucy didn't even look up. 'What happened?' Monica asked.

'Oh, who knows. Back to being best friends again though, it looked like.'

Monica thought about this for a moment, wondered exactly what had been going on there. How many of these little mysteries came into a child's life before they were separated from you entirely? How many was the right number to allow for the child to become an independent human being? And how many, and what, led to those dark alleys of strangeness? To a Barry Sutherland or a Pauline Tosh. When did the fantasies of power and magic that Lucy had been drawn to out of vulnerability – that Miranda Salisbury, Brodie King and Joseph Moon had embraced, to make them feel powerful – when did they become corrosive fantasies that prevented someone from properly engaging with their life? From being able to fit into society?

Monica sighed.

'Would you like a beer, Crawford?' Angela crouched down to the fridge and came back with a cold bottle of Beck's. 'How's Heather?'

Crawford hesitated then accepted the beer, obviously remembering that he was now 'on holiday'. He took a mouthful. 'Not great. I mean, we've kind of broken up. Wasn't working out between us. Better to go our separate ways.'

'Aye, that's right.' Angela nodded sagely. Monica knew her mum didn't approve of Heather's wealth, her laid-back style, her mid-Atlantic accent which she'd regarded as pretentious. 'Sometimes it's better going your separate ways.' Lucy was now watching on, taking it all in.

There was a knock at the door and Monica got up to answer it. Pleased not to have to listen to her mum administering relationship advice to her colleague. Outside there was a skinny teenage boy. Monica realised that he had a cat carrier beside him.

'Is this your cat, Albert?' he asked nervously. 'He's been round at ours, came in asking for food. Then we saw your flyer. We thought he was a stray . . .'

Monica looked through the door of the carrier at a wide cream-coloured face inside.

Barry Sutherland was convicted of the abduction and murder of Freya Sutherland, the murder of Rolf Stilger, as well as three counts of wilful fire-raising. The fibres recovered from Freya's nostrils matched carpet purchased by Barry's uncle in 1993, and fitted to the interior of several of his vans. His uncle had been engaged as a groundworks subcontractor on the tidal defences at the time of Freya's disappearance.

The body of Patrick Salisbury was found buried in a shallow grave behind Miranda Salisbury's childhood home. From there he had haunted Brodie King, Joseph Moon and Miranda Salisbury for twenty-four years. Miranda's mother essentially corroborated Miranda and Brodie's account of his death. Patrick Salisbury had previous convictions for embezzlement and tax fraud, and was wanted on charges of fraud by the police in Germany. No one had missed him in the two decades he had been in the ground, and there was no particular clamour for justice on his behalf. The jury accepted King and Salisbury had acted in self-defence, and they were eventually acquitted of manslaughter. Salisbury's political career was over but she reinvented herself as an advocate for child victims of sexual abuse. The notoriety did King no harm. He emigrated with his family to France, set up a successful restaurant on Cap Ferret and became something of a local celebrity.

Two days after the tabloid story about Crawford's heroics, the same newspaper published a follow-up headlined HERO COP'S SEX SHAME and featuring video stills of Crawford and a woman. The story included details of the 'love rat cop' who had 'blabbed details of murder investigations' during 'pillow talk'.

Chapter 78

The drive to the west coast was slow but uneventful. There was snow on the mountainsides and heaped up by the road as they drove down the Great Glen towards Fort William, seventy miles to the south-west of Inverness. Lucy was in a good mood in the back of the Volvo. It was the week before Christmas, and her excitement had been heightened by each opened door on the Advent calendar. Monica watched the back of Crawford's red Audi ahead of them on the road.

Finally Crawford indicated left on the outskirts of Fort William, the flashing amber lighting the grey snow. Monica followed him into the car park beneath a block of flats. She had agreed to help him move his belongings to his new home, his new beat. When she parked he was already outside the Audi, stretching his back as he looked up at the uninspiring grey block.

'It'll just be until I get somewhere better.' He shook his head. 'Back on the west coast of the Highlands, back in uniform. I asked for Glasgow.'

'You're still young. They'll have forgotten about all this in a few years.'

Crawford nodded, obviously not convinced. In the police, having a tabloid sex-tape story against your name wasn't conducive to career advancement. He'd only avoided dismissal because none of the details of the cases had actually been recorded on the videos, and because of his exemplary service record. 'I guess I'll wait for all this to die down, think about another job. God knows what, though.'

Monica allowed herself a moment of sadness. It had taken her this long to find a partner she enjoyed working with, someone who had become part of her life. She thought of the times that she, Crawford, Lucy and her mum had gone for picnics or had Sunday lunch at her flat. It had been so nice, even though she hadn't always thought so at the time. Like a little family, after so many years on her own down in Glasgow and London. So many lonely days between cases that she had buried under long walks, in busyness and not understanding why she couldn't ever seem to let herself make a close connection.

But maybe this was more of the same. Maybe she'd been drawn to Crawford and allowed herself to feel close to him because it would always be temporary. Deep down she'd known it could never go anywhere with a junior colleague, ten years younger – a serial womaniser with an underlying wildness that meant he was always going to struggle within the structured confines of the police. The unconventionality that made him a great detective also meant he would burn out, fuck up eventually.

Sleet was falling more heavily now. Crawford hugged himself in the black leather jacket he had taken to wearing all the time. He'd grown his hair longer and it was sticking out from under his black beanie. The outfit looked more Al Pacino in *Serpico* than ever, and Monica wondered if he'd adopted the look for effect. Though perhaps he was too young to even have seen the film?

'How are Jessica and the kids doing?'

Monica was surprised by the question, but then realised that Crawford was outside the loop of the Incident Room now. Jessica's response to her husband's conviction had been one of the more surprising parts of the case. 'She says she's standing by Barry,' Monica said. 'She believes that what happened with Freya was an accident, that he was raised badly and was just a damaged kid at the time. That he deserves a second chance after everything he's done for charity over the years.'

Crawford raised his eyebrows. 'I guess you never know how you'll react. Can't be easy with three kids. But Barry wasn't exactly a damaged child when he killed Rolf Stilger.' He shook his head, then added, 'I forgot to ask, about the Sutherlands' cat that went missing. Did he ever turn up?'

'Bramble? Harriet found him curled up under a tree, sleeping with Butter, the ancient cat that used to belong to Freya. Just like he'd never been away.'

Monica felt the chill wind pick up, billowing the fabric of the red Gore-Tex jacket she was wearing.

Crawford cleared his throat. 'Emilija got in touch.'

Monica wondered for a moment who he was talking about, then realised he meant the woman who had recorded him and sold the story to the press.

'Said she was sorry, she needed the money. Her mum doesn't keep well in Lithuania.' He shrugged. 'Told her no hard feelings. Francis MacGregor asked her to pass on a message.'

'What was it?' Monica assumed some kind of *Fuck you, I won. No one points a gun at me.*

'Job offer. Driving, advice, good money, she said.'

'What did you say?' Monica was surprised, though she shouldn't have been. Crawford was one of the best detectives she'd worked with – he would be an asset to any criminal gang.

'What do you think?' Crawford said, sounding outraged that she would even ask. 'Told her I'm a cop.'

Monica nodded. Beyond her ex-partner was the grey block of

flats, and beyond that the snowy bulk of Ben Nevis – the highest mountain in the UK – which hung over Fort William like an open invitation to trouble. She wondered how Crawford would fare out here. So far from the action that he craved, and without the demands of serious crime investigations to focus his mind. She'd been there herself. Knew how empty life could feel without the adrenaline of knowing that your work, your life, actually meant something.

Lucy was pressed against a window of the Volvo, making funny faces at Crawford. He pulled a face back at her and she fell about laughing. 'I left a Christmas present for Lucy with your mum. It's a little mane, to put on the cat. Makes him look like a mini lion.'

Monica thanked him, then remembered the bag with a Christmas present and home-made seasonal chutney that her mum had put in the car for him. She went to the boot of the Volvo and took out his two cases. Stood them on the pavement, balanced the present bag on top.

'Do you want a hand up with these?'

'It's fine, boss. It'll be dark soon – you should get on the road.'

She ducked back into the boot and found the second bag, this one with cake and a plastic container of soup, also from her mum. She smiled as she handed it to him, wanting to say, *I liked working with you, Crawford. I'll miss you.* Instead she heard herself say, 'Keep out of trouble.'

He laughed at that, waved again to Lucy through the window. 'I'm planning on it, believe me.'

Spits of icy snow were now landing on Monica's face and hands. Blowing in with the salty air from somewhere far, far out in the North Atlantic Ocean. It always was colder here than in Inverness. It rained much more too.

'Call me some time.'

She got back in the Volvo, put it into reverse. Crawford was still smiling and waving beside his cases and the red Audi packed full of the rest of his stuff. He looked small against the mountain behind him.

Monica turned the car, wound down the window so Lucy could wave to him, then accelerated out of the car park without looking back in the rear-view mirror, until the mountain was just another mass of grey against the darkening sky.

Acknowledgements

Firstly thanks to you, for reading my book! And thanks to all the readers from around the world who have taken the time to read, review my books, get in touch via social media, share pictures or blog about them. And thanks to all those who have got in touch privately, your enthusiasm and encouragement is hugely appreciated. Writing a novel can be a tiring and solitary pursuit, feeling those connections is so inspiring and energising. Special thanks to Instagrammer Jane Kelsey, Martin Ball down under in Melbourne Australia, and Lisa Schmitt in Germany, for your amazing enthusiasm in posting about and sharing my novels. Thank you to all the bookshops that have stocked my books and let me pop by to sign copies over the years!

Specials thanks to the people of Inverness and the Highlands for allowing me to take such huge liberties with this beautiful city and this amazing area. I was nervous about how my first novel would be received locally, but the endless kindness and enthusiasm I've encountered from Highland readers and booksellers is truly heartwarming.

Thanks to my sister Dr Tanya Baron for advice on the medical side of things. To PC Parr for police advice and filling me in on the proper use of police radios! And huge thanks to Detective Superintendent Mike Sutherland for his generous time talking to me, sharing some of his vast experience, and straightening out some of my errors in procedural understanding. Though the mistakes and liberties are obviously still all mine!

Thanks to my wonderful agent Camilla Bolton, Jade Kavanagh and all at Darley Anderson agency. To Jade Chandler, Dredheza Maloku, Liz Foley, Mia Quibell-Smith, Kate Neilan, Hugh Davis, Gemma Wain, and all at Harvill Secker, Vintage, and Dead Good Books. Can't thank you all enough for your amazing work on my novels. And to Dan Mogford for designing the most beautiful book covers that capture the spirit of the novels.

My fellow Caledonia Crime Collective members, Emma Christie, Andrew Greig, Allan Martin, Deborah Masson, Marion Todd, and Jonathan Whitelaw, thanks for your comradeship, enthusiasm, and just being an amazing bunch of fun and creative people.

To my uncle, Neil Halliday, for flying the flag for DI Monica Kennedy down in the Midlands, and inviting me along to speak to his students at Telford College. A tough audience, but rewarding!

Finally, huge thanks as ever to my wonderful partner Sarah Woodcock for her editorial input, her psychological expertise, shared cold swims, and helping me stay sane and happy while I was writing *Under The Marsh* during the covid lockdowns of 2020.

penguin.co.uk/vintage